NO FORCED ENTRY

NO FORCED ENTRY

Be Careful Who You Let In

A Novel

ROBERT MAX

STATION HOUSE PUBLISHING
TRUST

This novel is a work of fiction. Any references to real people, companies, events, establishments, organizations, institutions, agencies, municipalities, or locales are intended only to give the fiction a sense of reality and authenticity, and are used fictitiously. All other names, characters, products, places, corporate entities, agencies, and incidents are the product of the author's imagination and are also used fictitiously, and any resemblance to actual persons living or dead or locales is entirely coincidental.

Copyright © 2018 by Station House Publishing Trust

All rights reserved.

No part of this book my be reproduced, distributed, or transmitted in any form or by any means whatsoever, now known or to be invented, nor is it to be scanned, uploaded, or stored in a database or retrieval system without permission in writing from the publisher, except for brief quotations to be included in an article or review.

Station House Publishing Trust
P.O. Box 51403
Sparks, NV 89435
www.robertmaxnovels.com

To contact the author, direct your inquiry to the publisher at the address above. The publisher is not responsible for websites or their content that are not owned by the publisher.

ISBN 978-0-9966105-0-6

For Mack, Sid, Howard, and Janet… all of whom, in what seems like a previous life, made this book possible in the most profound ways.

In my present life it is for Lynn, Benny, and Dreamy… in my heart every day.

NO FORCED ENTRY

PROLOGUE

This feels like a fairly safe neighborhood, Dana Bennett thought at 2:15 p.m. as she walked into the food store near the corner of Queens Boulevard and Continental Avenue in the heart of Forest Hills. She'd shopped there before, even though she didn't live in that part of New York City. She was in a carefree mood that pleasant, sunny Sunday afternoon in April, so the idea that she'd never have a chance to eat the food she was about to buy never entered her mind.

She lovingly selected the ingredients for a savory pot roast while ignoring the attention of several men near the register. She paid with cash, crossed the boulevard carrying a reusable grocery sack in each hand, and began the two-block walk to the apartment she visited at least once a month, never looking behind her. Walking slowly despite the weight of the bundles, she found herself enjoying the delightfully perfumed warmth of spring while being careful not to turn an ankle on the cracked and uneven sidewalk, obscured here and there by a pastel carpet of fallen cherry blossoms. She wore indigo jeans, a powder blue T-shirt, and beige canvas shoes with a woven wedge-heel just high enough to transform an exquisite figure into an irresistible one. The small purse, also beige, she'd hung from her shoulder bumped her right hip in counterpoint to the rhythm of her stroll.

Lulled by the peaceful, non-threatening character of the quiet residential block, she casually absorbed her surroundings—the bloom-strewn string of cars parked along the curb to her left and the freshly-cut fragrant green lawns separating six-story red brick apartment buildings set back from the street. A handful of elderly residents, seated on benches in the shade of graceful elms that made the congested neighborhood feel like a park, smiled hello as she passed. She noticed those mundane afternoon things, but her thoughts were more focused on the next few satisfying hours, as her husband was out of town for the weekend.

She turned right at the second corner, crossed another one-way tree-shrouded street, and headed for the path that led to a well-kept but aging building with brass-trimmed glass entrance doors. One of the inner doors that led to the lobby, fitted with a key-lock that could be buzzed open by any tenant answering the intercom on the wall to the right, was held aside by a hinged doorstop with a rubber foot. With the groceries growing heavier by the minute, she hurried across the terrazzo floor and summoned the elevator at the far end of the lobby. When it arrived, she checked the convex security mirror in the corner at the car's ceiling, as she did in any elevator so equipped, entered knowing there was no one unseen within, and managed to press the button for the fourth floor without putting down the bags. As the door slid closed, she felt a touch of claustrophobia and waited anxiously, trapped by the close graffiti-resistant walls. The whole car shuddered before stopping its ascent, triggering a wave of queasiness that turned her stomach, only to be exacerbated by the momentary sensation of weightlessness. The door opened and she rushed out, short of breath. She turned left and rang the bell for the apartment situated in the corner of the battleship gray fluorescent-lit hall.

"Hello, Sweetheart. Are you all right? Let me help you," said the man expecting her. He took the bags from her hands and stepped back into the cozy apartment, holding the door open with his shoe.

She followed him inside, turned left at the first archway, and entered the tiny kitchen, immediately making room for the provisions between the porcelain sink and chrome toaster-oven on the white Formica countertop. She noticed the damp paper towel hanging on a rack perpendicular to the wall as she moved a bare-bones cell phone, plugged into its charger, out of the way.

"It's always so wonderful to see you," he said, hugging her. Then he held her shoulders at arm's length. "You look a little pale. Let me get you something to drink." He pulled a plain juice glass from cupboards that had been painted gloss white more than a few times. Then he opened the old refrigerator, grabbed a bottle of ginger ale, and filled the glass for her, topping if off as the foaming head settled. "I'm so glad you're here." He watched her drink and said, "Does your husband know how lucky he is?"

"I don't know. Men have a way of taking the women they love for granted."

"Not this one."

"I brought your favorite meal," she said, putting down the glass before unpacking the bags. She noticed the sunlight streaming through the canary yellow lace curtains and began to feel better. "How have you been?"

"To tell you the truth, I've been better. There was a little more excitement around here on Friday than I cared for. I'll tell you one thing. The neighborhood isn't what it used to be."

"That doesn't sound good. What happened?"

He turned away for a moment, the mere thought of what he was about to recount weakening his knees. He steadied himself by holding the edge of the counter until he was ready to speak. But before he could utter a word, they both heard the doorbell. "It's probably my neighbor. I'll get it."

Dana Bennett finished neatly arranging the groceries and looked through the archway into the living room. Every inch of wall space not occupied by shelves crammed with books was covered with beautiful original paintings arranged like a mosaic right to the ceiling. One of the things she loved most about her visits was the artwork and literature that made the small apartment a pleasant and uniquely interesting haven. She noticed the elaborate collapsible wooden easel set up in the center of the room and made a mental note to ask if he'd finished another painting or was about to start one. Then she heard Maxwell talking to another man.

"What are you doing here? Nobody said you were coming."

"I'm here for the painting. Where is it?"

"I can't give it to you now. You'll have to come back another time."

"I can't do that. Where is it?"

"You don't understand. I can't give it to you today."

"No, *you* don't understand. Give me the damn painting right now."

"All right. Calm down. Take it easy. I'll get it for you. It's under the bed."

"Don't bother. I'll get it myself."

Then Dana saw the man for whom she'd come to cook dinner backing into his own living room.

"What are you doing? I said I'll get it for you. What else do you want?"

"The cell phone we gave you. I'll get that, too. I know where to look."

The first muffled shot hit the artist in the chest. He collapsed in the middle of the room near the empty easel. The man who'd fired once came into view as he approached his victim. Dana saw him point a large silver handgun with a black silencer toward the floor. She flinched as a spit of flame left the gun and the second bullet slammed into the fallen man's head, dislodging a hearing aid.

She tried to scream, but there was no air in her lungs. She ran from the kitchen, but the man wearing a long black leather coat saw her and reacted quickly, blocking her way before she could reach the front door. She turned and ran for the bedroom, panicked and flailing. Then it felt like she'd been cut in half. She landed face-first on the worn carpet, her chin skidding across the threshold. Barely able to move, she turned her head to the right as slowly as she dared, just in time to see the man standing over her. From the odd angle, the long coat made him seem ten feet tall.

She saw him looking down at her before he squatted near her face for a close-up. Talking to himself, she heard him say, "Wow. What a waste."

Dana Bennett watched him stand, back away a few feet, and aim the gun at her head. Utterly helpless, she knew what she'd witnessed, she knew she was next, she knew there was nothing she could do to continue living, and she knew she'd never again have the chance to tell her husband that she loved him.

1

The feeling you get in the pit of your stomach when red lights appear in your mirrors is a difficult one to describe, isn't it?

One uniformed officer in an enormous white SUV with massive push-bars on the front bumper and intensely bright alternating flashers in the grill pulled up behind me. I saw him look in the direction of his computer console; a display usually mounted near the center of the dashboard, and surmised he was probably running my new plates. Two minutes later he stepped out. I kept my hands high on the wheel so they would be in plain sight. My window was already down. When he was beside my car, standing slightly behind my door, leaning forward to look in at me, I said, "Hello, Officer."

"Can I see your license, registration, and evidence of insurance, please?"

"Those things are in my wallet. Is it all right if I reach for it?"

"Yes."

"Have I done something wrong?" I asked, digging into my back pocket.

He didn't answer.

I extricated the requested documents and handed them over. My driver's license was a temporary certificate, as I hadn't received the laminated photo version yet. Surrendering my New York license at the DMV when I'd registered the Porsche had stirred mixed feelings. On one hand, I'd been born in New York, learned to drive in New York, and had gotten my first car in New York, all of which may sound a little adolescent or shallow, but that's still a big deal to a red-blooded American male. Speaking of adolescent and shallow, I'd had my first piece of ass in that car, too, but that's a different story. On the other hand, giving up my New York license made my relocation and the start of my new life in California official and complete.

I glanced up at the Pine County Deputy as he scrutinized my papers in the sunshine. His name tag read M. Johnson. He was about thirty, maybe five or six years younger than yours truly, and tall enough to make me feel like I was sitting on the ground. He wore a dark green baseball cap with a seven-pointed gold star embroidered above the visor, which was pulled low on his forehead above a mean-looking pair of wraparound sunglasses. His uniform was particularly crisp, much more so than the sloppy cops I'd dealt with in New York City. I could see the outline of Kevlar body armor beneath his tan uniform shirt.

"Are you having a problem here, Mr. Bennett?"

"No, Sir. There's no problem."

"Is there a reason you've stopped at this particular location?"

"Actually, there is." I knew he'd ask something like that. "I'm new to the area and I've discovered that this spot resembles a painting my uncle painted many years ago. I'm just looking around." I knew he'd heard his fair share of strange stories on the side of the road, but I would have bet anything he hadn't heard that one. I plucked my iPhone from the passenger seat, recalled the photo I'd snapped of the painting on Monday night, and handed it to him.

He held it beside my head in the shadow of the Porsche's roof so it would be out of the noonday sun. He viewed it perfunctorily before returning it to me. "Do you have any other plans here, Mr. Bennett?"

"Not really."

"I've seen you parked here several times this week at sunset. You're not looking for trouble, are you, Robert?"

"No. I'm not."

"You're not casing that house, are you?"

"No, Sir."

"You're not stalking someone there, are you?"

"No. I'm not. I told you why I stopped. That painting has been in my family for years. I moved here from New York a week ago. I noticed the similarity on my way home from my new job in Placerville and I'm curious about the coincidence."

He stared at me, not knowing what to make of my explanation. I suppose the whole thing did sound pretty odd.

"Wait here. Stay in your car," he said, before returning to his vehicle with my papers.

I watched him in the mirror. He got behind the wheel again, took off his shades, spoke into his radio and waited, watching me watching him. As the minutes passed, the trepidations I'd had earlier about embarking on this questionable quest for who knows what returned to haunt me. To be completely honest, I'm not really sure what I was hoping to find in the white house that was situated in a small clearing across the river, but the more I'd thought about it, the more I thought it would turn out badly, this time lucky if I didn't get arrested for trespassing, or shot. Still I'd kept going. It was a beautiful day for a spring drive in the mountains. I had a full tank of premium and nothing to do on the first Saturday after a week at my new job. In a way, it was just one of those things. You know you shouldn't do it. You know it's probably pointless. You know you could be courting disaster. But you do it anyway. And now, here I was.

I expected him to approach my car once more after speaking again into his radio, but instead he just sat there watching me through the windshield. I could see the contemplation on his face and knew that the cynical law enforcement mentality dictating his next move found it difficult, if not impossible, to believe me. Then I had the sense that he began to write something down, although I couldn't see his hands.

As the minutes ground by, I became acutely aware of the thin cold sweat that had erupted under my collar. Then, in the mirror, I saw him step out again. He adjusted his equipment belt, apparently making sure his gun was where it was supposed to be, and returned to my door.

"You look like a pretty smart guy, Mr. Bennett," he said, returning my papers. "Does the phrase 'a word to the wise is sufficient' mean anything to you?"

I looked up at him, but couldn't see his eyes because the shades were back in position. I nodded.

"Good. Listen to me very carefully. I know who you are. I know what you drive. And I know where you live. Do you understand what I'm saying to you, Robert?"

If I were truly stupid I would have said something like: *Are you threatening me?* Admittedly, I've put my foot in my mouth a few times over the years, but I was determined to not let this be yet another such memorable moment. I nodded again.

"I didn't hear you?"

Suddenly it felt as if I'd joined the army. "I understand."

"Good. Have a nice day, Mr. Bennett."

He made it halfway back to his vehicle before stopping short, pivoting, and returning to my door. "Would you mind showing me that photo again, Mr. Bennett?"

I reached over, picked up my phone, recalled the picture, and handed it to him.

He took off his sunglasses and studied it carefully this time, comparing the painting to the scene across the river.

I watched his hard brown eyes for a glimmer of recognition. Knowing that police officers, like artists, are trained observers, often seeing telling details ordinary people may not notice, I found myself hoping for some validation.

After giving it ample consideration, the deputy's shrug doused my mounting excitement like a cold shower. "Personally, I think you're making more out of this than necessary," he said. "I see a white house next to a river, but there are more differences here than similarities. I think you're just wasting your time."

Really? Was the connection luring me here all in my mind?

He returned my phone, strode back to his SUV, climbed in, and drove away.

This encounter with the police wasn't nearly as frustrating as my last. "I'm sorry, Mr. Bennett," the detective had said in New York as the investigation lost steam. "We're doing everything we can, but unfortunately we don't have much to go on." That's what they'd said until they started looking at me—for the second time.

I'd been married in my old life to a girl I was absolutely crazy about, head over heels madly in love and all that happy horseshit, until she was murdered, one of two people shot to death in what New York's Finest called a double homicide. Of course, the cops ran *me* through the mill, elevating my embarrassment to a museum-quality art form with my friends, neighbors, and co-workers. I know that the spouse is always the person they look at first in a murder investigation, but that didn't lessen the humiliation. Having little else to go on, the detectives said it probably began as a push-in robbery. They referred to this type of homicide as a random crime. "And random crimes are the hardest to solve, especially when there are no witnesses, cameras, fingerprints, fibers, DNA specimens, and so forth, because there's no connection between the perpetrators and the victims."

It sounded a little like a cover-your-ass statement, which pissed me off and even caused me to consider working the case myself. You know, canvassing the area, as the cops call it—hanging around, talking to people in the neighborhood, finding out if there'd been any other push-ins, things like that. But I'm an architect, not a detective, so I decided instead to get the hell out of New York. At least the decision to split was my own and I'm not some dumb-ass jammed up in the witness protection program, forced to look over my shoulder every minute for the rest of my life. Finding happiness under normal conditions is hard enough, don't you think?

I'd landed at Reno-Tahoe International Airport a week ago with only the clothes on my back and a valise full of clean underwear. I'd quit my job, gave up our old apartment in Brooklyn, including all of the carefully selected possessions within, sold my BMW M3 coupe, and said goodbye to my two lifelong married buddies. It was pretty simple, really. Get away from the places Dana and I had frequented, the places where people expected to see the two of us. Get away from the things that reminded me of what we had together—the things I'll never have again. Start over. Make a clean break. Walk away from everything in my old life and start a new one far away. If only I could have left my mind behind.

I took a cab from the airport to the Porsche dealer and bought a new metallic-silver 911 Carrera 4 S for my commute from Lake Tahoe to Placerville, a small town in the foothills. I knew the sixty mile trip would probably become tiresome, if not impossible when the snows came next winter, but I thought the ride would be therapeutic. Call it what you will; a shallow substitute for love, or the motorized manifestation of a premature midlife crisis. The fact is I love to drive. And I'd wanted that car for a very long time.

I'd rented a condo in Tahoe Keys, an upscale neighborhood which, except for being surrounded by snow-capped mountains, reminded me of Fort Lauderdale because a system of waterways arranged like streets behind the houses allowed the lucky residents to dock their boats in their backyards. All things considered, it was a rather tranquil and picturesque arrangement. Or to put it another way, it was nothing like Brooklyn.

Sunrise arrived on Monday just as it had every day for millions of years before Dana was killed. It spilled in above the vertical blinds, through the high windows that reached the vaulted ceiling, illuminating my sparsely furnished existence. I was determined to be optimistic on the first official day of my new life. I really was. It was like convincing a lion to be a vegetarian.

The crates in the next room were the only exceptions to my plan. They contained the complete collection of Maxwell Bennett paintings, which totaled thirty-nine works. I'd had them professionally packed and shipped to ensure their survival. I say that as if they have great monetary value, which they do not, for they are utterly unknown to the world. The paintings have never been sold, reproduced, or published. They have never graced an auction, museum, or gallery. They are, however, priceless to me, not only for their beauty, or because I appreciate the talent needed to create them, but because they are tangible proof that

Maxwell Bennett lived. Mack, as we called him, was my father's baby brother.

I showered, shaved, and boiled some water for my tea that Monday morning. I put on some new clothes—a pair of pleated khakis and a light blue oxford button-down—and looked through the window at the sailboats moored in the Tahoe Keys marina. A floating grove of masts and halyards before a backdrop of ski run-carved mountains and a sky bluer than any I can ever recall seeing over the Big Apple reminded me that my new life was about to begin.

I put my glass mug in the sink, locked the door behind me, and walked past the condo association-maintained lawn to my new car. I started the Porsche and listened to the engine's unique growl. The scent of new leather entered my head and a lost smile graced my face as I set out to find the architectural firm of Sherman and Essen.

I was in a new place, wearing new clothes, driving a new car on my way to a new job, but all I could soon think about was that I was still alone in the world. I remembered watching the sun come up over the Atlantic with Dana from a blanket on the dunes at Long Island's Montauk Point after spending the night gazing at the stars in the summer sky. Another time we'd imagined our future together as we watched an endless procession of big puffy cotton clouds drift by in slow motion over Shelter Island, our limbs and minds intertwined on a quilt, cloistered by a sea of tall grass, sharing our love in the open air of a straw room with no ceiling. We'd watched the ducks on a pond in Amagansett and marveled at the way two wayward souls find each other in a world of solitary indifference. And we'd burned our lips on roasted marshmallows, and on each other, wrapped in a warm and soft patchwork beside a crackling fire in sunset's fading light on the beach at Oyster Bay. As much as I cherish those moments, they return to me now and then with an uncanny clarity and there is nothing I can do to stop them—the warmth of the sun on our faces, the sweet fragrance of wildflowers carried on gentle breezes, and the chill of evening drawing us closer as we'd kiss away the beckoning goose bumps that would spring to life at the end of days that should have lasted forever.

I lowered the window to clear my head. The pine-scented, mountain-chilled morning reached in and slapped my face as if to say, *snap out of it!* I downshifted, pushed the accelerator into the carpet, and hugged the apex of the next bend at the correct point in the radius, a difficult task in a blind curve. If I'd been in a less agile machine I would have plowed into the deer standing in the middle of the lane, obviously trying to commit suicide. Using a quick-reaction avoidance technique I'd learned at a racetrack-based high performance car-control course saved the day. Nevertheless, it was easy to imagine the Porsche's low front-end knocking the legs out from under the animal, sending its body through the windshield. Marginally happy to be alive, a sentiment that had abandoned me a year ago, I scaled back a notch and arrived in Placerville an hour and ten minutes after I'd left.

I pulled into the small private lot and parked beside a large black S-class Mercedes-Benz sedan. Confident my car would feel right at home and make friends easily, I walked to the sidewalk and up the block toward the steps that led to an old Victorian house. I thought the pastel trim was appropriate. It coordinated well with the dramatic periwinkle hydrangea blooms that hugged the foundation. I stopped for a moment to look at the quiet residential hillside street lined with mature oaks. The warm, dry spring air that had crossed the broad Sacramento Valley now passed through the foothills on its way to the mountains. I drew a deep breath, gave myself a silent three-second pep talk, and checked my watch. I'd never been less than ten minutes late for anything in my old life. Maybe this really was a new beginning.

I was greeted in the anteroom by a pretty receptionist in her early twenties. Seated behind an antique oak desk, she had vivid blue eyes and long, straight blonde hair.

"How can I help you?" she asked.

I was tempted to say, *I'm here to inspect your surfboard.* But instead I said, "I'm here to see Mr. Sherman. My name is Robert Bennett."

I restrained myself from flirting with the beautiful blonde smiling back at me for a few awkward moments before William Sherman appeared, looking like we'd shopped in the same store. He was a happy guy in his late forties, despite the fact that his curly brown hair was abandoning him, one of nature's cruelest ironies; take the crowning lion's mane from the men with the strongest hormones. He welcomed me with great warmth and introduced me to everyone in the building, starting with his daughter, whom I'd just met. Glad that I hadn't made a schmuck out of myself right off the bat, I decided to listen twice as much as speak, remembering why God has given us two ears and just one mouth.

Warm was not a word I would use to describe his partner, Heinrich Essen, who could have been a U-boat commander in *his* previous life, but I decided to keep an open mind and not judge a book by its cover, affording him the same consideration he was apparently affording me. I guessed that the Mercedes was his. Sherman continued the tour, leading me, at last, to my new office.

I spent the morning getting situated and going over the nuts and bolts of the operation. I rearranged the furniture, making the office my own, dialing in the fundamentals of feng shui, marshalling all of the positive energy in the universe, aligning my desk and everything on it with the appropriate planets, and all the rest of that touchy-feely crap. Basically, I just wanted to be able to see my sporty new car through the tall Victorian windows while sitting at either my high-tech computer or my low-tech drafting table, now afraid that, when I wasn't looking, Essen would convince my Teutonic twin-turbo autobahn-special to turn me over to the Gestapo.

Sherman took me to a small, festive Mexican restaurant on Main Street for lunch where we got to know each other. "Harold told me what happened," he said.

I stared at the condensation on the outside of my iced water goblet and drew on it with my fingertip as I said, "It was pretty bad. But it was a year ago. I'm on the way back now." I really didn't want to talk about it with my new employer. I simply didn't know him that well.

In fact, I'd asked Harold Rice not to get into the details with Sherman, his old college buddy, when he called him. "You know I love working for you," I'd said to my old boss. "I really do, but I've got to get out of New York. I've tried to get past it, but I can't. Not entirely. Not here. I've got to start over someplace else. I don't know what else to say about it."

"Take a vacation," he'd replied. "You haven't had much time off since it happened. Why don't you go down to the Caribbean for a while and get your pipes cleaned. There are some great resorts down there for singles. You'll come back a new man. I guarantee it."

"Thanks for the time and the suggestion, and for everything else you've done for me, but I don't need time off. I need to get out of this city and not come back. I need to start my life over in a completely different place. I've thought about it for a long time now. I really don't know if it's the best thing to do, but I do know that I've made up my mind."

"Where do you want to go? Where will it be better?"

"I don't know. Just as long as it's far away, and it's a place I've never been with Dana. I've been thinking about Northern

California—maybe somewhere on the coast like Monterey, or even in the mountains. That's got to feel different."

Rice looked at me squarely for a while before saying, "I'm sorry to see you go, I really am, but if that's the way it's got to be, I've got an idea." Then he simply picked William Sherman's number out of his contact list and phoned the man right in front of me. After getting past the pleasantries and some catching up, which included the last time they'd golfed together at a championship course of world-renown, an annual ritual, he told him about me and what had happened in my life. To my amazement, he then convinced the man to hire me, despite the fact that I did overhear the phrase "basket case" somewhere in the conversation.

"Have you found a place to live yet?" Sherman asked as a large plate of enchiladas was slid in front of him.

"I rented a condo in Tahoe."

"Tahoe? Isn't that a little far?"

"A little, but I love to drive, especially on a twisty two lane blacktop like Highway 50. Women have their aroma therapy candles. I have a new Carrera 4 S. It's got to be better than lying on a stinking couch and spilling your guts to some diploma-laden, psycho-analyzing pompous ass for two hundred dollars an hour, which, come to think of it, is just about what the car costs."

Sherman chuckled a little. "The drive is going to be impossible next winter. The pass at Echo Summit is a snowy mess half the time."

I thought about the morning's ride over the summit, the road clinging to a shear rock face on one side and jutting out in space on the other a thousand feet over a place called Christmas Valley. "I'll be okay. The car has all-wheel-drive. If I can't do it, I'll move here. I haven't had a chance to look it over yet, but this seems like a nice little town. In the meantime, it's one hell of a way to start the day. The scenery is incredible, especially at Twin Bridges. Are you familiar with it?"

Sherman nodded.

"The grandeur of it all is breath-taking, isn't it?" I asked rhetorically. "Especially the way those gigantic granite monoliths rise near the road and climb in the distance to reach the cobalt sky. How could you get tired of it? There's even a spectacular waterfall way the hell up there. I can only imagine how it'll look covered with snow."

"That's Horsetail Falls," Sherman said. "It feeds the American River that runs beside the highway. You should hike up there while the spring runoff is strong. It's a beautiful place."

I nodded, but didn't mention how I'd missed Dana as I raced the roaring river down through the mountains. I remembered thinking that if she'd been in the empty seat beside me, I would have touched her cheek, or taken her hand in mine and brought it to my lips, as I had so many times, never thinking that our lives together would be cut short by fifty or sixty years. It was, however, the memory of the last time we were in the mountains together that brought me back to a day when we'd both almost died.

We'd gone away for a romantic weekend in the Adirondacks. I'd booked a secluded cabin on the shores of historic Lake George two hundred miles north of the city, where we intended to make some history of our own. As it turned out, we did.

We arrived on a beautiful Saturday afternoon in late April three years ago. The plan for the rest of the day was to explore the sprawling lake and a few nearby islands by canoe, which we did until the weather abruptly turned and we were suddenly paddling against a fierce wind, spray blowing off little whitecaps and from the tips of our paddles as we desperately struggled to get back.

Have you ever capsized a canoe in wickedly cold water a quarter of a mile from shore? Maybe it wasn't as bad as it seemed. Maybe it was worse. I don't know. But that night we made love over and over again, sometimes tenderly, the melding of two inherently gentle people. And then furiously, trying to somehow reach each other on a new level, not only elated to be alive, but to still have one another. "I was so afraid I'd lose you," she'd said, looking into my eyes, my face in her hands, our skin touching from head to toe. "I was more panicked about losing you than I was about dying myself." She was crying and smiling at the same time. "I don't want to live without you. I never had to think about it before, but now I know. Hold me. Make love to me." She kissed me like I'd never been kissed. "Make love to me, Robert, and don't stop. Don't ever stop!"

As hard as we tried, it seemed we couldn't hold each other tight enough that night, or any other night since. Besides the trivial things we learn every day, and I'm smart enough to know that I do indeed learn something new every day, the last year without my wife taught me that once someone else makes your spirit complete, it's difficult going back to being a partial person.

I refrained from telling Bill Sherman that story, not wanting him to think that hiring me had been a mistake, that I was still an inconsolably preoccupied blithering mess.

"Why did you become an architect?" he asked.

I sat back in my chair, smiled, and said in a lighthearted sort of way, "It's a little late for an interview, isn't it? I thought I had the job."

"You do. I'm just curious. There's no right or wrong answer."

"Because of my father."

"Your father was an architect?"

"No. He sold things to earn a living; first food, then beer, then automobiles. Food and beer turn to shit in no time. Cars last longer. But he hadn't designed them. He'd only sold them. Don't get me wrong. I've always had a great deal of respect for my dad. He had a unique sense of style and charm, which I truly admired, and a work ethic second to none. He's the one who taught me that a job worth doing is not only worth doing well, but should be completed using every ounce of one's ability, preferably while wearing a Brooks Brothers suit and tie. For the most part I find myself living to his standards without trying, except for falling a little short sartorially, as you can see. But in the end, what proof exists that he ever lived? What had he created other than me?"

William Sherman thought about this for a minute while probably feeling a little self-conscious about his outfit. Then he began to nod. I can't say that he was impressed, but it was marginally clear that he understood the need for immortality.

Perhaps I should have left it at that, but something made me say, "If I had designed the pyramids, I would have signed them."

"That sounds a little pretentious, but I like a man who's proud of his work. I think we'll get along just fine."

"I'll do a good job for you and the firm."

"Harold had only good things to say about you, although he does think you're a little too cynical."

"That's something else I inherited from my father. He was a world-class worrier. Not that I could blame him after our first major confrontation with futility."

"He's not still with us?"

"No. His heart gave out a few years after my mother died. She perished from some incredibly rare form of cancer when I was ten. Starting over in another part of the country was not a decision I could have made then."

I can still remember the specialists parading around the hospital in their white lab coats and stethoscopes. One afternoon they took pictures of my mother for a medical journal. I've wondered from time to time what really happened to those photos, since I've never seen the publication for which they were allegedly intended. Because I was a child, taking pictures of my mother naked seemed wrong. But that was, of course, the whole point. If she'd had her clothes on, how could anyone have seen all those purple spots?

I haven't undergone psychoanalysis, but it's a pretty safe bet that any shrink worth his salt would probably make a big deal about the fact that the only two women of significance in my life had both been taken from me by malevolent forces beyond my control. Factoring in that little tidbit, how well-adjusted could I be?

Sherman winced a little and asked, "Do you have any children?"

"No"

"You had no one else in New York?"

"My wife and my uncle, my only blood relative, were both murdered at the same time a year ago in his apartment in Forest Hills, a quiet neighborhood in Queens, one of the five boroughs that comprise New York City. The police think it was a home invasion. Maxwell lived alone, and Dana had taken it upon herself to bring him groceries, prepare a home-cooked meal in his apartment from time to time, or take him out to lunch when the weather allowed it. I know it sounds a little corny, but he loved her like a daughter, the daughter he'd never had. He'd told me so. She was there that day. When I left for a convention I had family. When I returned, I had no one."

"I can see why you wanted to leave."

"My uncle was an artist. It wasn't his day job, but it was his persona. I'm convinced he saw the most mundane things like no one else. He would stop and point out the intricacies of time-sensitive shadows and why they fell the way they did, or the way sunlight intensified color as we'd walk past a garden. It was almost as if his crystal blue-green eyes absorbed textures and colors and hues and depth, the things most people take for granted without a second glance or thought, and stored them the way a battery stores energy. He had incredible eyes. They were so bright. That's what I remember most about him. That, and the fact that he looked like David Niven."

"The late English actor?" Sherman asked.

I nodded. "Mack is probably the source of my professional abilities. He was a master of perspective."

"I thought you said his name was Maxwell."

"It was. That was his given name, but to me he was always Uncle Mack, although I can't remember why."

Bill Sherman seemed genuinely interested in my description. Then he commented, "It does sound like he did have quite an influence on you."

"Undoubtedly."

"What did he do for a living?"

"He worked in the subway for the Transit Authority. Despite a difficult life, I recognized a certain inner sparkle in his eyes up to and including the very last day I saw him alive. The way it all ended is a damned shame. He'd survived the Korean War and a bad bout with prostate cancer, only to be shot to death in his own living room. Apparently, he couldn't survive New York City."

"Did the police ever make an arrest?"

I moved my head in the negative just enough to be perceptible and realized that I'd had more than enough of memory lane for a while so I said, "Tell me a little about yourself and the company."

He did and I liked what I heard. I know about buildings; about what constitutes curb appeal, about floor loads, and if it will stand in a hurricane, but I've never been a very good judge of character. Structural integrity is easier to appraise than human integrity. Still, I had a good feeling about William Sherman— father, businessman, experienced architect, historian, avid gun collector, and veteran. That aside, he tried to pick up the tab to welcome me, but I paid it to say thanks for the opportunity to start my life over in California.

I spent the afternoon familiarizing myself with California licensing requirements and Pine County codes. I wanted to stay past five, but Sherman assured me that tomorrow would be another day. It was good to hear someone else say those words. I thanked him again for making me part of his team and headed for my car.

I was soon driving east on Highway 50, the early stages of sunset settling over the mountains. When I'd had a favorite time of day, this was it. The setting sun bathes the faces of nature in gold. Trees seem more defined, shadows emerging and growing Earth's third dimension. Spring leaves dangle like emeralds. Stone seems softer. Lakes and rivers sparkle as if strewn with sequins.

I settled back in my seat and set the automatic speed control, a little more at ease with the decisions I'd made lately—decisions responsible for my being in California. A disturbing, yet strangely calming truth came to me in an annoyingly philosophical moment: No matter how hard we try to be in control of our lives, anything can happen to anyone at any time—anything at all.

The sun was in my mirrors, touching the horizon behind me. It lit up the narrow valley like a projector beaming from the rear of a theater, golden rays streaming past me, skimming over the river to my right that still ran down the western slope of the Sierra Nevada toward the sea. As I rounded yet another bend in the road it shone, as if with purpose, upon the side of a white house located on the opposite bank. It was at that moment that the obsession began.

I considered pulling over, but the cars behind me were too close to permit any sudden moves. I sat up in my seat as I passed the only house on the other side of the river and the narrow footbridge that made it accessible. I had to go half a mile before a turnout presented itself. I pulled over, waited for the thin traffic to clear in both directions, and swung a U-turn, wondering why I hadn't noticed the house in the morning. That question was answered as I passed the bridge again. The house was barely visible from the westbound exposure. I drove to the point a little further downriver where the house first came into view, turned around again, and pulled over where the shoulder permitted a clear line of sight. I turned off the engine and just sat there, staring at the scene—a simple white house beside a rushing river. I sat there until the setting sun no longer illuminated the west wall directly, from the shrub-covered ground to the tip of the roof's apex.

When the details finally succumbed to the gloom, I restarted the car and drove slowly past the white Lexus SUV parked perpendicular to the road and facing the river in a small paved area near the bridge access. Then I continued back to Tahoe and shut the Porsche down exactly where I'd started fourteen hours earlier. I pulled the car's tool kit from where the salesman told me it was stowed and took it into my apartment. I filled the tea kettle with bottled water, probably from a tap in the Bronx, and pried open the wooden crates in the living room. One by one I extricated the paintings of Maxwell Bennett until, at last, the one I sought appeared in my hands. I set it on the beige carpet, leaning the framed oil-on-canvas against the wall.

I made a cup of tea and sat on a barstool at the breakfast counter staring at the painting for as long as I'd stared at the house beside the river.

There were some obvious differences between the house in the painting and the one I'd passed on the way back to my new home. The one in the frame was three stories, the real one was two. In the painting, the white house appeared to rise from the waterline, as if in Venice, but the real house had been set back, accounting for high water. And one had a small porch, the other did not. But still, the resemblance was uncanny, at least to me. Perhaps that's why I pulled out my phone and snapped a photo of the painting.

    I finished my tea, washed up, and decided to have dinner in the restaurant at the marina. I headed for the door, but stopped on the way out for one more look at the painting, unable to imagine the ways in which it would change my life.

·

2

I watched Deputy Johnson drive away that Saturday morning five days after I'd first noticed the house and thought, I don't like being wrong, and I like being told I'm wrong even less. What had started out as the best day in a long time was rapidly going downhill, and it had little to do with my descent from South Lake Tahoe's 6,252 foot elevation.

I awoke that morning thinking about the house beside the river, instead of thinking about Dana—how beautiful she was, or how I ached to hold her, or imagining the horrible way in which she died. I couldn't do anything to bring her back to life, to bring her back into *my* life, but I could try to find out why I felt so inexorably drawn to that simple white country house. Common sense told me the whole thing was nothing more than a coincidence. What more could it be? But at least I could check it out. Either there'd be more to it, or there wouldn't. I could go there. It wasn't that far away. And presumably, people were alive inside. It wasn't a grave.

I dressed in cleaning attire, drove down Tahoe Keys Boulevard to the do-it-yourself carwash, soaped, rinsed, and dried the new love of my life, returned to my condo, and did the same to myself. I pulled on a fresh pair of jeans, a light denim shirt, and a pair of running shoes. In no time at all I was back in the driver's seat, an undeniable eagerness mixing with the relaxed feel of the weekend.

That whole week, in fact, hadn't been too bad. I'd immersed myself in a strip mall project. The proposed shopping center was to be in El Dorado Hills, a sprawling area in the lower foothills above Folsom, between Sacramento and Placerville. The initial plans were fairly attractive, but admittedly they were somewhat less impressive than other notable projects in history, like the Taj Mahal, Notre Dame, or the Guggenheim.

Still, despite my hard work, it felt as if I were just going through the motions. At that point in my life I wasn't really sure what I was looking for, although I suppose some romance and great sex, or any sex at all for that matter, would have been nice.

I forced myself to stay away from Jenny, Bill Sherman's daughter, not wanting to be presumed a lecherous old bastard, even though thirty-six is not all that old. Beautiful, smart, and sexy, she was a natural blonde in her early twenties with vivid blue eyes and great legs. Having her in the office every day could have been a problem but, fortunately, she was a student at Cal Poly in San Luis Obispo here on spring break, and only filling in for the vacationing receptionist. Did I really just say that?

I wasn't doing that badly. I had a pleasant job working with nice people in a nice place, although the Nazi was questionable, especially after learning that Heinrich "Make Ready the Forward Tubes" Essen did in fact have relatives living in Argentina. I wasn't exactly rolling in dough, but the only worry about my next meal was deciding where to eat it. I'd moved to one of the most beautiful places on the planet, where, from every window of my condo, I had a splendid view of snowcapped mountains, an enormous shimmering alpine lake complete with oceanic white caps on blustery days, and a tranquil marina filled with sailboats. And last but not least, I had great wheels that went really fast. What else could I have wanted?

But needless to say, something was missing. I knew what it was, of course. Or should I say *who* it was, but I'm really trying to keep from being morbid. I mean, that's why I'd moved all the way across the whole damn continent. The point was to start fresh. And I was trying, but the hole in my life must have showed somehow.

Sherman had asked if I had any hobbies. Stamp collecting and bird-watching come to mind whenever anyone asks that question. I could have killed two birds with one stone by becoming an ornithological philatelist, collecting stamps with birds on them, but I don't think I could have handled the excitement.

As it turned out, something did happen in my life that began to occupy my free time. At first, it was only in my mind, a strange obsession connecting the simple white house beside the river that I had to pass on my daily commute with the house in the painting my late uncle painted in 1981. I wrestled with the silliness of the whole thing. There had to be thousands of similar structures throughout the country, even accounting for its proximity to a narrow river. Of that I'm certain. After all, I am an architect.

Still, it was something I couldn't ignore. Beyond that, I really can't explain it. Call it fate, or destiny, or kismet, or whatever you want, as long as it means it was meant to be. I couldn't pass the house on my way home after work without stopping to look at it every evening. I would pull over and just sit and study the property until the sun abandoned the quaint rural scene. A few times I'd gotten out of the car for a closer look at the river, swollen with runoff and filling the narrow valley with the unmistakable sounds of rushing water. I watched it swirl past boulders visible just below the surface and around exposed rocks closer to the banks with frothy displays. But despite the swift water's turbulence, I felt the undeniable tranquility that hung in the spring air of early evening. To a city boy, the setting seemed almost idyllic.

Now, parked beside the river, things looked a little different while facing east in late morning instead of at dusk. The changes I noticed were subtle, associated mostly with the length of shadows, or the lack thereof, as the sun approached its zenith. I looked at the photo on my phone and tried to determine the time of day in the painting. There were no shadows to speak of, indicative of midday as well, but the abstractly violent sky could have warned of a brewing storm. I'd never given it much thought, really, but my interpretation of the subject matter had always been quite literal. Even at that moment, giving the details of the painting more scrutiny than ever before, it still didn't occur to me that the stormy sky could have been a metaphor for the despair and turmoil in the artist's mind.

I looked at the large blue tree beside the house in the painting and remembered my uncle asking, "Have you ever seen a blue tree?" At the time I didn't know what point he was trying to make, but I definitely had the sense that that tree, a tree painted entirely in blue, had a very special significance for him.

I looked across the river in search of a big blue tree but, of course, it wasn't there. I shook my head at the mystery and cleared the screen on my phone. Why had he painted a blue tree? And why didn't I have the sense to ask him about it while he was still alive?

I looked at the long and narrow footbridge spanning the river and considered my next move. Deputy Johnson's opinion played over in my mind: "I think you're just wasting your time." It almost sent me on my way, back whence I'd come. But once my mind wraps itself around something, even if it's an odd notion, I can't let it go. I knew if I didn't do what I'd set out to do, I'd probably be back in the same spot the following Saturday. Then a few clichéd sayings came to mind, the likes of: Nothing ventured—nothing gained; no guts—no glory; a journey of a thousand miles must begin with a single step; and my own personal favorite, for which I'll take the credit: If you don't ask—you don't get.

I started the Porsche again, drove the two-hundred feet to the small paved area near the bridge access, parked beside the white Lexus SUV that had been there every morning and evening that week, secured the car out of habit, and walked across the bridge. I stopped briefly at mid-span, first for a view directly upriver at the gorge and snow-capped mountaintops of the Sierra Nevada. The sun was glistening on the fast-flowing water headed my way. Then I turned to the west for a glimpse downriver, the fresh and clean early spring breeze suddenly in my face. I could feel the warmth from above and the chill from below. I held the railing and looked over the edge at the crystal-clear snowmelt spilling beneath me in an unstoppable torrent. A little unnerved at the thought that the iron pipe in my grasp might give way, I continued to the other side, stopping near the porch that wasn't in the painting. I gave the house and surrounding property the once over and immediately ascended the few steps that led to the front door, not wanting to appear like a trespasser if I were being observed. The door was white with raised panels surrounding a small rectangular window formed from irregularly-shaped pieces of glass held together by leaded seams. I pressed the button beside the jamb and heard a chime ring inside. A minute later I noticed movement within and the door opened.

"Amy, you're early. I didn't think you'd be here until…" The elderly woman stopped in mid-sentence, realizing I wasn't the person she was apparently expecting. "Oh. I beg your pardon. Can I help you?"

"Hello. My name is Robert Bennett. I don't know where to begin except by saying…" I stopped in mid-sentence too, surprised by her reaction. Her jaw dropped, parting her thin lips as her pale green eyes widened. I've never seen a ghost, nor have I been present when anyone else has seen one, but if a spirit had introduced itself to the woman in the doorway, I couldn't have imagined her looking any different. I waited a few seconds, wondering what the hell was going on, and could only think to ask, "Are you okay?"

She steadied herself by holding onto the door. She tried to find her breath.

I said, "Maybe you should sit down."

She ignored my suggestion and said instead, "Is Maxwell all right?"

I don't really know how long I stood there before speaking again. And I can only imagine the look on my own face. "You know who I am?"

She nodded and stood aside. "Why don't you come in?"

I stepped over the threshold and into the house. If Rod Serling had been standing in the corner saying something about a painting, obsession, and a man from New York City, I would have listened to the small mob of brain cells telling me to turn around, walk off the porch, get back to my car, and get the hell out of there before the door closed me inside.

She led me into the parlor and said, "Please sit down. I'll make some tea." She turned and hurried off.

I must have stood where I stopped for a minute or two, locked in a state of disbelief. I can't really remember my exact thoughts, but concepts like different dimensions and parallel universes must have been swimming around in my head. I do remember, however, that a faint undercurrent of fear, just enough to make me shiver, was mixing with the curiosity that had pushed me this far.

There was nothing threatening about the room per se, although it was a little dark despite the sunlight beaming through two sash windows; one beside the door, albeit hindered by the porch overhang, and one at the front corner of the west wall further to my right. I noticed a different exposure through each. Both were trimmed with maroon taffeta floor-length drapes tied back with decorative gold tassels, which struck me as being particularly elegant. I knew the light of day entering through the bi-parting French patio doors cut in the back wall's southern exposure was filtered by the tall pines that stood behind the house. I could see the bridge, otherwise known as my escape route, through the window beside the entrance door.

Just before the kitchen to the left, I saw that carpeted stairs dividing the floor plan led straight to the second floor. I glanced up the stairway sheathed in beige Berber as far as I could and saw only a few framed photographs on the left-hand wall arranged in an ascending fashion. I was tempted to approach and scrutinize the pictures to see if I recognized anyone or anything, but I refrained from entering a staircase that undoubtedly led to the bedrooms, not wanting to appear overly intrusive in a stranger's home.

Instead, hearing my own footsteps on the polished hardwood floor, I ventured further into the living room in search of something that might have meaning to me, and also to get a feel for the type of person or persons who lived in the house. Beyond a small closet or bathroom under the stairs, I saw white bookshelves along the entire length of the left wall. They appeared to be filled from floor to ceiling with hardbound first editions.

I scanned the rest of the furnishings, starting with the Persian rug in front of the river rock fireplace at the center of the opposite wall, setting the stage for a French provincial grouping. It consisted of two floral brocade armchairs with a small round table and lamp between them, both facing a delicate coffee table perpendicular to the hearth, and a light green sateen settee with its own end table and lamp. In my opinion, the décor was decidedly feminine, with fringes on the lamp shades and knick-knacks everywhere.

But for me, the most striking aspect of the room was the artwork—four paintings, each with a brass lamp affixed to its frame but not presently illuminated. I recognized the one on the back wall, to the right of the French doors, as being the work of Leland Drake, an artist known for his charming scenes of rural America. I am by no means a connoisseur, but I do know a few things about art thanks to my wonderful, talented, and very well-read uncle.

Still alone, I began to meander, looking at everything on and between the harvest gold walls trimmed with white baseboards and crown moldings, trying to find clues that would help explain what was happening, and what I'd gotten myself into. I scanned the little hand-painted candy dishes, saucers, miniature Grecian urns, diminutive Oriental dynasty vases, and creamer pitchers on the tables. Many of the curios seemed strangely familiar, and an undeniable feeling of *déjà vu* came over me. It gave me pause at the time, but I dismissed the chord of recognition, not knowing much about those sorts of things, thinking they were the types of dust collectors commonly found in touristy gift shops.

I studied the faces in framed photographs that stood amidst the bric-a-brac. They were mostly portrait shots snapped at various times in the twentieth century: Black and whites taken around the time of the Titanic, World War II, and through the Fifties and Sixties. More recent photos were in color. Strangely, I remember noticing that facial expressions and poses changed along with hair and clothing styles, all of which seemed to loosen up and become less formal as time went by. But I knew no one.

I moved to the mantel to examine the photos there, another half dozen, all apparently taken more recently. The last photo on the right was of an extraordinarily beautiful woman in her late twenties or early thirties. She had shoulder-length auburn hair and piercing pale green eyes. I attributed the intensity of her eyes to her youth. I recognized no one, but suspected in that mesmerizing moment that she was the granddaughter of the woman who'd opened the door.

I raised my gaze and looked at the painting above the mantel. The work was an original oil-on-canvas depicting a majestic square-rigger under full sail on the high seas. It was a stately painting set in an appropriately ornate, gilded frame. My eyes wandered to the lower right corner. There was only one name there. That was the way my uncle signed all of his paintings. The name was Bennett.

3

"Is he all right, or did you come here with bad news?"

I turned and saw the woman of the house holding a plate full of cookies. She wore a dark blue dress hemmed a few inches below the knee, and I thought the single strand of pearls that hung around her neck was appropriate. She was thin, but not frail. And either she applied a modest amount of make-up every day, or she'd planned to go out. She was rather pleasant looking, and must have been quite attractive in her youth.

I didn't know where to begin, what to ask, or what to explain. I envisioned the dish hitting the hardwood floor and shattering into a million pieces, the cookies crumbling amongst the porcelain shards, if I answered directly. I took the plate from her and set it on the coffee table. Then I turned, extended my hand, and when she took it I said, "I'm afraid I do have bad news."

"I see," she said, plainly.

I thought I saw her lower lip quiver.

"We've never been properly introduced," she continued, not allowing her emotions time to surface. "I'm May Drake. Won't you sit down?"

I lowered myself onto one of the floral chairs, and she seated herself in the corner of the settee, the table between us. My head was almost spinning. I couldn't very well say, *I've heard so much about you.* Nor could I say, *my uncle never even mentioned your name.* It was my impression that if this woman had been British, she couldn't have been more proper. The last thing I wanted was to seem rude. I resolved to choose my words very carefully, and where applicable, abide by the two ears/one mouth policy. I said, "There is so much I want to know about you."

She smiled ever so slightly. "What happened to Maxwell?"

"He died in his apartment a year ago."

She lowered her eyes and looked at her clasped hands. "Was it the cancer?"

I could feel the anger that consumed me in New York return as I remembered my uncle's modest apartment turned bloody crime scene. *It was the cancer, all right. The two-legged cancer that prowls the streets in search of lives to destroy!*

She continued before I could answer. "I know he had cancer years ago."

I picked up one of the curios on the end table beside me, a three inch-tall urn. I looked at the pastel flowers painted on black enamel. The rim was decorated with gold, like a piece of fine china. A small round piece of green felt had been glued to the bottom. "No. That wasn't it. He was murdered."

"Oh, my God." She winced, covering her mouth with both hands.

Certainly, the crime of murder was not confined to New York, but the brutality of the city seemed a million miles away from this idyllic place. If the degree of violence that had taken Dana and my Uncle Mack from this world was hard for me to accept, it would have been impossible for this small-town, genteel woman.

"Maxwell bought that for me more than fifty years ago," she said, her eyes following the antique in my hand. "We were in San Francisco. I remember it as if it were yesterday. He bought two of them. He said that if we each had one when we spoke on the phone, or read a letter, we would always remember that day and how we felt about one another." She paused, as if transported back in time.

It occurred to me to say, *apparently, he was right,* but I didn't want to break the spell.

She looked up at me and said, "He was quite romantic, you know. He was a kind and wonderful man—a gentleman in every sense of the word. He bought many of the precious little things you see here, some on subsequent visits, and others were shipped from New York. There were always two, one for me and one for him."

I put the *objet d'art* back on the table very carefully, now knowing exactly why the keenly detailed porcelain pieces seemed so familiar.

She continued with a smile of remembrance. "Each time one arrived in the mail, it contained a letter neatly rolled up and tied with a ribbon. It seemed as if the prose were the gift, and the exquisitely painted treasure was only the wrapping. I knew that he'd gone to great lengths to find each prize and prepare it for its journey. He must have done the same organizing his thoughts and putting them down on paper. Even though we ultimately lived our lives apart, I've always found great warmth and comfort knowing the way he felt about me."

So this was the woman who'd almost changed the course of Maxwell Bennett's life. Memories of faded and soundless home movies shot before I was born were coming back to me. My parents were visiting the house in Richmond Hill, an old two-story on a tree-lined block in a blue-collar neighborhood in Queens. I can recall seeing on the flickering film the enclosed porch and long one-lane driveway to the right of the house, which led to a single car garage with dark green barn doors. Equally clear in my mind is the small square grass-covered backyard that butted up against the brick wall of a firehouse whose entrance, I'd been told, was around the corner. They'd spent many a Saturday or Sunday at my aunt and uncle's place, but what made that particular day different was the fact that Uncle Mack was gone.

Maxwell and Sophie were brother and sister—my father's siblings. Neither had ever married. Sophie was a sales associate selling fine scarves at the original Saks Fifth Avenue department store in Manhattan. She preferred to be called Sid. In fact, calling her Sophie would provoke a look that could scare you right out of the room. What I remember most about Aunt Sid, besides the fact that she taught me how to use a clothes iron and an ironing board, was that her favorite color was yellow. What I remember least was that she'd had more than her share of health problems.

As the story goes, Mack had been gone a week. He'd loaded up his shiny black 1961 Thunderbird and was headed for California to spend the rest of his life with a woman about whom my parents may have known little. I'd learned some of the intricacies of my uncle's life from my father as the years went by. In a nutshell, he'd graduated from Long Island University, but had cast off admission into med school in order to work full-time, first at a sign shop, and then in the subway for the New York City Transit Authority, to help pay Sid's medical bills, essentially sacrificing his career goals for his sister. Now, something I'd known all along, but had never really considered, was becoming obvious. He'd not only forfeited his professional life for someone else; he'd given up his personal life as well. *What else is there?*

On that sunny and tranquil afternoon, Sid and my parents were sitting on garden furniture under a peach tree in the backyard, probably wondering how far Mack had gotten when the Thunderbird thundered up the narrow concrete driveway, skidding to a stop just short of crashing through the closed swing-out garage doors. Mack was irate, to say the least. Or to borrow a phrase from my father's lexicon, the man was "fit to be tied." That was quite apparent in the film taken with my father's eight millimeter Kodak movie camera by a visiting neighbor who just happened to be shooting at the time. My dad told me that he'd had to walk his brother around the block just to calm him down. Mack had made it as far as Indianapolis before turning around. We never heard another word about it, although we did watch the film several times over the years. Each and every viewing reminded us just how pivotal that day had been in our lives for it returned their brother to Sid and to my father. And it gave me back my extraordinarily compassionate uncle.

I observed the woman who would have been my aunt sitting alone in the corner of the love seat and imagined Uncle Mack beside her, holding her hand. I couldn't help but think they would have looked nice together. It didn't take long for me to realize that if he'd kept going that summer so long ago, and had spent his life here, he wouldn't have been in that apartment. He would still be alive. And Dana wouldn't have been there either. They would *both* be alive.

I looked past May Drake at the painting on the far wall behind her. It depicted a sunlit-stretch of seashore. "Are you related to Leland Drake?"

"He's my ex-husband." Her expression changed from one of introspection to one of disenchantment. "I met Leland after knowing, but not quite accepting, that Maxwell wasn't moving here to be with me—that he'd chosen instead to care for his sister. At first I resented her, but I soon realized she wasn't my rival. I've always respected his decision. I know it was the most difficult decision of his life. It didn't mean he loved her more—or me less. She was his sister, for God's sake. It was just something he had to do. That was the kind of man he was." May Drake lowered her eyes and said, "The irony is, it just made me love him that much more."

We both heard the tea kettle begin to whistle.

She stood and said, "I'll be right back."

After she left the room, a burning curiosity compelled me to identify the two remaining paintings, one on either side of the fireplace. Both were signed, but the names meant nothing to me, so I picked up the untouched plate of cookies and joined May Drake in the kitchen.

It was situated at the northeast corner of the house to the left of the stairs. I expected to see the entrance to a formal dining room at the far wall, but there was none, only the U-shaped sweep of countertop and cupboards. I'm an architect, not an interior designer, but I've always had an eye for detail—spatial arrangements, color and lighting—things like that. Although the kitchen had obviously been remodeled to include several modern appliances, it still managed to exude a warm and homey old-world charm. I noticed decorative plates adorning the walls, and a variety of leafy green plants in hand-painted ceramic pots topping cabinets that stopped a foot short of the ceiling. I imagined this elderly lady standing precariously on a step ladder, extending her reach with a watering can.

The room was spacious and airy with two windows—one above the sink on the left wall for a picture-perfect shot upriver, and one carved out of the home's north-facing front wall for a view of the bridge. This was in stark contrast to the closet-size kitchens of my Brooklyn apartment-dwelling youth, where the one and only galley window faced a dismal courtyard if you were lucky or a brick wall if you weren't.

I placed the cookies on a large dinette table in front of the bridge-facing window and glanced outside. A few cars traveling the two-lane blacktop beyond the river helped me realize just how rural the setting was for this woman's life. "So this is what a country kitchen looks like."

She nodded. "I've been very comfortable here."

I noticed the yellow lace curtains framing the view and thought of my Aunt Sid. I always think of my late aunt whenever I see yellow lace curtains. They're like a posthypnotic suggestion. There'd never been a view like this through *her* urban windows—neither from the house in Richmond Hill, nor from the two subsequent apartments—one in Kew Gardens and one in Forest Hills.

My mind compared the two women. If Sid were still alive, she would have been about ten years older. Both liked yellow, both liked porcelain decorations, and both had loved my uncle—albeit in different ways. Both women had a certain air of dignity about them, although Sid's sense of humor was better. I froze that observation, noting that I'd just met May. And certainly, the nature of the conversation thus far had hardly left any room for jest. I did have the sense that Sid's life had been considerably more difficult, although perhaps less lonely, given the fact that she'd had Mack, and that this woman was divorced. I knew virtually nothing about her ex-husband, Leland Drake, except for his celebrity. I wondered if he'd dumped May for a younger woman when he'd made it big, a so-called trophy wife. She didn't seem bitter, but then, she'd spoken only of Maxwell Bennett, not Leland Drake.

I thought of the little hand-painted pieces of her life in the other room and realized that for some people life moves forward, and for others life stands still. Apparently, I'd made the decision to move forward. That's why I was in California.

Then an odd thought shifted my mind from the philosophical to the devious, where it was undoubtedly more at home. Had my uncle, in fact, bought the lifetime supply of duplicate dust collectors for the reason he'd given May, or had he really purchased every matching twin for Sid? That was a question that could never be answered.

I asked, "How do you know who I am?"

"Maxwell and I kept in touch over the years. He was proud of you. That you'd gone to college. And that you'd become an architect. Obviously, artistic ability runs in the Bennett family. I'm sorry your mother passed away when you were so young."

I pulled back inside, unnerved that a total stranger knew more about me than I did about her. I said, "It's quite a coincidence that the two men in your life were both artists."

She paused for a moment, almost as if no one had ever made that observation before. "Not really. My life has always revolved around art. I owned a gallery many years ago. How do you take your tea, Robert?"

"Just a little sugar, please. Your ex has done quite well for himself. I've seen his work in many places. Even on greeting cards, come to think of it. He's obviously very talented."

She nodded, but didn't agree. Then she asked, "How did you find me?"

I'd been afraid that question would come up. I didn't think

that trying to explain the inexplicable was really necessary, or even a good idea. It would have, of course, been the same thing as saying, I'd never heard of you. I simply smiled and said, "I suppose I just got lucky."

May Drake smiled tentatively. "Have you tried one of my oatmeal cookies?"

"Not yet."

I gently placed the fine china tea cup and saucer on a macramé placemat as we seated ourselves at the table near the front window. Then some movement outside caught my eye. I turned and saw a young woman walking toward the house from the bridge. I glanced across the river and spotted a late model bright red BMW Three Series convertible with the top down now parked next to my car. I focused on the woman nearing the porch and noticed her cinnamon-brown waist-length leather jacket, faded blue jeans tight all the way to the ankle, and short saddle-colored lace-up leather Victorian boots. "You've got company, May," I said.

She glanced outside. "That's my granddaughter, Amy. She's here to take me to lunch. Why don't you join us?"

"Will she know who I am? I don't want to make things awkward for you."

"Thank you for that, but she knows about Maxwell." She paused and corrected herself. "I mean she knows who he was. We're very close."

I stood and followed May Drake to the front door, where she introduced me to the girl in the photo.

4

Lunch was interesting, to say the least. I mean, these people could have been my long lost relatives. If my uncle had married May, Amy would have been my cousin. I was certainly glad that wasn't the case.

We talked about the things people talk about when first getting to know each other—where we live, where we came from, what we enjoy, where we've gone, and what we've done—the things that make us who we are. I suppose, however, it's more accurate to say that people will tell you what they want you to know, as opposed to what they don't want you to know. Learning those things takes more time, if you can get that close. And I wanted to get that close to Amy. I knew it from the minute I laid eyes on her.

The restaurant was a charming little place that served Bavarian cuisine beside the river—knockwurst, bratwurst, spätzle, schnitzel, and sauerbraten—all of which taste much better than they sound. I made a mental note to tell *Herr* Essen about it, although I had the feeling he not only knew about it already, but attended secret meetings there on Thursday nights.

The conversation seemed to flow quite naturally. By the time the schnitzel arrived, I'd learned that May Drake had earned a degree in art history from UCLA and had met a tourist named Maxwell Bennett in the art gallery she'd owned in San Francisco. When I asked why she'd chosen that field she replied, "Because I wanted to fill my life with beautiful things."

At first I equated this with wealth, which I wouldn't have faulted.

But May continued, "The arts and sciences separate humans from animals. I wanted to fill my mind with celebrated human creations. Art throughout history, including architecture, has advanced civilizations all over the world. The *Renaissance* helped lift the people of Europe out of the Dark Ages. Art is the observable expression of human imagination, perhaps the most wonderful aspect of what makes us people."

This confirmed something I already knew. The woman across the table in the demure navy blue dress and pearls was the perfect picture of dignity, although I did want to point out that we, too, were animals. In a world characterized throughout history by barbarism, pillaging, domination, fanaticism, and ruthlessness, this lady was the personification of enlightenment. I might add that my appraisal had nothing to do with her mentioning architecture, which I don't believe was solely for my benefit.

I also noticed that Amy exuded an obvious and undeniable sense of pride, as if May were her daughter instead of her grandmother. In fact, she stood, stepped behind the woman, and kissed her on the cheek, their faces side by side—two sets of pale green eyes illuminating the restaurant. "That's my grandma."

May Drake reached up and cradled Amy's face in her palm.

"I love you, too, Sweetie."

I smiled at both women. The resemblance was apparent. I know it's been said that if you want to see what a young bride will be like later in life, look at her mother. I flashed on the thought that starting off with Amy and ending up with May, if you get my drift, wouldn't be that bad. I wouldn't go so far as to say that my uncle had made a mistake by turning around somewhere in Indiana, which would have meant abandoning his sister, but continuing on to California would not have been a bad move either.

Throughout lunch I said as little about myself as possible, though trying not to sound secretive or evasive. This was quite the exercise in diplomacy, especially considering the fact that until a couple of hours ago I had no idea these two people even existed. I left out the entire *white house beside the river in the painting obsession*, which was, of course, why I'd stopped in the first place and how I'd met them, saying instead that Maxwell had spoken about May, and that I'd felt an obligation to let her know what had happened to him. In my own defense, it did seem like the right thing to say, even if it wasn't true. Don't think any less of me knowing that I stretched it a little further, saying that I'd always wanted to meet the woman about whom my uncle had felt so strongly.

I didn't want to talk about my wife; how we'd met, what she did daily as a nurse in NYU Medical Center's Cardiac Intensive Care Unit, how adored and respected she'd been, how happy we were, or how much I loved her. And I didn't want to mention how hard the last year had been living without her, or even that she'd been murdered only a few feet from my uncle. Truthfully, I didn't want to turn lunch, which had become a voyage of discovery, into a morbid requiem. I also didn't want Amy to get the impression that I was on the rebound, or that I was desperate and therefore pathetic; although, if I didn't say now that I'd considered the merits of the sympathy angle as a possible means of bringing us closer, I'd be lying. In the final analysis, my wife *had* been killed and that was why I'd left New York, so I mentioned it—that she'd gone to cook dinner for Maxwell and was murdered when he was. I mentioned it and moved on, actually surprised that I didn't tear up. As much as I hate to say it, looking at Amy made moving on, for the first time in a year, easier than I thought possible.

Amy had the kind of face that could make a man forget everything else in his life, good or bad, past or present. It was the kind of face that could leave a man speechless for fear of saying the wrong thing, the kind of face most men could only dream of seeing by the light of a candle, or kissing, or seeing on a pillow.

She made no mention of a husband, fiancé, or boyfriend during the course of the conversation, nor did she wear any symbolic rings on her slender fingers. I guessed that she was in her late twenties and therefore easily old enough to have been married, at least once, but no one came up.

Although it seems as if I'm easily impressed, I'm really not. But I kept being surprised by the substance of these two women and the friendship between them, even though separated by at least fifty years. I was amazed that Amy knew, not only of my uncle, but about the depth of her grandmother's feelings for him and that he had been the one true love of her life. That just didn't seem like something she would have known, or should have known, unless she'd found a secret diary. But I suppose it was all right, really, since her grandfather, Leland Drake, and her grandmother were divorced. Obviously, Leland had not been the love of May's life, an irony compounded by the fact that she still used his name.

I turned to Amy and asked, "What do you do?"

"I work for my grandfather."

Instead of imagining her ordering paints and brushes, or arranging gallery showings, or whatever it is that an employee does for an artist, I, of course, envisioned her posing nude on a chaise, or perhaps on a marble pedestal in front of a drape beneath a skylight in a paint-splattered studio. "What do you do for him?"

"I run his company."

"You do?" The only company Maxwell Bennett ever had, that I knew about, was Aunt Sid. Occasionally, cousins Betty and Harry would come over while they were still alive, but that was it. They were considered company because they'd call first and bring a nice piece of coffee cake. My uncle had no office, no studio, and no warehouse. There'd been no shipping and receiving, no distribution, no advertising, no accounts receivable, and no payroll. I do remember a plastic art bin resembling a tool box filled with ointment-size tubes of paint and an assortment of artist's brushes. He would paint in the middle of the living room on a folding wooden easel with brass hinges that he otherwise kept hidden away in the hall coat closet.

Amy nodded and said, "I have a graduate degree in business and marketing. It's not from the Wharton School, but I like to think I'm qualified. I suppose I had an advantage during the one and only interview, but that was years ago and sales are up four hundred percent. Either he's one hell of an artist, or I know a thing or two about marketing."

I returned the grin and said, "Maybe both. My uncle respected your grandfather's work." I lied. I don't know why I said that. It just came out. It was just something someone would say for the sake of conversation. This time the someone was me, and I regretted it the moment it left my lips. First of all, I had no idea how Maxwell Bennett had felt about Leland Drake. And secondly, it made me realize the lying was getting out of control.

"Did he, really?" Amy asked, a dubious expression on her face.

I nodded.

"That's a meaningful compliment. I know your uncle was also a great talent. It's easily recognizable in the painting above grandma's mantel. It's her most prized possession. Isn't it?" Amy asked, turning toward May.

The elderly woman across the table nodded, although this time her smile seemed a bit weary. I thought she was holding back more than a tear or two, a lifetime of lost love funneled into one afternoon.

Suddenly I could feel things winding down, if not utterly deteriorating. The arrival of the strudel and coffee was timely. I knew this day had taken an unexpected turn for May. She'd been looking forward to spending time with her granddaughter. I'd recognized the anticipation on her face when she'd opened the door, expecting to see Amy. Instead, she saw me, death's messenger standing on her porch. Now I was seated at the same table.

May Drake excused herself, which I expected. I stood as she did, and also expected Amy to accompany her to the restroom, but she didn't.

"Did your uncle sell his work?" Amy asked as I sat again.

"No. Not to my knowledge. Not one."

"Where are they all? He must have created dozens of paintings in the course of his life."

"I thought there were thirty-nine, until today. Now I know there are at least forty."

"Where are they? Do you know?"

"I have them. They're in my condo, although I haven't had a chance to hang them yet."

"I'd really love to see them."

I've never won the lottery. In fact, I seldom pick more than one correct number out of six, so I can't say I know how it feels to win, but those last six words were winners. "I'd like to hear your professional opinion about the collection," I said, telling myself that's all she meant. "And I'd like to meet your grandfather."

"You would?"

"Yes, especially in his studio. I know how my uncle painted. I watched him a few times in his apartment. I'd really like to see a famous artist's studio."

She suddenly looked a little put off.

I realized I'd overstepped my bounds. Such a request could only put her in an awkward position, especially coming from Maxwell Bennett's nephew. Drake knew of my uncle and what he'd shared with May. The conversation had revealed that much. Having gone in the wrong direction and about to overstay my welcome, I envisioned being dropped at my car and watching Amy drive out of my life as quickly as she'd driven into it. In the span of two minutes I'd gone from elation to deflation. "I'm sorry. I had no right to ask such a thing. I certainly didn't mean to put you on the spot."

For a moment she seemed to be somewhere else, staring at something far beyond the restaurant. Then she turned toward me and forced a smile. "It's all right. I'll see what I can do."

"Forget it. What I'd really like is to see *you* again. I've always known the best time to ask someone out is immediately after I've made an ass of myself."

Her eyes connected with mine. Then she reached into her purse, took out a business card, wrote her home number on the back, and handed it to me. "I'd better check on my grandma."

She stood and so did I. I motioned for the check before the two new women in my life returned. If the waiter had snapped to attention, clicked his heels, and said, "*Jawohl, mein herr,*" I wouldn't have noticed.

5

Mondays suck, don't they? As I sat at my desk in the modest architectural firm of Sherman and Essen, I wondered if there'd been one day that routinely sucked more than the others before Julius Caesar took a few minutes between orgies to invent the calendar.

But Mondays don't seem quite so bad if you've got something to look forward to. I should have been on top of my game, whipping up an architectural masterpiece, drafting plans that would make the El Dorado Hills project a real knockout, if a strip mall could ever be called a knockout. I was actually in a good mood. I'd almost forgotten what it felt like. I know it sounds a bit immature, but each time the phone rang I found myself hoping it was Amy. I hadn't given her my work number, but I had mentioned the name of the firm. Is that wishful thinking, or what?

The fourth incoming call of the morning was, however, very different. I answered, "Hello, this is Robert Bennett."

"Hello, Mr. Bennett. This is Detective Sheldon Stein of the One-Seventeen Squad in New York City. How are you?"

Fantasyland was over. The real world was now bristling through the line. As much as I wanted the brutal scumbag responsible for murdering the people I loved captured or killed, I'd also done everything I could to keep the past behind me and as far away as possible. Isn't that why I'd moved nearly three thousand miles? I had, however, given my new contact information to Sheldon Stein and Joe DiCarlo, the two detectives who'd caught the case. "I want to know if you find the son of a bitch," I'd said, ignoring Stein's partner, who'd already issued the warning, "Don't leave town without telling us where you're going," as if anyone guilty of anything would really do that before starting a life on the run.

"Hello, Detective. I'm all right. How are you?"

"I'm fine. I'm sorry to bother you at work, but there's been a development in the case."

"Please tell me you've caught someone."

"We've made a burglary arrest, but I'm not so sure the person we have in custody is the shooter. We believe he's responsible for numerous burglaries in the Forest Hills area. We've recovered a lot of stolen property, some of which may have belonged to your uncle and your wife. I was hoping you'd be able to identify a few things, including a painting."

"Whose name is on it? Paintings are always signed."

"Not this one."

"But none of my uncle's paintings were missing. They were all still hanging on the walls when I got there."

"I'm just telling you we recovered a small painting that's unsigned. It's also unframed, with no wire or hook on the stretcher with which to hang it. That tells me it has never been displayed. I'd like you to look at it."

"How should I do that?"

"In person. It will hold up better in court."

"I'll fly back Thursday. I'll see you Friday morning. Will that be all right?"

"That'll be fine. Thanks for your help. Have a safe flight."

I hung up the phone and just stared at it for a while. I didn't know what to think. I wondered if Detective Stein was being truthful about the reason for requesting my presence. In today's high-tech world, surely I could identify anything digitally photographed and sent electronically. I wondered if what he'd said about holding up better in court was true.

Cynic that I am, I concluded that if Stein was lying, there could only be one reason. He'd spent a year putting a case together against *me*. Having the suspect buy his own plane ticket would be cheaper for the city than flying a detective across the continent to extradite the alleged perpetrator from California. This plan wouldn't cost *them* anything! He'd mentioned an unsigned painting. What the hell was that all about? Maybe it was just a clever ruse, a ploy to get me back there. Talk about a hook. If ever there was a way to reel me in, that was it. I imagined walking into the precinct a free man and being escorted out in handcuffs. It was a story the cops could tell over and over again, each time getting a bigger laugh. They'd tell all the rookies and reminisce at Stein's retirement bash. "Hey, remember the time you convinced that architect to fly back from California so you could slap the cuffs on him right here in the house? That was a good one. He went down for premeditated murder, two counts. Talk about a stupid bastard!"

I didn't know whether or not to take my own ramblings seriously. I could probably be called a lot of things, but naïve isn't one of them. I felt like phoning Stein to ask if I should book a round trip or buy a one-way ticket. The detectives had been fairly cordial during the interviews a year ago, keeping the good cop/bad cop thing to a minimum, although they did offer me a deal. They'd said, if I confessed, the DA would only ask that I serve time concurrently for two counts of murder in the first degree instead of consecutively. Then they went on to explain that the reduced sentence would mean twenty-five to life, but with good behavior I'd be eligible for parole in as little as fifteen years. Now that's what I call a bargain: A decade and a half in a drafty cell, sixteen thousand four hundred and twenty-five lousy meals in a row, even if they were on the house, and a perpetually sore anus, all in exchange for confessing to a crime I didn't commit. I must say, it did sound awfully tempting, but I went with a verifiable accounting of my whereabouts instead. I knew it was time to switch gears at Sherman and Essen when I found myself wondering if penitentiaries retained full-time proctologists or if they were simply on call.

I left my office and found Bill Sherman in his. The door was open. I knocked on the jamb and poked my head in. "Do you have a minute, Bill?"

"Sure. Come in and have a seat. What's on your mind?"

I entered, closed the door behind me, and sat in one of the brown leather visitor's chairs in front of Sherman's large antique oak desk. He was quite at home in a tall executive swiveling version, his back to large-pane sash windows that showcased a sun-drenched garden brimming with vivid flowers and lush green shrubs. I said, "A detective in New York just called me. They've made an arrest. They want me to come in and identify some recovered property."

"That's great. I'm glad they finally got the son of a bitch."

"They didn't say that exactly. They said they made a burglary arrest, but they don't know if he's actually the shooter."

"What does that mean? If he's not the triggerman, who do

they think he is?"

"It's a very complicated case. It's hard to explain."

Sherman leaned forward on his elbows. "You can't stop there. If you don't mind, tell me the details."

"It'll take a while. Do you have the time?"

"The sooner you start, the sooner you'll finish."

Spoken like a true employer, I thought. "All right. There'd actually been two separate crimes on two different days. On Friday, while Mack was out, his apartment was ransacked. They took cameras, watches, a laptop, and a few other things of value. My uncle was a real gadget hound. They also stole my deceased aunt's jewelry." Images of Sid's collectible Borel watch and two gold rings with large aquamarines in Tiffany settings flashed through my mind again, along with the knowledge that Mack truly cherished the things his sister had treasured while she was alive. I suppressed the residual anger that still haunted me and kept going. "They let me read the police report. It described a residential burglary—forced entry through a fire-escape window, the looting of drawers, cabinets, and closets, and egress through the front door, which had been left unlocked. The document was filed that evening by the officers who'd responded to my uncle's 911 call. That was the first crime. At the time, I knew nothing about it. I'd left that morning for a damned convention in Las Vegas."

It's funny how we remember things of little or no significance, isn't it? The NYPD report was called a UF-61. That number stuck with me when I'd noticed it at the corner of the form because that was the model year of my uncle's beautiful black Thunderbird. And at the time I hadn't even remembered the fleeting moments captured, so long ago, on my father's eight millimeter Kodak when Mack pointed the car's bullet-nose toward California and they all watched its jet-thruster taillights disappear in the distance.

"I went to that convention," Sherman said. "It was a colossal waste of time, wasn't it?"

"Except for being in Vegas."

"You've got a point there. What was the second crime?"

"The push-in happened Sunday. Dana had gone over to cook dinner for my uncle, even though I wasn't going to be there. It was her idea, and she'd do it at least once a month, sometimes twice, with me or without me. I wanted to take her to Vegas, but she couldn't arrange the time off." I tried to remain in control of myself, thinking for the umpteenth time that she would still be alive if only she'd accompanied me on that damn trip.

Sherman nodded, as if he understood just how special Dana was. I could see it in his eyes.

I paused for a few seconds to collect myself, overcoming that falling apart feeling known to sneak up on me now and then, even when I'm not discussing what happened with someone. "Anyway, the police theorized early on that either the perpetrator had followed her to the door, shoving her in when Mack opened it, the typical M.O. of a push-in, or that either of them had opened the door for someone who then forced his way in at gunpoint. Stein and DiCarlo liked the second theory better because the groceries Dana brought were neatly arranged in the kitchen and were not all over the floor."

"Sounds logical," Sherman observed.

"I suppose so. The bastard took the jewelry they were wearing, credit cards, and cash. He also tore the place apart, apparently looking for anything else of value. It could have been just another robbery. Why'd he have to murder them?"

Sherman winced a little. "So there'd be no witnesses."

I nodded. It was a question that didn't need a reply.

"Do you know how it happened?" he asked.

"My uncle was shot to death in his living room. Dana was

shot in the back as she tried to flee into the bedroom. That's what the detectives said. Then she was shot in the head."

"Do you know anything else about it?"

"No. They only told me that much after they stopped looking at *me*. The husband is always the first suspect, isn't he? I was in a Boeing 767 at forty-three thousand feet when it happened. The Medical Examiner estimated the time of death to be between two and four p.m. I was somewhere over the Midwest when they needed me."

"That's what I'd call an airtight alibi." It was an odd time for Sherman's sense of humor to kick in, but I suppose he was trying to lighten the moment.

"I guess so. Whatever it was, it was enough for them to leave me alone."

"Did you discover the bodies?"

"No. I went home from the airport. One of my uncle's neighbors, an elderly woman, found them. She said the door was unlocked when she went over to ask him to change a light bulb because she couldn't find the superintendent."

"Do the cops think the two crimes were related?"

I nodded. "They think the burglar told the other bottom feeders in the neighborhood about an easy target."

Sherman made a skeptical face. "That doesn't make any sense. Why would someone else go in after the most valuable items in the house had already been taken?"

"That's what I thought. I'd asked the same question."

"What was their answer?"

"Criminals are stupid."

"That does sound like something the police would say. When are you going back?"

"I told Stein I'd see him Friday. I'll be here through Wednesday, and I'll be back in my office Monday. This is the last thing I expected, Bill. Are you okay with it?"

"I'll have Jenny make the arrangements for you, if you'd like. Just give her the details."

"Thank you, but I'll handle it. Do you think I can get a special witness rate on the airfare if I have a note on NYPD letterhead?" I asked with a smile.

My new boss laughed. "I doubt it. Maybe if you'd been served with a subpoena."

"Maybe."

"If you're anything like me, and I think you are," he observed, "you'd charter a jet if it would help put away the killer. I think you'd do anything to make that happen. And I'd be the last person in the world to stand in your way."

"How could you know me that well?" I asked. "I've only been here a week."

"Go on. Do what you've got to do."

I went back to my office, mustered a different kind of courage, and dialed the number on Amy Drake's business card. I touch-toned my way through the automated phone system after hearing, "Thank you for calling Leland Drake Incorporated. This call may be recorded for quality of service. If you know the extension of the person..." I was soon speaking with Amy's assistant, thinking along the way, *it's a good thing I'd become an architect instead of a switchboard operator.* A minute later I heard Amy's voice.

"Hi. I'm glad you called. I just finished telling my grandfather all about you. He wants to meet you."

I haven't been speechless many times in my life, but I was at that moment. Not because I'm in awe of celebrity. I'm not. I'm sure Leland Drake puts his pants on the same way I do. Drake's willingness to grant me an audience was nice, but it didn't take my breath away. Being on Amy's mind did.

"Hello? Robert, are you there?"

"Yes. Like I said at lunch, I'd love to meet him, but I'm afraid that'll have to wait. I'm going back to New York this week. Apparently there's been a break in the case. They may have even recovered a stolen painting."

"Really?"

"That's what the detective told me this morning. I want you to have dinner with me when I get back. I'll be in San Francisco Saturday evening after I land at SFO. I'll rent a car and pick you up."

The line was suddenly quiet. I assumed she'd heard me, so I just waited for a reply.

Then she said, "You don't have to rent anything. I'll pick you up at the airport. What time does your plane arrive?"

"I haven't made the arrangements yet. Thanks for the offer, but because I'll drive a rental on the trip down there, I'll have to rent another one anyway to get back to Tahoe."

"I was planning to visit my grandmother Sunday. I'll drive you back."

I knew at that moment it was time to get off the phone before I said something stupid like, *you don't have to do that.* "All right. I'll call you."

"Have a good trip."

"Thanks." I hung up and just sat there, wondering where I'd be during the wee hours between Saturday night and Sunday morning. If Sherman and Essen had kept a defibrillator on the premises, this would have been a good time to bring out the paddles. One thing I knew for sure: If Stein and DiCarlo locked me up when I walked into the station house, one way or another, I was breaking out.

6

Have you ever noticed that, if not for the engine whine, a pin-drop could be heard during takeoffs and landings? I think it's because most people can't carry on a conversation and pray at the same time. I particularly like it when a planeload of people applaud just after the landing gear touches down. Those people must really love to fly. When was the last time you heard a bus driver get so much as an attaboy?

I rented a car for as long as I'd be back in the Big Apple, my hometown. The rental agency didn't have anything armored available, so I made do with a Chrysler 300 in standard trim. The agent asked if I was a member of the Auto Club, so I flashed my membership card.

I then asked, "Do you have a special witness rate?"

"Excuse me?"

"Never mind."

I left the airport and drove to a hotel located on Queens

Boulevard just north of the Long Island Expressway. I'd reserved a room there because it was fairly close to the precinct. It was also halfway between the homes of my two lifelong buddies, one on Long Island and one in Brooklyn, in case I decided to visit them. I didn't think that was very likely since I'd only been gone a couple of weeks, but at least it made the option convenient—as convenient as anything could be considering the fact that the city's highways were adequate only at three o'clock in the morning.

Already late in the afternoon because of the travel time and three hour difference from California's Pacific Standard Time, I called Stein to tell him I'd arrived and that I'd see him in the morning. I remember thinking he sounded surprised that I'd actually come back, which made me a little nervous. In the next fifteen hours I seriously considered changing my mind more than once about showing up.

In fact, I had mixed feelings about being back there at all. A lot of memories were flooding over me. This was where I'd grown up, where I'd gone to school, where I'd become a person. It was where I'd loved the people who'd given me life and nurtured me; the people who'd made me who I am. It's where I'd fallen in love with the girl who'd fulfilled my dreams. It was also the place that took it all away.

I'd made a clean break, moving far from the sights, sounds, and smells of New York City. I was living in a new place, high in the mountains beside one of the largest alpine lakes in the world, a glacier-carved basin sixteen hundred feet deep and filled to the brim with crystal clear ice water from streams and rivers alive with trout and salmon. People were snowshoeing and cross-country skiing right outside my door. The air was sweet and clean, and the most common sound was the wind whistling through tall pines. I had a new job, a new car, and new clothes. And it may have been a little premature to say I'd met someone new, but that's the way it felt.

Now I was back in the turmoil, dirt and litter swirling in the street, intolerable traffic in an impatient daily crush, horns blaring, and shrieking sirens desperately trying to save another victim. It was all coming back to me in a rush, like the rush that defined the city. I suppose I never quite realized just how close I'd come to losing my mind, but merely being where it all went wrong was dumping me exactly where I'd left off. I remember feeling the urge to turn around, drive right back to JFK, and fly the hell out of there without even checking in at the hotel. But if putting in my two cents would keep the wheels of justice turning, I had to stiffen my spine.

I walked into the station house a little after nine the next morning. Inviting isn't exactly the word I'd use to describe the décor of the One-Seventeen, as the cops call it, but maybe that was the idea. Even if I have a lot on my mind, I'm apt to notice the details of my surroundings—institutional green enamel walls every bit as charming as the buzzing fluorescent lights overhead. Either the planning commission wanted anyone brought into the precinct to get used to life on the inside the minute they entered the system, or they'd had a really hard time finding a reputable interior decorator.

The desk sergeant asked, "Can I help you?"

I had to look up to address him, as the desk wasn't really a desk but more a judge's courtroom bench, which, come to think of it, isn't really a bench. In any event, it did convey the concept of authority. "I'm here to see Detective Stein. He's expecting me."

"Up the stairs, first door on the right."

"Thanks." I knew that. I'd been there before.

The door to the squad room was open. The half-dozen steel office desks inside were arranged in pairs facing each other so partners could easily converse. I figured that out myself. I also noticed that no one sat with his, or her, back to the door, a fundamental of feng shui, although I doubted seriously if any of the personnel in the building knew that. Perhaps Mr. Shui had been a cop somewhere in Asia before changing careers.

I saw Detective Sheldon Stein sitting behind the last desk on the right, the one closest to the Squad Commander's office at the back wall. He was on the phone. I knew he was in his thirties, although he had a baby face below tousled wavy brown hair. He seemed more easy-going than intimidating, which made him a natural at playing the good cop, but his appearance didn't exactly inspire confidence in his ability to bring in the bad guys. He noticed me immediately and held up his pointer finger, signaling that he'd be free shortly. I heard him say into the phone, "I'll do what I can. In the meantime, you should make the notifications I've just advised." He hung up, switched gears, came out from behind his desk, and said to me as he extended his hand, "Hello, Mr. Bennett. I'm glad you could make it. Thanks for coming in."

We got past the customary small talk in short order, for which I was thankful, not wanting to be there in the first place. I was in no mood for idle chitchat. *Show me the possessions I flew across the whole damn country to see, tell me about the arrest and who the scumbag is, how you think the prosecution will go, and let me get the hell out of here.*

"Let's get right to it, shall we?" Stein said. "I'll take you down to the evidence locker in the basement and let you view what we've recovered."

He led and I followed.

"How was your flight?" he asked as we entered the stairs.

"You know what pilots say, don't you, Detective?"

"What's that?"

"Any landing you can walk away from is a good one."

"They should know."

When we stopped at the first floor to sign for the locker key,

Stein told me to give my I.D. to the sergeant. He explained, "In order to safeguard the chain of custody, the desk officer makes a log entry every time he releases and receives the evidence key. This will also help document the fact that you were here to identify the stolen property in person."

I handed my new California interim license to the officer I'd met on the way in and said, "By the book is good. We don't want the perp to walk because of a technicality, do we?"

Instead of responding with something like, *no, we don't*, or *we always do everything by the book*, he ignored me and looked at Stein with an expression that said, *where the fuck did you find this idiot?*

He handed Stein a key attached to a short wooden stick, and the detective said, "Let's go. You can pick up your license on the way out."

I wasn't sure I wanted to follow him anywhere. It seemed as if I'd just been duped into surrendering my identification and was now being led off to the lockup, key and all. Either that or we'd just been given the key to the toilet.

"Where's your partner?" I asked, as we headed for the basement. *Warming up the rubber hose?* "Shouldn't he be with us as a witness for this chain of evidence thing?"

Stein didn't answer, except to say, "That's not necessary."

I followed him, although reluctantly, down another green enameled corridor to a storage room. We entered a door on the right and he switched on the ceiling fluorescents. I could smell the unmistakable mustiness that seemed to permeate most basements.

"Have a seat," he said, pointing to the table and chairs at the center of the floor. "And put these on." He pulled a couple of medical examination gloves from a box on the table and handed them to me. Then he stretched a pair over his own hands. "You're not allergic to latex, are you?"

"No. I'm only allergic to poverty."

I looked around at the metal file cabinets lining the walls as Stein unlocked a gray steel wardrobe. I noticed labels indicating that the contents of the drawers had been arranged alphabetically. I said, "I don't suppose these files are filled with birth announcements, graduation pictures, wedding invitations, or vacation photos."

"Hardly."

I watched Detective Sheldon Stein empty five Manila envelopes onto the light gray Formica tabletop in front of me, creating five piles of jewelry, each solely consisting of watches, rings, bracelets, earrings, and necklaces respectively. "We know this is all stolen property from numerous burglaries in Queens, but we don't know what came from where or who owned what. See if you can positively identify anything that belonged to your wife or uncle."

If I'd been a pirate I suppose it would have looked like treasure, but all I could think about was that the jewelry spilled before me belonged to people whose lives had been turned upside down. It seemed as if the sparkle that would have otherwise gleamed from the gold, silver, gems, and pearls, had been dulled, as much by the circumstances of its presence as by the lackluster fluorescent light.

I spotted my aunt's aquamarine rings in an instant; one round and one emerald cut, both in pronged gold settings. I picked them from the pile of rings and stared at the gems, one at a time, almost hoping to see Sid's or Mack's image in the flat table at the center of each cut stone, but all I saw was the cold reflection of the impersonal light above, at least until the tears flooding my eyes turned everything to a blur.

I pulled a few tissues from my pocket and wiped my face. Then I felt a hand on my shoulder.

"I'm sorry," Stein said. "I know this must be difficult for you."

I ignored him and picked through that particular pile of evidence in search of Dana's wedding band and three carat princess-cut solitaire, the rings for which I'd scoured the city, and now hoped to find for the second time. But they weren't there. Neither was Mack's worn-smooth Long Island University ring.

I focused on the mound of watches and discovered my aunt's Borel, a fine timepiece in a thin gold case with a black leather strap. The unique design, a kaleidoscope-like motif made to rotate like a sweep second hand, was idle. I turned the crown and the unmistakable pattern in between the face and the crystal was suddenly moving, just as it had been the first time I saw it. It fascinated me when I was a child, long before I knew what life was about, and then as an adult, long after I'd learned what death was about. Sid and Mack were both gone forever, but the little watch they'd cherished, the intricately crafted novelty that had ticked away the precious seconds of their lives could be brought back to life with only a twist. If only that could have been done for them. And for Dana.

I examined the other watches, hoping to find Dana's Movado and the wafer-thin gold Omega that Mack had prized and worn daily, but neither was there. I did spot a rectangular Cartier with a black leather band that I knew belonged to my uncle and pulled it from the heap, placing it beside the Borel. I stirred the pile of earrings with my finger, but nothing caught my eye as familiar, so I moved to the necklaces. There were several common gold chains that could have belonged to my aunt, but nothing I could swear to. "Is this all of it?" I asked.

"Yes, why? What are you looking for?" Stein asked, sounding more like a salesman than a detective.

"My wife's pendant. I'm sure she was wearing it. She wore it every day."

"What does it look like?"

"It's a fourteen karat yellow gold heart."

Stein stepped closer and pulled a heart-shaped locket from the tangle of chains and asked, "Is this it?"

"No. It's a little thing I had custom-made—a one of a kind. It's a filigree design the size and thickness of a nickel with the word *Pretend* cut through and through diagonally in script."

I could tell that Stein didn't know what to make of the message. He didn't ask, and I didn't explain.

"It sounds like something with a lot of sentimental value."

"You have no idea."

Stein nodded and said, "You're right. I don't."

"If these things were stolen a year ago, why did the mutt you arrested still have them?"

"Believe it or not, he was holding on to the goods because the price of gold was going up. He thought he could fence the loot for more if he held on to it longer."

"Oh, I see. The burglar was an investor."

"More like a broker," Stein said.

I thought about his analogy and said, "I get it. He used other people's assets."

"Exactly."

"I thought you said criminals are stupid."

"They are. He got caught, didn't he?"

I said, "I know you're the detective and I'm the architect, but none of that makes any sense. I thought burglaries were committed by junkies to pay for their dope. They wouldn't hold the loot that long. They'd turn it for a quick fix, wouldn't they?"

"You're right," Stein agreed. "That's the usual, but this perp was a little more sophisticated than most. What can I tell you?"

I asked, "Where's the painting you recovered?"

"Right here," Stein said, slipping a small unframed oil-on-canvas out of a large padded evidence envelope. It was a foot square.

My eyes must have widened, as if suddenly gazing upon a mural. I recognized the picture, although I'd forgotten about it entirely. To prove to us, or perhaps to himself, that he could paint as well as anyone, including the most renowned masters, Mack had, many years ago, duplicated a famous work—the portrait of a Toulouse-Lautrec kind of character. I remembered him holding the little painting in one hand and the large open art book from which he'd copied it in the other for a side by side comparison. I also remember thinking the first time I saw the piece that it was not particularly attractive. But I was amazed, nonetheless, by my uncle's talent. Now, sitting in the basement of the One-Seventeen, in a storage room filled with its fair share of the city's eight million stories, I tried to recall the original artist's name, but like many of the people responsible for the very existence of the files around me, his identity proved elusive.

"Do you recognize it?" Stein asked.

"I do. And so should you."

"I should? Why? Is it a famous painting?"

"It is."

"Why isn't it signed?"

"This one isn't signed because my uncle painted it. It's a copy."

"You mean a forgery."

"No. I mean a copy. Don't get carried away, Detective. If he'd signed the original artist's name it would be a forgery. And he wasn't going to sign his own name to an exact copy. So, he left it unsigned. It was only a test."

Stein regarded the small painting with a critical eye and said, "No offense, but this isn't a very pretty picture."

"That's what I thought the first time I saw it. The original is probably worth ten million dollars. That shows how much *we* know."

"It's probably worth that much because the artist is dead."

"My uncle is dead and his paintings are only valuable to me."

"Sorry. That reminds me though; there was something else I did want to ask you."

"What's that?"

"Let's review the two crimes."

"All right."

"The first crime was the burglary on Friday. Your uncle was out for the day and when he returned home he discovered that someone had broken into his apartment. He dialed 911, and the dispatcher had a sector car respond. The officers determined the points of entry and egress, examined the scene, talked to the neighbors, canvassed the area, and filed a report."

"A UF-61."

"That's right. How did you know that?"

"Suffice it to say I have an eye for detail."

"Apparently. On Sunday evening the same team responded again to your uncle's apartment. This time the 911 call was made by a neighbor who'd discovered the homicides when she tried to ask your uncle for help with a light fixture. The officers made the necessary notifications and, as you know, Detective DiCarlo and I caught the case. I was curious as to the presence of an elaborate easel in the living room until I realized that the paintings lining the walls had been signed by the deceased."

"That's where my uncle painted, in his living room. He didn't have a studio."

"I see," Stein said, before continuing. "I interviewed the responding officers at length, since they'd been the first to arrive both times. They agreed that a painting had been on the easel on Friday after the burglary, but it was not there on Sunday after the homicides. Do you know anything about this?"

I sat there, on an old and uncomfortable wooden chair, recalling my uncle's apartment turned crime scene. I remembered the empty easel, because I remember standing in front of it and thinking it would never again hold another Maxwell Bennett painting in progress. "You're right. The easel was there, and there was nothing on it. I don't know what he was working on, if anything. He usually kept the easel folded away in the coat closet. He wasn't prolific. He'd painted for most of his life, but all that work only yielded thirty-nine paintings. I have them all except for that one," I said pointing to the weird little copy. I stopped myself, suddenly remembering the majestic sailing ship depicted in the oil-on-canvas above May Drake's river rock fireplace, the name Bennett signed characteristically in the lower right-hand corner. The surprise I'd felt in May's house slapped me again in the basement of the One-Seventeen, but I didn't let it show.

"If what you say is true," Stein said, "thirty-nine paintings are not enough for an artist his age. That's considerably less than one a year over the course of his adult life. Maybe he painted pictures you knew nothing about."

I'm not sure how long I sat there contemplating Mack's life and how little I actually knew about it. I considered telling Stein how a house by a river in one of my uncle's paintings had come to life in a bizarre twist of fate, but ultimately decided against it. Involving the police in my new life didn't seem particularly appealing.

"Well? What do you think?"

"I'm sorry. What was the question?"

"Could there be Maxwell Bennett paintings out there you've never seen?"

"I suppose it's possible. What can I say? I thought I had all of them. I went through his possessions myself, drawer by drawer, closet by closet when I emptied his apartment. The only paintings there were the ones hanging on the walls, all of which are now in my condo in California. I don't know what your officers saw on that easel, but I'd like to ask them about it myself."

"I can arrange that," Stein said. "Is it possible that your uncle sold or delivered the painting on the easel to someone that Saturday?"

"To my knowledge, which apparently is lacking, he never sold a painting in his life."

"Could he have given it away?"

"His best friend didn't say anything to me about it at the funeral, but I could ask him." I took out my cell phone and obtained Maxwell Martin's number by dialing 411. I heard his voice a few seconds later.

Two friends named Maxwell. What were the odds? My two best buddies have the same birthday; December seventh, a date which will live in infamy, as so eloquently stated by Franklin D. Roosevelt. Talk about making it easy to remember! What about those odds? That's why I, unlike the police, believe in coincidence.

Maxwell Martin and I exchanged the requisite pleasantries and I then asked if my uncle had given him a painting the day before he was killed. The answer was no, and he knew nothing about it. My uncle's closest friend for more than sixty years did tell me, however, that they had indeed talked over the phone that Saturday at length, mostly about the break-in the day before. Never had he heard my uncle more upset, never in his life, except of course on the days when Sid and my father died. The conversation stalled when I heard Martin sobbing at the other end of the line. I tried to steel myself against the infectious emotion but failed. When he collected himself I heard him say, "I miss him, Robert."

"So do I, Maxwell. So do I." I ended the call, wrote down the man's name and phone number, handed it to the detective, and said, "I don't know who else to ask." *Except May.* "What are you getting at, Detective? Why are you asking about a painting?"

"If there was a painting in his apartment on Friday evening after the first burglary, and it wasn't there on Sunday evening after the murders, maybe the person or persons responsible for the homicides took it."

"Why didn't they steal any of the paintings hanging on the walls?"

"We don't know."

"I see." I thought about this for a minute before asking, "Are we finished here? Did you recover anything else?"

"No."

"There were no cameras or binoculars?"

"No. If there were any, the suspect must have already moved them."

"What's his name?"

"You don't need to know that now."

"Why not? I think I should know his name."

"I don't think so. I know how you feel, and I don't want you doing anything stupid."

"You know how I feel?"

"I think so."

"No, you don't. You have no idea how I feel. The only two people that meant anything to me were both shot to death while I was in Las Vegas. How could you know how I feel?"

"You're right. What's happened to you has never happened to me, but this isn't my first homicide. And you're not the first next of kin I've met. I deal with death and grief day after day. Besides, you're lucky you were out of town. If you'd been in that apartment, you probably wouldn't be here now."

"That's right. I would have thwarted the whole damned thing and they'd still be alive."

"No. I doubt it. You'd be dead, too."

"Are we done here?"

"Yeah. I'll rebag everything, keeping the items you've identified separate. Sit tight."

I watched Stein go though some kind of bagging, sealing, and labeling ritual. "Will I ever be able to recover those items?"

"After the trial."

"Or the plea bargain."

"That's right. One of the reasons I don't want you doing anything stupid is because I don't think the guy we have in custody did the murders. He's got a sheet as long as your arm for breaking and entering, but he's never been caught carrying a gun. Most burglars don't carry because they don't want that charge. He did the burglary, all right, but not the murders. We'll probably offer him a deal if he gives up the shooter."

"I know how it works. And the word bargain doesn't belong anywhere in this bullshit process. Everyone should get what's coming to them. Period. End of story."

"I'll do my best," Stein said, pausing to look at me. "For whatever it's worth, I think you did the right thing. Starting over in a new place was a good idea."

"And I was fine for the first time in a long time until you called and dragged me back here. Now I'm right back where I started. It feels like they were killed yesterday."

"I'm sorry to put you through this, but it was necessary. You've just tied the suspect to the victims. That gives us leverage. You'll be okay. Like everything else, it just takes time."

"So does mold."

"Penicillin is made from mold," Stein said.

"Thanks for the information, Mr. Cup Half Full. I'll remember that if I ever get the clap."

7

Stopping at the front desk to return the key, I said, "The room was a little musty, there was no view, and it brought back bad memories. Other than that, the stay was okay."

"If you'd like," the sergeant replied, "I can refer you to our larger facility on Riker's Island. I'd be happy to make the reservation for you."

I don't know what I expected Sgt. Humorless to say, but that wasn't it. I might have even preferred another silent civil service *go fuck yourself*, but at least I'd gotten him to loosen up a little.

Stein said, "Could you have sector Charlie ten-two?"

The sergeant nodded and asked, "Where do you want me to send them when they arrive?"

"We'll be in the coffee room," Stein replied.

"Any luck downstairs?"

"Mr. Bennett identified five items."

"Good. Your timing was down to the wire. The van is

scheduled to be here this afternoon to make the pick-up."

I asked, "What pick-up?"

Stein said, "Evidence isn't stored in the precinct for more than a few days. It gets transferred to a central location we call the property clerk."

"I see." I looked up at the sergeant again and began to feel a stiff neck coming on. "Can I have my license?" I asked, adding a little authority to my Mr. Nice Guy voice, which accomplished absolutely nothing.

I could have sworn he glanced at Stein before saying, "I haven't finished with it yet." I wasn't fast enough to notice if Stein had put the kibosh on my request, nor was I fast enough to come up with a fitting comment.

We went upstairs and saw Joe DiCarlo with the coffee pot in his hand. I regained my wit, despite my decaying nerves, and said, "Caught you red-handed."

DiCarlo glared at me with an expression that made the wolverine with the sergeant's stripes downstairs seem downright cuddly.

Stein said to his partner, "You remember Robert Bennett."

"Of course. How could I forget my favorite suspect in an unsolved double?"

"It's nice to see you again, too, Detective."

"How'd it go downstairs?" DiCarlo asked his partner.

"Good. Mr. Bennett confirmed five items: Two rings, two watches, and the painting."

"Great," DiCarlo said, pulling a chair away from the table in the center of the room. "Have a seat right here, Robert. You don't mind if I call you Robert, do ya?"

Joe DiCarlo was a burly Italian in his fifties. He wore a short-sleeved white dress shirt, as he had the last time we'd met. I remember thinking then, that based on the diameter of his forearms, his tattoos must have cost double the going rate.

"Why should I mind, *Joe*? That's my name." *Just don't put me in a headlock.*

I sat down thinking this is surprisingly informal. The coffee room was nothing like the stark, no-nonsense, shackle bolted to the table, one-way mirror equipped interrogation room they'd grilled me in a year ago. That was my impression until I noticed the video camera in the corner above the door. I knew then that every answer, every word, every expression, every reaction, even my body language, could be reviewed, dissected, and analyzed over and over again. *Think before you speak! Think!* That's what I told myself.

After ushering me to the chair facing the camera, DiCarlo seated himself with the table between us, all the while sporting an expression that said, if this had been a vehicle stop, the summons would have already been written. "Did your uncle have a cell phone?"

"Yes, he did."

"Do you have it?"

"No."

"Do you know where it is?"

I thought about it for a minute, having emptied out his apartment. "No. I gave all of his things to charity, except the paintings, when I terminated the lease. But now that you mention it, I don't recall seeing his cell, only the charger, which was on the kitchen counter."

"Could it have been in the pocket of something you gave away?" Stein asked.

"No. I checked everything. Maybe it was in his pocket when he was killed."

Stein said, "No. It wasn't. The clothing he was wearing at the time is in evidence. It's not there."

"Maybe the son of a bitch who killed him took it, along with his watch and ring."

"Could be," DiCarlo admitted. "That's what we're trying to determine."

"What about Dana's cell?" I asked. "Was it in her purse?"

"Yes, as a matter of fact, it was," Stein said.

"What difference does it make about the phone, anyway? Maybe he lost it."

"Maybe he did. Maybe he didn't," DiCarlo said, staring at me. "Don't you think it's a little odd that the perpetrator would have stolen your uncle's cell, but not your wife's? We know he took the time to go through her bag. It had been emptied onto the floor."

"How the hell should I know? You're the detective."

"What cell company did your uncle use?" DiCarlo asked.

"I don't know. What difference does it make?"

"Checking phone records is standard operating procedure in a homicide investigation," Stein said.

"Okay. Did you check the phone records for his home phone?"

"Yes, we did," Stein said.

"And?"

"Nothing that led anywhere."

"Of course, not. What are you looking for? He was a retired transit worker living on a fixed income. He was a brilliant and talented man who wasted his life sitting in a token booth in the stinking subway, going deaf from the trains. What did you expect to find in his phone records? Wait. I know. Maybe he was a drug dealer. No. That's not it. I've got it. He was a pimp. That's it. He must have been a pimp."

"Are you finished, Mr. Bennett?" DiCarlo asked.

"Yeah, I'm finished."

"Good. You do what you do, and we'll do what we do. Okay?"

"Fine."

"You never know what a phone record will turn up," Stein said. "Maybe he owed somebody money. That's possible, isn't it?"

"I doubt it."

"Why?"

"Because he would have come to me."

"Why? Why would he have gone to you?"

"Because I told him to."

"What do you mean, 'you told him to?'"

"I told him if he needed money, I wanted him to tell me. I wouldn't have let him go hungry any more than I would have let my father go hungry if he were alive."

"Maybe he was too embarrassed to ask you for anything," DiCarlo said. "Maybe he didn't think he should go to a nephew. Maybe he knew other people he could ask. You didn't live with him. He probably did things you knew nothing about."

When I didn't answer, DiCarlo leaned forward and said, "Maybe somebody owed *him* money. What do you think about that?"

"What? That's ridiculous. I know how he lived. He'd reuse the same paper towel when it dried. He didn't have enough money to loan anybody anything. His only extravagance was a nice watch or two. I was a joint tenant on his checking account in case something happened to him. Some people have stocks and bonds. Some have annuities. Some have CDs. He had a hand-to-mouth account."

"'*In case something happened to him?*'" DiCarlo repeated my words, as if he'd caught me in a trap.

"Yes, in case something happened to him, like a heart attack." I considered my father and the coronary that put an end to his worrying. At least he'd died of natural causes. I shook my head and said, "If you're so interested in his cell, why don't you check with *all* the carriers? There aren't that many."

"We did," Stein said. "There's no record of him being a subscriber with any of them, which is very odd because there was a charger in his kitchen as you said, and you just confirmed that he did in fact have a cell."

"What if it was pre-paid?"

"We've looked into that, too," Stein said.

"Then I don't know what to tell you."

Joe DiCarlo put his coffee down and asked, "So, if your uncle lived from hand to mouth, as you say, where does the sixty grand come in?"

"What sixty grand?"

"The sixty grand in your uncle's safe-deposit box," DiCarlo said casually.

"He didn't have a safe-deposit box."

"Oh, yes he did. We found it and opened it with a court order."

At that moment, two uniformed police officers presented themselves in the doorway. The one on the right, said, "You wanted to see us?"

Stein said, "Thanks for coming in. This is Robert Bennett."

I stood and shook hands with both officers as they identified themselves.

"Mr. Bennett's wife and uncle were the victims in that double homicide you responded to a year ago on 113th Street," Stein continued.

Steve Jensen glanced at his partner and got the nod. "We remember the job," he said, apparently speaking for both of them.

Gwen Millhouse asked, "Do you mind if we have a cup?"

DiCarlo motioned toward the coffee.

"How can we help?" Jensen asked. He was tall and handsome, with thick brown hair and sky blue eyes.

I watched Officer Millhouse pour two coffees. She, too, was very attractive, even with minimal makeup. Her chestnut hair was pulled back into a French twist, which, I surmised, provided less to grab in a scuffle. Her brown eyes were large and soft, like Dana's, turning her into the proverbial girl next door. The NYPD was missing a recruitment opportunity if they didn't have these two on a poster. I know a book shouldn't be judged by its cover, but there was something about Gwen's appearance that said this gal really knows how to have fun, if you know what I mean. She sugared one coffee and handed it to her partner, without him having asked for it, which told me that there was probably something going on between them. These partners had to be a perfect example of Bennett's Law of Close Proximity; a theoretical physical constant as predictable as Newton's gravity, which can be stated thusly: If a man and a woman are in close proximity to one another on a daily basis for extended periods, and at least one of them is even slightly attracted to the other, it's only a matter of time until they're having sex every chance they get. What could be more constant or physical than that?

Stein asked, "Do you remember our conversation about your responding to the two jobs at that location; the burglary on Friday and the homicides on Sunday?"

"What about it?" Jensen asked, the hot-drink paper cup in his left hand.

I noticed the gold wedding band on his ring finger.

Stein said, "You'd told me there'd been a painting on the easel in the living room Friday, but not Sunday after the homicides. Do you remember that?"

"I remember."

"What can you tell us about that painting?" Stein asked.

Officer Jensen raised his eyebrows and said, "I don't know. I don't know much about art. If you asked me who pitched a perfect game, or who had the highest number of RBIs I could tell you, but the only thing I know about paintings is that you put a frame around them. I saw a painting there, but I couldn't tell you anything about it."

I asked, "What did it look like?"

"What do you mean?"

"What was the subject matter?"

"To tell you the truth, I don't remember."

Trying to jog his memory I asked, "Was it a street scene or a landscape, a seascape or a still life? You know; a bowl of fruit or a vase full of flowers?"

"I don't remember."

"Was it framed?"

"I don't think so, but I really don't remember that either. There were other things for me to do there besides admire the pictures. I'm a police officer, not an art critic."

I noticed a subtle smile appear on his partner's pretty face and understood it to be an expression of approval, proud of him for standing up for himself. I could tell in the five minutes they'd been in the room that she really had a thing for this guy. I imagined his wife living with her worst fears every time he went off to work, wondering, but for the wrong reasons, if he'd be coming home again. *I'm putting in some overtime, Honey. Don't wait up.*

The more I looked at Officer Millhouse, the hotter she seemed. I mean, if Victoria's Secret made Kevlar bras and panties, she would have bought the whole line. I'm telling you, this female cop gave new meaning to the word *backup*.

Maybe it was just me. Maybe it had just been too long since I'd gotten any. I asked, "What about you, Officer Millhouse? Where were you?" *And have you ever considered changing your first name to Brick?*

"I was there. I helped my partner secure the scene."

"Can you tell us anything about the painting that was on the easel?"

"Not really."

I'm not psychic, but I knew immediately she was holding something back. I suspected she didn't want to make her partner look bad—that she knew more about art than he did, or that she was more observant. I also knew I wasn't going to get the chance to interview her alone. "What do you mean, not really?" I asked. "Do you remember the subject matter of the picture?"

She feigned trying to remember the details, which I recognized as stalling. Stein picked up on it as well and said to her partner, "Why don't you come with me for a minute, Steve? I've got something I think you'll like." Sheldon Stein walked out of the room and Officer Jensen followed, coffee in hand.

Joe DiCarlo asked the question I was going to ask. "What was in the picture, Gwen?"

"I grew up in a small town in Maine, on the coast. You know; a white church steeple, a gazebo in the square, lobster boats in a little harbor, gulls, and a lighthouse. It reminded me of that. It reminded me of when I was a little girl. The painting was in the middle of the room, right in front of me. I couldn't help but look at it. It was a peaceful picture of the way life used to be in the summer where I was raised. It made me want to go back, back to my hometown, back to the quaint fishing village I couldn't wait to leave. The place in that painting couldn't have been further away from where I was standing at the time. I'm sorry, Mr. Bennett."

I understood the stark contrast to which she referred: Serene versus macabre.

"Not that I don't love being a police officer," she continued, this time addressing Detective DiCarlo as if he were her boss. "I love *The Job*," she said, sounding like she'd been summoned to Internal Affairs. "There's nothing I'd rather do."

"I'm sure that's true," he said. "Can you tell us anything else about the painting or the crime scene?"

She shook her head. "Not that I can remember."

I asked, "Was the painting signed?"

"I didn't notice."

"Was it finished?" This may have been more difficult to answer if the painting was nearly finished, knowing that original works are not painted from left to right or top to bottom but rather in layers. The final layers or details are known only by the artist before they're transferred to the canvas. Anyone else wouldn't know if they're supposed to be there or not. Only the artist can say when a painting is actually complete.

"I don't know," she said. "It looked finished."

"Was it framed?"

"No."

DiCarlo asked, "Would you be able to identify it if you saw it again?"

"I think so."

"Excellent. Thanks for coming in, Officer Millhouse. You did good."

While I had the chance I said, "I have one more question for you, Officer."

"What's that, Mr. Bennett?"

At that moment, Stein and Jensen returned.

I ignored them and inquired, "Can you tell us in what style the painting was done?"

"I have no idea. Unfortunately, there are no art courses, that I know of, at the police academy."

The others chuckled a little, and I managed to catch the wink Jensen gave his partner.

I ignored them. "Was it realistic, emulating a photograph, or was it unnatural, perhaps a little surreal? Could it have been composed of geometric shapes like cubes? That would be Cubism. See what I mean? If you had to, what would you say about it?"

"It definitely wasn't like a photo. I could see the brushstrokes. It's funny. It made things look too nice. The colors were bright and beautiful. It was so calm and inviting. Maybe that's why I wanted to go back. That's all I can tell you. I'd like to be more helpful, but I looked at it for only a minute or two a year ago. That's the best I can do."

"Thank you. You're very observant," I said. I considered saying *I know a nice little place that serves wonderful New England clam chowder*, but DiCarlo intervened.

"That's all, Officers. You can resume."

She took another sip of coffee, spilled the rest into the sink, and dropped the cup in the trash before they both left.

Stein said, "I gave him a couple of tickets to a Mets game. You should have seen that guy. He lit up like a light bar."

"That must have cost you a few bucks," DiCarlo said.

"They were a gift. I don't like baseball."

"What about the sixty thousand dollars?" I asked.

"What about it? We were hoping you could tell us," DiCarlo said.

"My uncle couldn't have had that kind of money. I would have known about it."

"Why," DiCarlo asked. "You weren't his sister; only his nephew."

"I told you. He had no one else. Why are you looking so hard at *him*? He was the victim, for God's sake. What the hell is wrong with you?"

"Look, Mr. Bennett," Stein said. "There are a few things we can't figure out. The burglary was pretty straight forward, your typical residential break-in. They happen all over the city. But we're not so sure about the push-in robbery. There aren't many home invasions in Forest Hills. Push-ins usually happen when the victim is followed home. They literally get pushed into their own house or apartment from behind when they unlock the door. We don't think that happened because the groceries your wife brought were neatly arranged on the kitchen counter next to the sink and were not all over the floor in the foyer. And we know, unlike the burglary two days before, in this case there was no forced entry. That suggests that at least one victim knew the assailant, or knew the person or persons who sent him. It means that Dana or Maxwell unlocked the door for someone and let him in. Since it was your uncle's apartment we assume it was Maxwell. Yeah, things were taken from them both and it looked like the place had been gone through, which could have been window dressing, but Dana wasn't sexually assaulted."

"Thank God for that."

"Thank God, indeed, but the skells who commit these crimes usually rape the women, even elderly women. The victims are off the street, out of sight, locked in their own home with the worst kind of criminal. That means the perp is in no hurry. He can do whatever he wants for as long as he wants. The women are usually raped and beaten repeatedly."

"I get it."

"That didn't happen here," Stein continued. "And your wife was a very beautiful woman. That doesn't fit. Another point is that they were both shot twice, execution style, but no one heard a thing. The neighbors were home all afternoon, but nobody heard a single gunshot, let alone four. That means a suppressor was probably used, but mutts who do push-ins don't use suppressors. Also, we know by the caliber that the murder weapon was an automatic, but no shell casings were found, which means the killer picked them up—something else highly unusual in your average robbery."

"Are you saying the murders were a hit?"

"Based on what I've just told you, we think that's likely,"

Stein said. "It was meant to look like a robbery, but it just doesn't add up."

"Are you crazy? You think someone put out a contract on my family? That's the best you could come up with? A whole year's gone by and that's your conclusion?"

"Actually we think the contract was on your uncle and your wife was just in the wrong place at the wrong time." Stein said.

"Do you want to know what I think?"

"What's that?" DiCarlo asked.

"I think you've both been watching too many mob movies."

Joe DiCarlo waved his finger at me. "You don't know as much as you think you do, Robert. You didn't know about the money in the vault. People who put that much cash in a safe-deposit box are hiding it, not saving it."

I really didn't know what to say, so I didn't say anything.

But that didn't stop DiCarlo. "And you're wrong about your uncle having no one else but you."

My eyebrows must have reached my hairline this time because he then said, "That's right. We know there was someone else in his life."

For the first time since the last grilling, I actually felt a lump in my throat. I prepared my sphincters for whatever was coming next. "And who would that be?"

"Have you ever heard of a woman named May?" DiCarlo asked.

I'm really not a very good liar. At least I don't think I am, but after cramming an hour's worth of contemplation into ten seconds, I tried my best to play dumb, not wanting the police to pick apart my new life. Getting caught in a lie in a murder investigation can go very badly. I'm smart enough to know that, but I'd gone to a lot of trouble and expense to start my life over, and that's what I was determined to do. "May who?"

"We don't know her surname," Stein said. "Can you help us with that?"

It sounded as if they were baiting me, setting me up in some way, so I said, "There was a woman in his life a long time ago. That could have been her name. Where did you hear it?"

"There were letters in the vault box along with the cash," Stein said. "No envelopes. Just letters signed, May. We know she lived in California."

"How do you know that?"

"Because she wanted your uncle to move there," Stein continued. "She said so in many of the letters."

"Were they dated?"

Stein nodded. "From June of '62 to September of '65."

"And this is New York's Finest? You *are* crazy. Do you really think a woman he knew that long ago could have anything to do with this? What's wrong with you?"

DiCarlo stood and walked behind me. Then he spoke directly into my right ear, his coffee breath making me twitch. "Listen to me very carefully, Robert. If you know anything about this woman, this would be the time to tell us. Do you understand?"

"Those letters were written more than fifty years ago!"

"We know that," DiCarlo said. "Now tell us something we don't know."

So I told them the story of how Maxwell Bennett long ago left Richmond Hill in his shiny black '61 Thunderbird to start a new life in California, which for some strange reason was sounding a little too familiar. By the time I'd finished paraphrasing that chapter in the Bennett family saga, which included his less than triumphant return, I'd hoped my own attempt to start over in the Golden State would have a happier ending. I said, "It's obvious to me. That woman had been the love of his life. Clearly, he'd cherished those memories enough to lock them away in a vault for safekeeping. Do you really believe letters written so long ago could have any connection at all to the murders? They were love letters, for God's sake, weren't they? Not death threats."

"Do you believe in coincidence, Mr. Bennett," DiCarlo asked, still behind me.

"Actually, I do."

"Well, we don't. We're the police," DiCarlo said. "We don't believe in coincidence. That's why we had the Federal Reserve trace the serial numbers on the bills in the box, some of which were consecutive, and do you know what they found?"

"No. What did they find?"

"That they'd shipped those bills to a bank in San Francisco. Last time we checked, Robert, San Francisco was in California. Northern California, to be more specific. According to the letters, May was in California. Northern California, as a matter of fact. That's two links to Northern California in the same safe-deposit box. And guess what? You've moved to California, haven't you? Northern California, as well. What are we supposed to think about that?"

"I moved there to start over. I had to. I tried to get past the grief for a year, but couldn't. I loved Dana from the first minute I saw her. I loved her more each day. I can't really describe the way I felt about her except to say I loved her more than anything in the world. I couldn't stand being in the apartment without her."

Stein offered, "You could have found another place to live somewhere in the city. You didn't have to quit your job and move across the country."

"We went everywhere together. It was impossible for me to go anywhere we hadn't been. Wherever I went in the past year—stores, restaurants, movies, everywhere, goddamn it, I went alone. I was reminded every day and every night of what I no longer had."

"Why California?" DiCarlo asked. "It's a big country. Why'd you move *there*?"

"My old boss was nice enough to get me a job there when I told him I needed a change. He called a friend of his and convinced the man to hire me. Call him. His name is Harold Rice. You talked to him last year. I know you went to my office when I wasn't there and embarrassed the shit out of me, asking about my relationship with Dana, trying to dig up dirt. That's all right. I know you were just doing your job. I'll give you the number again, in case you lost it. I know I gave it to you before, when you were busting my balls the last time."

"We already talked to him," DiCarlo said. "And that's what he told us, but when I asked him why he called someone in California in particular he said it was because that's where *you* said you wanted to go. Your exact words, to the best of his recollection, were 'Northern California.' I think that's interesting, Robert. Don't you?"

"What I said was, 'It had to be a place I'd never been with Dana.' We loved traveling. We'd been all over the country together, including L.A. to visit her sister, but we'd never been to the northern part of the state. And I'd never been there before myself."

"Why California at all?"

"Because it's clear across the country. That's why."

"You could have gone to Portland or Seattle," Stein volunteered. "They're on the other side of the country. I hear Seattle is a pretty nice town."

"You could have gone to Anchorage or Honolulu for that matter," DiCarlo added. "They're even further."

I looked at both detectives in disbelief. "Are you fucking kidding me? Why don't you name a few more cities? I haven't had a geography lesson since I was a kid. Maybe I should have asked your advice before I went anywhere at all, since you're both undoubtedly so worldly and well-traveled."

DiCarlo pointed his finger at me. "I warned you once already about your smart mouth, Architect. If I have to warn you again, we'll finish this interview in the E.R. because that's where E.M.S. will take you after you've fallen down the stairs. And as you know, we have a lot of stairs in this building. Do you understand what I'm saying?"

"Listen to me—both of you. You can threaten me all you want, but that won't change the fact that I had absolutely nothing to do with the deaths of my wife and uncle. Nothing! Did you forget that I was in Las Vegas that weekend for a convention? That I was on a plane when they were killed?"

"That just means you weren't there to do it yourself," DiCarlo reasoned. "We've already determined that it was most likely a case of murder for hire. That alibi doesn't work for you anymore. You could have paid someone to do it knowing you'd be out of town. The timing was probably part of your plan."

"Why?" I shouted. "Why would I do that? Tell me why!"

"Because your uncle was up to something, you were in it with him, and so was someone else in California. That's why you moved there. You planned on going there from the beginning. You waited a year thinking things would cool off. That a year was long enough. That the case would go cold."

"Are you out of your mind? You're talking about my family. My father's brother! My wife, for God's sake! How many times do I have to say it? I loved her!"

"Things got out of control. We know that. We already agreed that your wife was in the wrong place at the wrong time. We talked to the personnel in the cardiac unit where Dana worked. We know she asked for that weekend off so she could go with you to Las Vegas, but the hospital was short staffed. She couldn't get all three days. Maybe you couldn't call it off. Maybe you just couldn't reach the shooter in time."

Have you ever been so exasperated that the only thing you could do was close your eyes and take a breath so deep you thought your lungs would explode? When I finally opened my eyes, both detectives were staring at me intently. "I knew getting me back here was just so you could pick up where you left off trying to implicate me. I knew it. I just knew it. I'm going to tell you this one more time. I had nothing to do with it. I went to California to start a new life because some motherfucker I know nothing about destroyed my old one. And if you believe that fifty-year-old love letters, kept in a safe-deposit box by a sweet old man who sacrificed his own happiness for his sister, have anything to do with it you're dreadfully incompetent. Both of you."

Joe DiCarlo shook his head calmly and said, "The newest bills in the box were put into circulation just two years ago. The letters may be fifty years old, but the money isn't. What do you have to say about that, Robert? And if I were you, I'd keep the wise cracks to a minimum."

I sat there, in the harsh green coffee room on the second floor of the One Seventeen, trying to answer that question, and many more, without digging myself into a hole so deep I'd never see daylight.

To my surprise, they actually let me walk out of there the way I'd come in—a free man. I picked up my California interim license on the way out and hit the street. Even though I hadn't been under oath, sworn to tell the truth, the whole truth, and nothing but the truth, words like perjury, conspiracy, and obstruction of justice would bang around in my head with the resonance of a lockdown, all the way back to San Francisco.

8

To tell you the truth, I didn't know what to do when I left the One Seventeen. Or even what to think. I'd really gotten clobbered in there. I mean, I'd gone back to New York to identify stolen property, which I did, but then got hit with the news that the cops thought my uncle's murder had been a contract killing, that he'd hidden away sixty thousand dollars—money that somehow came from California, that they had May's first name, that they suspected a connection between the two, and that my moving to California had somehow further implicated me!

Maybe I should have been more upset about still being the NYPD's prime suspect after a year-long investigation, but what infuriated me most was the possibility that Mack had been involved in something that had gotten Dana killed, as well as himself. That *really* ticked me off. I tried to imagine what that could have been, or with whom he could have been entangled, but it was easier to envision the surface of the moon.

I sat in the Hertz car for a while outside the precinct, trying to figure out where to go. I was in no mood to schmooze with my old friends and relive old times. Old times were getting pretty old. I considered taking them into my confidence separately with an ear toward getting some advice, as they are both extraordinarily sharp, although their minds work in different ways. To date, I hadn't told anyone about my having discovered the house in the painting, or about May, or Amy. I was assessing the value of gaining another perspective or two when I remembered something Benjamin Franklin once said, although not to me personally. "Three may keep a secret, if two of them are dead." No wonder they'd put that guy's picture on the hundred dollar bill.

I didn't want to have anyone else killed (just kidding), so I headed for the airport and booked myself onto the first flight back to San Francisco. I wasn't in possession of any firearms (with or without silencers), sharp objects, or questionable liquids, and there were no fuses sticking out of my shoes, or anywhere else for that matter, so they let me on the plane. Of course I didn't say anything about being a suspect in a double murder. I wanted to ask the flight attendant if I could sit in the seat closest to the flight-data recorder, which I knew was strategically placed to best survive a crash, but I was already in enough trouble, through no fault of my own I might add, so I kept my mouth shut. I would say that being wrestled to the cabin floor by the air marshal and escorted back off the plane in handcuffs by the FBI would have ruined my day, but my day was already ruined.

Once I settled down in a window seat on the starboard side, I wondered if I should have stayed in New York longer. One tidbit of logic was inescapable: The best way to get myself off the hook would be to find the real killer or the bastard responsible for orchestrating the murders, if in fact the police had it right. But what could I have accomplished there? A year had passed.

The crime scene tape had long ago been removed. I'd emptied out my uncle's apartment and donated everything to charity—everything except the thirty-nine paintings now in my Tahoe condo. His apartment had probably been rented to someone else by now, if the law allowed it. Even if none of that had happened and it was still a crime scene, and I somehow managed to get in, what would I have looked for? What could I have learned that the police didn't already know?

I wondered about the missing painting so poignantly described by Gwen Millhouse, the peaceful picture I'd never seen of the New England coast. What had happened to it? Why had that painting been stolen and no others?

If it had been stolen by the killer, it could very well have been an integral part of the motive, unless the painting simply rekindled fond childhood memories for the hit man, as it had for Officer Steamy. That was certainly unlikely, even for those who do believe in coincidence. After all, aren't most hit men from Detroit or Cleveland? Who ever heard of hired muscle from Boothbay Harbor?

My mind jumped from one ridiculous scenario to the next. Maybe Mack sold the painting, but the buyer didn't want to pay for it, so he killed him and stole it, like a big drug deal gone bad. Maybe there were cryptic messages hidden in the painting which could have incriminated a cartel kingpin, or exposed a foreign agent. That thread of whimsy-gone-wild made me recall something that had flattered Dana and me, something which made that comic supposition one tenth of one percent less far-fetched. Maxwell Bennett had painted our wedding present: An abstract pastel watercolor still life; a unique rendition of a flower bouquet sans vase. Set on the vertical, it spanned eighteen by twenty four inches. I'd never seen anything quite like it, which yet again made me marvel at his ability to paint in many different styles. When first I'd gazed upon it he'd asked, "What do you see?"

"I see a beautiful painting of flowers," I'd replied. "What do you mean, what do I see?"

"Look closer and tell me what you see."

So I stepped forward, which is contrary to the way one ordinarily views a painting, especially an abstract. The closer I got, the less depth the arrangement seemed to have, although the subtle details of the stamens, petals, and stems became more identifiable despite the abstract nature of the work. "At this distance I can really appreciate the amount of work you've done here, but to tell you the truth, I think it looks better at a distance."

"Don't you see your name in there?"

"My name? What are you talking about?"

I moved closer still and examined every little line, every hairline stroke, and then, low and behold, there it was. As if printed by someone's weak hand, running up at a slight angle, there were a series of craggy letters decipherable only to someone who knew they were there. I cocked my head a few degrees to the left and read the hidden characters: *Robert & Dana, always!*

I didn't know what to say. I'm not ashamed to admit I'd gotten a little choked up. I simply turned and gave him a long hug. I believe he knew what I was thinking.

"I know you'll have a lot of flowers at your wedding," he'd said, "but I was planning to give you *these*. Just like your love for each other, these will never die."

That overwhelmed me, even then, when Dana was alive. The only words I could summon were, "I love you, Uncle Mack. You're the greatest."

I have that painting, but I can't look at it without crashing. It's in my condo, hidden behind whatever I could stack in front of it in the closet. I'd carefully hung the collection on the walls in my new place the day after I'd told Amy about it. I'd hung them all:

Large and small, vertical and horizontal, oils, acrylics, and watercolors; all but that one.

If I said I hadn't been thinking about Dana while deciding which painting went here and which one went there, I'd be lying. But as the painting of the white house beside the river became the centerpiece of my Tahoe Keys condo turned gallery, my thoughts shifted to Amy. I really wanted her to see the paintings of Maxwell Bennett because I had the feeling that she, perhaps more than anyone I'd ever met, except May Drake, could truly appreciate them. And if I said that using my uncle's paintings as a lure to bring her back to my place hadn't crossed my mind, I'd be lying again.

I thought about my uncle's missing cell phone. I'd seen it a few times when I visited, although I don't know where he got it. It was a real cheapy. As far as I knew, he only carried it for emergencies, because the odds of finding a pay phone in New York City that hadn't been vandalized were just about the same as finding a winning lottery ticket on the sidewalk. I never saw him use it, nor do I believe he ever used it to call me. The more I thought about it at thirty-seven thousand feet somewhere over the Great Lakes, the more their interest in it made sense, both for the numbers he may have programmed into it, and for the record of incoming as well as outgoing calls that was probably also in some, as of yet, undiscovered databank. If indeed he'd been involved in something that had brought death to his door, he may well have unwittingly arranged it with that very instrument.

The more I considered the possibility that my uncle had been involved in some illicit activity, the more absurd the notion seemed. Still, there was the enigma of the recently circulated sixty thousand dollars that had made its way from San Francisco to a safe-deposit box in Queens. Only at that point, while I was in a plane hurtling through space at five hundred miles per hour eight miles above North America, did the obvious question pop into my head: Had there been anything else in the box besides the love letters and the money? It hadn't occurred to me to ask that while I'd had the chance, in person, where I could've observed Stein's and DiCarlo's responses as well as hear them. *Schmuck!* They hadn't volunteered any more information, but that didn't mean there hadn't been more.

I suddenly realized why Stein had taken me down to the evidence room in the basement without his partner. It must have been part of the old good cop/bad cop routine. The pressure hadn't yet been applied. Maybe they'd thought I'd open up to the easy-going half of the team, the sincere and sympathetic Mr. Nice Guy, especially while I had my aunt's and uncle's most prized possessions in my hands. I remembered Stein's hand on my shoulder. *"I'm sorry. I know this must be difficult for you."*

As I tried to recall the details of that conversation in the depressing catacombs of the precinct, an interrogation thinly veiled with the pretense of identifying evidence, one visual in particular came to mind—that odd little painting of a Toulouse Lautrec-looking dude that Mack copied years ago from a book. Stein had vocalized his conclusion in so many words. Maxwell Bennett had painted a forgery. No longer were the murders thought to be a random act of violence, otherwise known as a crime of opportunity. The investigation was now clearly focused on the victim and his artwork. The next questions could have been: If he'd produced one forgery, why not more? How many were there? Were they being sold? And if so, by whom?

The NYPD was far ahead of me, but I hadn't been looking. I've said it before and I'll say it again. I'm an architect, not a detective. I didn't know the questions to ask in New York, or whom to question. But now I had something the police didn't, something they thought important enough to warrant my flying across the country for a face-to-face interview: May Drake's identity and address. There were letters from a woman in Northern California, currency from a bank in Northern California, and now I was again on my way to Northern California—the trifecta of coincidence. Maybe it was time to ask a few questions of my own.

9

The runways of SFO jut far into the bay, which means if you're on final approach from the south it looks like you're going to land in the water. This can be a little disconcerting, especially if you're a control freak like I am, because no one has ever seen an Airbus A320 with pontoons. I suppose you've just got to have faith in your fellow man or woman—faith that your pilot can get you down, faith that your psychiatrist can get you up, faith that the police will arrest the right person, faith that the jury will know the truth when they hear it, and faith that both your lawyer and your lover can get you off.

At that point in time I remember thinking that the limited optimism I'd mustered in my new life was suddenly being sucked back into the black hole of my old life. Then the pilot proved himself, receiving the usual round of applause, not only for putting the big bird down safely on good ole *terra firma*, but for also getting us through enough clear-air turbulence to have shaken a memorable martini. I resolved to move forward, although I will admit I did briefly wonder if San Francisco would vibrate itself to pieces while I was there. I banished that specter from my mind remembering the adage: It is pointless to worry about things over which one has no control. I can't remember where I'd heard that, or from whom, but of one thing I'm certain. They weren't my father's words, may he rest in peace.

The direction of the investigation was, however, cause for concern. And if that isn't an understatement, I don't know what is. I wasn't about to let the police besmirch my uncle's memory. And I certainly wasn't going to let them indict *me* for the murders of the only two people I truly loved in this world. Apparently, living on the opposite side of the continent, and trusting the police to do their thing back in New York, was not working exactly the way I'd hoped.

I needed to talk to May Drake. I thought about the questions I might ask. I tried to imagine what she might reveal, but that was, of course, ridiculous. I would say that such speculation had been nothing but a waste of time, but it did lead me to one inescapable conclusion: If I were to infer that she'd had anything to do with Maxwell Bennett's murder, it would be safe to assume I'd be rendered *persona non grata* on the spot, unwelcome in the white house by the river, in her life, and therefore in Amy's life.

Considering the big picture, that shouldn't have mattered. Not one bit. Not with what was at stake. But I wasn't willing to let that happen. Not just yet. I told myself that getting closer to Amy first could have its advantages, in more ways than one. It was only logical to think that having her on my side could open more doors, if in fact her grandmother had anything to do with my uncle's death, as the NYPD suggested.

I remembered with romantically-charged anticipation her offer to pick me up at the airport, but I was a day early. And to tell you the truth, despite my desires, I'm more independent than that. So, I simply rented another Hertz car and, needless to say, found the lone black Mustang GT in the parking garage with no trouble at all. When offered the V8 pony car at the counter I thought, why not? San Francisco was, in fact, the city in which the classic film *Bullitt* had been shot. Considering the way Steve McQueen's '68 Highland Green Mustang fastback looked after one of Hollywood's greatest chases, I decided to accept the zero deductible damage waiver. Events in the unfolding drama known as my life, starring yours truly, had become a little too unpredictable, and I found myself more than willing to sign for all the horsepower and insurance I could get.

I pulled Amy Drake's business card from my wallet and called her at the office. Although having left New York at one o'clock in the afternoon, bucking the west to east jet stream for five hours, and playing musical rental cars at opposite ends of the country, it was only four p.m., thanks to Pacific Standard Time. Even though I'd gone back in time three hours, I didn't feel any younger. But I did feel more aggressive. Until now, wanting to know Amy better had been part social and part hormonal, although not necessarily in that order. Suddenly it seemed more like a matter of survival.

I considered just dropping in and surprising her, but I didn't know her that well. And I do know that showing up without calling first can be the best way to get your feelings hurt. I was feeling aggressive, but not cocky.

A minute after her assistant put me on hold I heard her voice.
"Robert, is that you?"

The needle on my voice analyzer was clearly in the warm zone, wishful thinking notwithstanding. "It is. Am I interrupting anything?"

"Only the usual. How are things going in New York?"

"Not quite as I expected."

"Is that good or bad?"

"I'll tell you when I see you. Do you have any plans for this evening?"

She paused long enough for me to imagine hearing words like: *As a matter of fact I do. I'm sorry, maybe some other time.* "Are you asking me to fly to New York?"

"Actually, I just landed a little while ago at SFO. I cut a day off the trip. I'm on the 101 heading your way. I was hoping to see you tonight. I'd like you to have dinner with me. I'll pick you up at your office."

Another pause lasted at least as long as the first. "All right. That way you can meet my grandfather. He's asked about you several times."

"He has?"

"Once a day, I think, since I told him about you on Monday."

"Why?"

"Because you wanted to meet him."

"No, not why did you tell him about me? I know that part. Why did he ask about *me* so many times?"

"I don't know. Maybe because he thinks I should be married or something. I don't usually tell him about anyone I've met."

"Do me a favor and thank him for me."

"Thank him for what?" she asked.

"Keeping me on your mind."

She paused again, long enough this time for me to think the cell call had been dropped. But before I could repeat her name into the phone I heard her say, "I shouldn't tell you this, but you didn't need his help."

"I'll see you in a little while." Somehow, I managed to contain myself until the call ended. Then I did a mental backflip, despite the unprecedented level of aggravation in my life. I signaled myself into the fast-lane and whipped the ponies under the hood as if the city in the distance were the finish line at Churchill Downs.

Leland Drake Incorporated was located on the Embarcadero, at the east end of Market Street. I stopped and looked around before going in. Even though this was bustling downtown San Francisco, I almost expected to see a few snow-capped mountains, a lush meadow full of wildflowers, a babbling brook, or an old and weathered sagging barn in the immediate vicinity. No such luck. But because the bay was just on the other side of the street, the view wasn't half-bad. In fact, all the ingredients of a painting were there: A majestic clock tower, a graceful suspension bridge, a half-dozen sailboats pushed to a rakish angle on the chop in the distance, a few circling seagulls in an azure sky with a puffy white cloud here and there, and an old man on a bench feeding pigeons in the foreground. Of course, all of the things you don't see in a painting were there, too—the time on the clock tower was wrong, the traffic on the Bay Bridge was at a standstill, and everything was covered with bird shit.

The tan brick building itself would have been so-so in SoHo. It was six-stories tall and old, but seemed to be in good repair. From the outside it appeared to be comprised of lofts. It wasn't particularly impressive architecturally, but the real estate agent's mantra undoubtedly applied—location, location, location.

But who am I to talk? At least Leland Drake had a building with his name on it. The three dimensional brass plaque to the right of the entrance was the size of a fireplace. The only thing I had with my name on it that was larger than a business card was my desk plate. The plate was mine. I'd paid for it, but the desk belonged to my new boss and his partner, the Nazi.

To be honest, I hesitated outside because I was a little nervous, not about meeting Leland Drake, but about seeing Amy again and wanting to say all the right things. I remember sniffing the white roses I'd bought from a flower vender around the corner, a sight as common in San Francisco as the homeless. I'd given the selection some thought on the sidewalk. A mixed bouquet would have been too generic, and red roses would have been too intense. I went over a few more things in my head and went inside.

The elevator opened on the top floor and I stepped into a large, high-ceilinged loft with white walls. The vast space had been subdivided into offices. I crossed the polished hardwood to a reception desk and was greeted by Amy's assistant, the man behind the radio announcer's voice that answered my calls. "How may I help you?" he asked. He was strikingly handsome, as if an employment agency had sent over an out-of-work actor or model to fill in. He seemed to look me over before I replied, something probably prompted by the roses in my hand. It may have all been in my head, but my first thought was that he was sizing up the competition because he was either doing Amy himself, or was trying to.

"Ms. Drake is expecting me. Please tell her Robert Bennett is here."

"Certainly." He picked up the phone, pressed a button, and said, "Mr. Bennett is here to see you." Then he returned the phone to its cradle and said to me, "Why don't you have a seat." He gestured toward a Danish black leather sofa. "She'll be out in a minute."

I took his suggestion and ambled to the seating at the opposite wall. A Leland Drake catalog was on the coffee table in front of the couch, so I picked it up and thumbed through it. I immediately recognized the style that had made Drake famous. The work obviously required talent, and was pleasant in a warm and inviting way, but it was a little too charming for me. I guess I'm not that charming.

If Amy Drake wasn't genuinely happy to see me, she must have had acting lessons, although now that I think about it, she could have beamed so at the sight of the roses. She wore a white silk blouse, a navy blue fitted skirt hemmed just above the knee, shear nylons, and dark blue closed-toe leather pumps. She was even more beautiful than I'd remembered. "I thought you might like these," I said, offering her the flowers.

She took the bouquet and inhaled their fragrance. "I love them. Thank you. They're beautiful." Then she kissed me on the cheek. "How are you?" she asked.

"Better now. It's great to see you again."

"I'm glad you called. Come with me and I'll introduce you to my grandfather. Then we'll take off." She turned and addressed her assistant, "You might as well call it a day. I'll see you Monday."

"All right. Good night. Nice to have met you, Mr. Bennett."

"You as well," I replied as I began to follow his boss.

I don't know what I'd expected to see in Leland Drake's office besides Leland Drake, but a mural or some paintings would have been nice. Bringing the outdoors indoors with a few vivid floral arrangements and a couple of tall, decorative green-leaf ficus trees beneath the loft's high ceiling and plentiful daylight would not have been a surprise. Even one of those soothing indoor burbling tranquility fountains could have been predictable. I suppose, based on his art, I was expecting warm and cozy. Instead, the word austere came to mind.

The office was huge and mostly empty, except for a large chrome and glass desk, a phone and a laptop, a modern leather swivel chair, a few starkly simple visitor's chairs, and a contemporary sidebar on casters. There were no drapes decorating the expansive windows that looked out on San Francisco Bay, which was a good thing considering the view. But the sparseness of the furnishings in such a large space gave the office a cold and temporary feel. I heard our footsteps echo through the loft as we crossed the parquet floor.

Drake stood and extended his hand across the desk as Amy introduced me. "How do you do?" he asked. "I'm glad you could stop by. Amy has told me a lot about you."

Have you ever noticed that some people shake hands as if your hand were a raw fish, and others do their best to impersonate a vise? Suffice it to say I was taken unawares by the strength of his grasp, instantly at odds in my mind with the gentle way an artist holds his brush. The fact that I'd guessed him to be about eighty only added to my surprise. I tried to ignore the bones in my hand folding onto one another as I glanced at Amy.

She seemed a little embarrassed by his opening comment. "I have some things to finish before we go," she said, immediately excusing herself. "I'll see you in a few minutes." Then she left the office.

My eyes wanted to follow her out, but that would have been inappropriate, as the man to whom I had just been introduced was her grandfather. I said, "I've heard a lot about you, too. I appreciate your work. I'm an architect, so I have a pretty good eye. And I know a little about art. My late uncle was an artist."

"Amy told me what happened. I'm very sorry for your loss."

"Thank you."

"Why don't you sit down," Drake said, indicating the chair beside me.

We both sat and looked at each other for a moment. He was a handsome man, lucky enough to still have his own brown hair, even if he did dye away the gray. He appeared to be slim and fit beneath his Ralph Lauren navy blue brass-button trimmed double-breasted blazer and powder blue shirt, open at the collar. All that was missing was a yachting cap, which he'd probably left on his yacht.

In those first few seconds I had the feeling he was measuring me with brown eyes the exact color of his hair. I wasn't sure if he was using them as artist's eyes (although I don't recall seeing any discernable inner light) or grandfather's eyes. To my knowledge he didn't do portraits, but I thought he might say something like, "You have good cheek bones and a strong chin." Or, on the other hand, he could have said, "My granddaughter is a very special girl," which I already knew. Instead, he said, "I know who your uncle was. I never met him, but I know who he was." Drake stopped and looked down at his hands, now clasped on the glass desk. "Maxwell Bennett was the love of my ex-wife's life," he said, without looking up. "He knew May before I did. After would have been better, but thankfully it wasn't at the same time. At least I don't think it was, although sometimes it felt that way. I suppose you could say she was on the rebound when I met her. All things considered, that wasn't the best circumstance."

Needless to say I was taken aback by the man's candor. I didn't really know how to respond so I just sat there, a little embarrassed, and a little sorry for him, although I do definitely recall feeling proud of my uncle, even if it was at Leland Drake's expense. I might also say I felt a certain surge in the Bennett family team spirit.

"From what I've seen, he was a good artist," Drake continued. "As much as I hate to admit it, your uncle had the gift."

"So do you. It's made you a celebrity. Maxwell Bennett never sold anything."

"That's a pity. He could have."

I nodded. "Which paintings have you seen?"

"Only the one above May's mantel. I know talent when I see it."

I remembered standing in May's living room and staring, for the first time, at the ship under full-sail crashing through waves and whitecaps. "I thought I possessed all of his works," I said, "but that painting proves I don't."

Leland Drake's eyes met mine and he said, "Amy told me that you moved from New York City to Lake Tahoe."

I nodded.

"If you don't mind my asking, why did you come to California?"

"After my wife and uncle were murdered, I was getting nowhere. I tried for a year. I tried to make sense of it, but couldn't. I had to look elsewhere."

He stared at me for a while, as if contemplating my explanation, before asking the next question. "How long have you known about May?"

I flashed on watching my father's home movies when I was a child, in which I saw my uncle leave Richmond Hill to start a new life in California and return a week later in an absolute tizzy. "For a very long time. I just never had a reason to come here before."

"How did you find her?"

I considered telling him the truth; that noticing May's house on the way home from my new job, because it resembled a house in one of my uncle's paintings, had been entirely by chance. I hadn't told *her* about the coincidence that led me to her door, so I didn't tell her ex-husband either. I simply said, "It's a small world, isn't it?"

Drake stood and walked to the sidebar. "Would you like a drink?"

"No thanks."

He poured a big dose of Chivas into a rocks glass and crossed to the windows. The daylight illuminating the bay had begun to fail with the day's end, and I could see Drake's transparent reflection in the plate glass. He brought the aged scotch to his lips and threw it back. Then he said, "It's a beautiful view, isn't it?"

"It certainly is."

"Well, at least they caught the bastard."

"No. They didn't. Not yet. What makes you think they did?"

"Amy said there'd been a break in the case and that the police recovered a stolen painting. If they found something that had been taken, I assumed they'd made an arrest."

"There were actually two break-ins, two days apart. The first one was just a burglary. My uncle wasn't home at the time. The second entry ended with the killing of my uncle and my wife, Dana. The police locked up the scumbag responsible for the first one, but they don't believe he did the second one."

Drake poured himself another drink and swirled it around in the glass before saying, "Of course he did. He went back to steal things he couldn't carry out the first time. Or he thought about things he'd seen there and decided he wanted them after all."

I remember staring at the celebrity artist standing in front of that dramatic backdrop, the whole scene resembling an advertisement for the twelve year old scotch or the designer clothing, and being stunned by the direction of the conversation. I really don't know what I'd expected from Leland Drake, but a discussion that could have taken place back in the station house wasn't it. My first reaction was to shut down the conversation, knowing that the police sometimes withhold sensitive information so as not to compromise an investigation. But I had intended to ask May a few choice questions, and this man was May's ex-husband, so I decided to let the discussion run its course.

"There's evidence to suggest the murders were committed by someone else," I said. "The lowlife in custody has a long record which includes numerous burglaries, but he never carried a gun. Both of my relatives were shot."

Drake started shaking his head. "That doesn't prove anything.

Maybe he decided to step it up a notch."

"The police have come to the conclusion that the murders were a contract; that someone went to my uncle's apartment specifically to kill him and that Dana just happened to be there at the time. They think it was just made to look like a push-in robbery."

"My God," Drake said. "What would make them think that?"

"Each of them was shot twice, but the neighbors, who were home at the time, never heard a thing, so the police believe a silencer was used. They also think my uncle opened the door for someone he knew." At that point I remembered Stein's observation that Dana hadn't been raped; a clear departure, according to the police, from the push-in robber's *modus operandi*. I stopped short of mentioning that tidbit. "Overall, they're pretty convinced it wasn't a random crime. And now, so am I."

Drake turned away and faced the windows again. "I never knew the man," he said, "but who would want your uncle killed?"

"Well," I said, buying a second or two while deciding whether or not to verbalize the thought that had just crossed my mind. Feeling more like a detective than an architect, I simply stated, "*You* would."

Indignation turned him around. "Pardon me?"

"Based on what you've already said, you would. It sounds like you had a reason to want him dead."

"I can see why you'd say that, but that was a very long time ago."

"If you don't mind my asking, where were you on Sunday afternoon, April seventeenth last year?" I've got to say it felt pretty strange articulating that question. Fun actually, but strange.

Drake hit a few keys on his computer, read the information on the screen, and said, "I do mind, but if you must know, I was the keynote speaker at a fundraiser for the San Francisco Museum of Modern Art. Let me remind you that your uncle took himself out of the picture, no pun intended. He didn't marry May, I did. He could have, but he didn't. He stayed in New York to take care of his sickly sister. I know the whole story. He blew it. No offense."

I did take offense. "May never got over it. Maybe you didn't either. Maybe you still blame him for your failed marriage. Maybe you never got over May."

"I've moved on. Quite nicely, I might add." He turned the laptop around so I could see the photograph he'd installed as the machine's desktop. "That's Mona, my new wife."

It was a full body shot of a woman in heels and a thong bikini. She was Amy's age and quite attractive, but in a trampy sort of way. A big boob job was also a good bet. Her name was appropriate, I thought, although unsure if it was because she was married to an artist or because she undoubtedly made easily imaginable sounds.

"Thank God for sildenafil," he volunteered.

"What?"

"You know, the little pill that puts lead in your pencil."

"I thought that's what you said. I don't have that problem. Erectile dysfunction for me is not being able to put up a building the way I envision it."

"But that means you've never had a four hour erection, right?"

"I can't say I have."

"Then you haven't lived."

"If that's what it takes, I guess I haven't. But I've got to say, I've never heard anyone refer to that medication by its generic name. Maybe you should have been a pharmacist instead of an artist."

Leland Drake ignored that observation and asked, "What painting did the police recover?"

"Excuse me?"

"You told Amy the police recovered a painting. Which one

was it?"

I sat there for a minute processing his question before saying, "My uncle has never sold a painting, and you've never met him, so what do you mean, 'Which one was it?'"

"I mean, what did it look like?"

I pictured in my mind the small oil-on-canvas portrait that had been stolen for some unknown reason during the first break-in, the painting Sheldon Stein had called a forgery. "It's not important. What is important is that I'm going to get to the bottom of this."

"*You* are?"

I nodded. "The police believe there's a California connection. They've got a few pieces of the puzzle, but I may have one they don't."

At that moment, Amy entered without knocking. I smiled and watched her cross the floor. She returned the smile, but then something caught her eye and her expression lost its favor. I realized it was the photo of her grandfather's young wife on the laptop, having been turned around to face me. Amy took my hand and pulled me out of my seat.

"I'm getting hungry," she said. "Let's get something to eat. I know a nice little place. Do you like Italian?"

"I love Italian. There's nothing like a good vendetta."

"Great," she said. "I've already made a reservation at Luigi's."

"Luigi's?"

"Don't worry. You'll love it."

I glanced at her grandfather and thought he looked noticeably troubled. Before I let Amy lead me out of the office, I broke free and shook hands with Leland Drake again, this time not only ready for the big squeeze, but offended just enough to get even.

10

Leland Drake had said of his ex-wife, "She was on the rebound when I met her. All things considered, that wasn't the best circumstance." *No kidding.*

But could the same have been said of me? And is that why I was so taken with Amy? How much time must pass after your lover leaves you, or leaves this world, for you to no longer be on the rebound? I actually wondered about that as I looked at Amy Drake. I was trying to be objective. I hate being a slave to my emotions. That's even worse than being a slave to my hormones. I like to think I'm stronger than that. And have more character than that. I'd like to think that my mind controls my actions. But, apparently, it doesn't.

Luigi's was an inviting little neighborhood *ristorante* located in San Francisco's North Beach. I knew the moment I walked in that the ambience was just right; the lights low enough to be very romantic, but focused enough to see what you were eating.

I noticed the large and beautiful paintings of Italy that hung in gilded frames on forest green walls, each illuminated by the same kind of narrow-beam spotlight that made every table an oasis. I particularly liked the contrast between the pure white table cloths, each hosting a candle, and the artwork, so vivid it couldn't be ignored. I don't wear a hat, but if I did I would have tipped it to Luigi's interior designer for creating the perfect combination of warmth and drama.

Luigi himself, long white apron and all, led us to the best table in the house. "So nice to see you again, Miss Amy," he said with a colorful Italian accent. He offered to take her suitcoat as she peeled if off, but she folded it instead and draped it over the back of her chair as I pulled it away from the table for her. He handed her a menu and said, "I didn't think it was possible, but you look more beautiful every time I see you."

This guy should have been a politician. I said, "I had the very same thought."

"You may have been thinking it, but did you tell her?" he asked, offering a menu to me along with the wine list.

"No. Unfortunately I didn't."

"Well, my friend, if you want to keep a beautiful woman, you've got to tell her she's beautiful every chance you get."

I can keep her if she's not murdered. Maybe the sign outside should read, Luigi's Italian Cuisine & Counseling. Advice with Extra Cheese! "I'll try to remember that."

Amy introduced me to the restaurateur formally. We shook hands and he said, "It's nice to meet you. I hope you enjoy your evening. Guido will be right over to take your order." Then he headed for the kitchen.

Guido? Is he a waiter or an enforcer? I said to Amy, "It sounds like you eat here often."

She nodded. "Sometimes, when I don't feel like cooking. The

food is very good."

"What do you recommend?"

"I like the Angel Hair Primavera. The garlic and oil is just right."

"If the food is as good as the advice, this place is a winner."

She smiled and I thought I noticed a hint of humility in her green eyes.

I could use words like mesmerizing or hypnotic to describe her face, but even they wouldn't convey the feeling of intoxication that entered my eyes and warmed my body from the inside like cognac.

At the risk of sounding less than romantic I said, "If you'd like some wine I'm afraid you'll have to order it by the glass. I don't drink and drive."

"I'm glad you don't. I'll have a cabernet occasionally."

Guido arrived and asked, "Can I get you something from the bar?"

How about a good criminal defense attorney? "The lady would like a cabernet. What do you have by the glass this evening?"

Guido named several wines and Amy chose one. Then we listened politely while he recited the evening's specials, each sounding like a dream for the palate and a nightmare for the arteries. Why is it that the better something tastes, the worse it is for you?

Amy said, "If you don't mind, Guido, I'll have my usual."

"Of course."

"I'll have the same." I was tempted to ask if he'd ever broken anybody's legs, but I let it go.

She looked at me and said, "I wasn't expecting to hear from you until tomorrow."

"Things didn't take as long in New York as they could have." *Twenty-five to life would have taken considerably longer.* "I should have waited to call you, but the truth is I wanted to see you again."

I did want to see her again, ever since the minute she and May had dropped me at my Porsche after our Bavarian lunch fest. I wanted to see her again for all the usual boy-meets-girl reasons, but I also wanted to see her before I saw May again, a meeting which would likely wear out my welcome at the white house by the river. If we could get to know each other, if I could get her to want to see me again after our first date, then I'd stand a chance of surviving my interrogating her grandmother. I know it sounds absurd, but that's what I thought. That's what the NYPD had done to my head.

"I wanted to see you, too," she said. "I'm glad you called. And I'm glad you had a chance to meet my grandfather, I think." Her smile turned skeptical. "How did you two get along?"

Like Al Capone and Eliot Ness. "Fine."

"What did you talk about?"

How the hell was I supposed to answer that? Let's see. *We chatted about how your grandmother loved my uncle more than she ever loved your grandfather. In less than five minutes I virtually accused your gramps of murdering Mack. He provided an alibi and went on to talk about what it's like to have a four hour erection. Then he proudly showed me a picture of the gold-digging slut who replaced your grandmother.* "The usual."

"The usual?"

"Yeah, you know, how I adore his work, that you're a very a special girl, things like that."

"Why do I get the feeling you're lying?"

Could it be because I am? "I don't know, but that's not exactly the feeling I was hoping for."

"And what feeling is that?"

"That you find me irresistible."

"I didn't know you're such an optimist."

Yeah. That's me, optimist extraordinaire! I'm surprised my picture isn't next to the word in the dictionary. "Actually, I only became an optimist the minute I saw you over your *schnitzel* last week. Until then, I thought the world was coming to an end."

"And you don't any longer?"

I thought about that for a moment. "I suppose I still do. The difference is, before I really didn't care. Now it feels like I do."

She looked into my eyes. "That's one of the nicest things anyone has ever said to me."

"If that's true, you've been hanging out with the wrong people."

"You may have a point there."

Amy's cabernet arrived, courtesy of Guido. He also filled our water glasses. I raised my clear goblet, quite annoyed at myself for being such a straight arrow, and said, "Here's to hanging with the right people." We clinked and sipped.

"Tell me about yourself," I continued. "All I know is that you drive a red BMW, you live in San Francisco, but I don't know where, you manage a corporation, and you're very close to your grandmother. I know I can't take my eyes off you, but that's more about me than you."

"What else do you want to know?"

"I haven't heard anything about your parents."

Her gaze dropped away. "They were killed in a car crash when I was fifteen."

Nice going, Bennett. What other questions would you like to ask? What was the second worst day of your life? "I'm sorry. I had no idea."

"It's all right. I only remember two things about my father anyway. He was very handsome, and he was the biggest asshole in the world, drunk more often than not."

That's three things, but who's counting? I envisioned a younger version of her grandfather and something about an apple not falling far from the tree came to mind—on all three counts.

"I still hate him," she continued. "I hate him more than miss him."

"I'm no psychiatrist but you probably hate him because he left you, so to speak?"

"No. I hate him because he was an asshole. And because he killed my mother, who was an angel. A beautiful angel."

Killed? As in murdered? I sat there for a minute trying to figure out what she meant. Finally I put two and two together, took a guess, and said, "He was drunk behind the wheel?"

"They tried to keep it from me, but I always knew that's what happened. There were no other cars involved. I thank God for that, but that's how I knew. You just don't hit a bridge abutment for no reason at all, do you?"

I wouldn't. Glad that I was such a straight arrow I said, "Maybe he dropped a cigarette in his lap. Or maybe they were arguing."

"If they were arguing when my mother went through the windshield, he killed her anyway."

You've got a point there. "You weren't in the car with them?"

She shook her head. "But for a long time I wished I was."

"I doubt you could have prevented it, if that's what you were thinking."

"No. But maybe I should have died with my mother. That way she wouldn't be alone with him now."

Amy's beautiful green eyes were filling fast thanks to Bennett the Magnificent, Master of Romance. *Good going. You really know how to put a girl in the mood.* "Don't think that way. She's not with him now. It sounds like they went to different places, if you know what I mean." I reached across the table, took her hand, and said, "You're right. If you think your father was a jerk, he probably was." *A veritable chip off the old block.* "But look at what he created."

"What did he create?"

"You. He created you. He created incredible beauty. Beauty and brains. But you'd better blot your eyes before your mascara streaks your cheeks and I've got to drop you off at the circus."

She used her napkin with one hand, leaving the other in my gentle grasp, which I took as a good sign. I expected her to excuse herself and escape to the powder room, but she didn't. Instead she said, "My mother's responsible for the way I turned out. My mother and May. My grandmother raised me after my mother died. She saw me through high school, college, and grad school."

"Your grandmother and your grandfather."

"No. They'd already divorced. They've been divorced for a long time."

"How did they meet? Do you know?"

"May owned an art gallery near the Ghirardelli. Leland walked in one day."

I thought about what May had told me. She'd met my uncle at a gallery. For a moment, I imagined how that might have gone… a dashing young tourist from New York City on holiday, with a keen eye and a deep appreciation for art, visits a San Francisco gallery and is soon swept up in a torrid and everlasting romance that most likely begins with the simple words, "May I help you?" I wondered if May had met Maxwell and Leland in the same gallery. Some women like a man in uniform. Some like a rebel. Maybe May just had a thing for artists. I'd never heard that one before, but why not?

I asked, "Do you have any sisters or brothers?"

She reached for her wine glass, looked at the red liquid within before taking more than a few sips, but didn't answer.

Asking about her parents had undeniably opened an old wound. Now, for a very long moment, it suddenly felt as if I had a scalpel in my hand.

Then, still staring at her wine, she simply replied, "No, it's just me."

Relieved, I said, "I don't have any siblings either. Both my mother and father passed away a long time ago. Not at the same time, but much too soon, no matter how you look at it, especially my mom. I was always very close to my uncle, my father's brother." I didn't know exactly how much she knew about Mack, but I was about to find out. I said, "To tell you the truth, I was surprised that you knew about what my uncle and your grandmother shared. That doesn't seem like the kind of thing a granddaughter would know."

She smiled for the first time in a little while. "May and I are friends. We talk about all kinds of things. Even things you wouldn't expect. She's like a best friend, a sister, a mother, and a grandmother all rolled into one."

"I never knew my grandparents. They died before I was born. Considering what you just said about you and May, it actually sounds like you're pretty lucky."

"I suppose in that respect. May was alone when I went to live with her. As it turned out, I became the daughter she never had as well as the granddaughter she did. I really loved living there with her. She's such a wonderful person. And it's such a beautiful spot. It's as pretty as a painting."

A Leland Drake painting or a Maxwell Bennett painting? "It's funny you should say that. My uncle did an oil of May's house. I have it. It's not an accurate rendering, but I'm certain it's of her place."

"That house has been in her family for years, since the thirties, I think. She grew up in it. She loves it there."

"How did you find out about my uncle? Did May just tell you about him over French toast one morning in the kitchen?"

Amy Drake shook her head. "While she was out one day I washed and ironed a few of her blouses. When I put them in her armoire I discovered a beautiful mahogany box. I can still see the hand-painted red rose on the porcelain medallion inlaid on its lid. At first I thought it was a jewelry box. Letters from your uncle were inside."

"Love letters?"

She nodded.

"You read them?"

"I suppose I shouldn't have, but I couldn't help myself. I took the box over to the window-seat, curled up on the cushion in the afternoon sun and read each one. It took quite a while. I read them all before she came home. They made me feel as warm on the inside as I did on the outside with the sun on my shoulders. It was almost like reading a romance novel. Not that they were dirty in any way, but I could feel the love he'd felt for her. The letters made me incredibly happy… happy that someone had felt that strongly about my grandmother, at least once in her life. It wasn't until that afternoon that I knew where all of the little curios that filled the house had come from. Your uncle had sent them, one with each letter. It was incredible. I'd never heard anything like that. It was so romantic I cried. I never knew just how special each one was."

"Leland must have loved your grandmother, certainly in the beginning."

"I'm not so sure," Amy said. "Even when they were together I never really sensed love in the air. My grandfather can be very cold."

At the risk of offending her, though emboldened by her candor, I said, "I felt that in the office, even down to the furnishings, but it didn't make sense to me, not considering the warm and comfortable nature of his paintings."

"Leland Drake is a shrewd businessman. He knows what will sell. He developed his signature style, the style that made him famous, because of its universal appeal. He doesn't paint because he loves to paint, like so many other artists."

"My uncle was one of the others. *And* he had great warmth."

"I know he did," she said. "I could feel it in the letters as his words came off the pages and tugged at my heart. He bared his soul in some of them. I know that's not easy for a man to do. I read them over and over again, whenever I had the chance. After a while it almost felt as if I knew him. He was a wonderful man, caring and sensitive. I couldn't help but think that if he'd moved to California they'd still be together. I remember hoping that someday someone would care about me that way, the way Maxwell cared about my grandmother."

I sat there for a minute, long enough to remember the man who was my uncle, but not long enough to miss the moment. I leaned forward, lifted her left hand toward me, and kissed it. I looked into her green eyes, past the reflection of the candle's flame and said, "That day may come sooner than you think."

Wouldn't you know it? Just as her perfect lips began to utter a reply, Guido shows up with the pasta. "Angel Hair Primavera for two. Would you like fresh parmesan?"

*I'd like you to get the hell out of here before I break **your** legs.* "Parmesan would be nice."

Guido grated a chunk of cheese right before our eyes, said, "Enjoy," collected the large oval tray and folding stand he'd brought, and disappeared.

"What were you going to say?" I asked.

She smiled a subtle smile and said, "Never mind."

"What do you mean, never mind? What were you going to say?"

After a moment, the gears turning in her head seemed to move her face from side to side. "Maybe I'll tell you later. It's important to have something to look forward to, don't you think?"

I nodded while my mind performed a ten second review. Last year I was looking forward to spending my life with Dana. This morning I'd been told all I had to look forward to were two consecutive life sentences unless I confessed. Then I could relish the prospect of being prison punked for a couple of decades. Now it sounded like Amy was suggesting something considerably more positive. Things were looking up, at least for the moment. "Having something to look forward to is what makes life worth living, especially if it's with someone you've taken into your heart."

She looked off somewhere, her memory apparently jogged by my words of wisdom. Then she made a curious comment. "Your uncle had said something like that in one of his letters. I don't remember the exact words, but I'm sure that was the idea." She turned to me again and said, "I don't know you very well, Robert Bennett, and I don't know how you could remind me of someone I've never met, but I think you may be very much like your uncle."

I stopped twirling my pasta, thought about what I'd just heard, and said, "That may be one of the nicest things anyone has ever said to *me*."

She smiled and said, "You're welcome."

"So how did you get May to tell you about it? You didn't tell her you read his letters, did you?"

"No, I couldn't tell her that. I told her I saw a beautiful wooden box in her armoire and asked if she would show me the jewelry inside sometime. I couldn't think of any other way to get her to tell me about a very special time in her life. The funny thing is, once she did, we spoke about it for hours. She'd kept it inside for so long she was thrilled to finally let it out. It was like going back. I could see it on her face. Just talking about him made it feel like he was there with us, reliving the time of their lives."

"The box didn't have a lock, did it?"

"No."

"You realize she knew you opened it and read the letters, don't you?"

Amy Drake nodded.

"That's all right," I said. "It sounds like she wanted to tell you about the love of her life as much as you wanted to know about it."

"Your uncle put his thoughts down on paper a long time ago. May received them a long time ago. I read them a long time ago, but time doesn't seem to matter. You popped into our lives last Saturday and connected the past to the present. You told May that Maxwell had died, that he'd been murdered, and that afternoon, after you drove away, she cried on and off for hours. At least I was there with her."

"I'm glad you were there, too. After all, if you hadn't been, I wouldn't be here with you now."

"No. I suppose not. It's funny how things happen, isn't it?"

"The way things happen isn't always funny, but I know what you mean."

"Speaking about the way things happen, what happened in New York?"

This girl knew a lot about my uncle, probably things I didn't, at least things earlier in his life. She knew a lot about May Drake, not only because she was her granddaughter, but because they'd lived together. And because they were *friends*. Friends know things about friends. So I told her everything except, of course, the part about the police considering me a suspect. Detective Joe DiCarlo's favorite suspect, in fact, or at least that's the way he'd put it.

I told her about both crimes at my uncle's apartment a year ago—the burglary on Friday and the murders on Sunday. I told her the police had made an arrest for the burglary just last week, but they didn't believe the Friday burglar was the Sunday murderer. "Someone wanted my uncle dead. That's what the police think. They think it was a contract killing."

Her hands covered her mouth, as if by reflex, and I heard the muffled words, "Oh, my God," slip through her fingers. "Who would want such a thing?"

"I don't know yet, but I will."

Amy looked down at her food for a minute. When she looked up she said, "Before you went back to New York, you said the police recovered a painting. Tell me about it."

"Years ago, my uncle copied a silly little portrait out of a book just to prove, if only to himself, that he could paint as well as anyone, even the so-called masters. That's what they found, a twelve-inch square oil of a Toulouse-Lautrec type character. I explained it to the cops, but they've got it in their little blue brains that they discovered the tip of an art forgery iceberg."

"Whose name did he sign on the painting?"

"He didn't sign it at all."

"Didn't you point that out to the police? It's only a forgery if the original artist's name is on it and he or she didn't paint it."

"I told them that, but they still think my uncle was involved in something that got him killed. And Dana, too."

"Based on what you just told me, the art forgery angle is ridiculous. What evidence makes them think it was a case of murder for hire?"

"Well, for one thing, they were each shot twice, execution style, as they say. The neighbors heard nothing, even though they were home at the time, which leads the police to believe a silencer was used. And push in scumbags don't use silencers."

"Maybe this one did."

"The police know the murder weapon was an automatic based on the caliber. An automatic ejects shell casings when it's fired, but they didn't find any at the crime scene. A skell wouldn't have picked up after himself. Only a professional does that."

"A skell?"

"That's NYPD jargon for street criminal."

"Is that all they're going on? Maybe this was a really

smart skell."

"They also insist that a push-in type would have raped Dana and that didn't happen."

"I suppose we should be thankful for that," Amy said, obviously identifying with another woman.

"I guess so."

"Are they assuming Maxwell was the target because it happened in his apartment?"

"Who else would have been? Dana?"

"There *were* two people involved."

That notion caught me totally by surprise. It never crossed my mind, and no one had ever suggested such a thing. I could feel my head shaking from side to side even before the words came out of my mouth. "That's impossible. Why the hell would anyone want Dana dead?"

"I don't know. How can I answer that? I didn't know her. Why would anybody have wanted your uncle killed?"

My head was spinning. It took a minute or two for me to slow things down. "If Dana had been the target, they would have gone to where she lived or worked, not to someone she was visiting. Sorry, but that doesn't make sense."

"You said she went to cook dinner for your uncle, didn't you?"

I nodded.

"Did she bring the groceries?"

"Yes."

"Maybe they followed her and thought she lived there." Amy looked straight at me. "Maybe she was having an affair."

I sat there for a while remembering our lives together, as well as the times we were separated by the odd hours and long shifts at the hospital. Had Dana actually been working? I can't say doubt had never entered my mind, knowing she'd worked closely with a small army of doctors—the cream of the income crop. After all, she was astonishingly beautiful. Even Stein had said so, and he'd only met her after she was dead. The two uniformed cops I'd met in the morning at the One-Seventeen, Officer Pin Up and her stud muffin married partner, came to mind in a particularly irritating way.

I looked again at Amy and asked, "Even if it were true, how would that have gotten her killed?"

"Haven't you ever heard of a crime of passion? Maybe she tried to end it and her lover wouldn't take no for an answer. You know, 'if I can't have you, no one else will.'"

I withdrew again, pulling myself back in time, trying to remember Dana's demeanor when she returned to me after a long stint in the ICU. I smiled with the memory, surprised now as I was then, that, despite the exhaustion, she would still want to make love to me before collapsing, happy that we were together and healthy. Seeing patients day in and day out who'd been brushed by death made her that much more thankful for what we had.

I focused on Amy again and noticed that she was watching me closely. I said, "I don't believe it. Sometimes Dana would call me from the hospital, especially if they'd lost someone, just to say she loved me. I simply don't believe it."

Amy Drake picked up her glass again, swirled the remaining wine, let it return to level, brought the rim to her lips, and finished it. "Maybe it was something else. Maybe it was revenge."

"For what?"

"Maybe someone died in her care and a relative thought she was to blame. Maybe she made a mistake and gave the wrong medication, or an incorrect dose. Or maybe she just wasn't as attentive as she should have been. Maybe someone thought she was negligent. Had she been named in any malpractice suits?"

I held up my hand and pointed a threatening finger. "Stop. That's enough. Leave it alone. Just leave it alone. Don't say another word about Dana. Not one more word."

"I'm sorry, Robert. I didn't mean anything by it. Really I didn't. I was just trying to think of things the police may have missed. I'm so sorry. I didn't mean to upset you. I should have known better." Her eyes started to fill again and a couple of tears escaped. She blotted them away with her napkin and looked into my eyes. "I think we have a lot in common. I'm glad you were at my grandmother's house last week. I didn't like the reason, but I'm glad you were there."

Have you ever noticed that servers have the worst timing in the world? Guido appeared out of nowhere and asked, "Can I get you some espresso and desert? We have spumoni, tortoni, cannoli, and Italian cheese cake."

We ordered two coffees, one desert, and two spoons. Guido collected our plates and hurried off.

At that point I considered being honest about the extraordinary coincidence that led me to knock on the door of the white house by the river, the one with her grandmother inside. Instead I said, "Maybe you could answer a question for me. It's about the painting I mentioned, the one of May's place. To tell you the truth, I'd forgotten snapping a picture of it." I took out my phone, scrolled through the camera roll, selected the photo I'd shown the Pine County deputy on the side of the road, and handed it to her. "What do you think of this?"

She studied it for a while, an expression of approval gradually manifesting itself on her gorgeous face. "I like it. It's very good. But it doesn't really look quite like May's house."

"You don't think so?"

"Not really, but I can see why you'd think it does, given the setting."

Disappointed, I leaned back and recalled a few of the deputy's disparaging comments, the only other person I'd asked to make the comparison. "Well, it looks like your grandmother's place to me. If it is, what do you think the significance is of that tree near the riverbank? The whole damned thing is blue. You've read his letters and discussed them with your grandmother. Do you have any idea why he'd paint a tree entirely in blue?"

"I don't know, but the sky is turbulent, if not downright stormy," she said looking at the picture again. "The tone of a painting often reflects the artist's state of mind. The blue tree is probably a metaphor for sadness. Trees are symbolic of life. And blue is always used that way in music and literature, isn't it? The turbulent sky could represent the turmoil and despair he felt when he made the decision to stay in New York and care for his sister instead of moving to California to be with my grandmother."

"That makes sense." *But if it's true, how has it been possible for Leland "Cold as Ice" Drake to have consistently painted so many warm and welcoming paintings?*

She returned my phone and leaned on her elbows, interlacing her slender fingers below her chin. "I'd like to see all of your uncle's paintings. Have you had a chance to hang them?"

I nodded calmly on the outside, but felt the thrill of romance bubbling on the inside. "Thanks to my uncle, my condo in the Keys looks great, except of course for the furniture that came with the place."

"I'm having lunch again with May on Sunday," she said. "If you're not busy I could come over in the evening."

I was planning to visit May Drake again on my own to ask the questions Stein and DiCarlo might ask, but that would go a little easier with Amy there for support. I said, "I really enjoyed having lunch with you and your grandmother. Do you think it would be all right if I joined you both again? To tell you the truth I wanted to ask her a few questions about my uncle."

Amy suddenly seemed wary. "I don't know if that's a good

idea. She was very upset after you left last week. What do you want to ask her?"

This was the moment of truth—literally. Things were going so well I decided to put all the cards on the table. "The detectives in New York told me about other evidence they'd discovered including cash and a bundle of letters from May in a safe-deposit box. It sounds really stupid, but *they* want to talk to her. They know from the content of the letters that she's in California, but that's all they know. They only have her first name. There were no envelopes so they have no address, and I didn't give them one. I didn't tell them about her at all."

Amy Drake was frozen in her chair. For the first time that evening, the warmth she exuded suddenly turned cold. She sat there for a few minutes in silence. The ambient noise in the restaurant seemed to rise around us even though the sound really didn't change. Finally, she spoke. "The police think my grandmother had something to do with the murders? Is that what you're saying?"

"They're just following leads."

"How old are *those* letters? Did they say?"

"About fifty years."

"The letters are fifty years old and they think my grandmother knows something now? That's absurd. Don't you think that's absurd?"

"I do. As a matter of fact, that's exactly what I told them, but they said the money in the box was only two years old and that they'd traced the bills to a bank in California by the serial numbers."

Amy's lower lip started to quiver as she went silent, averting her eyes. Then she said, "So that's what this is about. I get it now. You called me to use me. You want to interrogate my eighty-year-old grandmother and you want me to help you do it. Is that it?"

"I called you because I wanted to see you again."

"Do you honestly believe my grandmother had anything to do with the murder of your wife and uncle? Do you?"

"No, I don't, but the police don't believe in coincidence. The money is from California, May's letters are from California, and everything was in the same box."

"You're insane, all of you, and I'm not going to listen to any more." She reached into her handbag, pulled out some cash, peeled off a couple of twenties, and tossed them onto the table. "Stay away from my grandmother, you son of a bitch. And stay away from me."

Before I could say another word she simply stood, grabbed her jacket, and stormed out of the restaurant.

Luigi was staring at me from across the room. There was a pronounced look of disappointment on his face. There wasn't a mirror in sight, but I'm sure, compared to me, he must have looked like the happiest man on Earth.

11

Needless to say, my evening with Amy didn't work out exactly the way I'd hoped. George Washington allegedly said, "…honesty is always the best policy." Always, George? Really? If you'd taken Amy to dinner instead of crossing the Delaware, would things have turned out better for you than they did for me? I suppose they could have, especially if she had a thing for men with dentures carved from hippopotamus ivory.

I left one of Amy's twenties on the table for Guido, paid the check, and got the hell out of Luigi's as fast as I could. I'd actually gone back in to pay it after following her out. She'd hailed a cab and was gone before I could even try to calm her down.

I knew as I watched the taxi disappear into the city that I still needed to talk to May Drake. What was going to be difficult at best was quickly becoming impossible. I could only assume Amy was going to warn her. Now, even if she agreed to see me, she would answer in a rehearsed way, having had the luxury of anticipating my questions.

It was nine o'clock on Friday night. If I called May before Amy could tell her my intentions and she agreed to see me, she was at least three hours away. Visiting an old lady at midnight couldn't be a very good idea. It would have to wait until tomorrow.

I sat in the Mustang for a while deciding what to do next. I could think of no prudent reasons to stay in San Francisco. A few imprudent ones did occur to me, however, like picking up some bar tramp and getting laid while I was still a free man. That's usually said of a man about to be married, but even worse in my case, it was in the literal sense. I'll admit I was a little cranked up after seeing Amy again. At first, looking for some action didn't seem like a bad idea. I'd never set out in search of a one-night-stand. I'm more romantic than that. But given the recent turn of events, to say nothing of my unmentionable frame of mind, the notion seemed workable. Things had certainly been a little tense lately, so disappearing into the night, getting lost in the anonymity of the city, and fucking my brains out with someone I'd never see again definitely had its appeal.

But I really didn't know San Francisco; where to go, and where not to go. And to be completely honest, I didn't feel like playing the dating game thing all over again. You know, struggling to say all the right words, being on your best behavior, or trying to be someone you're not just to score—something I've never done. Besides, one failed attempt at romance per day is my limit.

I briefly considered staying the night so I could take the world-famous tour of Alcatraz the next day, just to get a firsthand feel for what DiCarlo had in mind for me, but the inane act of sightseeing didn't seem particularly appealing after one of the worst days of my life. I just wasn't in the mood. It's funny how a couple of little things like being interrogated by the NYPD for hours, and then ruining the best date imaginable, could put my frame of mind in the dumpster. Maybe I'm just too sensitive.

I woke up the huge herd of rented horses sleeping under the hood, worked my way through the city, and headed back to Tahoe via the Bay Bridge. The crawl hour traffic had dissipated, so I soon brought the speedometer up to my usual nine miles per hour over the posted limit and set the cruise control. That made me the slowest car on eastbound Route 80, except for the Suburban behind me.

I had a lot on my mind, to be sure, but apparently not enough to keep me awake. I exited near Vacaville and swung into the Chevron station on the right. The Mustang's tank had been full when I'd picked it up at the airport, so I didn't need fuel yet. I stopped in front of the building instead of beside the pumps, got out of the car, took a deep breath, and stretched this way and that. I looked around and noticed that the black Suburban which had been behind me for some time had pulled into the Shell station across the street. I knew it was the same one because the amber parking light on the passenger's side was out.

I went inside, used the restroom, bought an energy drink to keep me conscious, and a bag of pretzels to keep me busy. I noticed the large condom display behind the register as I paid and noted that I didn't need anything there.

I returned to the Mustang, more annoyed than ever. I kept replaying the whole thing in my mind—bits and pieces of what the cops had said in New York, how Leland Drake had been nothing like I'd imagined, and how incredibly well it had gone with Amy until I'd screwed everything up. She was a one-in-a-million woman—the way she looked, the way she spoke, the chemistry between us. I know I sound like an adolescent, but quite to the contrary, life has taught me how truly rare it is to make such a connection. I should have been more concerned about being a suspect in a double homicide than how a date turned out, but

I couldn't help it. My mind just kept seeing her face. I'd felt the same way after my first date with Dana. No one else had ever had that effect on me. At least *I* hadn't been the one to screw up that relationship, except of course for not being there to thwart the attack that took her away from me.

I thought about what Amy had said about Dana being the target, not Mack. That notion was too wild for even my paranoid imagination to embrace. Who could have wanted Dana dead badly enough to have had her professionally murdered? What could she have been doing, and with whom, about which I knew absolutely nothing? I concluded for the second time that evening, in as few minutes, that such a theory was completely preposterous.

Then again, the same could have been said about my uncle, but things unknown to me had certainly happened in his life. The very nature of his murder proved that, as did the "hidden" sixty thousand dollars. Even the existence of a painting in his apartment I'd never seen, deemed missing by the police, was a surprise. That thought made me remember officer Millhouse, who had described so clearly the painting on Mack's easel of a New England fishing village. I tried to envision the painting based on her description, but imagined *her* instead—restless and bored in the small town she couldn't wait to leave. One thing led to another and she was soon reclined on a blanket in the tall grass near the beach.

The last thing I needed at that moment was a woody, and I don't mean an old station wagon with a couple of surfboards on the roof. I was heading home alone to my bachelor pad in Tahoe.

What I did need, however, was to be angry. Maybe a mild state of rage would keep me awake. And Lord knows I had plenty to work with. I remembered seeing Dana and Mack lowered into the ground, the dirt shoveled over them. No longer could they see the beautiful light of sunshine, or feel a warm summer breeze.

They'd never hear the melody of a song, or enjoy a bowl of hot soup. And I'd never have the pleasure of being with either of them again. All I could do was walk away and leave them there to rot.

I started the engine and backed away from the store. I noticed at the driveway-cut that the Suburban was still in the station across the street. I turned left and headed for the freeway on-ramp. At the stop sign, I punched it and the car did a good job of transmitting to the pavement my growing need for vengeance. I heard the tires screech in agreement as I laid down two long rubber streaks, the acceleration pushing me back in the seat. I glanced at the mirror and saw a cloud of tire smoke backlit by the lights of the gas station. The throaty dual pipes filled my ears, changing pitch each time the automatic transmission shifted at redline, rocketing the black Mustang up the long gradual incline in the darkness. We shot through the hole in the right lane and across three lanes of traffic, as if coming up from the back of the pack on the straight at Talladega.

I wondered if the police would ever catch the bastard. I wondered if I'd ever see him in court. And I wondered, somewhat seriously for the first time, if I'd be the one to catch him. Wouldn't that be something? I found myself wringing the leather-wrapped steering wheel in my grasp at a hundred miles an hour.

I backed off the gas, but it was too late. Red and blue lights filled the mirrors in an instant. Why is there never a cop around when you need one, but you can count on one being there when you don't? I suppose a woody might have been a better choice than rage after all.

I worked my way over to the shoulder using the right turn signal, safe driver that I am, and pulled as far off the road as I could. I switched on the interior lights and then held the top of the wheel so the cop could see my hands. At that moment, I was blinded by intense white lights saturating the inside of the Mustang, glaring in the mirrors. A police officer approached a minute later and knocked on the window. Squinting, I lowered it and cranked my head around.

"Good evening, Sir," the officer said from a position beside the Mustang, slightly behind my door. He wore a tan Highway Patrol uniform with royal blue trim.

"Hello, Officer."

"Do you know how fast you were going?"

"Apparently, too fast."

"Apparently. Please give me your license and rental documents."

For a moment I wondered how he knew the car was rented, but then I remembered seeing the bar-code sticker affixed to the left corner of the rear window. I handed over my interim California license and said, "I'm going to open the glove box. That's where the rental agreement is. All right?"

"Go ahead."

When I gave him the Hertz data he said, "Wait in the car."

Knowing when I saw him next he would have a completed speeding citation in his hand, I said loud enough to be heard above the roar of the freeway traffic behind him, "I have an explanation you've never heard before."

He stopped backing away and stared at me for a few seconds before smiling thinly and saying, "I doubt it, but I'll listen."

I said, "A year ago my wife and my uncle were both murdered in a double homicide in New York City. They were shot to death. Today, the detectives had me identify personal belongings they'd recently recovered that had been stolen from my family. I just got back. It stirred up a lot of grief and anger that I tried hard to put behind me. When I realized it was pushing me over the limit I backed off, but not soon enough. I'm sorry."

The highway patrolman stared at me for a few more seconds

before saying, "You're right. I've never heard that one. Are you sure you didn't rent this car to see how fast it would go?"

"No, Sir. They offered it to me at the airport, so I took it. What red-blooded American male would have turned it down?"

"Someone who prefers a hybrid. Stay in the car."

"Yes, Sir."

Then I saw the black Suburban race by in the far lane, the one that had been behind me before my pit stop. It was almost impossible to see the driver inside through the darkness and glare, but it seemed as if he turned his head to watch me as he flew past. Then again, so did everyone else. *Let's all gawk at the poor jerk who got caught.*

I checked the inside rearview, but could see nothing in the blinding glare. Given that Stein and DiCarlo had let me walk, I doubted that a warrant had been issued for my arrest, so checking my I.D. over the radio, which this officer was undoubtedly doing, didn't worry me. What did worry me was the realization that I could be going to jail for exceeding the posted speed limit by thirty-five miles per hour. If my license was suspended, how would I get from Tahoe to Placerville on Monday when I was due back at my new job? Things were clearly going from bad to worse.

"I'm sorry for your loss, Mr. Bennett," the officer said when he finally returned with my documents. "It sounds like you've had enough distress for one day, so I'm just going to give you a warning. There are a lot of other people out here with families at home waiting for them. Don't put them or yourself in danger. Slow down and keep your mind on driving."

"Thank you. I will."

"Good night, Mr. Bennett."

"Good night, Officer."

I waited for a safe break in the traffic, signaled, and carefully resumed my drive to Tahoe, thoroughly surprised that I hadn't been cited, or arrested. I managed to control the amazement, disbelief, anger, and disappointment swirling through my head about everything that had happened in the past year, especially in the last twenty-four hours, until I reached Fresh Pond—about forty miles short of the lake. It all went to hell when the black Suburban with the burned-out parking lamp reappeared in my mirror.

12

Believe me; nothing wakes you up like fear. My mind was suddenly moving faster than the Mustang as it began its assault on the winding, gradual uphill blacktop that weaves its way through the dense woods on the western slope of the Sierra Nevada. Almost immediately, I felt a thin film of sweat dampen the inside of my clothes, my forehead, and my palms as they tightened around the wheel. What were the odds that another black Suburban with a failed parking lamp on the right side would be behind me a hundred miles from where the first one had been? If I'd had a bookie, I would have punched him up on my cell and plunked down my life savings on that long shot.

Granted, there was really only one practical route to Tahoe's South Shore from where I'd been, so seeing the same vehicle going the same way was possible. But I couldn't help agreeing, perhaps for the first time, with my buddies at the One-Seventeen that coincidence was, indeed, a dirty word. *"We're the police. We don't believe in coincidence."* That's what they'd said. I remember every word. If ever the police imply that you're a murderer, and you're not, you'll probably remember every word of that conversation, too.

If I'd had the sense to read the license plates the first time, it would have been easier to erase all doubt as to whether or not this was the same rig, but I hadn't been that smart. Of course there'd been no reason to note the tags when the gargantuan SUV stopped across the street at a different gas station, but that's beside the point.

The question now was: How did it get behind me again? Passing me as I sat on the shoulder, my retinas treated to a free light show courtesy of the California Highway Patrol, had given it a fifteen minute head start, especially since I'd taken the gracious warning to heart and had been motoring at the speed limit for the last two hours. Didn't that mean it had to wait for me? It wouldn't have stopped for fuel again. I replayed the gas station scene in my mind. He'd stopped at the pumps, but I didn't actually see anyone fit the hose and nozzle into the vehicle. In fact, I hadn't seen anyone get out. If he'd needed fuel for the journey into the mountains, wouldn't he have bought it then? I'd gone into the convenience store to do my business and when I came out the Suburban was still at the pumps across the street.

I thought about executing a few test maneuvers to determine if, in fact, the Suburban was following me. I could stop at a turnout to see if he would just keep going, but that scenario had already been inadvertently tried thanks to the Highway Patrol near Vacaville. It had blown by, and yet, there it was, behind me again. So I concluded there was little to be learned by reenacting that move. Add to that the fact that this portion of Highway 50 was significantly less traveled than Interstate 80, I really didn't want to make myself more vulnerable than necessary.

I considered making a U-turn, since there was no median or divider even though the road had two lanes in each direction. But that would be as inconclusive as stopping if the Suburban just kept going, only to wait for me again, playing a motorized version of cat and mouse.

I reasoned that the most effective move might be to use the next exit, but that meant taking Ice House Road, a narrow ribbon of pavement that threaded its way through a remote and desolate corner of the mountains. I wouldn't have been more alone on the dark side of the moon, so that was out.

I knew of no other exits, except for campgrounds, the dead-end into a ski resort twenty or thirty miles ahead now closed because it was almost midnight, and a few spurs that led to remote alpine lakes in the middle of nowhere. There simply were no other routes to where I was going. That's what I'd gleaned from the detailed map spread across my kitchen table a week ago. Highway 50 had but one purpose: To traverse the sierra on its way to Lake Tahoe and beyond into Nevada via the breath-taking pass at Echo Summit.

The only option left was for me to put as much distance between us as the Mustang GT and my driving skills would allow. I'd learned the intricacies of the road in my new Porsche commuting that first week to and from Placerville, alternately practicing the best lines through the curves and obsessing about the white house by the river. I knew Highway 50 narrowed to two lanes between Ice House Road and South Lake Tahoe, except for passing areas. There were enough twists and turns, some of which were quite blind, to give me the clear advantage, even if the bastard behind me in the overstuffed SUV had driven in the Paris to Dakar Rally.

Before I shoved my right foot into the carpet I decided to give the three ton coincidence behind me the benefit of the doubt.

After all, I'd gone from the lingering disappointment of a date gone wrong to virtual panic in the blink of an eye. As I passed Bridal Veil Falls, the road still four lanes, I slowed in the right lane offering the Suburban the opportunity to move over and pass at its own pace. I prepared myself to make an evasive maneuver if necessary, and to memorize the illuminated rear license plate if I had the chance.

At first, he slowed as I did. All right, so maybe he wasn't in a hurry. Maybe he wasn't paying attention. Maybe he'd been mesmerized by the tedium of the trip and didn't realize we were both losing speed. But the slower I went, the slower he went. And the slower we both went, the faster my pulse went. Even though I'd been sitting on my ass for the last two hours like a couch potato with wheels, I could soon feel my ticker pounding away as if trying to break out of my chest.

Suddenly, the Suburban began to close on me, its headlights instantly looming in my rear window. I felt the accelerator pedal through the sole of my shoe as I waited until the last second to stand on it. Knowing the car had enough power to leave the SUV behind, I remember thinking: *I'm glad I didn't rent some gutless little econobox four cylinder sardine can that couldn't get out of its own way in the name of saving a few bucks.*

You may think that paranoia had gotten the best of me, but let me remind you I'd lived in New York City until two weeks ago, and aside from the usual late night empty-street jitters that are a part of life in any city, I'd never thought that someone wanted to kill me. Even after Dana and Mack had been murdered, it never occurred to me that I might be next. Why would it? The police had, until recently, characterized the homicides as a robbery. Only today, a year later, did I learn that the police had instead concluded that someone had entered Maxwell Bennett's modest apartment not to rob him, but to kill him. Now someone was following *me*, or so it seemed. What was I supposed to think?

For an instant I expected it to ram my rear bumper. I'd waited too long. But it didn't. Just like that, the Suburban changed lanes without signaling and I watched the big SUV approach in the side mirror. Through the glare, I could see that there was no license plate on the front bumper. That chilled me again, thinking it had been removed because this bastard, whoever he was, was up to no good. I'd only been in California a couple of weeks, so I didn't know if a front plate was required like it is in New York, or not, like it isn't in Florida. As it began to pass, its lights at eye level, I realized that the parking lamp below the headlight closest to me was out because the whole assembly, including the lens, had been smashed—damage impossible to see at night from a distance. So there it is. His lousy driving explains that, I thought. Compared to this guy, the Captain of the Titanic should have been knighted for good judgment behind the wheel—posthumously, of course.

I watched it pull alongside and begin to take the lead, but then, just before its rear plate came into view, it slowed and fell back to a position equal to mine. At thirty miles per hour on a fifty-five mile per hour highway, it began to pace me, making me feel small and vulnerable. I tried to see inside, but it was just too high, or I was too low, or both. I knew it was time to go, to stop playing with this son of a bitch and get the hell out of there.

But I really wanted to read his plate, so I slowed to twenty. And so did he. There was still no one behind us, so I mashed the brakes, hoping the lighter Mustang would stop in a shorter distance. If I could see his plate number, I could get his information with a little help from Stein and DiCarlo. I thought it might be a lead. And it might save my life, one way or another.

But at only twenty miles an hour my performance advantage evaporated. I should have sped up and then tried the maneuver, but I'm sorry to say I just didn't think of it. In a couple of seconds we were both at a dead stop, side by side on an empty four lane highway in the dark. When the front door's window began to open, I knew it couldn't be good. I also knew it was time to leave.

I stomped the gas pedal into the carpet as if trying to push it through the floor. The acceleration pinned me in the seat and I soon saw another cloud of white tire smoke in the mirror, this time backlit by the Suburban's headlamps. Then I watched those lights get smaller and smaller.

Four lanes soon changed to two on the road I'd come to know and love in a week. I also knew the American River was beside me to the right, raging with the sierra's spring runoff. That meant I'd be swept away by an icy torrent and drowned in the darkness if I misjudged a turn. But I was willing to bet the farm that my car-control skills were better than those of the mystery man in the Suburban somewhere behind me.

I began talking my way through the curves, using what I'd been taught in the HPDE courses I'd taken at Lime Rock and Watkins Glen. I'd put that high performance driving education to good use a dozen times or more in my BMW M3 at open track events while I lived, loved, worried, and worked in New York. What I'd learned on the track bettered my lap times. Using that knowledge now, I set up for a tight left, completed all the braking before the turn, and throttled-steered through it countering the drift. The tires seemed to scream, "What the hell are you doing?" And I wondered if I'd learned enough to keep me alive in what felt like the race of my life.

I soon powered past the deserted Bavarian restaurant where I'd had lunch with Amy and her grandmother, and had taken her phone number, smitten over a plate of warm strudel. I took my right hand off the wheel just long enough to flip the place the bird.

The road straightened in the high beams and I stretched each gear by keeping the pedal jammed into the carpet before braking for the next curve, a right-hand sweeper. I hugged the guardrail that occasionally separated the road from the river and actually began to enjoy myself a little as the thundering dual exhausts reverberated off the steel barrier. The double yellow line was soon pulled taut again and I tried to bury the needle sweeping across the deeply-recessed speedometer, passing a few cars in the process as if they were all standing still.

When I'd conceived the plan to outrun the Suburban, counting on the car's superior agility, I'd forgotten to factor in the proverbial deer in the headlights. I spotted the first two grazing on the tasty gravel between the oncoming lane and the hillside across the road. I passed them so fast they didn't even have time to pick up their antlers and watch me go by, but I'm pretty sure one must have said to the other, *"What the hell was that?"* If more were ahead on the pavement, at least their deaths were going to be humane, never knowing what hit them. I, on the other hand, had enough time to imagine several hundred pounds of venison crashing through the windshield.

Whenever the road unfurled I checked the mirrors, no longer scanning for the Suburban, but instead for flashing colored lights. I looked ahead and, recognizing May Drake's white Lexus SUV lit broadside like a billboard in the Mustang's high beams, wondered if Deputy Johnson, who quite professionally broke my balls while I sat in the Porsche, was positioned somewhere nearby in the bushes. Talking him out of a good arrest in the middle of the night was going to be like talking a great white shark out of a tuna salad sandwich.

When I reached the pass at Echo Summit and slowed along the two lane ledge high above Christmas Valley, I could see, as if from a plane, the runway lights of Lake Tahoe's airport and the enormous lake beyond shimmering in the moonlight. I recognized the casinos along the South Shore at Stateline Nevada, lit in the distance like a mini Las Vegas. I considered checking into one of the hotels as a precaution, in so doing making it harder for anyone to find me.

But I was tired, and my tired brain, overwhelmed by a day I'll never forget, began to reject the notion that someone was actually after me. The murders had been committed a year ago and no one had tried to kill me yet. The reason to race across the sierra in the dark, clocking an elapsed time certainly worthy of a place in the Guinness Book of World Records, slowly dissolved into the nebulous haze of a nightmarish imagination.

The Suburban was no figment. But I had toyed with him, antagonizing and provoking a total stranger into a state of road rage on an empty stretch of pavement at night in the mountains; a dangerous series of chess moves which ultimately proved nothing.

As it turns out, I'd made two mistakes that night. The first was being truthful with Amy. The second was going home.

13

I pulled into the parking lot outside my condo in Tahoe Keys after midnight, positive no one was following me. I had no tail, and I wasn't getting any tail. Needless to say I was happier about one than the other. Overall though, I remember being vaguely content just to be alive and not in jail for homicide, speeding, or anything in between.

That feeling lasted about ten seconds. As I reached into the trunk to retrieve my valise, I heard a car door close behind me. I turned in time to see a man step out of the shadows. He walked around the fender of a white Ram pickup that had been backed into the corner space against the building. He wore a black baseball cap pulled low over his eyes and a three-quarter length green camouflage jacket. His right hand was in his coat pocket. He was a tall bastard and I had the sense that he was equally fit. I remember wishing I had something in *my* hand other than the Hertz keys, but there was nothing to reach for.

He stopped about ten feet away and said in a voice as chilled as the midnight mountain air, "Do you remember me, Bennett?"

I couldn't see his shadowed face very well in the wan spill of a distant street light. Mentally drained and physically exhausted, I struggled with his question. "Do I know you?"

"I asked you if you were looking for trouble. Do you remember that"?

That did sound vaguely familiar. "Who are you? What do you want?"

"I want to know how you know May Drake."

I stood motionless, trying to connect the voice to the questions.

"I want to know why you murdered your wife and your uncle."

That had to be a cop question. Then it came to me. "Where's your uniform, Deputy Johnson?"

"I told you I know where you live."

"So do the cops in New York. I don't have time for this now. They put me through the wringer this morning, which feels like a week ago. I can't keep my eyes open. If you'd like, I'll meet you tomorrow in your office, if you have an office. Or if you prefer, we can talk on the side of the road, but right now I've got to get some sleep."

"I've been waiting for you for hours. You'll tell me what I want to know tonight."

Then an agitated voice echoed across the parking lot from a window on the second floor of the condo complex. "Hey! Keep it down, will ya? People are trying to sleep."

I said. "Write down your number and I'll call you tomorrow to arrange a time and place."

"Let's go into your apartment. We'll talk now."

"I told you, I'm beat. I can't keep my eyes open. I'm not awake enough to answer any questions."

"Listen to me, Bennett. We can talk in your house or you can spend the night cuffed to a desk in the office. Which will it be?"

"Fine." I grabbed my luggage, slammed the trunk, and led the way to my door, which was just around the corner of the closest building on the right.

Once inside Johnson asked, "Do you have any weapons on you?"

"Only my intellect, which is at twenty percent of normal right now."

"Then you won't mind assuming the position."

Apparently, the portion of my mind usually in the gutter was located in the quadrant still operating because it took only a few seconds for me to sort out which position he was talking about. I leaned against the wall in the entryway and was frisked for the first time in my life. I won't say I liked it, but it was clearly the most action I'd gotten in a long time. "Weren't you supposed to do this outside on the hood of your truck, or on the ground or something?"

"If you'd like, we can go back out and start over."

When the groping stopped I said, "I'm going to use the bathroom. Is that all right with you?"

Johnson spoke in a very matter of fact tone. "The NYPD likes you for a double homicide. If you try anything I'll just shoot you twice in the chest and the case will be closed. Do you understand me?"

I remember trying to think of a witty retort, but couldn't, too tired and too shaken to do anything except nod.

When I opened the bathroom door after relieving myself and washing my face in an effort to flush the drowsiness from my eyes, the first thing I saw was the muzzle of a large black handgun. I'd never faced a gun before.

Johnson had barricaded himself behind the frame of the nearest doorway across the hall so that only one eye was visible over the sights. When he saw that I hadn't come out of the bathroom with the New York murder weapon blazing, he lowered his gun and stepped out from behind the wall. If he was trying to intimidate me, as well as protect himself, it wasn't a bad technique. Then he said, "When I asked you a week ago what you were doing there you came up with some bullshit story about a painting. What kind of crap was that? What were you *really* up to?" The gun was still in his hand, but now it was down near his thigh.

I looked him in the eye and said, "Listen to me. The only living things I've ever killed were insects. You can put your gun away now."

"I asked you a question and I haven't heard the answer yet."

"Let me show you something." I led the way into the living room, turned on a few lamps, and pointed to the painting I'd made the centerpiece of my uncle's collection. I'd arranged a dozen Bennett oils on the long wall behind the dated beige and brown plaid sofa that enabled the realtor to list the place as furnished. "Does that look familiar to you?"

"That's the painting you showed me on your phone."

No shit, Sherlock. "My uncle, Maxwell Bennett, painted all of these."

He glanced at the others on the wall but offered no opinions.

"I was driving back from Placerville and the house across the river reminded me of this painting. That's why I stopped."

"You're telling me you didn't know who lives there?"

"That's what I'm telling you. I only stopped because of the painting. That's the truth."

"You'll have to do better than that, Bennett. The houses don't even look alike."

"I guess they do to me. I've admired that painting since I was a child. Last week I looked at that house every day, each time I passed it on my way home. Something drew me to it. Something made me stop there. Maybe it's some sort of telepathic thing because my uncle painted it. I don't know what else I can tell you."

"You listen to me, you lying sack of shit. The cops in New York want to talk to a woman named May. You were sitting outside her house. Do you expect me to believe that you were there because of a coincidence?"

Christ! There was that word again. "Believe what you want. I'm telling you the truth. That's what happened." I asked, "Did you question *her* yet?"

He ignored me. "What was May Drake's connection to your uncle?"

"They used to be an item. He was supposed to move here so they could be together, but never did. That was fifty years ago. She married someone else, another painter, if you can believe that. His name is Leland Drake. She must have had a thing for artists. I met him today, as a matter of fact. A real asshole, if you ask me. After he made it big he left her for a bimbo less than half his age. Now he needs pills to make it big."

"How did you meet him?"

"I went to see his granddaughter after I landed in San Francisco. She introduced me."

I didn't read the change in Deputy Johnson's expression at the time, but when I think about it now I can remember the downward transition from dubious disdain to loathsome envy.

He asked, "How do you know Amy Drake?"

"I met her at the house that Saturday shortly after meeting May."

"Apparently, you didn't waste any time."

"Excuse me?"

Johnson broke off eye contact and pretended to study the wall full of paintings.

I thought about this little exchange. I hadn't mentioned her name so I concluded, despite the fatigue plaguing me, that he knew Amy. Perhaps very well, or perhaps not as well as he would have liked. Now, his being at my house with his own truck on his own time in the middle of the night began to make sense. I considered raising the question: Why was a patrol officer, on duty or off, conducting this interview instead of a detective?

Then he asked, "Why did you kill them?"

I almost said, *don't be a fucking moron!* But even in my exhausted state I had the presence of mind and marginal good sense to realize, based on what I'd heard and seen so far, that antagonizing Deputy Johnson would be an error. "Mack was my only relative." As the words rolled off my tongue I realized that I had referred to my uncle by his birth name two minutes before, so I said, "Maxwell was his name, but I called him Mack. We all did. To me he was always Uncle Mack. And Dana was the best thing that ever happened to me. Why would I kill them?"

"That's what I asked you."

"I was in Las Vegas at a convention that weekend a year ago. When I left they were fine. When I got back they were dead. My wife was there to cook dinner for my uncle. They were both murdered in his apartment. Sheldon Stein and Joe DiCarlo, the detectives on the case at the One Hundred Seventeenth Precinct in Queens, said she was in the wrong place at the wrong time." No matter how many times I'm forced to tell the story, I can't get through it without misting up. I stopped talking long enough to catch my breath and blink a few times. "Excuse me. I'm going to get a tissue." I looked down and saw that the gun was still in his right hand. I said, "Please don't shoot me when I come back."

I went into the kitchen and dried my eyes with a paper towel better suited to sanding raw wood. Then I filled the tea kettle and lit the burner. When I turned to leave the room I saw Johnson watching me from the doorway. His hands were empty, which I took as a sign that I was winning him over. Then he opened his mouth.

"So you hired someone to do your dirty work. The NYPD called it a contract killing. Obviously, you knew the Vegas convention would be the perfect alibi. That's why you picked that weekend to have them killed."

I wanted to scream. How much more of this could I stand? But instead of jumping up and down or vibrating until I burst a blood vessel, I closed my eyes, took a deep breath, held it for a few seconds, and let it out slowly. Then I sat down at the colonial dinette set, an early American hemorrhoid special that came with the condo. How is it possible that the colonists had the keen foresight to establish a republic that has endured for considerably more than two hundred years, but they couldn't figure out that putting some padding on a chair might be a good idea? I leaned back until my tailbone hit the wood and the wraparound backrest dug into my ribs. Then I leaned forward, resting my elbows on the matching table.

"This is everything I know," I began. I told Johnson about the two break-ins, one on Friday when no one was home, and the one on Sunday that ended the only two lives that were important to me. I told him they'd locked up some son of a bitch scumbag bastard burglar for the first one, but didn't think he was responsible for the killings. I told him about the recovered jewelry and the unrecovered painting, the one that had been on the easel in the middle of the living room after the burglary, but not after the murders, as described by Officer Pin Up. Needless to say I used her given name. I told him about the safe-deposit box with the serialized cash and the letters from May that had obviously shifted the focus of the investigation to California. I went a little too far when I said, "They don't know May's last name, or where she lives."

"You didn't tell them?"

"No."

"Why not?"

I attempted to talk my way out of this, but didn't do very well. "I tried to continue living and working in New York for a year, making the best of a life suddenly empty. It wasn't possible, so I decided to move. My old boss knew someone in Placerville. He got me a job. I'm an architect. That's how I wound up here. I've gone to a lot of trouble to start over." I was about to mention the hopes I'd had for a relationship with Amy and how I wasn't going to let anything jeopardize that, but stopped short, afraid that the deputy sheriff standing in my kitchen may have had those same feelings for Amy at one time—or still did. This whole business of coincidence and anything even vaguely resembling a coincidence was rapidly becoming a royal pain in my ass. "I made a mistake. I should have told them about May."

"That's right, you should have. Withholding information in a criminal investigation is a crime. It's called obstruction of justice."

"Look, I'm one of the victims. My world was turned upside-down when the only people who meant anything to me were killed. It took a three thousand mile move to make it feel like I was finally getting on with my life and now, all of a sudden, because I'm in California, and they found a safe-deposit box filled with money and letters from California, I'm a suspect a year later. It's unbelievable. Being a suspect is unbelievable, for God's sake. Until this morning I still thought it was a push-in robbery. That's what Stein and DiCarlo called it from the beginning, or at least, that's what they'd told me. The only thing I'm guilty of is not being there to save the people I loved when they needed me."

He stared at me for at least two or three minutes without saying anything. Then he pulled out the chair opposite mine and seated himself, still wearing his camo jacket. He took off the ball cap and dropped it on the table. The square edges of his crew cut and jaw embellished his no-bullshit demeanor. His eyes were brown, but instead of being warm and soft they seemed as cold and hard as two marbles. With no cordiality at all he asked, "When did they find the safe-deposit box?"

"I don't know. They didn't tell me."

"Was there anything else in it besides the money and the letters?"

I'd wondered the same thing on the flight back. "I don't know. I didn't think to ask that while I was there and they didn't say."

"Did your uncle leave a will?"

"Yes."

"Were you in it?"

"Yes. I was his only living relative."

"So you stood to profit from his death."

Realizing that the object of each question was to get me to incriminate myself, instead of finding the real killer, I stopped talking.

He stared at me, waiting for me to say something he could twist around into something else.

I resolved to speak very carefully, or at least as carefully as my fatigue would allow. I said, "Listen to me. I loved my uncle. And I loved Dana. Mack lived on a meager pension from the Transit Authority. He worked in a token booth in the subway for thirty years and all he had to show for it was a hearing aid. He was almost deaf from the trains. I have more money than he ever had."

"You said they found sixty large in the box."

"That's what they told me."

"Why was it in a safe-deposit box and not in a savings account, or in a CD, or in mutual funds?"

"I have no idea. I never knew about it until today." *But maybe you should have been a financial advisor instead of a cop.*

"I'll tell you why," Johnson said. "Because he was hiding it; hiding it from the IRS, from you, and from everybody else. It sounds like he was involved in something he shouldn't have been. The question is, with whom? Figure that out, and we'll know who to put away for murder."

"Does that mean I'm off the hook?"

"I said he was hiding it from you. That doesn't mean you didn't know about it. But it does mean you couldn't get access to it, at least not until after probate."

I looked directly at Deputy Deadpan and asked, "Do you have an uncle?"

He stared back at me, but didn't answer.

"He's probably got a few bucks in the bank, right? Would you kill him for his life savings, no matter how much it was?"

He just sat there with a pretty good poker face.

"Well, I wouldn't kill *my* uncle either."

We stared at one another until I arranged two glass mugs with tea bags on the counter, filled them with boiling water, and let them steep, much the way Deputy Johnson was steeping.

Despite the stress and fatigue, I was suddenly feeling a little giddy. That may explain why I actually remembered the classic short story about a woman who bashed in her husband's brains with a frozen leg of lamb, invited the detective to dinner, and served him the murder weapon. Fortunately, I was awake enough to realize that relating that story to the humorless cop at my table would be an implicit admission of guilt that I could never undo. I set the hot tea in front of him, bag and all.

He said, "When people break the law for profit, it's usually in connection with something they've become familiar with. A drug user becomes a drug dealer, and so on and so forth. Maybe your uncle was doing something under the table with his art. Would you know anything about that?"

I thought about the small copy that had been recovered along with the jewelry I'd held in my hands that morning in the basement of the station house; the foot-square oil that had, despite my explanation, set the wheels in motion for Stein to think that Mack had been involved in an art forgery scheme. As much as I wanted to protect my uncle, and doubted that such a thing was even remotely possible, I also couldn't ignore the so-called evidence that had the cops, now at both ends of the country, smelling blood in the water. I sat down, blew across the surface of my tea, and told Johnson about the recovered painting in question, including what Sheldon Stein had suggested.

The first words out of his mouth were, "Why didn't you tell me about this before?"

"I forgot about it, I suppose because it sounds utterly ridiculous to me. If you knew my uncle, you'd think it was ridiculous, too."

"Where did he sell his paintings? Do you know the names of the galleries or art dealers?"

"To my knowledge he'd never sold anything. I thought I had them all right here, but apparently May Drake has one, and one is missing, taken at the time of the murders."

"Maybe there were others you never saw. Maybe he'd been selling paintings for years to supplement his pension."

That sounded logical enough. "I thought I knew him better than that, but I guess anything is possible."

"Maybe he'd been forging artwork and selling it to a black market dealer. Then he wanted more money. Or maybe he decided to quit, so to keep the secret from unraveling he was killed."

I began to feel pretty uncomfortable in a different sort of way, like my skin was starting to crawl. I said, "If the police in New

York figured out a long time ago that this had been a case of murder for hire and not a push-in like they claimed early on, shouldn't they have told me sooner?"

Johnson considered this and shrugged. "Not necessarily. By making you feel like you were in the clear, you could have slipped up. If they'd been following you all along, like they did today, or had your phone tapped, they could have scored."

"They followed me today?"

Johnson nodded. "To the airport. Then they called us."

I thought about the black Suburban I'd eluded. "If my uncle was murdered to shut him up, don't you think Stein and DiCarlo had an obligation to tell me that just in case I was next?"

The deputy's eyebrows rose, as if he hadn't thought of that. "That's unlikely. If someone wanted you dead, you'd be dead by now, or you'd know about it."

"That's the way it felt an hour ago."

"What are you talking about?"

I told him about the Suburban; when I'd first noticed it, when it passed me, and when it appeared behind me again and wouldn't pass a second time while the road was still two lanes wide in each direction.

"There's really only one way to get to South Lake Tahoe from the Bay Area." he said. "I've traded places with the same vehicles all along the way."

"What about our little tango at Ice House Road?"

"Haven't you ever heard of road rage?"

I would have nodded, but I didn't want to give him the satisfaction of being right. Instead I just curled my lip.

He asked, "Did you get the license number?"

"No. It had no front plate and I couldn't get behind it. All I can tell you is that it's a recent model, it's black, and the right front parking lamp is damaged."

"If you thought someone was following you, you shouldn't have come home."

"After I lost him, the melodrama subsided. If you'd been on duty tonight instead of sitting here in the parking lot, your radar would have exploded."

He smiled for the first time, probably in his life. He stood and turned toward the sliding glass patio doors a few feet away. Because the kitchen lights were on and the marina outside was black as pitch, except for a string of distant globe-shaped streetlamps far beyond the boats and obsidian water, all Johnson could see was reflection; his, mine, the uncomfortable furniture, and the glaring brass fixture hanging above the table. He switched off the lights, approached the glass, and stood there giving his eyes the time they needed to adjust to the darkness. He spoke without turning as he scanned the patio and common grass area that extended to the wrought iron railing at the water's edge. "You must be innocent. Nobody with anything to hide would live in a fishbowl. Why don't you have any drapes or blinds or something? You're just begging for a burglary of your own."

"I'm here only a couple of weeks. There weren't any when I moved in and I haven't had the chance to do anything about it."

"If you hadn't wasted time snooping around somebody else's house, you would have had the time to take care of your own."

I couldn't see his face, still near the glass, so I couldn't tell if he was kidding. Then I realized I didn't care. "I'm going back tomorrow to talk to May."

"No you're not."

"There are things I need to ask that woman."

"Like what?"

"I don't know, but I'll know when I see her."

He turned and looked at me in the gloom. I still couldn't see his face, just the large and shadowy silhouette of authority.

"You'll stay away from that house."

"No, I won't. My ass is the one on the line. I'm not going down for something I didn't do. I'm driving to the house in that damn painting again tomorrow. Maybe she knows something. Maybe she'll tell me the truth because she loved my uncle. I know she did. Probably still does. You can come with me if you want."

He stood there in the darkness with his back to the glass. I couldn't see the wheels turning, but I knew they were. "All right, I'll meet you there at ten o'clock. But don't go in without me."

"Why? Do you think I'll need backup?"

"Listen to me, Wise-ass. If you talk to May Drake tomorrow without me, I'll lock you up for obstruction and criminal trespass. Is that clear?"

I considered my small victory and decided to quit while I was ahead. "Make it eleven. I need the sleep."

"In the meantime, if you don't want to be a target, do yourself a favor and tack a sheet up over this glass." He walked out of the kitchen and out of my condo.

I locked the deadbolt behind him and dragged my suitcase into the bedroom. I shook out the bedcovers, making certain that if I were going to be alone between the sheets, I was really alone between the sheets. As I stepped out of my shoes and started peeling off my clothes I heard a knock at the door—three to be precise. Only a couple of minutes had passed, so I returned to the foyer in my socks, unlocked the front door, and said as I pulled it open, "What do you want now?"

It took a second to realize that the man standing in the glare of the entrance bulb wasn't the man who'd just left. He was a scary-looking sleaze ball in a black shirt and an open black leather coat that hung past his knees. Both hands were behind his back, as if he'd been standing *at ease* while waiting for the door to open. In the blink of an eye he swung a chrome handgun with a black silencer around and aimed it at my face. Then he answered my question. "I want to finish the job I started in New York."

14

I can now say definitively that seeing your life flash before your eyes when death is at your doorstep doesn't really happen. Glimpses of my childhood, including kissing the little neighbor-girl in the closet, or getting laid for the first time in the backseat of my first car, or the smile on Dana's face when she said, "*Yes*," never popped up. My mind just went blank as I waited for the white-hot flash and penetrating pain.

If I'd had more time I might have asked who'd ordered our deaths, and why. Or I might have pleaded for my own life, although I've always had enough pride to never beg for anything. But the shots came fast, two in rapid succession, all in the span of one breath.

I flinched, but felt nothing. I don't know if I would have processed what was happening more readily if I'd been wide awake instead of half asleep, but it seemed as if the blasts were too loud to have been fired from a gun with a suppressor. Of course, I'd never actually heard suppressed rounds other than in a movie, like most people, so I really had no frame of reference for comparison. Something else that made no sense at that moment, the moment that would have been my last, was that the blasts seemed to come from my left instead of from right in front of me, and I mean *right in front of me!*

Then I watched Mr. Scumbag collapse where he stood, little more than an arm's length away. He wasn't blown backwards or lifted off his feet by the invisible impacts, as one would imagine. He simply crumpled and fell backwards onto the asphalt walkway that led to other units and buildings in the complex. I'm not sure if the dull thud that accompanied his demise was the sound of his head hitting the pavement, or the gun landing on the welcome mat between us after slipping from his black gloves.

When I realized he was still alive, grimaced eyes showing the pain of his wounds, my first thought was to pick up the pistol gleaming just beyond the threshold and kill the man who'd come to kill me. I wanted so badly, in the brief seconds that followed, as the sounds of running footsteps approached, to grab the gun that killed Dana and Mack, hold it to his head, and pull the trigger over and over and over until his skull and his brains were pulp—just a wet pile of red fucking mush on the pavement. Does that make me a bad person? You know the argument: If you do that, then you're no better than he is. Bullshit! People talk about closure. Is closure sitting though a trial that ends with a guilty verdict, only to be followed by appeal after appeal? Is closure a plea bargain that permits a murderer to lift weights and play basketball in a sunlit yard while your loved ones are fodder for vermin in the ground? Is closure fifteen years on death row, only to be undone with some cockamamie argument about cruel and unusual punishment postulated by a judge who still has *his* family? Personally, I don't believe in closure. It doesn't exist. But if it did, the next best thing would probably be pressure washing the bastard's brains off your walkway. Alas, that might be true only if he hadn't been sent by someone else.

Fortunately, Deputy Johnson was not consumed by rage, as I was, so his actions were geared more toward being productive. He approached still aiming his gun at the man now sprawled on the ground and said to me, "Get back! Get back!"

I complied, moving a few feet further into my condo, a few feet further from the gun.

He picked it up, looked at it for a second, I suppose to see if it was cocked, and tucked it in between his belt and his jeans. He knelt beside the man and performed a rudimentary frisk with one hand in search of a second weapon, finding a long slender switchblade and two loaded spare magazines. He then pulled out his cell phone, dialed 911, identified himself, requested backup, an ambulance, and a supervisor from his department. After ending the call he said to me, "Stay inside. I'll be right back." Then he ran this way and that, apparently making sure the gunman had no accomplices. When he returned, he crouched beside the contract killer at my door. The man was having trouble breathing, blood oozing and bubbling out of his nose and mouth, red rivulets seeping down his cheeks.

Johnson repositioned himself behind the top of the man's head, I think so he could not be sprayed with blood. He spoke slowly and deliberately. "Listen to me," he said. "An ambulance is on the way. If you tell me who sent you, I'll let them take you to the hospital. I'll help them save you. If you don't, I'll hold them back and you'll bleed out right here. Do you understand me? Who sent you?"

The killer gagged and made a few gurgling sounds in the cold night air.

"Who sent you? Tell me who sent you."

He grimaced and winced, but made no to attempt to say anything.

Johnson said, "You're dying. Are you going down for this by yourself? Tell me who sent you."

We could now hear sirens in the distance. The deputy said, "Listen. Can you hear that? Help is coming. Tell me now. Who sent you?"

But the wincing and grimacing stopped cold, along with the chance to hear the name of the person or persons who'd presumably paid for more than one murder.

I said, "Weren't you supposed to identify yourself and order him to drop his gun before you shot him? He'd be alive now to talk."

Johnson looked at me as if I were an idiot. "With any warning he would have turned on me or taken you hostage. Would you have preferred that?"

I shook my head.

Johnson said, "You're lucky to be alive. Another second and you'd be lying there like that instead of criticizing me."

"I'm not criticizing you. I just thought if…"

"Don't worry about it. He'll tell us what we need to know even if he's dead. You stick to drawing your buildings and let us do the police work."

We both heard sirens now that couldn't have been more than a block or two away. I said just loud enough to be understood above the hysterical noise, "Thanks for saving my life. Don't worry about my statement. I clearly remember hearing you say, 'Drop the gun,' before you shot him."

Deputy Johnson looked at me. Then he nodded. "Wait here or you'll get shot." Then he put his own gun away, pulled out his badge, held it up like a sign, and headed for the street, disappearing around the corner.

I stood there in the doorway staring at the dead man, making sure he was really dead and not somehow faking, about to pull out another gun that Johnson missed and pick up where he'd left off. As the seconds passed and I contemplated what had just happened right before my eyes, I began to feel sick. I'd come much too close to dying at the hands of the man who'd killed my father's brother and my wife. It's hard to describe how I actually felt at that moment. The best I can do would be to say it was like someone dumped a cup of sadness into a blender, added a tablespoon of misery, sprinkled in a few shakes of loneliness, dropped in two scoops of frozen fear, plopped a dollop of plain old-fashioned anger into the mix for good measure, hit the slop button on the control panel, and then poured the whole stinking concoction, lumps and all, down my throat.

There really isn't much more I can say about that night except that everyone working midnights in uniform in South Lake Tahoe responded to Deputy Johnson's call for help: The local PD, the California Highway Patrol, a platoon of Johnson's Pine County coworkers, the fire department, and an ambulance crew. The only peace officers conspicuously absent were park rangers, probably because they couldn't deploy a cadre of wildlife activists to baby-sit the bears on such short notice.

They established a crime scene with enough yellow tape to cordon off a Nazi death camp. They knocked on doors, several of which were vacant vacation rentals, and questioned the slumbering neighbors in the occupied units, including the irate tenant who'd bitched about the noise in the parking lot even before things really took off. Apparently, a description of the evening's festivities as given by the alleged victim, yours truly, about his close encounter with the alleged perpetrator, the cooling piece of shit on the walkway, and a corresponding report provided by one of their own, Deputy Johnson, was not sufficient. What could untrained civilians roused from their nonsensical dreams add to the investigation?

The ranking officer from the sheriff's department had one of his men load me into a patrol car and take me downtown for a written statement, where I fell asleep twice before the document was completed.

Then somebody in the office said something I remember quite clearly, even though I can't remember who said it. "You shouldn't go home again. A hotel would be better. Somebody still out there wants you dead." That was something that had lodged itself subliminally in the back of my mind when the hit man died in the middle of Johnson's impromptu interrogation.

What a difference a day makes. That morning I was a suspect in a year-long double homicide investigation. Less than twenty-four hours later I was the target in an attempted assassination. What the hell happened? In the morning the police were trying to put me away. At night they were trying to keep me alive. I sat there, in an office newer but no more charming than the one in the New York City precinct, contemplating my fate. I said at last, "I can't go anywhere. I don't have a car here."

Twenty minutes later I was standing in a room on the sixth floor of the Atrium Hotel. I thanked the two Pine County soldiers in the war on crime for their help and concern, and asked them to have Deputy Johnson call me in the morning, but not too early. Then I secured the door with every lock, bolt, and chain the establishment had to offer.

I used the plumbing, stripped naked, and stretched out on the cool sheets. I covered myself, switched off the energy-saving lamp on the nightstand, and in the dark of a would-be safe house thought about how close I'd come to dying. The fear I'd experienced earlier returned in a nauseating wave that stole my breath, so I struggled to review the other, more inspired, events of the day. It wasn't long before my frazzled mind saw Amy's beautiful face. I tried to conjure up an excuse or two to call her again, but was soon teetering on the edge of sleep's void. As I tumbled in, torn from the angel I hoped would save me, I heard the words of warning that had been uttered in the sheriff's office. They reverberated through the abyss as if repeated by God himself. "Somebody still out there wants you dead."

15

They say you can't die in your dreams. I was just about to break that unwritten rule when Deputy Johnson saved me again, this time with a phone call. It took a few seconds for me to realize where I was. Have you ever been so relieved to wake from a terrible dream that each and every cell between your cerebral cortex and your toes feels like it's winding down from an orgasm?

Of course, in most cases that's the end of it and you don't even give it a second thought. You're just happy to be awake, separated by consciousness from the horrendous danger that turned a dream into a nightmare. But not for me. Happy to be awake was fleeting at best. After realizing where I was, I remembered why I was there.

"I'll pick you up in an hour," Johnson said. "Be ready."

"What time is it?"

"Nine o'clock."

"Make it two hours. I didn't lie down until four."

"One hour, or I'm going to the Drake house without you."

"I need a change of clothes."

"We can stop at your place on the way. I'll cover you."

That comment set me back another notch or two, but I recovered enough to ask, "What about breakfast?"

"What's with you? Do you want to get on with it or not?"

"I'm hungry. If you ate already, I'll get something downstairs before you get here."

"Do yourself a favor, Bennett," he said in his usual *all work and no play makes Jack a dull boy* voice. "Stay in the room until I get there."

It took me a little longer to recover after hearing that. I extricated myself from the comfort and safety of the covers, conducted the first business of the day, and stepped into the shower, where, instead of performing a joyful rendition of *Singing in the Rain*, I watched a few scenes from a thriller I'd seen the night before. I adjusted the water to be as hot as I could stand it to dispel a chill that swept through me, no doubt caused by a degree of high-definition, 3D, in your face, film *noir* realism I'd never experienced before.

I toweled myself off, wiped the steam from the mirror, and stared at the would-be victim above the sink. I knew I was lucky to be alive, although for the past year I hadn't considered my ability to go through life's daily motions in those terms. I won't say that there, alone and naked in a strange hotel room without so much as a toothbrush or a change of underwear, I was struck by an epiphany that changed my life, but a curious, if not profound, perspective did cross my mind. Perhaps the woe-is-me theme that had set the tone for the story of Robert Bennett was the wrong soundtrack after all. Maybe I was alive for a reason other than to be depressed. If I hadn't been in Las Vegas that weekend a year ago, I would have probably died with Dana and Mack in his apartment in Forest Hills. What were the odds that a string of coincidences since had led me this far? For me, Providence had only ever been the capitol of Rhode Island. But maybe I was still alive for a greater purpose, a purpose that, in fact, had nothing at all to do with designing a few walls and a roof someday that would make the palace at Versailles look like a hovel.

I was ready to roll when Johnson knocked, albeit in dirty clothes and in need of a shave. After checking the peephole, I opened the door and was a little surprised to see him in plain clothes again. In fact, he was wearing the same black baseball hat and green camo jacket. Because we were about to pay May Drake a visit, I expected him to be in his olive green Pine County uniform.

I stepped out of the hotel suite, pulled the door closed behind me, and followed the deputy down the corridor, which was actually a four-foot wide carpeted ledge bordered by a wrought iron railing to our left that jutted into the day-lit atrium six floors above the lobby. When we reached the elevators, he pressed the illuminated button on the wall before approaching the railing where he quickly scanned the ground-level far below. Then he moved back to a position beside the elevator doors.

I'd never had a bodyguard before, but then, no one had ever tried to kill me either. Where to stand or how to position myself while waiting for an elevator had never been a concern. Suddenly I felt vulnerable and awkward. Then I heard the adjacent steel door to the fire stairs open.

I saw Johnson fast-draw a big black handgun a split second before a man in a maintenance uniform holding a metal toolbox in his left hand emerged from the stairwell. Johnson quickly positioned the weapon down behind his right thigh, his trigger finger alongside the gun's frame. My first thought was that I was going to watch this deputy in plain clothes shoot a hotel employee for coming out of a stairwell at the wrong time. But I wasn't about to distract Johnson by yelling or interfering in any way. I had to believe that he knew what he was doing. After all, he did save my life less than twelve hours earlier.

I heard an electronic bell ring as one of the elevators arrived. The door opened and I saw that the car was empty. Apparently, the worker heard the bell as well because he smiled and began to hurry toward us and the waiting elevator. He was a middle-aged Hispanic with straight jet-black hair that started only an inch above his eyebrows. I read the plastic tag on his shirt and learned that his name was Jose.

But Johnson held up his left hand like a traffic cop and ordered the man to keep his distance. "Stop where you are! Deputy Sheriff! Don't come any closer!" Then he spoke to me without taking his eyes off the worker. "Get the door, Bennett."

I scurried into the car and held the doors open while Johnson backed in. I heard a Spanish accent color the words, "But I just want to use the elevator."

As the doors closed us inside Johnson said, "Take the next one, Jose." He opened his coat and jammed the gun back into its brown leather shoulder holster. With the situation behind us, I realized that this gun was a revolver and the one he'd used the night before had been an automatic. I thought about this as we were lowered to the lobby and surmised that he'd had to surrender the weapon used in the shooting.

We walked out of the building and into the driveway where I recognized Johnson's white Ram pickup parked under the portico. Again I was surprised, this time expecting to see the marked Pine County Ford Expedition that he was driving when he checked me out the first time near the river. I said, "I was hoping to ride in your cruiser."

He unlocked the truck and walked around the hood. "What

makes you think you'd ride in the front and not in the lockup?"

I climbed in, and, once he was beside me, said, "Actually, I expected to be dragged behind it."

"That can be arranged, but for now buckle your seatbelt."

"Yes, Sir."

As we drove out of the parking lot I said, "I was afraid for a minute back there that you were going to shoot Jose."

"You should have been afraid that Jose was going to shoot you."

"He was a maintenance worker."

"Listen to me, Bennett. If you want to stay alive, you'll have to start thinking less like a deer in the headlights and more like a cop. Do you have any idea what I'm talking about?"

"Yeah."

"I don't think you do. You didn't yesterday. And you haven't done much better in the first ten minutes of today. You live on the ground floor and have no window coverings. You were sharp enough to spot the tail that started in the Bay Area, I'll give you that, but then you went home. What the hell were you thinking? You opened your door for a murderer when he knocked, and then stood there with a thumb up your ass waiting to get popped. I saved your life and you complained that I didn't take the time to warn the professional sent to kill you. You'll have to do better than that if you want to stay alive. Get it? Lose the civilian mentality that makes the average person a victim looking for a place to happen or just paint a big fat bull's-eye on your chest right now and stand in the middle of the fucking highway."

"Are you always this empathetic?"

"I'm sorry you lost your people, Bennett. I really am. But you've got to get past that. You've got to snap out of it. You're a smart guy. Listen to what I'm trying to tell you."

I sat there for a few minutes feeling fairly inept as the town went by in the bright sunlight of a cool and crisp high sierra spring morning. Finally, I said, "I thought I'd lost him."

"And it didn't occur to you that he might know where you live?"

"I guess I just didn't take it seriously enough."

"I trust you won't make that mistake again."

"Not likely."

"Now we just have to find out who sent him."

"Who was he?"

"His name was Joseph Fabiano, or at least that's what his I.D. said. We're running his prints. We'll know more when we see his sheet. My guess is that it's a long one. Have you ever seen him before or heard his name? He called himself Joey. He lived in North Beach in San Francisco."

I strained my untrained civilian brain trying to make a connection. Something did sound vaguely familiar but I couldn't place it. "I don't think so. What did he do besides kill people? Do you know?"

"He ran a strip club near San Mateo called Night Fire. Ever been there?"

"No."

"Tell me the truth, Bennett. What do you know about it? Did you bring this upon yourself?"

"What are you talking about?"

"How many times have you been there?"

"I've never been there and I've never heard of it. Just watching without being able to touch never did anything for me, okay?"

"Come on, Bennett. How many times have you brought your hose to Night Fire? Did you owe Fabiano money?"

"What's wrong with you? Do all cops play mind games with the public, or just the ones I meet? One minute you're helping me and the next you're implicating me. Are you trying to play good cop/bad cop all by yourself? Stop the truck. Let me out. I'll go to the club without any help and I'll find out who sent that bastard. I'll do it myself."

"Calm down. You're out of your element here, Architect. Don't go screwing things up on your own. You'll just get in the way of the investigation and wind up dead. I'll go out on a limb here and keep you informed if you stay out of it. If not, I'll arrest you for obstruction. Do you understand?"

I didn't answer. I remembered seeing San Mateo on a map and thought it was about an hour south of San Francisco. If I was right, my Porsche would make short work of that. Besides, I wasn't getting much action the civilized way. Maybe I needed to change my own M.O.

Johnson looked at me when we stopped for the traffic signal at Al Tahoe Boulevard. "You didn't answer me, Bennett. I'm not fuckin' around. I'll keep you in the loop if you do what I tell you. If not, I'll put you in the lockup. Don't make me regret sharing information with you."

Then I started laughing. I couldn't help it.

"What the hell are you laughing at?"

"You're pretty funny, Johnson. You've got a sense of humor and don't even know it."

"What are you talking about?"

"'How many times have you brought your hose to Night Fire?' That was a good one. Got any others? Have you ever considered a career in stand-up?"

He tried to keep a straight face, but couldn't. He laughed a little but quickly reined himself in.

The signal changed and we started moving again. I asked, "What else do you know about him?"

"You didn't answer me."

"Yeah, yeah. All right. I won't go there. Are you happy now?"

"Ecstatic."

"How do you know he called himself Joey?"

"He had a few business cards in his wallet."

"I'm surprised a hit man had any I.D. on him at all. Aren't you?"

"No. If he was pulled over for a traffic violation, he wouldn't have wanted to be detained unnecessarily. He was professional enough to carry his wallet in a special pocket in his coat modified with a zipper to make sure he didn't drop anything at the scene."

"The detectives in New York said no shell casings were found in my uncle's apartment, even though the murder weapon was a nine millimeter automatic. That's one of the things that led them to believe it was a professional job and not just a push-in robbery."

"What else made them say that?"

"They suspected a silencer was used because the neighbors heard nothing. I don't know much about guns, but I do know the one I saw last night had a silencer stuck on the end of it."

"Actually, it's called a suppressor."

"Thanks for the lesson. What else do we know about the gun?"

"It was a Taurus nine millimeter with the serial number filed off. No surprise there, but we've got a technique for identifying the deeper distortions in the metal made during the stamping process. There were no prints on the gun except mine, on the magazine in the gun, or on the ammunition in the magazine. And the same is true about the two spare mags in his coat pocket. Based on what he said to you, I'm sure the ballistics report will confirm that the gun was the one used in New York, unless he changed the barrel. We already know it was the same caliber, but because we don't have any shell casings we can't compare the indentations in the primers to the firing pin. Where the gun came from might be helpful, if we can resurrect the serial number." Then Johnson appeared to think out loud. "No casings left behind, and no prints on the rounds in the magazine anyway, in the event he couldn't find them all. Aside from the fact that he should have used a revolver, he had it down, all right."

"What else do you know about him?" I asked.

"We're in the process of getting search warrants for his residence and the club. We'll seize his computers and scour his emails, but something tells me he's much too careful for us to find anything. We'll canvas his neighbors and check with the utility companies. We'll know more when we hear from the IRS—that is if he ever filed taxes. We'll check his credit and bank accounts. He had seven one hundred dollar bills in his wallet, along with his license, but the best evidence may be what I found in the Suburban. Before we impounded it, I looked for another gun. Instead I found two cell phones and five grand under the seat, presumably connected to the contract on you."

I felt that dose of news enter my bloodstream through my ears and numb my brain. I envisioned a business envelope with a thin stack of bills inside being handed to Joey Fabiano from someone in the passenger's seat, or through the window as payment for my death. All the years of schooling, of college, of studying to make something of myself, the hopes and dreams I'd had, all the things for which I'd worked so hard to prove to myself and to everyone who knew me that I was of value had been reduced to a few pieces of green paper hidden under somebody's ass. I sank down in the corner of the truck and watched the world go by through the glass beside my face—a man condemned to die. The worth of my life had been set by a total stranger.

Johnson must have seen me shrink into oblivion. I suppose that prompted him to ask, "What's wrong?"

Given the events of the preceding twelve hours I was tempted to say, *that's got to be, without doubt, the dumbest question anybody has ever asked me*, but instead I simply said, "It isn't every day that you find out exactly how much you're worth."

"Cheer up. You're probably worth twice that. Half up front and half after the job was done is probably how it was supposed to go. Does that make you feel better?"

"Not really, but I'm glad to see Johnson the Clown coming out of his shell, even if it is at my expense."

"Apparently you bring out the best in people."

"Yeah. That's it. That's why somebody paid to have me whacked. It doesn't make any sense. I've never heard of that little prick. And what the hell did a strip club in California have to do with my uncle who lived three time zones away?"

Deputy Johnson turned right onto Tahoe Keys Boulevard and said, "It makes sense to somebody, Bennett; somebody willing to pay a lot of money, presumably ten large for your uncle and another ten for you, plus expenses."

I thought about all that cash and a little bell went off in my head. "Was the currency under the seat new or old?"

"I'm not sure. Mixed, I think. Why?"

"Stein told me they knew from the serial numbers that the money in my uncle's safe-deposit box was from California, but they didn't tell me what bank it came from. If they know it was from California, they may also know exactly where the treasury sent it, right down to the branch. We've got to run it down. All of it; the cash you found last night and the cash in New York. Maybe it all came from the same bank? If it did, a name might jump off the list of depositors and fall into your lap."

"Even if we could narrow it down to a particular bank, the list would be a mile long."

"Then you've got your work cut out for you."

Johnson lifted his black ball cap and scratched his head. "Establishing a link between the bills in our possession and a name on a list of bank customers would be impossible."

"If you really want to be negative, Deputy, don't forget to

throw in, 'It'll never hold up in court.' Didn't you just say the money is evidence? It's a place to start, isn't it?"

"I've got a better place."

I looked at Johnson and asked, "Where's that?"

He watched the road ahead as he spoke. "The murders were a year ago, right?"

"Yes."

"And you lived there until you moved here two weeks ago."

"So?"

"No one tried to kill you in New York, right?"

"Correct."

"So, your sudden presence in California stirred the pot. Your appearance *here* has made somebody very nervous, nervous enough to kill you. Somebody who thought he'd gotten away with murder. Who have you surprised? You said you moved across the country to start a new life. The police don't believe you. Neither does the person or persons who've paid for your death. Apparently, people on both sides of the law are asking the same question: *Why are you really here?*"

As my mind spun out of control Johnson drove right past the entrance to my condo's parking lot. "You just missed it. That was my driveway."

"Relax. I'm checking things out. You don't want me to drive us into an ambush, do you?"

An answer wasn't really necessary, so I just sat there, doing my best impersonation of the Less twins—Helpless and Useless.

He drove around the block to the west of Keys Boulevard a few times, each time scanning the parking areas that served my condo and all of the buildings adjacent. When he was confident that nothing and no one seemed out of the ordinary, he finally entered the lot that still harbored my new silver Porsche and the black Hertz Mustang GT I'd rented at SFO. He backed into the spot he'd used the night before when he'd surprised me in the dark. As he shut it down, I asked, "How did you know he was here?"

"It's a good thing you described the Suburban to me when you did, including the damage to the parking lamp. I noticed it parked over there as I headed for my truck." Johnson pointed to a vacant spot a few spaces to our left. "I realized he'd probably been watching us in your kitchen through the slider, waiting for me to leave." The deputy reached into his jacket and pulled the large revolver from the shoulder rig I'd seen in the hotel elevator. "Let's go," he said, stepping out of the truck. He led the way to my condo with the gun down beside his thigh, instructing me along the way to unlock the door without standing in front of it.

I resisted being preoccupied by the blood stains on the walkway, still cordoned off with yellow plastic crime-scene tape, and opened the door.

He tore the tape out of the way and entered first, raising the gun to a combat position. "Wait here," he whispered, once inside the vestibule. "I'll let you know when it's safe." Then he moved from room to room like a one-man SWAT team. A minute later he reappeared at the far end of the hall. "Clear."

I brushed my teeth and changed my clothes from the ground up, pulling on a fresh pair of jeans and a black shirt. I still needed a shave, but wasn't about to waste time unnecessarily in the combat zone. Besides, the status of stubbles had somehow been elevated from stigma to fashion statement. At some point in recent history, I don't know when exactly, hadn't it become stylish to look like a slob? It was also a small step away from Ivy League toward sinister. I completed the GQ look with a black windbreaker.

I pulled the dirty laundry from the suitcase and replaced it with clean clothes. Then I dragged it back to the entryway, suspecting I would not be returning to Bennett central anytime soon.

"Ready when you are," I announced.

Mike Johnson said from the living room, "I really don't know much about art, but I think your uncle was a good artist. His paintings make you want to be there. Do you know what I mean?"

I joined him in the Bennett gallery for a parting reminder of my uncle's legacy. "I know exactly what you mean. I've said the same thing myself. In fact, that's my own personal test. If you want to live in the painting, or at least visit for a while, it's a good one. Given the circumstances, I'd crawl into any one of these right now if I could."

"You don't have to crawl into that one," he said, pointing to the oil I'd hung at the center of the wall. "We can walk into it."

Even though Mike Johnson had saved my life, it seemed that now, perhaps for the first time, he finally believed me. I smiled a little and gestured toward the exit. "After you, Deputy."

He took the lead again, ready to be on point, and asked as he reached the front door, "Do you still want to stop for breakfast? We've got time. I told May we'd be there by noon."

I stepped outside and placed my valise on the welcome mat, exactly where the nine millimeter automatic that killed Dana and Mack had landed. I relocked the door, picked up the bag, and said as calmly as I could, "Not really. To tell you the truth, I'd rather just get to it."

16

I nibbled on a few morsels of interest while en route to the house in the painting, the juiciest of which was the thing Deputy Deluded still had for Amy Drake. That was clear to me. And he had "a wonderful wife and two beautiful children." Come to think of it, have you ever heard a wife and children described any other way? Of course, any comparisons would be completely unfair, as I'd never met Mrs. Second Best. But based on the things Johnson said, and the way he said them, even though he was clearly downplaying his persistent feelings for all the obvious reasons, I can say with some degree of certainty that Amy Drake was, and would likely always be, even more wonderful. I do, however, owe the man my life, so don't ask me to repeat that in court. And please don't ask me to compare Dana to Amy. I'd already bought the ticket for that guilt trip.

Mike and Amy had gone to high school together. She went on to earn an MBA and manage the Drake art empire. He went on to make Pine County a safer place. She was destined to make her fortune in the business world. And he was destined to save my life.

Not that I'm complaining. What started off a week ago on the side of the road as a lesson in intimidation was slowly turning into some sort of impromptu partnership. It was an odd progression. In the grand scheme of things, I'd gone from next of kin to person of interest to prime suspect to victim to ally. For Johnson, protecting May Drake from me had shifted to protecting me from May Drake. That may sound fairly ridiculous, given her description and demeanor, but her name was certainly first on the list when answering the question, whom did I surprise?

Johnson signaled our departure from the westbound lane and we crossed the double yellow line. He parked the pickup facing the river to the right of the ever-present white SUV and turned off the engine, but made no attempt to get out. He leaned forward for a moment, hunched over the wheel, to survey the scene before us. Then he leaned back and simply stared through the windshield at the house above the opposite bank. "I've known May for a long time," he said, "since before I became a cop and this stretch of highway became my post. Amy's parents were killed in a vehicle accident in Sacramento when she was fifteen. That's where they lived until her grandmother took her in. That's when I met them both."

I already knew most of that. I'd heard it before—the night before in Luigi's, as a matter of fact. Remembering Amy's face in the candlelight made it extraordinarily easy to intrude like a voyeur on Johnson's private memories. I could almost see what he was mentally viewing; the two of them walking hand in hand across the narrow bridge, young lust blossoming beside the river that cut through the mountains from the snowy wilderness, two teenage lovers racing up the steps to her room for forbidden sessions of carnal discovery under a fluffy quilt while grandma was at the market twenty miles away.

Johnson shut down the porno projector before I did and said, "It's pretty hard for me to imagine that the nice old lady living in this house is hiding a secret that could have led to a case of murder for hire."

I realized he was suddenly trying to justify the impending browbeating of an elderly woman who'd probably served him sandwiches and lemonade after school, and after he'd violated her granddaughter in her own home.

Presumably guilt ridden, he needed a little moral support. And although I probably wouldn't be the best role model in that area, I gave him some. "I know what you mean. I liked May the moment I met her. Picturing her with Joey the Hit Man is a tough one, but that's probably a good example of why cops shouldn't work cases where there is personal involvement, right?"

He appeared surprised, as if I'd disclosed something a civilian wouldn't have known.

"Look," I said. "The NYPD wants to question her. I should have told them where she was, but I didn't. Now we're here and they're not. I was planning to talk to her today myself. As it turns out, I'm glad you're with me. You can run the show." What I meant was; a deputy sheriff should know better than I what to ask. And a cop would be more likely to scare the crap out of her than an architect. "Come to think of it, shouldn't you be in uniform? You're more intimidating when you're in uniform, unless you take out your gun. Then you've got it nailed."

"I've been reassigned to a desk pending a review of the shooting. This is an unofficial visit. Nevertheless, I'll ask the questions, Bennett."

"That's all right with me. Have at it."

He nodded and reached for the door handle. We walked across the pedestrian bridge and two minutes later we were all sitting in May Drake's living room, surrounded by paintings and knickknacks.

"What can I help you with, Michael?" she asked, after we'd gotten past the customary pleasantries. I'm certain she was surprised to see *me*. But it was impossible to make a critical distinction: Was she surprised to see me with Deputy Johnson, or was she surprised to see that I was still alive?

"It's about Robert's uncle."

"I was afraid you were going to say that."

"Why?"

"Robert told me what happened in New York when he was here last week. It's been on my mind ever since. I'm so sorry, Robert," she said, turning toward me. "It's just so terrible. Have the police caught anyone?"

Before I could answer Johnson said, ignoring her question, "As I understand it, you and Maxwell Bennett were quite close at one time."

She nodded and smiled thinly, as if the memory slightly overshadowed the tragedy. "That was a long time ago, before I was married. We communicated again over the years after I was divorced, but it was never quite the same."

"When was the last time you and Maxwell spoke?"

"Two birthdays ago." She looked down at her hands clasped on her lap. She wore a dark gray pleated wool skirt that draped over her knees and a light gray silk blouse with a ruffle over the buttons. The pearl earrings adorning her delicately wrinkled face were appropriately discreet. "When he didn't call on my last birthday, I knew something had happened. I just knew it. He never forgot, even after all these years. It never occurred to me that he could have been… murdered."

"At first the police thought it was a home invasion," Johnson said, "but it appears to have been significantly more complicated than a robbery."

I watched her carefully and saw her wince at the words "home invasion." Knowing that Amy could have warned May of my intention to return, she was now presumably prepared for whatever questions arose. She covered her mouth with her left hand and said, "Oh, dear, I'm afraid I'm going to need a tissue or two. If you'll excuse me, I'll be right back." She stood and walked silently across the Persian rug toward the door under the stairs. She opened it and stepped inside the small bathroom, closing the door after her.

I wondered if Johnson was going to pull his gun, as he had when I'd left the room to use the bathroom, in case she returned with a gun of her own. He made no strategic moves so I sat tight, trying to keep my imagination in check, which wasn't easy thanks to the humiliating tongue-lashing I'd endured for not being more alert to danger, or as he'd put it, being a victim looking for a place to happen.

She returned a couple of minutes later with a box of tissues, making room for them on the table beside the settee by carefully rearranging a few knickknacks. Freshly composed, she sat and asked, "What do you mean, more complicated? What do you think happened?"

"We believe someone was sent to kill him," Johnson said.

She winced again and started to shake her head in disbelief. "Oh, my. Why would anyone want to do such a thing?"

"We were hoping you could help us find the answer," Johnson said.

She looked genuinely confused. "Me? How could I help you?"

"We found evidence indicating Maxwell was involved with someone in California. What can you tell us about that?"

She blushed, obviously taking *involved* to mean romantically. "Yes, we were involved, but that was a lifetime ago. I don't know what else I can tell you."

Johnson shook his head. "This was more recent; within the last two years."

"I told you he called."

"Do you remember what you talked about?"

"We chatted for a while, more like old friends than old lovers, I'm sorry to say," she offered with surprising candor. "But that was the extent of it."

"Do you remember if he said anything that was cause for concern or made you feel uneasy?"

"Not especially."

"Did he mention if he was having money troubles, or if he was having difficulty with anyone he knew?"

"No. Not that I recall."

"Do you think he felt threatened in any way?"

"I don't think so. We talked about this and that and reminisced a little. That's all. Unless someone you know is dying, there really isn't much new to discuss when you're old," she observed. She looked away, I thought toward the painting of the tall ship on the high seas that hung above the fireplace—the Bennett oil I never knew existed. "I'm afraid it's all in the past; a lovely place we can never go. And now that he's gone, we can't even talk about it."

I expected Johnson to mention the money and letters in the safe-deposit box, but instead he pulled a piece of paper out of his jacket. He unfolded it to its original eight and a half by eleven inch size and handed it to May Drake. As it passed before me I saw that it was an enlarged full-color photocopy of Joseph Fabiano's California driver's license. "Do you know this man?"

"One moment, I'll need my glasses," she said as she stood.

She returned a minute later studying the photo. "Joseph Fabiano," she repeated. "I've never seen him."

When she began to return the copy I took it before Johnson

could react. I ignored his brief understated expression of disapproval and studied the photo myself, which looked appropriately like a mugshot. I memorized the address on the I.D. and handed it back to the deputy before an upwelling of hatred could drown out his line of questioning.

Johnson asked, "Have you ever heard the name? He called himself Joey."

"No," May Drake replied, sitting again. "Who is he?"

"We believe he's the man who killed Maxwell and Dana, Robert's wife. Are you sure you don't know him?"

She suddenly seemed a little indignant. "Why would I know that horrible man?"

"The police in New York found your name mixed in with a few of Maxwell Bennett's things. They wanted someone in my department to talk to you. I volunteered, thinking it would be easier for you with somebody you knew. I'm sorry if this is upsetting for you."

That wasn't what Johnson had told me. But it was all part of the learning experience. And what I was learning was that in police work the ends justify the means.

May Drake folded her arms across her chest as if suddenly chilled. "Have they caught him?"

"As you may have noticed, his license was issued in California, not New York."

"So you're saying no, no one's found him."

"Actually, I shot him last night when he tried to kill Robert."

If the abhorrent shock that appeared on her face was an act, then there was clearly room between the ranks of the abundant dust collectors all around us for a daytime Emmy.

After a long moment she turned to me and said, "I'm glad to see you're all right."

Are you? I didn't reply.

She looked at Johnson again and asked, "Is he dead?"

I was about to nod again, expecting to fall into synchronicity with the deputy, when he said, "He's in a coma. When he comes out of it we'll find out who sent him. We know someone paid him to commit murder because I found the money, or at least half of it. We're certain he was paid to kill Maxwell. Unfortunately, Robert's wife was there when he showed up."

If May was going to seem worried, this was the time. But she didn't. "I hope you can get it out of him."

"We always do." Then Johnson changed gears. "Did your husband know Maxwell?" he asked, apparently going to the second name on the list of people surprised by my arrival.

"My *ex*-husband," she corrected.

"Sorry, your ex-husband."

"He knew of him, but I don't think they ever met."

"It's quite a coincidence that both your ex-husband and Maxwell were artists."

She smiled perfunctorily. "I owned a gallery in San Francisco many years ago. Each of them walked through those doors."

"Forgive me for being blunt, May, but did your relationship with Maxwell contribute in any way to your divorce?"

"No. I was married to Leland for twenty-two years. It should have ended earlier, but Maxwell had nothing to do with it. Leland just wasn't the man I thought he was."

I was willing to accept that statement for its colloquial meaning, but apparently Johnson wasn't. "What do you mean by that?" he asked.

"He came into my life at the perfect time." She began to speak slowly and with great retrospection. "He was handsome and suave and charming. He made me feel like the most beautiful girl in the world. He was thoughtful and caring, always saying the right thing. He brought flowers and chocolates and cards. You could say he was just what the doctor ordered."

She fell silent, apparently lost in the reverie of better days. I thought Johnson was simply allowing her time to enjoy the memories as the silence grew awkward, but he surreptitiously signaled me to stay out of it. When it became clear nothing else was forthcoming he asked, "And by that you mean he helped you get over Maxwell?"

She nodded. "He knew I'd been involved with another man just before we'd met. I'm afraid I couldn't hide it very well. I was heartbroken and hard to reach, I suppose. But he wouldn't give up. He was determined to win me over. He was very patient."

Being a pragmatist, a cynic, an uninvolved third party, and above all a man, I had a different view. Leland Drake was an opportunist. He saw a vulnerable piece of ass, knew how to sell himself, and wouldn't give up until he scored. That was that. Not that I would ever stoop to that level, you understand, but I do know a thing or two about the male psyche. If I hadn't met Leland Drake, I may have given him the benefit of the doubt; that his intentions had in fact been honorable, if there is such a thing, but our unexpected face-to-face the day before had forever sullied my opinion of the man's character.

Indeed, that was what she meant by, "Leland just wasn't the man I thought he was." I knew that's where Johnson was going, and I was already there.

"Forgive me for pushing the issue," Johnson continued, "but if your ex-husband wasn't the man you thought he was, who did he turn out to be?"

She came out of the clouds and landed hard. "As time went by he turned cold. There was nothing I could do. I tried. I really did. But the more success he achieved, the more distant he became." She averted her eyes before continuing. "I knew when he no longer had any interest in me, he couldn't be trusted. His new wife is Amy's age, for God's sake. He's a filthy bastard. That's who he is. It was hard for me to believe he could change that much—that anyone could. At first I told myself, that's simply what happens when someone doesn't love you anymore. It happens all the time, doesn't it?"

"I'm afraid so," Johnson agreed.

"Then I began to think he'd really been that way all along and I just didn't see it." She suddenly looked directly at the deputy and said, "I was responsible for his success. All he had when we met was charm and ambition. He wanted to be wealthy in the worst way. I remember repeating the starving artist cliché to him, but to his credit he had bigger ideas. From a business perspective, I knew his grandiose scheme actually made sense because others like Warhol, Kinkade, and Behrens, to name a few, were doing it and seeing success. He simply wanted to copy the business model for selling art to the masses. I had faith in him so I used the gallery and all of my resources to launch his career. One thing led to another and, as it turns out, he was right."

Fascinated, I blurted out my first question. "How does that business model work?" I thought I saw a little admonishment out of the corner of my eye, but I ignored it.

"The key is selling art in quantity by producing, distributing, and marketing copies. Leland knew he could make a name for himself using the power of marketing. He had style and was very persuasive. He knew he could insert himself into the right circles and hobnob his way to fame and fortune. All he needed was the right product and some publicity. It was all about building a brand, eventually using name recognition alone to sell art—the way authors or entertainers use their celebrity to sell books and music. Like the others I mentioned blazing a trail across the art world, he too saw the potential to turn what had been a painting by painting business into an industry, not only by mass producing reproductions, but by offering what were essentially copies at different levels of quality." She stopped herself when she realized she'd answered my question.

But I wanted to hear more. I asked, "What do you mean 'different levels of quality?'"

"The original would, of course, always be worth the most, fame continually driving the value higher. Then there'd be the giclee lithographs and serigraphs on canvas, closely replicating the original in texture and vibrancy. Some could even be hand-embellished for a value-adding personal touch. Then there'd be numbered prints, produced in limited quantity to support their worth. Also, the original's value would be tied to the number of prints sold. Multiply all that by introducing each series in different sizes. Then there'd be the fine-art jigsaw puzzles, tapestries, calendars, greeting cards, post cards, wrapping paper, placemats, coffee mugs, and so on—basically, anything on which an image could be replicated. Things anyone could afford."

I must have seemed amazed because she then said, "I know it sounds impressive, but to me the art itself has always been what matters most. Artists paint because they're creative. They paint because they love to paint. They paint because each work is a representation of how they see the world, or perhaps the way they'd like it to be. Leland painted to make money and only to make money. The funny thing is, he was artistic, but he wasn't a very good artist."

The deputy and I exchanged glances, each aware that an incalculable degree of animus had risen to the surface of May Drake's emotional well. Even Johnson appeared willing to let it go at that, attributing her less than glowing opinion of Leland Drake to the spurned wife syndrome.

But she hadn't finished. "He could sketch well enough when we met, but his use of color was abysmal. I tried to be tactful in my criticism, especially because of his feelings for me. And he took it well, including my suggestions, promising to learn. 'No one is born great,' he said, 'but you inspire me. If you'll give me the time, I'll become great. I'll do it for you. *Nulla viene realizzato senza impegno!*' Nothing is accomplished without commitment! That's what he told me."

"Is that Latin?" Johnson asked.

"No. It's Italian. A year later we were married. He soon gave me that painting," she said, pointing to the twenty by twenty-four inch oil-on-canvas seashore landscape in a gilded frame that hung on the back wall beside the French patio doors.

I stood and moved in for a closer look. Johnson stayed seated, apparently uninterested.

I heard May Drake say, "It took only one year for him to be able to paint like that. He saw the potential in reviving American Impressionism, an enchanting style characterized by the use of pure color, short brushstrokes, and the realistic representation of light. It was popularized by a handful of American artists named Childe Hassam, William Merritt Chase, Mary Cassatt, John Singer Sargent, Willard Metcalf, Theodore Robinson, and a few others who reportedly studied in Paris with the so-called French masters, including Monet in Giverny, in the late eighteen hundreds. Unfortunately, the movement lost favor after the 1913 modern art exhibition held in a New York City armory, of all places."

"I understand the realistic representation of light," I said, turning to address May, "but what do you mean by pure color?"

"Applying paint directly from tube to canvas, instead of mixing it on a palate, makes the painting infinitely more vibrant." She got up and stood beside me. Then, looking at the painting, she said, "He did what he said he would. He learned to be great. And I tell myself he did it for me. I would have taken it down long ago, but it reminds me that at one point in my life I'd actually been an inspiration to someone." She hesitated for a moment before emptying her thoughts. "No woman wants to age. If I could have stayed young for him I would have. Maybe things would have turned out differently."

As I studied the painting, I asked, "Is this the original?"

"It is," she replied.

"It must be very valuable."

"It's insured."

I considered the priceless nature of its origin, as well as its depreciated sentimental value, and found myself wondering to what extremes I might go to win over Amy Drake.

I heard the deputy ask if May was in possession of her ex-husband's home address and phone number.

"I'll get it for you," she said.

Mike Johnson stood and thanked May Drake for seeing us as she handed him a small sheet of note paper. I approached, took her hand, and said, "I'm sorry there've been so many disappointments in your life, but you've got a beautiful home and an even more beautiful granddaughter."

That made Johnson a little uncomfortable so he headed for the door, soon letting in the spring runoff's white noise.

"I know," she said. "I'm glad you weren't hurt."

"Thanks. So am I."

Once on the porch, Johnson turned to May and said, "It was nice to see you again. It's a shame it wasn't under better circumstances."

She nodded. "If you have any other questions, call me. I'll do whatever I can to help."

"Come to think of it, I do have another question for you, as a neighbor."

"What's that?"

"Apparently, personal service is becoming a thing of the past. My bank is giving me a hard time with a small personal loan, even though I've been a customer there for years. I was hoping you could tell me what bank you use."

The temporary look of confusion on her face melted away and she said, "I've used the Pine Bank branch in Pollock Pines for a long time. Never had a problem."

"Thanks. I appreciate it. I'll give them a try."

We walked off the porch and headed for the bridge. When we climbed into the truck I asked, "What's the loan for; tip money at Night Fire?"

He smirked and cranked the engine. "Unless we do a hell of a lot better next time, you'll need it for an extended stay at the No-Tell Motel and I'll need it for ammunition." Then he waited for a break in the eastbound traffic, backed away from the river, and pointed us back toward Tahoe.

"I thought you did a good job."

"How's that?"

"She gave up a ton about her ex."

"Like what? That when guys get rich and famous they dump their wives for younger ones? You didn't know that? She's just bitter."

"She's bitter, all right," I said, "but she's got him pegged, even if it did take her twenty-two years to figure it out. I met him yesterday. It only took me twenty-two minutes to know he's always been a son of a bitch. The more I think about it, the more willing I'd be to bet that he played her from the beginning. *Nulla viene realizzato senza impegno,* my ass! Give me a break."

Johnson asked, "Where was he when you met him yesterday?"

"In his office in San Francisco. The Drake building is on the Embarcadero. I went there to meet Amy. She works for him. I wanted to take her to dinner when I got back from New

York. Sorry."

"No need. What did you and Drake talk about?"

"You wouldn't believe it."

"Try me."

"All right. We talked about my uncle, and I was surprised at how much Drake actually knew about him. It all seemed amazingly fresh in his mind. But I was even more blown away when Drake conceded that he'd always been second best, even though he'd been the one to marry May. I think that's when I asked him if he could account for his whereabouts when Mack was murdered."

Mike Johnson yanked the truck into a turnout and screeched to a stop. "What?"

I nodded. "That's what I asked him."

"You're fucking kidding me, right?"

"No, I'm not. I don't know how it happened, really. One thing led to the next and before I knew it I was Detective Bennett. Stein and DiCarlo had grilled me like a freakin' kielbasa that morning. All that bullshit they put me through was absurd. I told myself on the flight back that I had to do something to save my own ass. I didn't go to Drake's office to interrogate him, but when he started berating my uncle it just happened."

"Wait a minute. How did he even know your uncle had been murdered?"

"Amy told him. And he knew I'd flown to New York to I.D. some recovered property, including a painting, which turned out to be the strange little copy I told you about."

"What else was recovered?"

"Some jewelry: A couple of watches and rings that belonged to my uncle and his deceased sister."

"Was that all of it?"

"Those were the only items I recognized. It made me sick.

There were piles of jewelry from other burglaries, hundreds of pieces—everything imaginable except the one thing I really wanted to get back."

"What was that?"

I described the small gold filigree heart pendant I'd had custom made for Dana. His subsequent comment regarding the item's sentimental value was similar to Stein's. He also chose to ignore the obviously private and personal meaning of the word *Pretend*.

"How much did you tell Leland about the investigation?"

"Quite a bit, I'm afraid."

Johnson telegraphed his disappointment. "Such as?"

I tried to reconstruct the conversation. "Drake assumed the police had the killer in custody because of the recovered items. I told him there'd been two break-ins and that the NYPD liked the suspect they had only as the burglar, not as the killer. Drake was convinced they had the right guy for both crimes until I explained why the cops believe it was a contract."

"Drake was convinced, or he tried to convince you?"

"I'm not sure."

Johnson pivoted in his seat to face me. "Let's make a deal, all right?"

"What kind of a deal?"

"I won't make believe I'm an architect if you don't make believe you're a detective. Are you okay with that, or do I have to lock you up for impersonating?"

"Sounds like a deal to me."

"Good. What else did he say?"

"He asked why I'd come to California?"

"To which you replied?"

"I think I told him I was getting nowhere in New York. I had to look elsewhere."

Johnson stared at me as if I were speaking another language. "I'm pretty sure I know what you meant, but did he?"

"I don't know. He stared at me the way you just did. Then he asked how I found May?"

"And you said?"

"It's a small world."

Deputy Mike Johnson looked through the windshield in contemplation for a while before saying anything else. "I don't know what this is all about," he finally admitted, "But I do know one thing."

"What's that?"

"The pot you stirred was in Leland Drake's office."

"I thought you'd say something like that. What makes you think so?"

"Think about it. Think about the way you answered his questions."

"What do you mean?"

"You said one thing and he heard another. You said you'd left New York because you couldn't function there and he heard you ran out of answers. You came to California to start over and he heard you came to find May. Then you show up in his office and ask where he was at the time of the murders, for Christ's sake! Could it be any clearer? He thinks you're a revenge-crazed relative running your own investigation. You must have rattled his cage pretty good. You wandered around in one of the murder capitals of the world for your whole life, Mr. Oblivious, and nothing happened to you. You have a conversation with Drake in the afternoon and Joey is at your door a little after midnight. If I hadn't been there, you'd be dead and no one would be the wiser."

My mind started replaying the visit in Drake's austere office with San Francisco Bay as the backdrop. It ended on fast-forward; Fabiano standing on my welcome mat, the black silencer on his chrome gun pointing at my face. "What about the phones? You said you found two cell phones in Joey's Suburban. Did they give you anything to work with?"

"Not yet. One was an iPhone. The other was a pre-paid basic phone. That's all I can tell you right now."

It's hard to adequately describe the ratcheting anger I felt sitting in Johnson's pickup as I thought about Mack's missing phone, but before the throbbing started I asked, "When are we going to see Drake?"

He glared at me. "I thought we had a deal."

"We do. You can be the detective if it makes you happy. Just consider it a ride-along."

He shook his head, checked the traffic, and maneuvered back onto the highway. "Do us both a favor, will you?"

"And that is?"

"Sit there and be quiet."

"But I've got one more question."

He ignored me for about a mile so I simply asked, "Does the name Drake sound Italian to you?"

17

If you think Deputy Sense O. Humor was a little touchy about my desire to be a part of the investigation, imagine his reaction when I asked if I could borrow a gun. Given the circumstances, it was a logical enough question, wasn't it?

Ever helpful and accommodating, he suggested protective custody instead. I would have considered the recommendation if the Pine County jail had a coed plan as well as complimentary dining, but when he reminded me that the very nature of protective custody was akin to solitary confinement I summarily declined, thanking him for his gracious hospitality. Even though my ability to fend for myself had proven to be a dismal failure, I had different ideas.

Since he was in such a cooperative mood, I asked him to help me drop off the Mustang at the nearest Hertz location. At the counter he suggested, however, that I stay away from my new Porsche, unless it had a remote start feature, and rent a less conspicuous set of wheels for a while. I think the word he used was "invisible." He also said something about hiring a food taster, but I'm pretty sure he was kidding, even if such behavior was, for him, out of character.

Resisting my tendency to be headstrong, I acknowledged the merits of his advice and rented something else; the most powerful yet common car they had—a Dodge Charger in chameleon clearcoat.

To my surprise, Johnson volunteered that he would take me along when he questioned Leland Drake. I wasn't sure why, except that he seemed to learn more from me than from anyone else. Ulterior motive or not, I wanted to be there. I asked when it would happen. He told me he wanted to check him out first. Then he'd have to clear it with his lieutenant, since such an interview was, literally and figuratively, far beyond the informal meeting we'd had with a woman he'd known for years. He took my cell number and told me to keep it on. Then he reminded me to think like a cop without actually trying to be one. "You should know," he said, "that I tried to arrange protection for you, but because of the budget cuts and layoffs I couldn't get it approved. Apparently, the state is broke."

My initial reaction was to protest, saying something like the following: *That's a fine how-do-you-do! I just paid nearly fourteen thousand dollars in sales tax and registration fees to license my new car. California could, at least, make an effort to help keep their newest legal resident from being assassinated, don't you think?* But it occurred to me before I opened my big mouth that I'd be better off without protection. If no one but me knew where I was, there could be no leaks. How many movies have you seen where a cop on-the-take spills the beans? I don't know if that really happens, but I certainly didn't want to find out the hard way. Besides, I wasn't about to be cooped up somewhere with a deputy watching my every move. I had something else in mind. As the saying goes, I had places to go and people to see.

I transferred my luggage, thanked him for all he'd done thus far, and headed out alone into the world for the first time since someone tried to kill me.

I called my new boss at home and invited myself over. William Sherman lived in a sprawling ranch house set on a hilltop overlooking a lush piece of land fronting Highway 49, the winding two lane blacktop so named in honor of the original '49ers (not the football team) and the gold discovered at Sutter's Mill only a few miles away. Following his directions, and making sure I wasn't followed, it took a little over an hour to get there from Tahoe, after stopping for a quick lunch at a restaurant I'd chosen at random—where I sat in the rear facing the entrance.

I was greeted at the top of the driveway by two huge German Shepherds, both of whom tried their no-thumbs best to paw their way into the car. I sat there until someone came out to get me, thankful I'd left the Porsche at home. I was also glad I'd, once again, accepted the zero deductible damage waiver.

That someone made a beautiful spring Saturday afternoon in the foothills even more beautiful. Jenny Sherman, aka the boss's daughter, bounced out of a shampoo commercial and came to my rescue, rounding up Scratch and Sniff. She wore a white tank top, aqua short-shorts, and white tennis shoes. "My dad told me you were on your way," she said with a vivacious smile. "It's nice to see you away from the office."

"It's nice to see you, too." *Anywhere.*

"We missed you the last two days."

You did? "I had some unfinished business in New York. It

couldn't be helped."

"Is everything all right?"

"Great." *If you've always wanted to be a target.*

"You're not moving back east, are you?"

Even though I was already looking at her, I *really* looked at her. Her deep blue eyes were extraordinarily vivid in the daylight, something I hadn't noticed in the office. No, that's not entirely true. I had noticed, but I'd voluntarily decreed them off limits—her eyes, her long blonde hair, as well as the rest of her delightful attributes. "No," I said, before I had a chance to forget the question. "There's nothing there for me any longer. Everything I need is right here." *Was that too flirty?* I was enjoying the attention more than I can describe, especially after getting the big brush-off at Luigi's, but I really didn't want to break my own self-imposed rules. "I need to speak with your dad for a little while. Am I interrupting anything?"

"No. He's in the garage. My mom's here, too. I'll introduce you."

Her mother was in the kitchen shifting gears on a bright red high performance electric mixer. I noticed that the resemblance was apparent even though the years had somehow rounded things off a bit and shortened her blonde hair to an androgynous length. We exchanged a few pleasantries, which included her saying, "I've heard a lot about you."

"All good, I hope."

Apparently I had everyone fooled because she answered in the affirmative and offered me a beverage. When I declined, Jenny led me through the house to the garage.

William Sherman was standing in front of a workbench illuminated by a bright gooseneck lamp. He was cleaning a shiny black semi-automatic handgun which had been disassembled on an unfurled white towel. He put down what looked like the barrel, wiped his hands with another towel, and welcomed me. He wore a jade green fly-fishing shirt and a faded pair of loose-fitting jeans.

I asked, "What kind of gun is that?"

"It's a .45 caliber Colt Model 1911. It's what the U.S. armed forces carried as a sidearm for more than half of the twentieth century. It's one of the tools that defeated tyranny and kept us free."

I smiled and said, "It may have its rightful place in history, but around here it looks like a pretty good way to keep your daughter's dates from getting fresh."

"That too," he agreed. "I usually time it so I'm dallying around with one of these babies when they show up."

"He's not kidding either," Jenny chimed in. "I'll leave you boys to play with your toys." She turned and headed back into the house, closing the door behind her.

"You've got a beautiful home," I said. "The house, the land, the countryside, the climate—it's all perfect."

"Thanks. I can't take credit for the countryside or climate, but I do my best to keep my family safe and secure."

"It looks like you've done a terrific job so far. I just met your wife. I can see why Jenny is such a great girl."

Sherman nodded. "Her sister is a good kid, too. She's on the cheerleading squad at the high school. There's a game today. She should be home in a little while."

I hadn't met Jenny's kid sister yet, but if they looked at all alike, it could well explain why the hair on Bill's head was half gone.

I said, "I'm sorry to bother you, and I'm sorry I had to take the last two days off, but I've got a problem. Everything changed last night and I'm compelled to tell you what happened for your own safety and the safety of everyone at the office, including your daughter."

William Sherman's jolly smile vanished, and I can only

imagine the thoughts that ran through his mind after an introduction to peril like that. *Oh, God. What kind of psycho did I hire? And how much trouble has he brought with him from New York?* Does that sound about right? He simply looked at me and said, "I'm listening."

"The guy who killed my wife and uncle came after me last night with the same gun."

Incredulity replaced the short-lived grim expression on Bill Sherman's face. "What happened?" he asked, apparently interested in the details.

I didn't want to tell him why Deputy Johnson was at my condo; that the NYPD had called the Pine County Sheriff's Department to make sure I was on their radar since I was once again at the center of the investigation, at least before last night's attempt on my life. I said, "A deputy sheriff saved me. He shot and killed him. It was much too close for comfort. Let's leave it at that."

"I thought you said the murders were the result of a home invasion."

"That's what the detectives in New York had originally told me."

"So why would anyone come after *you*?"

"Yesterday they said something completely different; that Mack's murder had been a contract killing and Dana's presence there had just been bad timing."

Sherman turned around, leaned back against the workbench, and folded his arms. "What was your uncle into?"

"I have no idea. I can't imagine him being involved in anything illicit. Mack just wasn't like that."

"So I'll ask again. Why did someone come after you?"

"I don't know, Bill. I really don't."

He stared at me, turned away, and then stared at me again, apparently deciding whether or not to believe me.

"Where did it happen?"

"At my place in Tahoe."

"I don't suppose he had time to say anything before he died, did he?"

"Only that he came to finish the job he'd started in New York."

"You know it's not over, right? You know whoever's behind this may send someone else."

"I know. That's why I won't be at the office Monday. The killer knew my address and another deputy told me not to go home again. I've got to assume they know where I work. I won't put anyone else at risk."

Sherman didn't say anything, which didn't surprise me. The man was an employer. He must have heard a variety of "call in" excuses: I've got a migraine. I've got the flu. I've got food poisoning. I've got jury duty. And now the *coup de grâce*: I've got to disappear for a while.

He turned to face the workbench again and leaned on his palms in contemplation. He stood there for a minute or two without saying anything before reassembling the semi-automatic pistol he'd been cleaning. I watched as his fingers fitted the pieces together and suddenly had the feeling he could have completed the task with his eyes closed. He ran the slide back and forth quickly a half dozen times, apparently to insure its smooth operation. Then he inserted a loaded magazine that was on the towel. He racked the slide one more time and clicked on the safety. "You weren't followed, were you?"

"No. I made sure I wasn't."

"Let's go into the house," he said.

I trailed him to the den, where he instructed me to close the door. He walked directly to a closet and opened it, revealing a safe the size of a refrigerator. It had a black limousine paint job accented with gold foil pin striping. He set the .45 on the beige carpet in front of the safe and reached for the golden dial. "My family calls this the Sherman Tank."

"Would you mind if I lived in it for a week or two?"

"Sorry. It's already full."

I voluntarily turned away and reconnoitered the room while he worked the combination lock. It was undoubtedly a man's room, paneled in rich walnut. If anyone asked, I would have approved the décor, which included matching walnut-stained shutters that controlled the view of the sprawling backyard, set-in shelves displaying leather-bound books and marksmanship trophies, and a brick fireplace with a lever-action Winchester rifle above the mantel. I was tempted to sit on the thickly-tufted cordovan chair trimmed with bronze tacks behind an elaborate walnut desk, but I mustered some self-control. I couldn't stop myself, however, from rolling the polished brass muzzle-loading artillery field cannon replica across the desk blotter's green felt insert, all the while being careful not to knock over the flat-panel monitor or green glass banker's lamp. The only thing feminine that could have possibly fit in, and would have fit in nicely I might add, would have been a French maid, *n'est-ce pas?*

Sherman swung open the massive steel door and pulled out a shotgun that had been stored vertically beside an assortment of rifles. He stood it in the corner of the room nearest the desk chair. Then he requisitioned a box of twelve gauge shells and closed the safe, but didn't lock it. He lifted a thick hand-tooled saddle-colored leather gun belt already rigged with a matching holster off one of the hooks in the closet and strapped it on over his jeans. He picked up the Colt 1911 and wedged it into the holster. Then he pulled a tan three-quarter length shooter's vest, the kind with a suede patch at the shoulder, off a hanger and slipped it on over his shirt, concealing the .45. Functional elastic loops sewn onto the front of the garment already held six red plastic and brass shotgun shells. Having now reached the necessary level of readiness, almost as if for years he'd been preparing for just such a situation, he turned to peer outside through the slats of the shutters. He spoke with his back to me. "What kind of gun did he have?"

"A chrome nine millimeter Taurus with a black silencer. I looked down the barrel."

"Sounds like a pro, but he would have been better off with a revolver. Then there'd be no brass."

I'd been through this already so I knew what he was talking about. I smiled and said, "Hey, whose side are you on?"

"Only making an observation. And just so you know, the plating was probably nickel, not chrome. And a silencer is really called a suppressor."

"I ignored the corrections and said, "He picked up the brass in my uncle's apartment. The police didn't find any."

Sherman seemed impressed. "Did they I.D. him?"

I remembered Johnson asking of my meeting with Leland Drake, "How much did you tell him about the investigation?" He hadn't been pleased with the answer. But William Sherman wasn't Drake. And I'd come to his home seeking cooperation. "His name was Joseph Fabiano. He called himself Joey. He ran a strip club near San Mateo. That's all we know so far."

"It sounds like you or your uncle ticked off somebody in the mob."

I might have offered the same observation if I knew only what I told Bill Sherman. Correcting him would have probably led to a more in-depth explanation, so I simply said, "It sounds that way, doesn't it?"

"You could have explained all of this over the phone, you know. It's not that you're not welcome in my home, but considering what you've told me…"

"That's why I was very careful on the way here. I'm not even driving my own car. It's a rental."

"I've got a wife and two girls to think about."

"I know. That's why I felt the need to tell you what's happened—so you'd be alert."

He nodded slightly while the cogs continued turning. "At least Jenny is going back to college tomorrow."

I let that go without commenting and said, "I also have a favor to ask."

He stopped nodding. "What's that?"

"It's a big one, but I don't know anyone else."

"I'll help you if I can."

"I need a gun. I know there's a waiting period to buy one and I don't have the time. I've got to be able to protect myself. I wouldn't think of asking such a thing if I hadn't come within a second of dying last night."

Sherman pursed his lips. "I can't do that, Robert. All of my guns are registered. If you were caught with one, the authorities would be at my door the same day and they'd take everything. If you shot someone, maybe an innocent bystander, I'd be just as libel as you. I've got a family to worry about. I'm sorry. That's something I just can't do."

"You're right," I said, thoroughly understanding, and feeling pretty stupid for even asking. "I should have known better. I suppose last night shook me up more than I even realized. All I can say is desperation makes a person do foolish things." Knowing my welcome had evaporated, I proffered my hand. "Thanks for seeing me. And thanks again for the job. I really like you and your operation. I think I fit in pretty well and I know I can make a meaningful contribution to your bottom line, but given the circumstances, I feel compelled to resign. I'm sorry if I've caused you any trouble."

Sherman didn't let go of my hand. "I believe everything you've told me, and I think you're a decent guy and an asset to the firm. I'm not accepting your resignation. Take as much time as you need. Call me when the case is closed. Unless Frank Lloyd Wright Jr. shows up to take your place, there'll be a position for you if you want it."

"Thank you. You're very kind."

"And if I had a *cold* gun, I'd give it to you, but I don't. In the meantime, you'll just have to watch yourself."

We started to walk out of the den together, but he suddenly stopped short and said, "Wait a minute. There is something you can have that might help you as a last resort." He walked back to the Sherman Tank, hefted the door and reached inside. He turned around and held out a small device the size of a remote control garage door opener. "Check this out," he said, pressing a button on the side of the little black plastic box with his thumb. A white-hot spark arced between two prongs at the end of the weapon, generating a rapid ear-grating crackle. "That's five million volts, but it's nonlethal because of the amperage. All you've got to do is slide this switch before you press the button. The red LED means it's ready to go. It's rechargeable in any 110 volt outlet with this folding plug." He demonstrated the stun gun as if he were selling it. "When the early ones were introduced they were four times the size and only fifty thousand volts. Now they're tiny and a hundred times more powerful. Keep it in your pocket. If you have to use it, it should do the job."

I took the gizmo, created lightning a couple of times, slid the switch to the off position so I wouldn't flash-fry my own nuts by accident, and slipped it into my right front pants pocket. I pulled some cash out of my left pocket, peeled off a hundred dollar bill, and held it out. "Will this cover it?"

He refused to accept the money and said, "I'd do more for you if I could. Now don't take this the wrong way, but don't come back here until it's over." He closed the safe, reached for a pair of binoculars hanging on another hook in the closet, and accompanied me to the front door. As we passed the kitchen, I bid goodbye to his wife and daughter.

Jenny said, "Where's your Porsche? I was hoping you'd take me for a ride."

"It's in the shop. Maybe another time."

"I'm going back to San Luis Obispo tomorrow."

"Your dad told me."

"Break's over, but I'm graduating in June. I'll see you then, I hope."

Jenny Sherman was a parent's dream come true. Instead of jetting off to Cancun or Aruba to star in a boozed-up spring break wet T-shirt video that could be added with pride to the archival family home movies, she'd worked the two weeks as a receptionist at Sherman and Essen. "Me, too," I agreed.

Bill and I stepped outside and he started scanning the road at the base of the hill with the binoculars. He traced Highway 49 from the southern-most point visible all the way to where it disappeared around another bend to the north, an unobstructed span of about a half-mile. "I don't see anyone," he said. "Take care of yourself."

I thanked him again, mounted up, and rode out.

I took 49 back to the junction at Highway 50, contemplating my next move as I watched my mirrors. The smart thing to do would have been to do nothing. I could have found a motel nearby, registered using cash, and waited for Johnson's call. Or, I could have turned left at the signal, driven back to Tahoe, and checked into any of a hundred touristy accommodations, ignoring along the way that damned white wooden coincidence by the river that had lured me in and dragged me back in time. Those would have been the smart things to do. The sensible things. The prudent things. Did I do either of them? No, of course not. Instead, I turned right and drove toward San Mateo.

18

I decided to stay in San Francisco as I crossed the Bay Bridge.
It was early evening when I reached the Marina District and checked into a motor lodge on Lombard. I walked across the street and tried to get a table in a busy neighborhood watering hole, figuring that if I was ultimately headed to a strip club, I first needed a manly plate of meat and potatoes. Besides, if you knew you were going to risk catching any number of sexually transmitted diseases a few hours later, probably by just walking in the door, why worry about a few lipids?

Directed to the bar by the hostess after providing an alias for the waiting list, I eavesdropped on a few typical Saturday night conversations. The majority of patrons were nicely dressed couples. Pheromones flying through the air, most seemed to be enjoying themselves, an alcohol buzz already in their blood. I observed the women: Their smiles, their eyes, their outfits, and their poses. I surmised most were in various stages of the mating ritual, some closer to foreplay than others.

I scanned the crowd in search of an available female who might be cajoled into a sympathetic one-night stand by saying something like, *I was almost killed last night and what I need now is a beautiful woman to help me celebrate being alive!* But there were none.

When the hostess, a statuesque brunette in a little black dress, informed me that my table was ready, I considered working *her* over, but didn't bother, guessing she'd heard it all before, maybe even my lousy line. I resigned to put sex out my mind, at least to the extent possible, and enjoy dinner—which I did, although the New York cheesecake did make me a little homesick.

Not that I missed the Big Apple per se. It was Dana, the love of my previous life. Amy had been a welcomed distraction, but the promise of something new and wonderful had blown up in my face despite my best efforts. I realized as I paid the check and walked out, that the pain of the losses I'd been made to endure would likely stay with me for a very long time.

Although I'd never been a Boy Scout, I've always believed in being prepared. That's why I'd gone to Bill Sherman's house. It's also why I walked into the pharmacy around the corner where I perused the self-serve condom display. I'd hoped to see phrases like leak proof or industrial strength, but found none. Nor could I spot the UL logo or the Good Housekeeping Seal of Approval. An endorsement by the CDC would have been reassuring, but in the end I had to decide between a desensitizing item, which seemed somewhat counterintuitive, and one that promised a warming sensation. *How warm must it be?*

Night Fire was an erotic inferno, if you know what I mean. The place looked kind of like a fun house, except for the enormous bouncer at the entrance, who never even gave me the once-over. I decided to check out the various attractions before making myself uncomfortable. The walls and floors were matte black beyond the cashier's cover charge cage. I'd never liked psychedelic black lights, but here they created an adult fantasyland where anonymity reigned and inhibitions, especially about parting with money, were left at the door. I saw girls everywhere. To Joey's credit, they were all beautiful. Some wore thong bikinis. Some wore bras and panties. They stood in the black halls that led to the private peep shows and they were willing dates at the entrance to the porn mini-theater. Something about a kid in a candy store came to mind, but there was nothing there for five cents.

Past the labyrinth, I realized the place was divided into two separate lounges. I peeked in the room to the right and noticed that the girl on stage behind the bar wore thigh-high black patent leather stiletto-heel boots and little else as she used the brass pole in ways the workers' comp underwriting board would have definitely disallowed. Another girl, barefoot and nearly naked, was actually dancing on the bar itself, navigating between the drinks, keeping her balance by holding onto a nearly invisible horizontal cable.

I turned to tour the left lounge and saw two women on stage who'd really cleaned up their act. Both were virtually nude, one lathering the other, alternately, in a shower show that never ran out of hot water.

I walked back into the lounge with the low wire act and ordered a drink. The music was loud and I had to shout a little to be heard. When the bartender set it down and signaled that it was ten dollars, I curled my finger so he'd lean in for my question as I handed him a twenty. "Is the boss around?"

"No. He didn't come in today."

"It must be nice to be the boss."

"Must be. What do you need?"

"I've got a business deal for him."

"You can try again tomorrow. He doesn't come in until six."

I nodded and backed away, leaving the drink on the bar. I looked past him at the babe in boots and ogled the goods, just like the other losers on either side of me. The girl was well-lit by a bank of theatrical lights in the ceiling. She was a beautiful blonde about Jenny Sherman's age. I took in all there was to see above the tall boots, including two small tattoos; a red rose high on the inside of her left thigh visible only when she spread her legs for an obscured glimpse at Eden, and a small orange and red three-pointed flame at the base of her spine.

She noticed the new kid on the block and stared at me. She licked her red lips, felt herself up, and personalized the view.

A little embarrassed, despite myself, I nodded in appreciation and put a ten in the huge brandy snifter tip-glass on the bar. Because she actually looked a little like Jenny, I imagined Bill Sherman's outrage and disappointment if he were to find his beautiful daughter displaying herself like that in a place like this.

I reached for my drink, but was thwarted by the barefoot chick dancing right on the bar as she stepped into position directly above me and squatted. Things were really getting up close and personal now. I elevated my gaze to her face, which was close enough to ask a question or two without raising my voice. But there was a certain blankness behind her theatrical expression of desire and I realized this wasn't the moment to further the investigation by interrupting her performance. I resisted the interlude, with the emphasis on lewd, as much as any hetero-male could have, but must admit that the closeness and scent of a seductive woman was getting to me. I dropped another ten in the tip-glass and set out in search of someone else to question.

I returned to the porn theater's entrance, where I was

approached by an Asian girl with a silky jet-black ponytail. She wore only a white lace push-up bra, matching panties, and white platform shoes. "I'm Lily. Would you like some company while you watch the movie?" She had less of an accent than I did.

"That would be nice."

She took my hand and walked me into the screening room-size theater. Several seats were occupied by more than one person. She led me to two seats in the last row and sat beside me. I glanced at the screen and saw, thanks to the magic of creative cinematography, a moving close-up. And by moving, I don't mean poignant.

She asked, "Would you like me to touch you?"

Can you put on a pair of exam gloves first? "Sure."

A few seconds passed and nothing happened. Then I realized she was waiting for the cash. I took out a twenty, handed it over, and whispered above the moaning, "We've missed the beginning. What's this movie about?"

She tucked the cash into her panties, unbuttoned my shirt and began caressing my chest. "It's about getting your rocks off. Would you like that?"

Who wouldn't? "I'd love it, but I'm recovering from major surgery to correct a rather serious case of assassinitis."

I don't know if she didn't hear me, or just wouldn't take no for an answer. She stood, maneuvered herself in front of me, and sat on my lap. "For another twenty I'll give you a lap dance you'll never forget. There's no need to be shy. No one can see us."

Reluctantly, I handed over another twenty and the motion started. I inquired, "Who owns this place?"

"Why do you want to know that?" she asked, without breaking her rhythm.

"I owe Joey some money, but he didn't come in today. I'd feel okay about leaving it with his boss."

"You can give it to me," she offered, holding out an open palm again.

"How did I know you'd say that?"

I burned through another twenty and asked one more time, "What's the owner's name?"

"Joey's the boss. He hires all the girls. That's all I know."

"I'd bet he requires an *in-depth* interview."

"You could say that."

"Would you like to interview for me at my hotel after you close? I've got plenty of cash."

"You're not a cop, are you?"

I remembered the deal I'd made with Deputy Delightful, but didn't hesitate long enough to raise a made-up eyebrow. "No. I'm not a cop."

"All right. We close at three."

The flick ended and the credits began to roll, which was a pointless waste of time because I never saw anyone's face. The theater lights brightened a little and she asked, "Would you like to stay for the next show?"

"I'd rather wait for the real thing," I said, thinking that getting the answers I was looking for would be more likely if I could talk to her away from this place.

"In that case, this is what you can look forward to, any way you want it." She stood in front of me in her platform shoes and bent over the vacant seat ahead of us so I'd get a good look at her from behind.

When she straightened up I noticed the orange and red three pointed flame tattoo at the base of her spine. I said, "I like your tattoo. I've seen it before on one of your friends here."

"That's the mark of Night Fire. Every girl that works here wears the brand."

"Is that Joey's idea?"

She nodded. "As far as I know it's always been part of the initiation."

"What are the other parts?"

"I'll show you later."

"I'm counting on it."

We left the theater and I headed for the restroom. When I came out I saw Lily talking to the gorilla at the door. Isn't it amazing how you can find trouble when you look for it? Despite our scheduled tryst, I feared I'd once again worn out my welcome. There were only two possibilities: Either she was clearing, with the alternate pimp, her after-hours rendezvous, or she was saying something like, "The dork I just danced for was asking a lot of questions. He said he owes Joey money."

I set out in search of the rear fire exit and found it at the far end of the room in which I'd talked to the bartender and watched Jenny Sherman's evil twin. From about twenty feet away I saw that one of those Emergency Exit Only alarm mechanisms was bolted to it. Then I noticed another gorilla on a stool a few feet to the left. He wasn't wearing any discernable uniform, but he was the only guy in the bar *not* watching the dancing babe. He was watching everyone else, including me.

He didn't seem to recognize me though, so I casually nodded hello and tried to blend in by getting another eyeful of the slut on stage. As I struggled to formulate an escape plan, I realized the act had changed. Boots had been replaced by an older, more buxom bleached blonde sporting a silver lamé G-string and a matching set of pasties with dangling tassels.

I decided to head back to a busy spot closer to the entrance and wait for a distraction at the door that might give me an opportunity to slip out. Fortunately, I didn't have to wait long before a party of perverts on a field trip filed in. I seized the moment, weaved between a few tramps, and slithered out past the paying crowd. I strode with purpose toward my rental car, but only made it halfway across the parking lot before hearing a deep voice calling after me.

"Hey you! Wait up, Buddy."

There were no other people in the lot. I ignored the demand and kept going, moving quickly.

"Hey, I'm talking to you. You in the black jacket. Wait a minute."

I still kept going, but I should have run because he caught me just as I reached the car.

He grabbed my shoulder and turned me around. "Lily told me you owe Joey money. Why don't you give it to me? I'll give it to him."

I had to look up to see his face. It was supported by a twenty-two inch neck. His shoulders were wide enough to block out the neon Night Fire sign behind him. He wore a black suit and his black hair was slicked back. I said, "I'll come back tomorrow and give it to him myself. No offense."

I turned toward the car door, but he stopped me again, this time a little rougher. "What's your name? Joey would want to know your name."

"Tell him Frank was here."

"Frank who?"

"Just tell him Frank. He'll know who I am."

"Frank who? Tell me your fuckin' name."

"Frank Lloyd Wright." What can I say? It had been subliminally planted there by Bill Sherman a few hours earlier.

He looked at me in a weird way, as if he'd heard that name somewhere before but had no idea where. "Give me some I.D."

Trying to show no fear, which was a good trick, I said, "Your job is to check I.D.s going in, isn't it? Not going out. I don't think your boss would appreciate you bothering customers this way.

Back off and I'll tell Fabiano you did a good job looking out for him."

This approach appeared to work for two seconds, but that wasn't enough time to get into the car. He grabbed me from behind and put me in a choke hold, his massive arms cinched around my throat. As my feet came off the asphalt I heard him say into my right ear, "Give me some fucking I.D. or I'll take it myself when you're fucking unconscious."

I tried to pull his arms down, but felt like a child being abducted by an adult. I couldn't breathe, the flow of air squeezed off as if someone had tied a knot in my windpipe. I let go to reach into my pocket with my right hand and the vise seemed to tighten that much more. Bright flashes of white light began popping in my eyes like silent fireworks. I grabbed the small plastic box Sherman had given to me and slid the safety switch to the *on* position with my thumb. I muscled my arm up, curled it back toward his head, jammed the top of the stun gun hard against his tree-trunk neck, and pressed the button. I heard the crackle almost as well as he did.

He dropped me, and dropped to the pavement behind me like a marionette with its strings snipped.

Fear didn't change to satisfaction until I was doing seventy again on 101 North. It took about ten miles for the spots before my eyes to subside. I rolled my head to uncrimp the muscles and blood vessels in my neck as my heart slowed to a reasonable rate. Then I yelled at the top of my happy lungs, "Fuck you, Joey, you murdering bastard! You're dead! You're fucking dead! You'll never hurt anyone else! And your big dumb-ass bouncer didn't even bounce when he hit the asphalt. How do you like that, you fucking son of a bitch!"

I finally settled down when I realized I hadn't accomplished anything. Aside from the shit-stirring scenario in Leland Drake's office as theorized by Deputy Mike Johnson, I'd assumed that the person or persons who'd sent Fabiano could well have been his boss at the club, if he'd had a boss. That went nowhere.

I considered going to see Drake again on Monday, although reconciling that with Johnson would be a tough one. At best, I'd be out of the loop after that. Some jail time for obstruction was certainly on the table. At least I had another day to think about it.

I decided to follow the never-ending path to a mythical place called closure, at least for the time being. I found the townhouse in North Beach at the address I'd memorized in May's house when I snatched the enlarged copy of Fabiano's driver's license. I thought the brownstone duplex with classy curb appeal would have looked quite at home near Manhattan's Gramercy Park. No one passing the ornate black lacquer raised-panel door with brass trim would have had any inkling that a fulltime degenerate and part-time murderer had lived inside.

I parked across the street and sat there staring at the residence, much the way I'd stared at the white house by the river. It was hard to imagine that the person who'd come and gone up and down the half-dozen stone steps in the light of day, or in the spill of two glary carriage lamps, had shot my wife and uncle to death three thousand miles away. I knew it was true, but that didn't make it easier to accept.

I sat there for the first hour remembering Dana and the heart and soul way she loved me. The second was spent reliving visits with my mother and father at my aunt and uncle's, first at the house in Richmond Hill even before I was born, thanks to the magic of home movies, then at the apartment in Kew Gardens, and finally in Forest Hills were it all ended. One by one they'd all passed away, the years turning like the pages of a book, until no time and no people were left.

I started the car a little after two in the morning. Twenty minutes later I locked myself inside the room I'd reserved on Lombard Street and sat on the bed, drained and assaulted. I could smell Lily on my pants, which turned me on before it turned me off, knowing Fabiano had fucked her. He'd fucked us all.

I tried my best to steam away any remnants of Night Fire in a long, scalding shower. I toweled off, wiped the steam from the bathroom mirror, and examined myself for bruises. Thankfully, there were none—one less thing to explain to Johnson.

I connected my phone charger so I wouldn't miss his call, set it on the table in the sitting area, and collapsed on the sheets—never more alone.

19

I answered the call on Monday at noon. In anticipation, I'd put on nicer new clothes—a decent pair of camel slacks, a blue and white striped dress shirt with an English spread-collar, and a navy blue blazer. I was in a busy diner on the far side of Lombard when my cell started vibrating.

"Where are you?" Mike Johnson asked.

"I'm in a restaurant having lunch." I knew that wasn't exactly the type of answer he was expecting, but I didn't want to kill the conversation before it started by telling him I was already in San Francisco. "What did you find out?"

"I'll tell you when I see you. I met with my lieutenant this morning and he cleared me to question Leland Drake. Do you still want to go?"

"What do you think?"

"I'm at the office we took you to the other night. Drive over and we'll go from here."

Evading the inevitable was impossible. "I'm not in Tahoe. I'm in San Francisco. I came down Saturday for a little sightseeing," which I actually did, in a depraved sort of way.

There was a long pause. He finally said, "I'm getting tired of this, Bennett. I thought we had an agreement."

"We do, Deputy. You can have all the fun and glory protecting and defending while I design buildings everyone takes for granted, but I thought it would be a good idea to take some time off in case Mr. Big knows where I work. When I realized that meant I was suddenly on vacation, I decided to drive down and be a tourist until I heard from you. We were going to wind up here anyway, right? Besides, if anyone is looking for me, they're probably looking up there."

"Why do I think you're full of crap?"

"Because it's in your nature not to believe anyone. That's why you're such a good cop."

"Right. So, what did *you* find out?" he asked.

"That sourdough bread is actually sour, and cable cars really use cables. Where should I meet you?"

"As long as you're talking about cable cars, go to the trolley turntable near the Ghirardelli. Do you know where that is?"

"Not really, but I'll find it."

"I'll pick you up there at three."

"Great. See you then." I hung up and finished my sandwich, somewhat relieved that Johnson hadn't intentionally forgotten to call, and that he hadn't hung up when I told him where I was.

I ordered a nice piece of Danish, wondered briefly if people from Denmark become homesick while eating their namesake pastry, and contemplated how I could waste the next three hours.

I climbed into Johnson's white Ram pickup at 2:55. He wore a gray Harris Tweed sports jacket with suede patches on the elbows, black slacks, and a white oxford button-down shirt with a maroon Jacquard tie. I inquired, "Are you still assigned to a desk?"

"Don't ask."

He took a couple of turns and we were soon headed crosstown via Van Ness on a cool and sunny Monday afternoon. I asked, "What else did you find out about Fabiano?"

"He'd been hooked more than a few times for pandering, assault, possession and sale of controlled substances, and receiving stolen property. And those are only the times he got caught."

"Does hooked mean arrested?"

Johnson nodded. "That's what we call it out here. I think the cops call it a *collar* where you come from, most likely from the days when they grabbed a perp by the back of his collar to take him in."

"If Fabiano had such a long record, why was he out, running a strip joint instead of being *in* the joint?"

"He beat a lot of it—probably had a good lawyer. His prints showed him in the system early on for an A & R he'd committed on Postal Service property, which got him five years in the federal lockup at Lompoc in Santa Barbara County when he was only eighteen. He was due to be paroled in three, but got another ten added on for manslaughter while he was inside."

I was taken aback even though the man had murdered two people that we know of, and tried to shoot me the night before last. "What's an A & R?"

"Assault and robbery."

I thought about the big bruiser I'd left on the pavement outside Night Fire and contemplated his connection to Fabiano. I also wondered how long it took him to get up, if he'd gotten up at all. That plagued me on and off over the last day and a half. I reminded myself again that Sherman had told me the stun gun was non-lethal, so I put it out of my mind once more. "What about known associates?"

"A couple of names popped up, but if you think I'm going to share them with you, you're dreaming."

I couldn't blame Johnson there. Despite my reputation for honesty, my actions of late were proving I couldn't be trusted, at least with regard to the promises I'd made to stay out of it. I knew I was lucky he'd shown up at all. "What about Drake? You said you'd check him out."

"There was no hit when I ran his name through NCIC."

"Forgive me, Deputy, but I don't remember any of my professors mentioning the NCIC. Perhaps you could tell me what those letters stand for."

"National Crime Information Center."

"And if you don't mind me asking, what is it?"

"It's an FBI database."

"Thank you. I know you're really good at what you do, but if you're going to be my training officer, expounding a little more on such things would be helpful."

"You really *are* dreaming, Bennett."

"Apparently. So, getting back to Drake, you found nothing on him at all?"

"He's a wealthy celebrity, probably hobnobbing around with High Society. What did you expect, a conviction for sticking up a convenience store?"

"Hey, that's almost funny, Johnson. I'm glad to see you keep loosening up, even if we're not getting anywhere."

Johnson turned left on Market Street and pointed the truck toward the distant clock tower on the Embarcadero.

I asked, "Where are we headed, Drake's office?"

"I spoke to your pals this morning. Stein and DiCarlo. They

said to say hello, by the way."

"That's nice. What about Officer Millhouse? Did I get any regards from her?"

"Nope."

"Of course not."

"They said the cash in your uncle's safe-deposit box had been sent from the Federal Reserve's twelfth district headquarters in San Francisco to a Norcal Commerce Bank branch right here on Market Street." He reached into his shirt pocket, pulled out a folded piece of note paper, and handed it to me.

I deciphered the scrawl and started scanning the numbers on storefronts to see if we were going in the right direction, and on which side of the street to look. "It should be ahead on the right. What about the money you found under the seat in Fabiano's Suburban? Were you able to trace where it came from?"

"No. The bills weren't new."

I spotted the bank in question with only two blocks remaining before the thoroughfare ended at the water. "There it is," I said, pointing to the sign above the sidewalk.

Johnson parked the truck around the corner on the ground floor of a multi-level parking garage and we walked back to the main drag in silence, except for him saying, "If you speak in there without being spoken to, I'll shoot you."

We entered the bank and Johnson stopped for a moment to observe the activity throughout the floor, I think to be certain we weren't walking into the middle of a holdup by sheer bad luck. Apparently satisfied nothing out of the ordinary was happening, he headed for the new accounts and loan application area, a significant portion of the bank characterized by large desks arranged in rows on rust-colored commercial carpet. He approached the nearest available employee, showed his badge, and said, "I'd like to see the bank manager, please."

"Certainly." The woman stood and walked to what might be described as an open office in the corner with more substantial furniture. She relayed the message to a white-haired gentleman behind the desk who stood and followed her back to us. He wore a dark gray, three-button, pinstriped flannel suit, a white shirt, and a black tie with silver stripes.

"I'm Stanley Collier," he said, extending his hand.

Johnson showed his badge again and identified himself. He introduced me as his associate and I shook Stanley's hand as well.

Collier then led us to his desk. After everyone was seated, he said, "How can I help you today?"

"We're in the middle of a rather unusual investigation," Johnson began. "We're following a money trail that started in this bank and stretched all the way to the East Coast. The Federal Reserve confirmed it by the serial numbers on currency confiscated in New York City. We're in the process of obtaining a court order to examine the detailed account activity of someone we believe to be one of your depositors, who may in fact be the victim of identity theft, but because of jurisdictional issues there've been a few delays. What we need to know now is if that person actually has an account in this branch. That's all."

The bank manager didn't respond at first. Then he said, "I'm afraid I'll have to wait for that court order before I can release any information at all about one of our customers. We take the privacy and security of our clients very seriously."

Deputy Johnson continued without hesitation. "I can appreciate your fiduciary responsibilities, Mr. Collier, but time is of the essence. Lives are at stake. We're trying to head off a very dangerous situation. Two people have already been murdered, and we've thwarted an attempt on a third person two nights ago. We're racing the clock on this one. How would you feel tomorrow if someone was killed tonight because you failed to simply say yes or no?"

Stanley Collier drummed his fingers on the armrests of his high back swivel chair. His skin was starting to glisten, even in the drab fluorescence.

Johnson spoke again before Mr. Uncomfortable could answer a second time. "There is one more issue for you to consider."

"What's that?"

"Because of the identity theft component of this investigation, we suspect some degree of negligence with regard to allowing an unauthorized party to allegedly gain access to the account in question." Then, to my surprise, Johnson turned to me and asked, "How long before you can have someone here to examine the bank's records?"

I curled my lower lip and replied, "If I make the call now, I could have the first team here when Mr. Collier opens tomorrow. But to tell you the truth, I think the negative publicity, a possible unintended consequence, would prove to be an even bigger inconvenience."

"You're probably right about that," Johnson agreed before turning back to the bank manager, who was eyeing me with disdain. "Mr. Collier, we need your help—and we need it right now. Does Leland Drake have an account in this branch: Yes or no?"

"The artist?"

"The one and only."

Collier froze for another long moment. Then he said, "Would you mind showing me an I.D. card that matches your badge?"

I just sat there and stared at the guy while Johnson produced a black leather wallet, unfolded it, and held it up for Collier to read.

"Pine County. That's a long way from here." Not only was he trying to cover his own ass, he was buying time while deciding whether or not to answer the question.

Johnson said, "New York is even further. We're running out

of time, Mr. Collier. Leland Drake: Yes or no?"

The man nodded slowly—almost imperceptibly, in fact.

"Thank you. That'll do for now. You've done the right thing. We'd appreciate it if you kept this visit confidential. Lives and reputations are on the line."

"I understand."

"I'm sure you do. Thanks for your time."

Once outside Johnson said, "Drake's office is nearby, isn't it?"

"Two blocks."

"Good. Let's see if he's in."

I checked my watch. "It's late. He might be gone for the day."

"Then we'll pay him a visit at home, and hope he's not gone completely."

As we walked toward the Drake building at the end of Market Street, I considered the implications of what we'd just learned. I carried a lot of emotional baggage those two blocks, including the anticipation of seeing Amy again. I've never been a very good mind reader, but when I glanced at Mike Johnson moving in stride beside me, I had the distinct feeling that he and I were finally on the same page.

20

"I'm so glad you're all right," Amy Drake said as she hugged me, almost as if dinner in Luigi's had gone off without a hitch, we'd gone back to her place, made love all night, and promised to call each other the next day. I had the sense she might have been even more physical if her old high school flame hadn't been standing right there with me, but that impression was more likely attributable to a bad case of wishful thinking, an affliction that distorted my judgment every time I laid eyes on her. "My grandmother told me what happened. It's unbelievable. I wanted to call you, but I only had your work number."

She also hugged Mike Johnson and said, "It's been a long time. How have you been? You look great."

"Thanks. So do you."

I couldn't have agreed more. She was gorgeous. She wore a couture plum suit with a fitted skirt hemmed a couple of inches above the knee, sheer nylons, plum pumps, and a pure-white

Nehru-neck silk blouse. Her sea green eyes set amidst the palest plum shadow were almost mystical. Silky and lustrous abundant auburn hair framed the living portrait to perfection.

"I heard you became a police officer," she said to Johnson.

"A deputy with Pine County."

"Are you married?"

"Yes."

"Wow, it has been a long time, hasn't it? Did I know her?"

"No. She didn't go to our school."

"Any kids?"

"A boy and a girl."

"Oh my God, that's wonderful. Show me your pictures," she said. "I know you've got pictures."

I studied her expression while Johnson dug out a different leather case than the one he'd produced for Stanley Collier. I suspected her mind was suddenly taking a frantic stroll down memory lane, wondering what it might have been like if she'd been the one to marry him, anxious to see the children that could have been her own.

She looked at the photos and smiled. "They're beautiful. Your wife, too. You have a wonderful family."

All I came away with was that she was a damn good diplomat and an even better actress. I could be wrong, but if I had to guess at the state of her feelings at that moment, I would say that she was over it. I would also say Mike wasn't, but I already knew that. Not that I could blame him. One look at her and you knew she was the type of woman no man with sight could ever forget.

"What about you?" he asked.

She shook her head. "I haven't had time for anything but my career. I guess you could say everything comes with a price."

Acknowledging the spacious office and splendid bay view Johnson said, "It looks like you've done well."

I would say the office was anything but austere, unlike her grandfather's. The light gray carpeting was plush, and I thought the cherry wood furniture conveyed authority without being overbearing. I'll concede that the trappings were appropriately gender neutral, except perhaps for the pink porcelain vase on the corner of her desk. It was filled with fresh flowers, but not the ones I'd brought. I did the calendar math. I'd selected white roses with unopened blooms on Friday and this was only Monday. I could have been dead already, but the flowers wouldn't have been.

"Thanks," she said. "I've worked hard for it, even if nepotism got me through the door."

She turned to me and said, "I'm sorry I walked out on you at Luigi's. It sounded like you were using me to get to May. It really did. I thought about it afterwards and realized you weren't. When I remembered you tried to protect her by not giving her name and address to the police in New York, I felt pretty stupid for being so hard on you and embarrassing you like that." Then, realizing she may have said too much in the presence of a policeman, she tried to change the subject. "Why don't you both sit down and tell me why you're here."

"We've actually come to talk with your grandfather," Johnson began, "but the lobby security officer told us he didn't come in today."

"No, he didn't," she agreed. "Is there something I can help you with?"

"I've got a few routine questions for him."

"About what?"

"If you don't mind, Amy, I'd rather speak to him directly."

"You can talk to him all you want, but I'd like to know why, Mike. He's my grandfather."

"I just want to get a few things out of the way. That's all. I've spoken to May and now I need to chat with Leland so I can move on to other areas of the investigation. There's nothing for you to worry about."

Reluctantly, she let it go and said, "May told me you shot the man who came looking for Robert."

"I had to. He left me no choice."

"That must be awful for you. I can't imagine shooting someone."

"Don't even try."

"May told me Saturday he's in a coma. Did he come out of it yet?"

"No," Johnson replied. "But there is one thing we do know. He's the one who murdered Robert's wife and uncle."

"How can you be sure?"

"We heard him say so, more or less. And I'm confident the gun he had was the one used in New York. Ballistics tests should confirm that shortly."

She winced, as if imagining the carnage. "Who is he?"

Johnson reached into his jacket, pulled out a white piece of paper, unfolded it, and handed it to Amy. It was the photocopy of Fabiano's license. "Have you ever seen him?"

She studied the image and shook her head. "No." Then she shuddered and held the duplicate at arm's length, letting it dangle between two fingers. "Get this away from me, please."

Johnson refolded the copy and put it back in his pocket.

"Why did he do it?" she asked.

"Someone paid him."

"I mean, why would anyone want that?"

"That's what we're trying to figure out."

"Do the doctors expect that creep to pull through?"

He hesitated for a moment, I assume dealing with the fact that Fabiano was already dead, and he'd been the one to end his life. "They do."

Concerned, she said, "I hope he does for your sake. It'll be easier for you to live with."

"To tell you the truth, I'm all right with it. He's a killer. I only want him to survive so he can talk."

Then Johnson smiled thinly and said, "It's great to see you again. I'm sorry it wasn't a happier occasion."

She hugged him once more, pecked him on the cheek, and said, "Take care of yourself and your family. You're very lucky."

I imagined him saying, *I'd have been luckier if it had all happened with you.* But, of course he didn't. Instead he headed for the door, perhaps to conceal those very words, or perhaps to give me a minute alone with Amy.

When he was gone I said, "I want to see you again."

She stared at me in silence and without expression, either to keep me in suspense or to buy time while composing her thoughts—I don't know which. Finally, she smiled and simply said, "I was hoping you'd say that."

I reached for her, pulled her to me, and kissed her on the lips—lingering as long as I dared, vaguely aware that lately I'd gotten pretty good at wearing out my welcome. I inhaled her and the faint scent of perfume that had mingled with her own essence blew across my heart like a whisper's breath over glowing embers. It took only a few seconds for an old familiar warmth to spread through each and every strand of my being.

As our lips parted and my eyes opened, her face only an inch from mine, something stopped me from asking, *was it as good for you as it was for me?* The dependable little voice at the back of my head was repeating a mangled fortune cookie proverb subconsciously filed away for future reference: *If you're afraid of hearing the answer, don't ask the question!*

21

Johnson used his cell to phone the Marin County Sheriff's Office as soon as we returned to his truck. He spoke to the ranking officer and summarized the case in a professional parlance, using an economy of words totally unknown to any politician. He concluded with a request for backup to meet us at Drake's lair, including a second unit to cover the rear. He supplied the address and set the ETA at one hour.

We left the city, considering along the way the possible reasons why Drake hadn't gone to work that day, which included a nagging suspicion that he'd already fled the country. Obviously, he hadn't gotten the call he'd expected from Joey late Friday night confirming my death.

I imagined the call he probably *did* get a year earlier after Fabiano had walked out of my uncle's apartment. It made me bristle with rage. Johnson let me vent for a couple of miles before subjecting me to another one of his humorless warnings. This lecture began as we crossed the Golden Gate Bridge and ended after we'd passed the hillside houses and houseboats of picturesque Sausalito. He then forced me to swear another vow of silence, this one to be implemented when we reached Drake's house, which I really didn't think was going to be all that difficult because I'd been living like a monk anyway.

In fact, it was his authoritative monologue that actually calmed me down, at least to some degree, pointing out that his methods were now getting results. He also shared the cop-to-cop telephone conversation he'd had earlier with Stein and DiCarlo. Although the NYPD had no idea who'd commissioned the murders, they did feel strongly that art was somehow an integral part of the motive, partly because of the strange little copy they'd recovered, the one I'd identified in the basement of the station house. They'd also told him about the larger painting that had been on the easel in the apartment at the first crime scene, but not at the second—a fact I'd mentioned in my Tahoe condo before Fabiano showed up. It was their belief that the killer had taken it and, unless it had been destroyed, the money-man behind the murders was now in possession.

"Based on Officer Millhouse's description of the missing painting, do you think you'd recognize it if you saw it?" Johnson asked.

"Probably."

"Good. Look for it when we get in there. I don't think I'll be able to get a search warrant. As it stands now, we don't have enough probable cause. Not yet, anyway."

"Great. How did I know you were going to say that?"

Leland Drake's sprawling estate was located in a wooded section of Marin just to the west of Mount Tamalpais. Even I could peg the two sedans parked on the shoulder about a hundred feet from the stately entrance as unmarked police vehicles. Four detectives got out to meet us as we pulled up behind the second car.

Everyone identified themselves by name, including me. Then Johnson laid down a little background. "Robert's not on *The Job*," he began. "A year ago a shooter named Joey Fabiano executed a contract on his uncle in New York City for reasons unknown. Unfortunately, Robert's wife was in the apartment at the time so she was also killed. No arrests were ever made. Fast-forward to this past Friday. Robert met Leland Drake for the first time and then, a few hours later, Fabiano tried to kill him. That's why I want to talk to Drake. That, and the fact that sixty thousand dollars found by the NYPD in the vic's safe-deposit box was traced back to Drake's bank by the serial numbers."

I was glad Johnson didn't misrepresent me as his partner so, if push came to shove, none of them would rely on me as armed backup. I know that's why he played it straight. Fooling the bank manager on Market Street was one thing. Involving four detectives at the home of the man allegedly responsible for a double homicide and one attempted murder was another.

"What happened to Fabiano?" one of the men asked.

"I shot him outside Robert's condo and he expired at the scene before he could tell us anything, but no civilian knows he went DOA, present company excepted." Johnson replied.

"What was Fabiano's game?" another asked.

"He ran a strip club south of San Mateo called Night Fire. He had a long sheet which included a stretch in Lompoc, extended ten years for manslaughter while inside."

"How was he associated with Drake?" the first man asked.

"Unknown."

"You said Robert met Drake for the first time three days ago," another asked. "How did that happen? Is he working the case himself? Did he hire a PI? What's going on?" Then the detective looked at me.

"It's a long story," Johnson said. "But suffice it to say it stems from a bizarre coincidence."

As if on cue, all four detectives exchanged dubious glances. There was that word again. Talk about burglary, robbery, rape, and homicide all day long and it's business as usual. But if you want a cop's neck hair to stand on end, just mention the word coincidence.

"What's he doing here?" the first one asked.

"He's helping with the investigation. He knows more about the case than anyone."

They looked at each other again.

"He's going to wait in the car, right?" the same one asked.

"No. He's going in with me."

They were all shaking their heads now. "Taking the next of kin along when you're going to hook someone is crazy," the fourth one said. "You've got to know that."

"I don't have enough for an arrest yet. It's just an interview."

"But Drake doesn't know that."

"You're right, but let's not make this into something it's not. I'm here to interview Leland Drake. I thought a little backup would be a good idea in case he's got other people in there. If he was going to run, he's already gone. If it turns into an arrest, I'll make it."

After a long moment the detective who had been the first to speak asked, "Where do you want us?"

"The estate looks enormous," Johnson said. "Does anyone know if there's another way in or out?"

"There is," the same cop replied. "The back of the property runs along Mill Road. There's a gate back there. It's a little overgrown, but it's there."

Johnson said, "I'd like one car to cover that exit. I'd like the other to follow us in the front and hang back at the entrance. Who can give me a portable?"

The one standing closest reached into his jacket, pulled a small Motorola walkie-talkie from his belt, and handed it to Johnson. Then he said, "You know you're talking about Leland Drake, the famous artist, right?"

Johnson nodded. "Yep."

The electric gates of Glenshire were closed. I read the name of the estate proclaimed in Old English characters above the ornate wrought iron, or should I say *overwrought* iron to be more accurate? Instead of buzzing the intercom and smiling for the camera, Deputy Johnson took out his cell and keyed the number May Drake had given him. He identified himself to the servant who answered the phone and asked to speak to King Drake. Once Drake was on the line, Johnson repeated his authority for the benefit of the art world royal directly, requested entry, and two minutes later the gates parted. He made no mention of the peasant in the passenger's seat, or anyone else.

Unable to see the main house from the road, we followed the meandering driveway across manicured grounds until the castle came into view. The garages and chauffeur's quarters were to the right. Johnson steered toward the porte-cochere to the left and parked under the pitched slate roof. I accompanied him to the massive oaken front door set in stone beneath a gothic pointed arch and said, "What, no moat?"

Leland could have opened it himself, I'm sure, but he undoubtedly wanted to afford the visiting civil servant the full effect of

Drakedom. We followed the butler across the marble floor in the foyer, past the grand stairs, and down a narrow passageway that should have been lit by flaming torches. It cut through the core of the house to a travertine courtyard.

Drake was sitting at a patio set, facing the pool, Jacuzzi, and formal gardens. I noticed a martini, and the shaker from which it was poured, on the round glass table in front of him, along with a copy of *Barron's* and a pair of readers with gold frames. He wore a powder blue golf shirt and a pair of khakis. He didn't turn to acknowledge us until we approached. Then he stood.

Johnson showed his badge and identified himself. He gestured toward me and said, "You've already met Robert Bennett on Friday."

Drake feigned cordiality well, but I knew he was less than thrilled to see me, especially since he'd paid to have me killed.

We seated ourselves on the cushy outdoor chairs situated around the table. Johnson could have said something to break the ice like, "You may remember I dated your granddaughter in high school. Or, you've got a beautiful little castle here," but he didn't. He just jumped right in. "How did you know Maxwell Bennett, Mr. Drake?"

If I'd had my way, I would have been even more direct, jamming the stun gun against his pharmaceutically assisted nuts, but only after a crackling visual demo that would have scared the reconstituted crap out of Frankenstein. *Why did you have my family killed, you son of a bitch? Why did you try to have me killed?* We'd made that leap by deductive reasoning after leaving May's on Saturday morning. Now we knew he had an account in the very same bank from which the cash in my uncle's safe-deposit box had come. That was good enough for me. Of all the banks in all the cities and towns of one hundred and sixty-three thousand square mile California, the most populous state in America, home to more than thirty-eight million people, with the sixth largest economy in the whole damn world, what were the odds?

Drake looked at Johnson and answered, "I didn't know him. I knew of him."

"How did you know of him?"

"My ex-wife. She was an emotional wreck when I met her. She was on the rebound. She'd met him before she met me. He was supposed to move west to be with her. He never did and she never got over it. That's the whole tear-jerker in a nutshell."

"What else do you know about him?"

Drake looked at me and said, "May told me more than I needed to know."

"Such as?"

Turning back toward Johnson, Drake ignored the inquiry and asked, "Why are you here?"

Johnson hesitated for a moment. Then he disregarded Drake's question and asked, "What kind of arrangement did you have with Maxwell Bennett?"

"Arrangement? What do you mean… arrangement? I just told you I didn't know the man."

"We think you did. You were involved in something together that went wrong. If you tell us what it was, things will be a lot easier for you. Cooperation goes a long way in court."

"I don't know what you're talking about and, apparently, neither do you."

"Really? Then how did your money get into his safe-deposit box?"

"What money?"

"The police found sixty thousand dollars in New York that came from your bank. That's what money."

"My bank?"

"Your bank."

"I'm an artist, Deputy. Not a banker."

"Excuse me. The Norcal Commerce Bank on Market Street only two blocks from your office. The one in which you have an account."

"Am I the bank's only depositor?"

Johnson leaned forward planting his elbows on the table. "Let me share something with you. I don't like it when people break the law. And I really hate it when people intentionally harm other people. But the thing I despise most about criminals is that they think the cops are stupid. Is that what you think? Do you think we're stupid, Mr. Drake?"

Drake shrugged. "You're mistaken. That's what I think."

"Am I mistaken that you sent Joey Fabiano to kill Robert Friday night?"

"I didn't send anyone anywhere. And I certainly didn't send anyone to kill anybody."

"How do you know Joseph Fabiano?"

"I don't know anyone by that name."

"Okay," Johnson said, leaning back in his chair. "Let's review, shall we? Maxwell Bennett was murdered in New York City. The police found money from your bank in his safe-deposit box, but you had nothing to do with that. Is that right?"

"That's right."

"Robert Bennett was in your office this past Friday afternoon asking where you were when his uncle and wife were murdered a whole year before, and then, a few hours later, the same murderer with the same gun comes after him, but you had nothing to do with that either. Is that right?"

"Right again."

"So why am I not surprised that the five grand I found under the seat in Fabiano's SUV also came from your bank? Oh, I'm sorry. Did I forget to mention that?"

I knew from the conversation we'd had earlier that the third happenstance was a bluff, but I doubted Drake did, although he still didn't look particularly frazzled, perhaps because he'd had three days to prepare for our visit.

"I'll ask you again," Johnson said. "How do you know Fabiano?"

"And I'll tell you again. I don't know anyone by that name."

"Let me show you his picture. That'll give you the opportunity to say, 'Oh, *him!* I didn't know you meant *that* Joey Fabiano.'" Johnson pulled out the photocopy of Joey's license, unfolded it, yanked the paper taut with a snap, and slid it across the table.

Drake put on his glasses, reached for the facsimile, leaned back in his chair, and looked at it for only a moment. Then he floated it back across the glass. "I've never seen that man before."

"Well, we'll see what *he* says when he regains consciousness, especially when we offer him a deal. You see, I shot him more than once outside Robert's place, but the doctors think he'll pull through. The funny thing about scum like Fabiano is that, even though they have no compassion for their victims, they always give it up in five minutes to save themselves. Personally, I don't believe in plea bargaining. Deals belong on car lots, not in court. If it were up to me, everyone would be prosecuted to the fullest extent of the law, but fortunately for the perps in the system it doesn't always work that way. Some of them catch a break for giving up information, but there's only room for one deal per crime and it goes to whoever talks first. Right now, since Fabiano is still in a coma, that could be you. But once he rolls over, you get everything that's coming to you, which means, not only a nice anus-stretching stint for conspiracy to commit murder right here in the Golden State, but also extradition to New York for a double, probably to be served consecutively. At your age that means the only way you're getting out is in a pine box. Is that clear enough?"

I'm giving you the chance to save yourself right now, before Joey gives you up. Why did you have Fabiano kill two people? Tell me what this was all about and the deal is yours. I'll help you write it." Johnson stopped talking and gave Drake a chance to mull over the things he'd just heard.

But Drake spoke immediately. "I don't know that character you keep referring to." He pointed to the photocopy, once again in Johnson's hand. "In fact, I don't know what you're talking about at all. Look around. I'm a wealthy man. I'm an artist, not a mobster. Why would I do such a thing?"

I did look around to see how the man who'd changed my life by ending the lives of everyone I'd cared about lived his life. The house had been constructed of limestone blocks, emulating many great castles and cathedrals in Europe. The architecture was decidedly gothic, replete with pointed arches, defensive parapets, and grotesque gargoyles protruding from the fascia just below the roof. The overall effect was to create an atmosphere of gloom and doom, which largely defines and characterizes the gothic age. It occurred to me, as I connected the man's home with his heart, that it was, indeed, the opposite of inviting. That was the second disconnect. His office at the top of the Drake building on the Embarcadero near Market Street had been the first. That, too, was incongruously cold, especially if compared to the delightful warmth for which his art had become famous.

Then I noticed a woman standing behind a second story window. She was looking down on the courtyard and the meeting taking place. In fact, she was now looking at me. She had long blonde hair and appeared to be naked, but the beveled-edge small glass panes that comprised the gothic window distorted the image. I guessed she was Drake's trophy wife, the gold-digging slut I'd seen on his laptop. But because I'd viewed the screen for only a moment, most of which was spent, to be completely honest, evaluating various physiological features other than her face, I couldn't be sure.

I was a little surprised that she didn't back away and retreat from view, knowing that I'd noticed her, but there she stood, looking directly at me. We stared at one another for what felt like a long time; long enough, as it were, for the questioning of Leland Drake, despite its importance, to become little more than garbled background noise. Eventually, a growing sense of embarrassment, which my inner pig tried to ignore, compelled me to look away.

I focused on the tête-à-tête at the table again just in time to see Drake turn to me and say, "I'm sorry Mr. Bennett has lost his wife and his uncle, I really am, but I had nothing to do with it. And to tell you the truth, I find it quite offensive that you've come to my home to accuse me of such a thing. This conversation is now over and neither of you are welcome here. It's time for you to leave."

Almost more than the denial, his choice of words hit me the wrong way, striking a raw nerve and jolting me back to reality. I didn't *lose* them. I would have lost them if we'd been in a crowd, I'd looked away, and when I turned around again they were gone. I would have lost them if they'd fallen overboard at sea when no one was looking. They would have been lost if their flight had plummeted from the sky. Amelia Earhart was lost. Dana and Mack weren't lost. Someone had taken them from me. And it wasn't even Fabiano. He'd just been an instrument, little more than the cold nickel-plated nine millimeter Taurus automatic he'd pointed at me. Someone had sent him to Maxwell Bennett's one bedroom apartment on the fourth floor of a red brick building on a delightful Sunday afternoon in the spring of the previous year to commit murder. Someone who was now two feet away from me, looking right at me, staring directly into my eyes and lying through his teeth.

"You're full of shit, Drake," I said returning his stare. "How would you like me to get out of this chair and show you what it feels like to be lost? How'd you like that, you old bastard?"

I heard Johnson say, "That's enough, Robert."

"Or better yet, how'd you like me to go upstairs and throw your beautiful wife headfirst through the window right in front of you. Then you'd know what it feels like to have someone you love taken from you. Not lost, you son of a bitch. Murdered!" I glanced back up at the corner window, but the damsel was gone.

"I said, that's enough," Johnson commanded in his most resonant and authoritative voice. "I think you should wait in the truck."

"Fuck that. And fuck the deal you're offering this old prick. I think *you* should wait in the truck and give me the time I need to hold court right here. This is a courtyard, isn't it? I've dreamed about being judge, jury, and executioner if the time came. Now I've heard enough. As far as I'm concerned, this is the time. And this is as good a place as any. In fact, knowing how my uncle died in his own living room, it would only be fitting that I beat the bastard responsible to death right in his own backyard. Go ahead, Johnson. Do me a favor. Wait in the truck. I'll only need ten or fifteen minutes. Then I'll turn myself in. I promise. Okay?"

Mike Johnson stared at me with a look that was hard to read, apparently thrown off guard by my forbidden outburst. I expected him to spring from his seat, drag me back to his pickup, and handcuff me to the door, but he didn't. Instead, his eyebrows slowly rose, as if he were actually considering my idea. Then he turned to Drake and simply stared at the man, giving him equal time.

Drake was silent, but the air of defiant confidence that accompanies great wealth—the ability to buy anything or anyone, was abandoning him.

Johnson looked at me again and said, "I can't do that, Robert.

But I may have to excuse myself to use the bathroom."

I cracked a devious smile and said, "You know what they say, Deputy. When you've got to go, you've got to go."

Johnson looked at Drake and said, "It's over. Tell me what your arrangement was with Maxwell and what went so wrong that you risked everything. I'll try to understand."

"I told you, I didn't even know the man."

"If you tell me, I'll help you survive it. I'll get the D.A. to argue the case like this: You panicked and overreacted. You tried to contact Fabiano to cancel the contract, but you couldn't reach him in time."

That sounded painfully familiar. DiCarlo had said the same thing to *me!*

I shivered a little as Johnson continued giving Drake a graceful way to confess. "Now you can't sleep at night because of the awful guilt. The jury will buy it. Think about it. I'm giving you a chance to save yourself."

"I don't know what you're talking about. And furthermore, I resent you coming into my home and accusing me of something I didn't do."

"All right," Johnson said. "In that case I'll ask a question you *can* answer without lying. Where's the nearest bathroom, or better yet, the farthest?"

Leland Drake stood and said, "I've heard enough. Get out of my house."

Johnson remained seated, but I noticed his eyes refocus on Drake's hands. I said, "I know where it is. We passed it in the passage of dread. It's halfway between the crypt and the dungeon."

It was at that moment that we heard the door through which we'd entered the courtyard open and close. I saw Johnson's right hand move reflexively into his jacket as we both stood and turned to face the portal, expecting to see either the butler, or a contingent of knights. Instead, we saw a statuesque blonde wearing only a black thong bikini and heels. She was sashaying toward us like a beauty pageant contestant strutting her stuff on stage during the swim suit competition. She approached without the requisite pirouette, however, and said to Drake, "I'd like to soak a little before dinner. I hope you don't mind."

I couldn't tell if Drake was annoyed, embarrassed, or thankful that she'd appeared. "That's fine," he said. "Our guests were just leaving."

"Won't you introduce me to your friends before they go?" she asked.

"This is my wife, Mona," Drake begrudgingly announced.

I extended my hand. "I'm Robert Bennett." Our eyes locked for the second time, and knowing I'd seen her naked, albeit at a distance and through glass, she held my hand four or five seconds longer than necessary. She was, indeed, the girl I'd seen on Drake's computer. And in person she was just as young, and even more seductive.

When the flirting ended, she repeated the social custom with Johnson, but for what I deemed to be of a normal duration. Then she looked at me again and briefly cast that unique and subtle smile that only emanates from deep within an interested woman. "It's nice to have met you. Visit us again." she said.

"Count on it," I replied.

She turned and kissed Drake on the cheek, as if he were *her* grandfather. Then, instead of standing beside him until we left, she turned and walked to the edge of the patio, then down the half-dozen steps that led to the spa so we could all watch her ass.

I've never been a violent man, but I knew beating Leland Drake to death right then and there would have filled me with a profound sense of satisfaction. Although it would not have brought Dana and Mack back to life, and such reprehensible behavior is not condoned by civilized people—two wrongs don't make a right and all that crap, I make no apology for wanting him dead, and for wanting him to understand why he would die. I don't know for sure if pummeling him into the travertine tile would have been the thing most likely to make me happy, if ever I could be happy again, but I can tell you this: Noticing the little orange and red three-pointed flame tattoo at the base of his young wife's spine as she stepped off the patio into the golden light of sunset was definitely a step in the right direction.

22

As Mona lowered herself into the Jacuzzi I turned to Leland Drake and said, "She's charming. Where did you two lovebirds meet?"

Pompous ass that he was, Drake mistook my facetiousness for envy. His scowl warmed to conceit and he said with a gloat, "At the club."

"What club would that be?" *Yacht, country, or strip?*

"The Mill Shadow Country Club."

"Wow. That sounds exclusive. The facilities must be impressive. But to tell you the truth, I don't play golf very often. I'd only join if I could get a good lap dance in the clubhouse while everyone else is chasing their dimpled little balls all over the place. Amenities like that are included, aren't they?"

"Goodbye. Let yourselves out the way you came in. The next time you want to ask me something, talk to my lawyer."

"Let's go, Bennett," Johnson said, gesturing for me to exit first.

I led the way back to the passage through which we'd come, but stopped just inside. I turned to Johnson and said, "He's lying."

He ignored me and said, "What the hell was that all about?"

"I'm trying to tell you. He's lying about not knowing Fabiano."

"Probably."

"Not probably. *Definitely!*"

"How do you know that?"

"Because the slut he called his wife was one of Joey's girls at Night Fire, that's how. That's the club he *really* meant."

"And just how do you know that, Bennett?"

"Did you see the flame tattoo above her ass?"

Johnson nodded. "What about it? Half the girls in America have a tattoo down there."

"That's no ordinary tramp stamp. It's the mark of Night Fire. Every girl who works there wears the brand. It's mandatory. It was part of Joey's initiation."

"I already asked once. How do you know that?"

"Never mind. Just be happy I do."

"I told you not to go there, didn't I? I warned you."

"Do you know what? I've had just about all of the warnings I can stand. How about a little gratitude for a change? You needed a reason for a search warrant and now I've given you one. Get on it."

Deputy Mike Johnson actually began to nod, which surprised the hell out of me. "Are you sure?" he asked.

"I'm sure. One of the girls with an identical stamp, a little Asian number named Lily, told me all about it while we were watching the Genitalia Film Festival. I actually asked her about it and she explained it to me. I'm telling you, all the girls in the place wear the brand—the exact same orange and red three-pointed flame in the exact same spot. Trust me on this, I saw it up close."

"All right. We'll take Drake down to the local lockup and hold him until we get the warrant so he can't destroy the missing painting, if he hasn't already. That'll give me a chance to sweat him outside his comfort zone. We'll take his wife, too."

"What about the butler?" I asked.

Johnson nodded. "Good thinking, Architect. We'll take everyone on the property."

He used the borrowed radio to call in the two Marin County cars. Six people in all had to be transported: Drake and his wife, the butler, cook, chauffeur, and gardener.

I thought I noticed some questionable eye contact between the chauffeur and Mona. And then between the gardener and Mona. I could have imagined it all, but I don't think I did. In fact, I could have imagined that she appeared to be the least upset of anyone in dealing with the police, almost as if she were used to it. If anything, it seemed as if she welcomed the excitement and the attention of strange men. When she'd held my hand a little too long, and batted her eyes at me right in front of her husband, I couldn't help but feel flattered, although in a perverted sort of way. Now not so much, suspecting that this exhibitionist/stripper/lap dancer/hooker would fuck anyone who could fog a mirror, and maybe even some who couldn't.

Johnson called his lieutenant and requested a search warrant for the premises, the subject of which was the painting that had been taken from Maxwell Bennett's easel. Ten minutes later the sheriff himself called Johnson. They'd talked earlier in the day, after Johnson's telephone conversation with Stein and DiCarlo. The only known information the sheriff lacked was the rundown on the events of the afternoon. What had started the week before as a notification by the NYPD to his department, that a person of interest in a double homicide in Queens was now living in his county, had turned into an attempted murder and the subsequent shooting of the suspect, one Joseph Fabiano.

To complicate matters, the person allegedly behind it all was a wealthy and respected celebrity artist. The sheriff was not about to let one of his subordinates make a decision that could result in a major media embarrassment, or worse—a costly lawsuit. He had demanded to be notified of any developments and had made it clear, according to Johnson, that he was to be the only one releasing any information or issuing executive orders. But when the time came for official action, he declared that the warrant should be issued by a New York court because the missing painting's relevance was the opinion of the New York authorities.

Johnson respectfully pointed out that the time it would likely take to get that accomplished would now move things well into the next day at best. Holding everyone in the Marin County lockup that long could be problematic, and it was imperative that the players be kept from moving or destroying the only evidence in the case that could link Drake to the crime scene.

Ultimately, the sheriff agreed and asked Johnson for a description of the painting that would be adequate and suitable for the wording on a warrant. Johnson handed the phone to me and conveyed the request. Although I'd never actually seen the painting with my own eyes, which I told the sheriff after identifying myself, I recounted Officer Millhouse's recollection of the picture that had made her homesick. I also relayed the fact that she was confident she could identify it if she saw it again. I thanked the man on the other end of the line and handed the phone back to Johnson. He recited the fax number into the phone, thanked his boss, and ended the call.

In the course of the next few hours, when threatened with complicity, Mona Drake admitted that she'd danced at Night Fire and confirmed Joey's initiation requirements. To his credit, Drake had told the truth about meeting her at the Mill Shadow Country Club. He had, however, omitted one minor detail. She'd been hand-delivered there by her pimp, none other than Joey Fabiano, a man he'd vehemently denied knowing. As it turns out, my little joke about the institution's amenities had been amazingly intuitive.

Juan, the gardener, admitted to having sexual relations repeatedly with Drake's wife, but insisted it was only because she'd threatened to turn him over to ICE if he refused. Mario, the chauffeur, admitted to having sexual relations repeatedly with her as well, but insisted it was only because she'd threatened to tell her husband that he'd forced himself on her in the back of the limo if he refused. Eve, the cook, was probably a good cook but was useless as a witness. Harry, the butler, would have probably been a better butler if Drake had treated him with any respect at all, but that condescension made him eager to roll over on his boss when given the opportunity, telling Johnson that although he'd never seen the painting in question, if it could be found anywhere, it was probably in a room believed to be Drake's studio on the top floor of the castle—a chamber that was always locked and strictly off limits to anyone.

Sometime later the warrant to search Glenshire emerged from the fax machine like an enormous lottery ticket.

23

I wanted to return with Johnson and the Marin County detectives to Drake's estate to execute the search warrant, but everyone agreed that playing it by the book, especially from this point on, which meant no unauthorized personnel where they didn't belong, would reduce the chances of the case being thrown out of court. Johnson promised to call me if he recovered the painting that had reminded Officer Millhouse of her youth.

For the first time in a long time I was actually optimistic. My mind went on a merry romp while I waited in the squad room, which once again included fantasizing about a relationship with the steamy female NYPD cop who would likely be the best witness in the trial if Johnson's search was fruitful.

That hormone-inspired moment retrained my one track mind on Amy, a woman I'd actually kissed only a few hours earlier, a woman I might, in fact, meet again outside the cold and formal confines of a courtroom. I pictured her beautiful face and captivating green eyes, her carnal scent still fresh in my mind. Then, true to the Bennett legacy, the cynicism in my chromosomes reached out and popped the warm and colorful daydream like a pin prick on a carnival balloon. There I'd soon be, positioned behind the prosecution, rooting for the district attorney, hoping to hear a guilty verdict for the charge of murder in the first degree with premeditation.

And there she'd be, seated behind her grandfather, hoping a money-is-no-object dream team of renowned attorneys at the defense table could set him free. Talk about a couple of star-crossed lovers!

I tried to occupy myself while waiting for Johnson's call. I wanted to interview each of the people taken from the Drake household myself, especially Mona, but that wasn't going to happen. They'd been separated and were being held incommunicado at least until the search was completed. Then they'd most likely be unemployed.

As the hours passed, my brief venture into the world of the optimistic became more and more unsettled until ultimately I began to feel like the proverbial fish out of water. Granted, Glenshire was enormous, and quite possibly laced with hidden passageways and secret chambers, but the wait was agonizing. At one point I imagined Johnson saying, *sorry I forgot to call*, as he carried the missing painting into the office like a triumphant warrior returning from the frontlines of the war on crime, but that never happened and the call never came.

My heart hit the floor when Mike and the Marin County team returned empty-handed. "Unless it's buried somewhere on the grounds, the painting that was described to you is not there," he said with a pronounced expression of disappointment.

It felt like the wind had been knocked out of me.

Then he reached into the right flap-pocket of his tweed sports jacket, pulled out a labeled and sealed transparent evidence bag, and held it up in front of my face. "But we did find this," he said, breaking into an uncharacteristic grin that stretched from ear to ear. "Do you recognize it?"

I looked at the small yellow gold heart that sat at an angle on a pile of tiny golden links along the crease at the bottom of the bag. The word *Pretend*, cut through and through in script, was readable even through the hazy plastic.

I felt like jumping for joy and collapsing into a miserable grief-stricken pathetic heap all at once. It took me a few minutes to compose myself. I dried the tears from my eyes, caught my breath, and said, "Oh, my God! I thought I'd never see that again. How did you find it?"

"We got lucky. It was out in the open."

"What do you mean?"

"A search warrant is very specific. It spells out exactly what you're looking for and the type of places you can look. You can't look for a three foot painting in a jewelry box. Whatever you found would be inadmissible in court. They call it Fruit of the Poisonous Tree. But this was sitting in a crystal dish on a dressing table in the bedroom. It was out in the open. Any evidence that's out in the open is admissible. It's a good thing you told me about it. With your testimony, the delicate necklace in this bag will be strong enough to convict Leland Drake."

I design things for a living. Big things: Buildings that shelter people from the elements and provide places for them to live and work—places that are, hopefully, as beautiful and impressive on the outside as they are comfortable and functional on the inside. But of all the things I'd ever designed, because it was for Dana, I've always liked that little pendant the most. Now I liked it even more.

Deputy Michael Johnson placed Leland Drake under arrest for the murders of Maxwell Bennett and Dana Bennett, and the attempted murder of yours truly. He might have done so when the innocent and naïve Mona Drake established an irrefutable connection between her former pimp and her present husband, but he'd chosen to wait for the *pièce de résistance*; what he thought would be the painting that had been on the easel in my uncle's apartment. What he found was even stronger—a custom-made one-of-a-kind personal item belonging to one of the victims. He read him his rights in a municipally austere interview room equipped with a video camera. I was permitted to watch from an adjacent viewing room through a one-way mirror. He tried to elicit a confession by pointing out that the little tattoo on Mona's back silently tied him to the triggerman even though a wife could not be forced to testify against her husband, although she did seem more than willing, as was her M.O. in general. He also informed Drake that he'd recovered Dana's pendant, evidence obtained with a valid search warrant linking him to the apartment in Queens where two people had been murdered. He went at him for some time, but got nowhere. He then let the Marin County boys process the arrest because it was made in their jurisdiction.

I watched them fingerprint Drake and a visceral hatred was slowly replaced by a calming sense of satisfaction. He stood there in silence, docile and defeated, distinguished on its way to extinguished, as his fingers were rolled, one by one, across the inkless electronic surface. Then his personal property was vouchered and he was led off to a private cell, which was actually a little homier than his home.

Leland Drake wasn't who he said he was. Or perhaps more importantly, he wasn't who everyone thought he was. His real name was Ralph Bertucci. Running his prints revealed his true identity and criminal record. Once upon a time he'd been convicted of an assortment of artistic crimes which included forgery, counterfeiting passports, driver licenses, bearer bonds, and stock certificates. Because a previous address was the federal penitentiary at Lompoc, Johnson contacted the prison authorities and learned that Bertucci and Fabiano had, indeed, been cellmates. That was something Johnson had suspected the moment Lompoc came up twice in the same investigation.

I couldn't help but think about May Drake. I'd considered, time and again, her cultured demeanor, remembering some of the things she'd said about art and the human spirit, about love and kindness, and about my uncle. He hadn't exactly left her standing at the altar, but failing to make California his new home so their lives could be joined in a manner more fulfilling than the postal service could provide, undoubtedly opened an abysmal void into which a sly con man with some questionable artistic abilities had soon stepped. Despite the fact that money did not appear to be a problem for the woman in the white house by the river, if I had to choose one word that best characterized the depth and breadth of her now solitary existence it would likely be *disappointing*. At that time, I hadn't even considered the fact that, according to Amy per our conversation over a couple of plates of pasta in Luigi's, May's son, the drunk, had died in a car wreck.

Now I not only felt sorry for myself. I also felt sorry for May Drake, who was really May Bertucci, but didn't know it yet.

Or did she? My first inclination was to believe she'd been duped, swept off her feet by a smooth-talking confidence man when she was most vulnerable, only to become an unknowing participant in some sort of ingenious and monumental game of art fraud. But what if she was in on it from the very beginning? What if she hadn't been played, but that together they'd played everyone else? What if she'd met Ralph when he was still Ralph and simply went along with the scheme, using her gallery, reputation, and business acumen to build an art empire based on a grand deception? Wouldn't that mean that she had, in fact, been the one to introduce Ralph Bertucci to Maxwell Bennett years ago? If that was the case, then most of what she'd said in the house, if not everything, had been Oscar-worthy lies, including having no knowledge of the murders. What if the whole damn thing had been her idea from the beginning? What if she'd created Leland Drake and crafted a world-renowned image based on exploiting the talents of Maxwell Bennett? Who better to know his potential? What if the resentment that had undoubtedly grown in the fertile garden of a woman scorned ultimately blossomed into a conspiracy to commit murder, when, a lifetime later, the fraud finally began to unravel?

Johnson and I had several telephone conversations in the days that followed, mostly filled with speculation about various elements of the case since Bertucci, AKA Drake, wasn't talking. It was my belief that Maxwell Bennett, my father's brother, my uncle, had actually been the one to paint each and every Leland Drake painting ever created. I'd come to that stunning, if not outlandish conclusion after obsessing about a painting I'd only heard about, but had never seen. Over and over I'd envisioned the painting that was described in the coffee room at the One-Seventeen, the one most likely lifted by Joey Fabiano, the one we couldn't find, neither with the search warrant for Drake's estate in Mill Valley, nor with the subsequent warrants for the Drake building on the Embarcadero, for Fabiano's townhouse in North Beach, and for the one and only Night Fire. The subject was a New England maritime town replete with a church steeple, a gazebo in the village square, lobster boats in a cozy little harbor, sea birds, and a classic lighthouse in the distance, which may have been done in a style reminiscent of American Impressionism— the signature style for which Drake had become famous.

So what the hell was it doing on my uncle's easel? I know my supposition sounds like a gigantic leap, but think of it this way. If Mack hadn't painted what certainly sounds more like a Drake than a Bennett, why had it been on an easel in the middle of his living room before he was murdered? What other explanation was there? There were only a limited number of possibilities: Mack had bought it, he'd stolen it, he'd won it, it had been a gift, someone had planted it there, it had fallen from the sky and he'd picked it up, carried it home, and placed it on the easel he'd used to paint his own pastime paintings instead of hanging it on the wall, or he'd painted it.

24

I decided not to return to Sherman and Essen for a while, not because I was lazy and wanted to play hooky, but because I still had a lot on my mind. No one had ever tried to kill me before. And I can tell you, if you've never looked straight down the barrel of a gun held by someone sent to cancel your ticket, it's something you won't soon forget. Thankfully, I've never been sent off to war, but I do believe I can now identify with those unfortunate enough to be afflicted with the debilitating and life-altering effects of Post-Traumatic Stress Disorder. Until recently, the losses I'd suffered in New York City; the deaths of Maxwell Bennett—my only remaining blood family, and Dana—my wife, made me believe I had nothing left to live for—that I really didn't care if I lived or died. But the little fracas that took place on my front doorstep in Tahoe actually changed my perspective. It's amazing how much you really want to live, even when you think you don't. It's ironic, I suppose, that I owe thanks to Ralph for trying to have me whacked, apparently the only remedy strong enough to jolt me out of the stupor for which he was responsible in the first place.

Education aside, I've never been particularly goal oriented, but I soon realized I did have two missions before me. One was to prove that Maxwell Bennett was, in fact, the real Leland Drake, if you will. The other was to win over Amy. I considered the latter for quite a while, psychoanalyzing myself and examining the reasons why I wanted to get close to her. Did I want to bed down with the new girl of my dreams for all the right reasons, or all the wrong ones? Did I want to connect with her in every way imaginable because I was already in love with her, or because I wanted to get even with her grandfather for the death of my wife? What better way to take it out on someone—*literally!* I'll admit, a vengeful streak electrified me from time to time, but I came away from that introspection relatively certain I really was the nice guy most people thought I was. Amy was clearly perfect; mesmerizingly beautiful, enviably smart, amorously charming, and devilishly sexy in the classiest way. I, of course, was again unquestionably ready for a meaningful relationship and clearly smitten. I concluded, trying to maintain what little objectivity I could muster, that my intentions regarding Amy Drake were free of malice.

Deputy Mike Johnson told me every time we spoke that I was to have zero contact with either May or Amy, both potential witnesses, until after the trial, fearing I might somehow cause evidence or testimony to be inadmissible. "Interfering with an ongoing homicide investigation could compromise the case, thereby resulting in a dismissal of any and all charges." That's what he'd said. As much as I wanted Amy, I didn't want that even more.

During the first post-arraignment phone conversation with Johnson, who'd promised to keep me in the loop, I asked, "What are the odds that May knew who Drake really was from the very beginning—knew about or even helped orchestrate the scheme from its inception and may therefore be complicit in the homicides even though she and Drake are long divorced?"

"I doubt it," he replied. "I've known May for years, ever since I dated Amy in high school." He paused briefly, probably remembering a romp or two in the hay with the girl that had gotten away. "Drake is a scumbag. That's obvious to me. He suckered May when they met and used her. He lived a lie knowingly, and caused her to live one unknowingly. He's not the first perp to use an alias and live under an assumed identity, and he won't be the last. That's the way I see it."

"No, he's not. But he's probably the first to do it on such a colossal scale."

"You may be right about that, Bennett."

During the second call I asked, "How are we doing?" I was staring at an array of newspapers and magazines arranged on the colonial dinette table in my Tahoe Keys kitchen. Drake's face was plastered on the cover of each one. The headlines read: *Artist on Trial*, *Fall from Grace*, and *The Demise of an Icon*. My personal favorite was *Leland Drake Indicted for Double Homicide*. If ever there was a magazine cover perfect for target practice that was it. The vile hatred I felt for the man rose in my throat like an acid tide. I looked away, toward the masts and halyards of the sailboats in the marina only steps beyond my sliding glass patio doors. "Do you think it'll stick?"

"Yes. The case would be even stronger if the Glenshire warrant had also turned up the painting taken from your uncle's easel, but I think we'll be all right."

I looked at an article titled: *Dream Team to Defend Leland Drake*.

I read the heading to Johnson and asked, "Are you sure we have enough evidence?" I could hear the skepticism in my own voice.

"Thanks to you, we've got physical evidence linking Drake to the scene. Ballistics tests proved Fabiano's gun was the murder weapon used in New York. That alone would have been enough to get Joey life if I hadn't killed him. Proving that Drake was involved in a conspiracy to commit murder, especially when the motive is unclear, will be a little harder. But, in my opinion, Dana's pendant seals the deal. We also know that Fabiano saved Drake's life in the yard at Lompoc. That's the manslaughter charge that earned Joey an extra ten years. And that's why Drake bankrolled Night Fire for Joey when he finally got out. After all, Drake had a ten year head start on the outside. Apparently the ties that bound them in prison became lifelong."

"Drake financed Night Fire?"

"Not directly, but we can prove a money trail through a dummy corporation."

Wow. From no women at all to a female-filled den of debauchery. All things considered, especially the sleaze factor, it was difficult now to adore a Leland Drake inspired world: Pastoral countryside, charming picket fence-trimmed farmhouses, golden fields of grain, garden flowers bursting with color in brilliant summer sunshine, beach dunes crowned with tall grass bent by an ocean breeze, and peaceful seaside villages; all inhabited by lascivious lap dancers, menacing bouncers, and gyrating naked pole-clutching strippers wearing only stiletto heels and the requisite three-pointed orange and red flame tattoo.

The third call began with the words, "You don't have to worry about Drake beating the charges anymore."

"Why not?" I asked.

"Because he's dead," Johnson announced. "That's why. You'll hear it on the news pretty soon."

"How did it happen?"

"He committed suicide. Hanged himself with a bedsheet."

"I thought he might do something like that. Shouldn't he have been on a suicide watch?"

"What do you know about a suicide watch? You're an architect."

"I am. But you've got to admit, I've gotten pretty good at this cop thing."

I heard him chuckle at the other end of the line, a rare occurrence for Deputy Mike Johnson. "Not bad, Bennett."

"Well, at least I don't need an alibi this time."

"No, you don't."

"I can tell you one thing. Being a person of interest, or a suspect, or whatever the hell you call it, in a homicide investigation is no fun. No fun at all."

"We try to make sure it isn't."

"Let me ask you a question, Mike."

"Go ahead."

"What happens to the case now?"

"It'll probably be closed by the D.A. The shooter's dead and so is the moneyman behind the conspiracy. It's over."

"Not really."

"Why not?"

"Because someone's got to prove that Maxwell Bennett painted all of the damn paintings that made Drake rich and famous. That's why."

"That's not going to happen, Robert. There's no one to do it. While the case was active, the NYPD's Art Squad got involved when Stein and DiCarlo turned up that little copied painting that you identified. The FBI and their art investigators, members of a twelve person team formed in 2004, got involved because the case crossed state lines thanks to the letters and currency from California in your uncle's safe-deposit box. It was actually their forensic accountants who found the fiscal pipeline from Leland Drake Incorporated to Night Fire. But now that Fabiano and Bertucci are both dead, the people allegedly behind it all, there's no prosecutorial reason to keep the case open. Since there's no one left to pursue, there's no reason to continue the investigation."

"Jack Ruby and Lee Harvey Oswald were both dead in no time, but their deaths didn't terminate that investigation."

"Come on, Robert. That was a little different, don't you think?"

"Why? Why is it so different?"

"Do I really have to explain it to you?"

"Yes."

"Give me a break, Bennett. Whether there were other shooters on that grassy fucking knoll will always be a matter of speculation. Everyone in the country wanted to know if there was a bigger conspiracy. That was a Presidential assassination, for God's sake! Compared to that, people won't care who painted a few paintings."

"Art collectors will care. Auction houses will care. Galleries will care. Museums will care. Insurance companies will care. I care. And my uncle would care."

"No disrespect, Robert, but if in fact he did paint the paintings that garnered Drake a fortune, he didn't seem to care if anyone knew the truth while he was alive."

"Maybe he cared more than we know, but being able to pay his sister's medical bills was more important. And I can tell you this much. Had he survived the hit, like I did, knowing Drake tried to have him killed—he'd want everyone to know. I'm sure of that."

Johnson was silent for a moment. Then he said in a helpless sort of way, "I'm sorry, Robert. I don't know what else to tell you. I've done everything I can. I don't see any jurisdiction continuing the case. Criminally, there's no reason to. If you want to pursue it civilly, you could hire a private investigator, an art expert, and a lawyer, but I don't know what's to be gained."

"It's a matter of pride, Mike. If my uncle painted Drake's paintings, he deserves the recognition. And Drake deserves to be posthumously stripped of his status in the art world."

"He's dead, Robert, apparently disgraced to the point of committing suicide. What more do you want? Justice has been served. Leave it alone. Leave it alone and move on."

"I've watched the news and read all the articles. Drake's true identity and criminal record have been disclosed time after time, but there's been no mention at all of any speculation that he didn't paint the paintings he signed, let alone that the victim could have been, in fact, the real artist. There hasn't been one word about that. Not one."

"No, there hasn't. The media outlets only regurgitated what was released to them at the press conferences. That's all they had. We shared the basic facts—Drake's true identity, which was neither a matter of conjecture nor speculation, and therefore couldn't compromise the case, except for a good mouthpiece possibly arguing that it would have been impossible to seat an unbiased jury in any venue. We had the murder weapon and the triggerman. And we could prove an ongoing relationship between him and Drake, despite Drake's denials, which were pretty lame considering the connection between Drake's new wife and her former pimp. When the press pushed us for more details, we threw them a couple of bones: The safe-deposit box cash, which a subpoena verified as originating in the bank on Market Street where Drake had an account, something you and I already knew, and a connection between the victim and Drake's ex-wife—the love letters that May confirmed were her own. But neither the NYPD nor Pine County had ever established a viable motive. We never had one, so we never divulged one. Therefore, one was never published."

I considered Johnson's explanation and understood why the best the media could do was to conclude that, identities and aliases notwithstanding, the motive revolved around some incredibly romantic, yet bizarre lifelong love triangle. "Didn't you tell your boss what *I* think? What *we* think? That Maxwell Bennett is the real Leland Drake. We know that Leland Drake isn't Leland Drake, for Christ's sake, so maybe the real artist is somebody else entirely."

"I shared your belief with the brass in the Department and the D.A., but nobody bought it. I'm not so sure anyone believes that but you, Robert."

"Why not?"

"Because there's no proof."

"What about the painting Officer Millhouse described in detail, the one on Mack's easel?"

"Oh, you mean the one we couldn't find, even with four warrants?"

I backed off, feeling a little stupid. "Yeah, that one."

"That might have been helpful, but he probably destroyed it when Joey brought it back. I would have," Johnson offered.

"What about you, Deputy? What do you believe?"

The line was silent for another long pause. Then I heard him say, "What I believe doesn't matter."

I could only imagine his expression as I said, "If that's true, then I won't worry about what you think when I date Amy."

There was suddenly contempt in Johnson's voice. "What are your intentions, Bennett? You're not still on a revenge mission, are you?"

I could have said, that's none of your business. You're not her father. Or, whatever you and Amy shared in the past is obviously over now, despite your regrets. But I chose to answer truthfully and respectfully, as Deputy Mike Johnson had treated me, not as a civilian, but as a partner, to say nothing of the fact that the man saved my life. "To be honest, Mike, I questioned my own motives here and came to the conclusion that I have feelings for the girl. I could be wrong, but I think she feels the same way."

"Wake up, Buddy. Her grandfather is dead because of you. That's the only way she can see it. How do you think that makes her feel?"

"Does she know he committed suicide?"

"Yes. The next of kin is notified immediately so they won't hear it on the news first. I told her personally. It wasn't easy."

"Does May know?"

"I told her, too."

"Listen, Mike. Drake's dead because he couldn't handle the embarrassment, or the prospect of being back in a penitentiary for the rest of his life without Fabiano there to protect him. He's dead because of the things he did. The lies caught up with him. There was no other way out. That's the way she'll see it. She's a smart girl."

"He was her grandfather, Robert. Right or wrong, he was alive and well before you showed up. To tell you the truth, I'm still on the fence about how you just happened to pass May's house the day after you arrived in California and recognize it as the one in your uncle's painting, especially since they don't even look that much alike. Now that the truth is out, which never would have happened if you'd stayed in New York, she's bound to see your sudden and unexpected appearance the way he did—that you came looking for him. There's no way she'll go out with you."

I considered Johnson's appraisal of the circumstances, admitted to myself that what he said made perfect sense and could very well be true, but ultimately went with the gut feeling that he was now just trying his best to keep me away from his old flame—that if he couldn't have her, neither could I. "I'm going to call her, Mike, and I hope you're okay with it."

"Go ahead. Make a fool of yourself. I don't care. Really. Knock yourself out. I'm a happily married man with a couple of great kids. She's all yours, if you can pull it off."

"I've got to try. The worst that can happen is she says no, right?"

"I don't know about that, Bennett. I've been a cop for ten years, made thousands of vehicle stops, handled a lot of crazy situations, and I've never been able to envision the worst-case scenario. I guess my crystal ball just isn't that good."

"Neither is mine. Wish me luck."

"You've got it. You'll need it."

"There's one other thing, Mike."

"What's that?"

"Thanks for taking me along and sharing the details of the investigation. I'm grateful. I'm sure it was an unorthodox way to conduct a case. I hope you didn't suffer a reprimand for it."

"To tell you the truth, I cleared it from the beginning with my lieutenant. Besides being one way to keep an eye on you, he agreed that spending time with the person likely to know the most about the victims and the other possible players was a good idea, especially since the NYPD considered you a suspect. You might have even slipped and said something incriminating."

"What did *you* think?"

"I thought so, too. But as it turns out, that was a good thing."

"Why?" I asked, beginning to get annoyed.

"Because if I hadn't shown up at your place after Stein and

DiCarlo called us with the knowledge that their suspect had relocated in our county, especially having stopped you outside May's house, you'd be dead now, and Fabiano and Drake would have gotten away with three murders in two states. That's why."

I suppose he was right, but that didn't make me feel better about being used, so I ended the call.

I dialed Amy's number without even putting down the phone. A moment later I heard her voice.

"Hello?"

"Amy. This is Robert Bennett. How are you?"

There was only silence in the wire. I heard neither breathing, nor a click. "Amy, are you there?"

Nothing.

"Hello? Amy? Are you there?"

"Yes."

"Are you all right?"

"I've been better."

"I called to express my condolences. Mike Johnson just told me about your grandfather. I'm very sorry."

"Are you?"

"I am."

"Why? Why would you be sorry? You must have wanted him dead. That's why you came here in the first place, isn't it? You came to California looking for my grandparents, didn't you?"

"No, I didn't."

"I don't believe you. You showed up and everything fell apart."

How do you think I feel? I met your grandfather, the forger from Lompoc, and a few hours later his henchman tried to kill me. "Finding May was purely accidental, Amy. I wasn't looking for anyone. I left New York to get away from the past and begin a new life as far away as I could. I started my new job and on the way home that first day, as I came around a bend in the road at early sunset, I knew instantly that I'd found the house in one of my uncle's paintings, one of my favorites, in fact. That notion haunted me for a week as I sat on the floor every night staring at the framed oil I'd taken out of a crate and leaned against the wall. Every evening on my way back to Tahoe, I considered stopping and knocking on the door, but, just like in the minutes before I called you, I didn't know what to say. Finally, on Saturday morning, obsessed with the idea that I'd actually found the house in a picture I'd looked at for years, I drove back and did it. I had to go. No longer was the house a work of fiction. Nor could I ask my uncle, why did you paint that house and the blue tree beside it? Who lived there? What did they mean to you? That's how it happened, Amy. I don't know why it happened. I have no idea. I've never believed in the premise that some things are meant to be, but what choice do I have now? What choice do I have but to believe that we were supposed to meet? Don't you see? If finding May's house was preordained, so was meeting you."

The line was silent for a long moment again before she said, "I don't believe you."

"Why not? I'm telling you the truth."

"Why didn't you tell me this before? I asked in Luigi's how you found my grandmother and you didn't say anything like this."

"I should have. I guess I thought May would have been offended in some way if I hadn't actually sought her out to bring her the news. I made a mistake. What can I say? I'm sorry."

"I still don't believe you. I don't believe you at all. And I don't want to talk to you. Don't ever call me again. I mean it."

"Amy. Wait. I'm telling you the truth. That's how it happened. I wasn't looking for anyone. I was minding my own business, starting over, designing a boring shopping center, and driving home alone to an empty apartment when I spotted a chapter in my uncle's life. I crossed a little bridge and stumbled into the world behind a painting I'd inherited. That's how it happened. Please believe me."

"Why should I? What difference does it make?"

"It makes a difference because I want to see you. I want you to believe me because I know there could be something special between us."

"You're kidding, right? You've got to be kidding."

"No. I'm not. I'm not kidding at all. Didn't you feel it in your office when I held you in my arms? When I kissed you?"

The line was quiet again.

"Amy. Talk to me. I felt it. I think you did, too."

"My grandfather was still alive then, Robert. Everything was normal then."

Normal? What the hell are you talking about? Some murdering ex-con pimp son of a bitch tried to kill me at my front door. Your revered grandfather wasn't who he said he was. He divorced your grandmother to marry a prostitute. He was famous for things he hadn't even done, which caused you to live your entire life thinking your name was Drake instead of Bertucci and manage a company that should never have been in business in the first place. That was normal? "Amy. Please. I've got to see you."

"I can't. Not after everything that's happened."

"But that's exactly why you should. Don't you see? We were supposed to meet. That's why I was standing in that white house by the river when you walked in."

"I don't know why you were there, and I don't know what to think."

"Listen to me, Amy. After everything we've *both* been through we should take advantage of the joy in getting to know each other better. It's there, waiting for us. I know it is. Let me prove it to you."

"I don't think so."

I was making progress. "Have dinner with me. If you don't

have a good time, you can pick up the tab." I suddenly realized that my pathetic attempt at humor would only remind her of how badly things had ended at Luigi's.

"I can't. It's not going to work, Robert. It's too complicated. Just leave it at that. Don't beg. And don't make me change my number."

"If you won't go out with me, I'd like to hire you. I'm in need of an art expert and I believe you're qualified."

"What do you mean you're in need of an art expert?" she asked after a noticeable moment of hesitation. "What are you looking for?"

"I'll tell you when we meet. It's hard to describe over the phone."

"Nice try, but you're beginning to sound desperate. It's not becoming."

"Seriously, I'll pay for your time."

"If that's the kind of relationship you want, there are lots of girls to choose from on the street in the Mission District. Just get off the highway after you cross the Bay Bridge. You can't miss it."

"I couldn't be more serious, Amy. I need to learn a few things about art and I'm willing to pay for the education. You don't have to give me an answer now. Think about it. Call me if you're interested." I gave her my cell number and ended the call before she could. I'd given it my best shot, laid out all the reasons why she should go out with me, most of which I truly believed, but I've never begged anyone for anything, and I wasn't about to start.

I went to bed, got up the next morning, showered, shaved, and went back to work.

The first words out of William Sherman's mouth were, "Are

people still trying to kill you?"

"No," I said. "It's over. I'll tell you all about it sometime if you want me to."

"I've read most of the articles," Sherman admitted. "But it'll be interesting to separate the spin from the truth." Then he shook my hand and, true to his word, welcomed me again to his architectural firm.

I took a moment to thank him for helping me personally when I needed help, and for his patience regarding my position at Sherman and Essen. Then I reached into my pocket, withdrew the garage door opener-size shocker he'd given me, and returned it to him. "Take my word for it," I said. "This little baby gets the job done. Thanks, but I don't need it anymore."

"You used it?"

I nodded.

"Now that's something I want to hear about. We'll talk later. Right now, you've got a ton of catching up to do." He brought me up to speed on the projects at hand, including the one I'd left behind, and walked me back to my office. "I'm glad you're okay, Robert."

I could see the sincerity in his eyes. It touched me, especially since I'd worked at Sherman and Essen less than two weeks before going back to New York to meet with Stein and DiCarlo. Then I'd disappeared for nearly a month. "Thanks. It's good to be back."

I planted myself in the big swiveler behind my oak desk, but my mind wasn't quite ready to deal with load-bearing walls, floor joists, and roof trusses, to say nothing of beguiling facades. As I gazed instead through the Victorian windows at the periwinkle hydrangea blooms, and beyond at my silver Porsche, I considered the way it had all turned out. Some aspects of the ordeal I'd endured were more satisfying than others. I particularly enjoyed the way the big palooka dropped to the asphalt in a heap like a sack of potatoes in the parking lot outside Night Fire, although having my neck in a vise was considerably less pleasurable.

Joey, of course, got precisely what he deserved. Watching him expire with the murder weapon at my feet left no room for doubt. Justice had been handed to the triggerman in the manner most fitting. By no means am I a biblical scholar, but something about "An eye for an eye" came to mind.

The same could be said of Ralph Bertucci, AKA Leland Drake. He'd ordered the death of another human being and had gotten two for the price of one. On the downside, remorse played no part in his suicide. I know this because I'd personally experienced his arrogance. Regarding the frauds and conspiracies he'd perpetrated over a lifetime, never should it be uttered, "He just couldn't live with the things he'd done." On the upside, however, the result was the same.

As for me? Well, I suppose I was meant to live. Just not happily ever after. In the end, we were all losers to varying degrees.

I forced myself to focus on the tasks at hand, rolled up my sleeves, and dug in, more than a month behind. Two hours later my cell started to vibrate in my pants, which, as it turns out, was entirely appropriate. Amy Drake was on the line.

25

I met Amy Saturday morning in the parking lot at the base of the Horsetail Falls trailhead in Twin Bridges. I knew exactly where it was when she'd set the time and place over the phone. I'd passed that very spot daily on my way to and from Sherman and Essen.

It was her idea, not mine. I would have preferred something more romantic; perchance a quiet little candle-lit table for two overlooking Lake Tahoe at sunset, the crystal waters shimmering within a ring of picturesque mountains that appeared to have been generously topped with powdered sugar, or perhaps a seductive rendezvous at the most intimate and elegant restaurant I could find in the storied City of San Francisco. But, happy that she'd called at all, I wasn't about to argue.

The fact is, the more I thought about the time and place that she'd selected, the more I liked it. She could have accepted my offer of consultancy, had me return to her office above the

Embarcadero and, dressed in one of her *haute couture* business suits, held class from behind a desk, probably keeping a ruler handy to smack my knuckles if I got out of line. Thrust back in time, I would be relegated again to adolescence, able only to ogle the teacher like a depraved little twerp forced to ignore his own raging hormones.

But this was going to be the real thing, the two of us alone in the high sierra. The morning air would be cool and fresh. The sun would be strong. The sky would be a vivid blue. The scent of pine would be clean. The snowmelt cascading over a thousand feet of vertical granite would embody the raw, untamed power of nature. Birds would be singing the praises of spring's renewal. It was going to be perfect, in the perfect setting for a new beginning.

Eager with anticipation, I arrived at the trailhead early. There were several cars already in the parking lot just off the highway, but there were no people in sight. I parked the Porsche in the far corner, away from the other vehicles to avoid a door ding. Then, unable to see the forest for the trees, I walked back to the road for an unobstructed view of the area, stopping along the way to use the government supplied outhouse, and paying the parking fee for two vehicles.

Highway 50 shot off to the right in a straight line down a long slope toward points west. I marveled at the American River Valley's own imposing monolithic version of Yosemite's notorious Half Dome as it rose beyond the road from the glen below to meet the sky; the likes of Ayer's Rock, or the Rock of Gibraltar, neither of which should be confused with Plymouth Rock, which has done pretty well for itself considering the fact that it is only slightly larger than a coffee table.

I walked a hundred yards or so back up Highway 50 to where I could get a good look northward at our destination—Horsetail Falls. The vista opened before my eyes to reveal all the grandeur and majesty of the Sierra Nevada: A granite range rising to more than ten thousand feet in the Tahoe region with peaks called Jobs, Freel, Tallac, Pyramid, and Mount Rose—geologic wonders of seismic up-thrust and glacial carving second only in North America to the mighty Rockies. The falls themselves, a massive white column that hung in stages like a drape from a point near the top of the mountain, displayed their power even at a distance that I estimated to be more than two miles. I couldn't see the trail, except where it started at the back of the parking lot, but surmised that it ascended the rugged terrain at least to a point near the falls, which was well into a region known as Desolation Wilderness.

I'd had a week to prepare for the hike and, despite being back at work, managed to outfit myself quite well, or at least as well as a guy from Brooklyn could imagine necessary. I'd purchased an expensive pair of insulated hiking boots, a royal blue long sleeve T-shirt woven from some space-age moisture-wicking fabric designed to prevent my sweat from chilling me to the bone once we reached the top, a pair of brown corduroy pants, a zip-front blue fleece which I deemed to be particularly suitable for an up-to-the-minute mountain man, and a bright yellow hooded windbreaker—in case the weather turned on me again, like it did in the Adirondacks, and we needed a helicopter rescue.

I also bought a backpack and stuffed it with two bottles of water, a nifty fire-starter, heat-generating hand warmers that would fit in the cute little zipper compartments of my new gloves, a compass and signaling mirror combo, a snake-bite kit, a Swiss Army knife with more blades and tools than a *Westside Story* reunion in a well-stocked hardware store, a two hundred and fifty lumen LED tactical mini-flashlight capable of beaming an SOS sequence ten miles, a foil thermal blanket large enough to sleep two that was folded into a packet smaller than a hot pastrami sandwich from the old Carnegie Deli, and a CO_2 powered pocket-size boating horn to scare any opportunistic bears away from my emergency supply of granola bars. I was fairly certain this was all overkill, as the entire trail wasn't very far from the road, but I wasn't about to let myself die from exposure after surviving the bone-chilling waters of Lake George three years ago and, more recently, a life-threatening bout of attempted murder. And I wasn't leaving any of my fingers or toes up there either.

 I've never been a Boy Scout, an Army Ranger, a Green Beret, a Navy Seal, or any other kind of survival expert. I've never slept in a tent at Base Camp, bonded with a Sherpa, traversed a crevasse, dug a snow cave, or scaled a rock face using ropes and carabiners, and I wasn't about to do any of those things that Saturday. Don't get me wrong. This wasn't a climbing expedition. It was merely a day hike, but the terrain leading up to the falls did look fairly daunting, at least from a distance. As I gazed up at the granite canyon below the falls, the perfect place for a perfect date and a new beginning suddenly didn't seem quite so perfect. What was I getting myself into? How cool would I look totally out of breath and panting like a dog after a Frisbee fest, or worse—clinging to a root protruding from a crack in the rock after losing my footing, hanging on for dear life, dangling like a leaf in the wind, and screaming my lungs out in the rarified air? The highest landmass in Brooklyn was either the painted yellow line down the middle of Fifth Avenue, also known as the "ridge" in Bay Ridge, or the Department of Sanitation Landfill beside the Belt Parkway at Pennsylvania Avenue. I'm not sure which held the title.

 I took a deep breath, filled my chest with cool mountain morning air, turned toward the sun, felt the warmth on my face, and made sure my balls were still where they were supposed to be. Then I looked at the cascading falls way the hell in the distance and said aloud, "If she can do it, so can I."

 I returned to the parking area, and as I tried to figure out which arm went through which strap on my backpack her BMW pulled up beside me.

"Hello Amy," I said as she stepped out of the car. I was going to add, "You look great," which she did, but I held back. A stylish pair of sunglasses hung around her neck and her silky auburn hair glistened in the sunlight as it brushed her bare shoulders. She wore a sea green spaghetti-strap tank top, which complimented her eyes. It was tucked into a pair of black leggings that sheathed her bottom, thighs, calves, and ankles like a still-wet coat of latex semi-gloss, disappearing into the tops of her fancy beige suede hiking boots.

"Hello, Robert," she said, walking past me and around the car to the trunk, making no attempt to kiss me, hug me, or even shake my hand.

She opened the lid, but, as she reached into the trunk, I took her left hand and gently turned her toward me.

She looked into my eyes, her gorgeous face expressionless and noncommittal.

I smiled and said, "It's great to see you again. I'm glad you're here. This is going to be fun."

She smiled perfunctorily and replied, "I'm not sure why I suggested this, Robert, other than to hike to my favorite place in the world. I told myself I wouldn't go out with you again, not after everything that's happened." She hesitated and turned her face away.

I said, "I'm sorry about your grandfather, Amy. I am."

She suddenly waved me off, as if she didn't want to hear it, or wouldn't believe it. "Don't say anything else." She pulled away and turned again to retrieve her gear from the trunk.

I looked in and noticed a large coil of lime green climbing rope, a string of anodized aluminum carabiners and expansion cams attached to a harness, and a bright orange helmet. A twinge of panic tightened in my gut, despite my testosterone-filled gonads being exactly where they were supposed to be, as my own male ego-driven words came back to haunt me. *If she can do it, so can I.*

I watched her strap on a little black fanny pack and position it above her left hip. Then she swung a small hydration pack behind her, slipping her bare arms through the padded shoulder straps.

"Here," I said. "Let me help you."

"I've got it," she warned, neither needing nor willing to accept my assistance. It had only been two minutes since her arrival and already I was beginning to get annoyed with the apparent hostility. She was intoxicatingly beautiful, especially up close, but I suddenly had the disturbing feeling that, maybe, as much as I hated to admit it, Mike Johnson was right—that this whole thing simply wasn't going to work out. *You know what? Here's an idea. I think you should hike to your favorite place in the world by yourself. Have a nice day.* I could have said that, or even something stronger and considerably more obscene (which in fact crossed my mind), gotten back into my car and split, but I knew she'd been through a lot in the past few weeks. I also wasn't ready to give up on a girl I was already in love with, even if, at least thus far, it was unrequited.

Instead I asked, "What's all that?" pointing to the climbing gear still in the trunk.

She was pulling on a specialized pair of gloves now, each with a wrist-cinching Velcro strap. "Relax," she said, sensing my apprehension. We won't need that today. That's for when I rock climb."

"I had no idea you're so outdoorsy."

"There's a lot you don't know about me." Then she slammed the trunk lid harder than necessary and attempted to walk around me, but I stopped her.

"Hey. Lighten up. This was your idea, remember? You called me and suggested this. If you don't want me to go with you just say so."

We looked at each other for more than a few seconds. I tried to read her mind, but had no idea what she was thinking. I did know, however, the most basic rule of negotiation: After the offer has been made, the person who speaks first loses. I therefore resolved to wait for her to say something.

She stared at me directly with a hard edge in her eyes that took too long to soften. Then she smiled just a little and said, "You're right. I did call you. I wasn't going to, to tell you the truth, but I had to."

"What do you mean, you had to?"

She examined her thoughts, or at least her choice of words, before turning away.

I tried to stretch the moment. "Why did you have to?"

"Never mind."

"Tell me what you're thinking right now."

She shook her head once and said, "Let's just go. We'll take it one step at a time."

I backed off and, realizing the need for some levity, said, "That's probably the best way to take a hike."

She chuckled and raised the sunglasses resting on her chest into position, the coated lenses conveniently hiding her eyes.

I stepped back to the Porsche's open door and began to hoist my pack to my shoulders, but stopped when she said, "Don't wear the fleece. You'll get too hot."

I dropped the pack on the seat again, peeled off the jacket and stuffed it into an already loaded compartment. Then I slipped the pack on, donned my own gloves, which I thought counteracted the appearance that I had absolutely no idea what I was doing, and locked the car. "After you, Mountain Girl."

She turned and struck off across the lot toward the trailhead. "Try to keep up."

"Don't worry about it," I said, instantly wondering if she'd selected that outfit for its functionality or entertainment value.

We passed the wilderness permit self-registration station without even slowing down.

"Shouldn't we stop and log in?" I asked.

"We don't have to. It's just a day hike."

"Don't we need a permit?"

"Don't sweat it. I've done this dozens of times. We'll be fine."

Always one to play by the rules, I stopped at the Park Service bulletin board to read the posted advisories, but she turned left, entered the beginning of the path, and kept going. I debated with the voice of caution in my head whether or not to take a minute to familiarize myself with the permanent weatherproof trail map in front of me, read the official warnings, and then try to catch up, or just rely on her knowledge of the area.

She was pulling away fast, taking long purposeful strides, obviously destination-bound. *Try to keep up!* Hadn't she ever heard that getting there was half the fun? What about stopping to smell the roses along the way, or at least to read the posted warnings?

I soon gave up on being prudent and inquisitive; afraid I'd exhaust myself or twist an ankle running after her between the bushes if I lollygagged, even in the name of caution. I should have gotten to the rendezvous point even earlier, I thought. That would have allowed the time needed to become better acquainted with the hike before she arrived. Now I was annoyed times two; annoyed with her, and annoyed with me.

As I took off after her, I started wondering how to turn this day into a joyous and amorous adventure, the true beginning of a one-in-a-million romantic relationship. It occurred to me that, once upon a time, even though Dana and I had been made for each other, *she* hadn't realized it as quickly as I had, which was from the very first minute I laid eyes on her.

You see, way back when, during the liberal arts phase of

my college career, otherwise known as the useless phase, I'd had the best idea a straight, single guy could ever have for writing a sociology paper—an idea which, by the way, I'm sure would be ridiculed and squashed today. Anyway, what started off as a curious notion soon became an interesting, if not deeply profound, theory. What if the most beautiful women are actually the loneliest simply because men are afraid to approach them? What if their social lives are the emptiest of all? Is it possible that they actually sit at home, bored and lonely, while their average-looking peers are out on dates, carousing and cavorting to the wee hours? Could it be true? And could that simple but ironic premise have been philosophically sophisticated enough to be the basis for a college term paper at one of the nation's most highly accredited universities?

It must have been because, believe it or not, my seersucker-clad, beard-scratching, pseudo-intellectual professor gave the project his hearty blessing. I then carefully crafted a twenty question survey designed to delve deeply into the social lives of the university's prettiest coeds and lay bare, among other things, their social disappointments and unsatisfied Saturday night cravings.

"Hello, my name is Robert Bennett," I began time after time, clipboard in hand as I sought out and approached the most attractive females on campus. "I'm writing a paper for a sociology class about the social lives of the most beautiful girls in the school. Would you mind answering a few questions?"

Needless to say some refused to believe that the whole thing was on the level, even though I named the course and professor. To tell you the truth, I could hardly believe it myself. But it *was* true and the flattery inherent in the question usually got the job done.

After considering headings like: *She's Not Out of My League After All,* and *Pinch Me, I Must Be Dreaming,* I finally settled on the publication-worthy title *The Fear of Rejection and its Unintended Consequences*. In the end the project was successful in every way imaginable, and even in one that wasn't. I'd proved that there was indeed a significant degree of truth to my hypothesis. The professor gave me an A. My own social life was never boring. And the very last girl to take the survey was Dana.

She'd, however, been in the sub-group that would have doomed my premise to failure for, as the saying goes, she was already seeing someone. And maybe I should have been more respectful of that. After all, if Dana had been my girl at the time, I certainly wouldn't have wanted someone like me to even be in the same room with her. But that's the chance one takes having a significant other who turns heads, isn't it?

Think of me what you will, I went out of my way after that now infamous sociology survey to bump into Dana wherever I thought she might be. I had to. I was crazy about her. To be honest, I don't think she was really ever that serious about the mope I replaced. If she had been, I doubt I could have stolen her heart.

"Pretend," I used to say when we talked here and there; in the halls, at the bulletin boards, in the cafeteria, and on the quadrangle—where the radicals protested, and the rest of us who actually belonged there would ultimately attend commencement on a humid June morning. "Pretend you like me enough to go out with me. Pretend we've got a date this Saturday and you can't wait. Pretend you're bursting with anticipation. Pretend you're giddy like a schoolgirl, because you are a schoolgirl. Dana," I used to say, "just pretend."

Of course, if she'd refused my machinations, if there were no such thing as a self-fulfilling prophecy, if pretending had never become the better part of reality, she would still be alive. She wouldn't be with me, but she'd be alive *somewhere*. Getting her to fall in love with me, making myself a part of her life, and making her the lion's share of mine is, however, all the responsibility I'm willing to shoulder in the matter of her death. That, and the guilt-laden fact that I was attending a lousy, stinking convention at the other end of the country while she was hand-picking the ingredients for Maxwell Bennett's favorite home-cooked dinner before arriving at his apartment to lovingly prepare it, just as if he were *her* uncle instead of mine. Then Joey showed up. The pot roast never made it into the pot. The rest is history, and so are they.

By the time I caught up with Amy Drake, the dirt trail that wound through a thinly wooded area near the road opened onto a vast expanse of sloping solid granite. It spread out before us like a great tilted golf course made of pale gray speckled stone instead of lush green grass.

Amy was headed diagonally across the bedrock to the right. For the first time, except perhaps for my appraisal of the entire region from the highway, I was now able to assess the true majesty of the valley before us as it unfurled and funneled up to the whitewater apex ahead. I noticed that the mountainside to our left was covered with tall pines, while the one to the right was an imposing sheer granite rock face, a natural stone wall at least a thousand feet high, or in city-boy architectural terms, the height of a hundred story skyscraper. Reminded of the way English ivy clings to a diminutive man-made wall, I studied, if only for a moment, the green foliage trimming the nearly vertical slab here and there on its way to the heavens.

In short order we reached Pyramid Creek, a raging torrent that had started at the top of the mountain, gushed over the massive falls still well in the distance, and was coursing through the canyon on its way to the American River. The whitewater before us imparted a noticeably damp chill to the air and filled it with the requisite white noise. It entered my head and joined the conflict. For me, this was a date, a chance to cultivate a relationship with the type of woman most men could only fantasize about—the exceptional woman you couldn't wait to touch, hold in your arms, squeeze with all your strength, and kiss until forced to stop by the rude intrusion of some untimely and annoying facet of reality.

I know I'd been lucky to a point. I'd had that before with Dana—an incomparable joy multiplied by the delightful expectation that our love would last a lifetime. I'd had that until it was taken away. Now I had the chance to have it again, nothing less than the extraordinary opportunity to make my life complete once more. That's what that spring day held for me. I didn't know what it held for her, other than just another weekend hike. And judging by the conversation thus far, it wasn't anything more than that.

When we reached a deep pool created by a makeshift dam constructed of boulders and submerged logs, I said, "Let's stop for a minute. I need some water."

She simply stopped and stared at the emerald green pool that, at a glance, appeared to be still but in fact swirled furiously beneath the surface with hidden tempestuous currents, impatient and angry down deep. "You said you need an art expert. Why?" she asked. "What do you want to know?"

Mentioning that over the phone had been a mistake, so I'd prepared for this, knowing the truth would be awkward, to say the least. *I want to know if it's possible to examine a painting and identify the artist solely by the style and technique used to paint it, so I could prove that my uncle was in fact the one who painted all of your grandfather's works.* How would that go over? Instead I said, "I want to learn the elements of style and technique that make an artist unique and recognizable."

"Why?"

"Because I want to paint."

"*You* want to paint?"

I nodded. "I've wanted to paint for some time now."

"Have you ever painted anything?"

"An apartment in Brooklyn Heights."

She ignored the humor as if she hadn't even heard it. "What makes you think you'd be good at it?"

"I'm an architect. I've got formal training in form and structure. I've got an eye for detail. I see things in three dimensions. I've got a feel for light and shadow. It's part of what I do. I'd like to pick up where my uncle left off."

"You can buy a roller and be a painter, but you just can't buy a brush and be an artist. You've got to have it in you."

"Don't you believe in heredity? Besides," I continued, remembering some of the things May Drake had said in her living room, "your grandfather wasn't very good when he met your grandmother. He learned to be great. It only took him a year, or so the story goes."

I slipped off my pack, sat it on the granite, and pulled out a bottle of spring water, allegedly bottled at some mysterious source from an aquifer beneath a mountain that, supposedly, looked just like this one. I offered it to Amy, who was now sitting on a rock the size of an ottoman. "Would you like one? I brought two bottles. Hopefully, this has less beaver poop in it than that does," I said, nodding toward the pool.

She slipped off her sunglasses, letting them hang around her neck on their keeper and shook her head without so much as a smirk at my facetious levity. Then she pointed to the hydration pack's tubing and mouthpiece attached to the shoulder strap beside her right breast. "I've got my own."

"So I see." I cracked the seal on the cap, took a few gulps, and paused for a moment to enjoy the surroundings. It was indeed a beautiful morning in the great outdoors. I drew a deep breath of crisp mountain air, admired the brilliant blue sky, and thought simply—it *is* good to be alive.

"You know," she began, "That bottle will be in a landfill forever."

As the sudden criticism set me back a little, I sensed that the jab was more than just a casual new age, ecology-minded, if not stylish, observation. I'd learned long ago that when you really like someone, they can do no wrong. Everything they say and do is cute, smart, and appealing. And when you don't, the opposite is, of course, also true. Apparently, this climb was going to be even harder than I thought; an uphill battle in more ways than one.

I swallowed a few more ounces and held the plastic bottle up before stowing it again. "No, it won't. I'll pack it out, recycle it, and it'll be reincarnated as a marvelous medical device like an i.v. pouch filled with medicine of some sort that will save someone's life." For me, being upbeat, positive, and optimistic required some Olympic-grade mental gymnastics, but if ever I was going to be up to the task, this was the time.

She seemed even more surprised by my positive reply than I was. So, with the first sign of a crack in the ice, I sat beside her. "It's really beautiful out here," I said. "I don't know about you, but I for one am glad you called and suggested this."

I was hoping for a reply in kind, but she said nothing.

I ignored the silence and said, "The closest thing we have to this in Brooklyn is the Discovery Channel in HD."

Again there was no reply.

I turned to look at her and although she was only inches from me, distant doesn't begin to describe the preoccupation on a face that could only have been more perfect if there was a smile on it. "Listen Amy, I have a favor to ask. It's not a very big one, so maybe you'll consider it."

"What's that?"

"Pretend you're having a good time. Could you do that? Just pretend you like me, at least for a little while. Okay?"

I hoped for a kiss, but waited for a chuckle, or at least a nod. I waited but nothing happened.

"Wow, this is a tough crowd. I've got an idea. Before I bomb completely, I think it's time to exit stage left. I'll let myself out." Without further ado, I simply stood, pulled on my backpack, and began to retrace my steps back to the parking lot.

I'd gotten about twenty paces when I heard her say, "Wait. Don't go."

I ignored her and kept walking, partly because I'd had enough, and partly to show who was really in control, which, of course, was only a pipe dream, as any honest man can tell you, no matter how demonstrably he pounds his chest.

"Robert. Wait. I'm sorry."

I stopped, paused a few seconds, and turned.

She was standing now, near the edge of the deep green pool where it spilled over the obstruction like a great flood that could not be contained. "Come with me." Then she smiled and said, "I'll pretend I like you."

As I approached, she pivoted and started to lead the way again, but I turned her around, held her shoulders, and looked into her eyes. "Listen to me, Amy. I know this is awkward, but you've got to relax. I wanted to know you the instant I saw your picture. From the moment I laid eyes on you. I want to know everything about you."

She returned my stare before asking, "What picture?"

"The one on May's mantel."

"Why did you come here?"

"Because you invited me, remember?"

"No. I mean why did you come to California? What were you doing in my grandmother's house in the first place? What did you want? What *do* you want?"

"I explained it to you over the phone."

"Explain it again. What do you want *now*?"

"I told you, I had to leave New York. I tried for a year after Dana was killed to make it right, but there was nothing there for me except memories. You can't live on memories, especially when there's no closure. That's why I moved across the continent; to put the pieces into perspective, to look in a new place for the things and people that would bring me peace so I could finally start over. California seemed like the best choice."

"I asked you a question, Robert. What do you want?"

I looked into the depths of her eyes and a hundred profoundly clichéd things came to mind, starting with the sun, the moon, and the stars, and ending with, truth be told, exploring every inch of her body in ways that would make the Kama Sutra look like a coloring book. I tried to hold on to the passing seconds, aware that each one seemed to bring me a little closer to paradise. At last, able to remain still no longer, my lips tried to answer hers with a tender kiss that mere words could never express. But she refused my explanation.

"Answer me, Robert. What do you want?"

Knowing the list was utterly too long to enumerate, and certainly too clumsy, I simply said, "You. I want you."

My lips touched hers again, but the ignition for which I'd hoped was tentative at best. I retreated an inch or two and waited for her eyes to open. Then I asked, "What else would you like to know?"

"Why are you so persistent? Why can't you just forget about me?"

"That won't happen. I'll never forget about you. You'll always be the one I wanted most. You'll always be the one that got away."

I could suddenly see an acknowledgement of sorts come over her, not a submission mind you, but instead an acceptance of the inevitable. It seemed almost clear. She'd obviously given this a lot of thought in the days and hours preceding our rendezvous, knowing full well where it was going.

"All right," she said, softly. "I'll pretend. Be patient with me."

"Have I ever told you that Patience is my middle name?"

"No. I don't believe you have."

"Well, if it isn't, it might as well be. For you, I have all the time in the world."

No longer conflicted, she smiled a coy smile and said, "Come with me and I'll show you something you've never seen before."

Apparently, I'd said all the right things for once. "I can hardly wait."

Then she raised her glasses into position, turned, and led the way to the mountaintop.

After we crossed the Desolation Wilderness boundary, great fields of granite soon gave way to dark pine forest where slanted shafts of sunlight penetrated an evergreen canopy supported high above by towering cedars and ponderosa pines. Slowly, we threaded our way through the shadows, stepping over fallen mossy trunks and around patches of mud softened by little rivulets of snowmelt that crisscrossed the forest floor. I realized the air was remarkably still as the smell of damp earth entered my head. I might have felt some sense of mythical enchantment had it not been for a tinge of fear, afraid that I'd come face to face with a bear or step on a rattlesnake. In fact, the most difficult aspect of the hike, so far, was taking my eyes off Amy's derrière long enough to watch my footing.

We emerged from the evergreens and I realized that the majestic valley had narrowed, funneling the ever-steepening trail into a jagged stone gorge near the bottom of the falls.

Here and there Amy held back unruly tufts of Juniper and Manzanita growing through cracks in the rock so I could pass unscathed. One by one we squeezed between enormous glacier-deposited boulders the size of trucks and scampered up tilted slabs of sandy granite on all fours until a thunderous roar enveloped us. My skin began to tingle as a misty chill settled upon me, a palpable warning that we were about to enter a treacherous place with no tolerance for mistakes.

When we reached a narrow plateau beside the chasm at the foot of the falls, the breath suddenly left my lungs as if it had been sucked out by the furious torrent suddenly churning and hurtling past us. Unexpectedly finding myself on a rock ledge that hung like a shelf over the raging flow, I fought back a brief wave of vertigo by planting my feet far apart and extending my arms like wings to maintain my balance. I then looked up and saw Horsetail Falls in front of us, falling in stages from high above, pouring off the mountain with a purpose that would have sent Noah rushing back to the ark.

I looked for Amy and saw her standing at the edge of the chasm. She looked tiny and insignificant at the base of the falls, like a twig that could be swept away, lost in the froth and carried off in a blur. There'd be nothing left but blood and pulp on the rocks below that the river would indiscriminately wash clean as if she'd never existed. It was frighteningly easy to envision.

I approached her from behind and, ready to grab her pack, said, "Step back. You're too close to the edge." I had to shout to be heard above the roar of the falls. It was like standing on a subway platform with an express train hurtling past the station at full speed right in front of you; the power rumbling under your feet, the wind turbulent in your face and ruffling your pants, the fear swelling in your gut that you might lose your balance and fall onto the tracks, or worse—get pushed.

We turned and found a safer spot to catch our breath and marvel at the forces of nature. "This is incredible," I said, leaning into her as we sat side by side on a rock just large enough for two.

"It is, isn't it?" she replied, this time raising her glasses to the top of her head. "I've been coming here since I was in high school. The Park Service opens the trail every year around this time. The spring runoff is always best early in the season and I'm pretty sure this is the wildest I've ever seen it."

Instead of enjoying the moment for what it was, a fresh start in a memorable place, I found myself wondering how many times she'd been here with other boys—with Mike Johnson in particular. How many times had they sat on this very rock, his arm around her shoulders? Had they made out here, the white noise of the falls blocking out the rest of the world? Had she shown *him* something he had never seen before, something he would never forget? Judging by the look of lost love on his face when we'd all stood in her office in the Drake building, I knew the answer. Clearly, whatever was going to happen here between *us*, if anything, was going to be more special for me than for her. That splash of jealousy made me feel like a teenager again, something I both enjoyed and detested at the same time. But at least I was the one with her now.

Not knowing what to say next, nor wanting to be compared to an old flame, I slipped off my pack and pulled out the bottle of water I'd opened, along with two granola bars. I offered one to Amy and said, "Here, we can look like a commercial for the company. All we need is a camera crew."

But she refused the snack and said, "We're only at the bottom of the falls. We're going to the top. I'll have one after we get there."

I looked around and saw no trail. It seemed to have ended near where we were. To the left of the falls the terrain looked like a monumental pile of boulders stacked haphazardly all the way to the top of the mountain—at least another four or five hundred feet. "How do we get there?"

"Up those rocks."

"I don't think so. This is a fantastic spot right here." For the first time in a long time I was actually aware of my own Brooklyn accent. "Forget about it," I said, doing my best New York City tough guy act.

"Come on. Put your pack on. It's not as difficult as it looks. I'll help you."

I gulped a few ounces of water and gazed up at the boulders beside the towering falls. I could feel my head moving from side to side in defiance. "I think this is far enough."

She stood, stepped in front of me, and slid my pack to the side along the ground so she could stand between my knees. Then, with her breasts at eye level and only an inch away from my face she said, "I thought you wanted to go all the way with me."

What? Was I dreaming? Or just trying too hard to read between the lines? I was, after all, an aficionado of innuendo, and equally adept at discerning the double entendre. I couldn't believe my ears. Talk about a change of heart. I sat there for a few seconds deciding how to react. Do nothing and you'll look like a geek, I thought. Be all over her like a cheap suit and you'll look like the horny toad you really are. I finally stood and wrapped my arms around her. "Are you sure you want to go there?"

This time she kissed me, her tongue quickly finding mine. After toying with me, she stopped and said into my ear, "I told you I'd show you something you've never seen before. I'll hold up my end of the deal if you'll hold up yours."

"What would you have me do?"

"Come with me," she whispered, pressing herself against me. Then she kissed me again, this time a little deeper. I could feel her pelvis against mine.

"I'd love to, but where?" I asked.

"Up there."

"Up where?"

She grabbed my chin and turned my head toward the rocks beside the falls. "There," she said, nibbling on my right ear. "That's the way to the top of the world."

"I must have missed the sign."

"There's a very private little spot up there beside Avalanche Lake. You won't believe it. It's like the Garden of Eden."

"I doubt if I'll be able to find a fig leaf at this altitude."

"Don't worry about it," she said, imitating my Brooklyneez. "You won't need one." She pushed me away and said with a devilish smile, "Let's go. It's not that hard."

I slipped on my pack and began to follow her again. *Not Yet.*

Over the years I've tried to talk to God a few times, questioning his wisdom when he allowed the people I loved to be taken from me, asking for a few things that seemed important now and then, and feebly conveying my appreciation for the blessings I've received, but I don't recall ever thanking him for creating the mind that invented Spandex.

I watched Amy from below as she scaled the boulders ahead of me, every inch of her—paying careful attention to the placement of her hands and feet on the rocks she chose to climb. Where possible, she favored the more angular ones because they had edges to grasp. One by one, stone by stone, climbing hand over foot and hoping I didn't end up ass over tea kettle, I duplicated her moves, or tried to, as we slowly ascended, the cascading falls only a few feet to our right.

I'll admit I'd gone to great lengths and spared no expense over the years in the name of romance, but never had I gone out on a limb this far. As the strength drained from my hands, arms, and legs, I wiped the sweat from my forehead with my sleeve and dug deep, assuring myself that it would all be worth it as I followed the girl of my dreams in my new life over the last few boulders at the very top of Horsetail Falls.

Then I saw it as the bottom of her tank top finally pulled free of her stretch-pants; a white gauze bandage two inches square. It was taped to the small of her back at the base of her spine.

26

I could only imagine one thing beneath that bandage. I tried to think it through before I opened my mouth. If it was what I thought it was, what did it mean? For one thing, it meant that she'd lied about not knowing Joey Fabiano. She'd held a copy of his driver's license photo in her hand and there, in her office, right in front of us, she'd denied knowing him, or ever having seen him.

If it was what I thought it was, it meant that she not only recognized him; it meant that she'd been a stripper at the club—that she'd worked for him. It meant that she'd fucked him for the job.

But it didn't mean that she was guilty of anything else, did it? Lily, the slut who'd ratted me out to the muscle at the door, wore the brand. She'd been the one to tell me about it, but that didn't mean that she'd had anything to do with the murders. All the tramps at Night Fire wore the three pointed orange and red flame. They had to. It was part of the initiation, along with a good couch-fuck for that lowlife bastard who tried to kill me. Mona, Drake's new wife, wore the brand. And now this—his own granddaughter! And I was upset because Mike Johnson had probably made out with Amy on a rock fifteen years ago, for cryin' out loud!

I tried to calm down before I made a total fool of myself. Maybe I was just jumping to conclusions, a bad habit of mine. Maybe everything I'd been through had made me paranoid. Maybe there was no tattoo. Maybe she'd just had a mole removed or something.

With one boulder yet to scale, I still hadn't reached the top of the falls. I looked up at Amy. She was standing above me now, peering out over the valley through which we'd come. From below, her curves seemed accentuated, almost making her a caricature of the perfect woman. For a moment, it seemed as if she were on stage, ready to start her act, looking out above the heads of the men in the audience who'd paid the cover charge at the door.

Then she realized that her shirt had pulled out of her pants. She looked down at me as she tucked it back in. She caught me staring at her, and I had the sense that she was wondering if I'd already noticed the bandage. "What's taking you so long, Slowpoke?" she asked.

Instead of answering, I considered lowering myself back down the mountain without ever reaching the top. I looked down, over the boulders I had just climbed. I'd never been afraid of heights before, but a sudden panic brushed me like an icy wind. What had I gotten myself into? Who was this woman, really? What was she capable of? And how the hell was I going to get off this mountain without breaking my neck? I had to make a decision and I was suddenly running out of time.

"Come on," she said. "You've only got another three feet to go."

"I need a minute. I've got a cramp."

She put her hands on her hips—the universal body-language symbol for impatience, her left hand falling on the black fanny pack she'd positioned there in the parking lot. Then she moved to my right, a little closer to where the water spilled over the edge. She looked down over the side and stared at the drop, her silky auburn hair hanging forward beside her face. She stood there for a minute thinking about something before moving back to a position above me again. "Are you all right?"

"Not yet."

She sat on the edge, braced her feet on the rock just above me, and reached down. "Give me your hand. I'll help you."

I could have backed away, but I didn't. I grabbed her wrist, she seized mine, and a few seconds later we were both standing beside the top of the falls gazing at the awe-inspiring endless vista.

"Have you ever seen a better view?" she asked.

I turned and looked at her, not knowing what to think. *If Drake was a fraud, if Maxwell Bennett had been the one to paint everything that Drake had signed and sold, and Amy was his second in command, was it even possible that she didn't know the truth? And why hadn't I thought of this before? How stupid could I be? I'd assumed that Drake alone had sent Joey to New York to murder my uncle. Why hadn't it occurred to me that they both could have contracted him? We'd assumed that Drake had sent that son of a bitch to kill me. After all, what kind of coincidence was it that Joey showed up at my doorstep seven hours after I was in Drake's office?*

Still worse, he'd knocked on my door only five hours after I had dinner with Amy, a date that ended in disaster. She'd stormed out; something I thought had been my fault. How long was it before I noticed the black Suburban? An hour? He must have been there outside Luigi's waiting to follow me home. She would have been the last one to see me alive if Johnson hadn't saved my life. Isn't that what the cops always ask: Who was the last person to see the victim alive?

She'd planned that date, not me. She'd chosen the restaurant. She'd made the reservation from her office after she'd left me alone with Drake. That's when she would have called Joey. She'd had plenty of time. He only lived around the corner, for Christ's sake! That's why North Beach had sounded familiar. She'd planned everything, including how it would end!

And now, she'd planned this date. She'd picked the time and place. She'd lured me into Desolation Wilderness. And like a lovesick little puppy, I followed.

I looked downward, beyond the steepest part of the climb beside the falls at the valley in search of other people. I spotted two hikers, but they were way down there, two tiny specks moving slowly on the trail at least two hours behind us. I considered calling out to them, but I also knew I'd never be heard above the roar of the falls. What would I have said, anyway?

I remembered the boating horn I'd brought as a bear deterrent, but it was in my pack. If a bear had popped out of nowhere, I couldn't have gotten to it under those circumstances either. So much for my careful planning.

I reached into my pocket for the shocker I'd used outside Night Fire, something I'd gotten quite comfortable carrying, but finding nothing there realized I'd returned it to Bill Sherman earlier in the week. The only weapon I had was the Swiss Army knife I'd brought, but, like the horn, it was also in my pack.

I considered simply grabbing her pack straps and flinging her off the edge right in front of us before she had a chance to complete whatever plan she'd devised, but considering a plain white gauze bandage was my only evidence, I thought that might be a little extreme and hard to explain, especially if the gauze was only covering a rug burn.

Then I felt her hand on the small of *my* back below my pack. My reflexes kicked in and every muscle I had stiffened as I braced myself. Fearing a shove, I quickly stepped to the side and backed up a few feet.

"What's wrong?" she asked, surprised that I'd moved away from her.

Instead of blurting out, *why did you lie about Fabiano?* I tried to remain calm and play along. "Nothing's wrong. Everything is perfect. I just feel a little uneasy being so close to the edge."

"All right," she said. "Stay right there. I'll take your picture." She stepped back about ten feet on the flat granite and unzipped the top of her fanny pack, leaving me a couple of yards from the edge of the falls, the spectacular panorama behind me.

I glanced at the surroundings behind her in search of the promised Garden of Eden, which would have given her words some degree of truth. But instead of glimpsing a high sierra Shangri-La, the landscape seemed, instead, quite grotesque. The Pinion Pines were short and deformed, and the lake that fed the falls was surrounded by mud.

She reached across her abdomen with her right hand, pulled a small black pistol from the pouch as if it had been a cross-draw holster, and pointed it at me. "How did you know?" she asked with little emotion.

Even though I knew it was coming, the fear that sliced through my mind seemed to sever my vocal cords.

When I didn't answer she demanded again, "How did you know?"

"Know what?"

"Where to look. How did you find us?"

"I didn't. I stumbled onto May's house. I recognized it as the house in my uncle's painting. I told you that."

"I don't believe you."

"That's how it happened. It was nothing more than a coincidence. The funny thing is, I left New York to get as far away from the murders as I could. If Joey hadn't tried to kill me, you would have gotten away with everything."

"Bullshit. You interrogated my grandfather the minute I introduced you to him in his office. Then it all made sense. You came to California looking for him. You found May first and used me to get to him. A whole year had passed and the cops had nothing. Then, out of nowhere, you show up. You were investigating the murders yourself, weren't you? Why the fuck else would an architect need an art expert? You just couldn't quit. You had to push it. Now you want to paint, do you? You've been full of shit from the minute you arrived."

"Believe whatever you want. Just tell me something: Who sent Joey to kill me? Who made the call?"

"What difference does it make?"

"I'd like to know just how stupid I've been."

"Let's put it this way," she began. "On a ten point stupid scale, you passed fifteen a long time ago."

"I thought so. But you were even more stupid than I was. If Joey hadn't tried to kill me, nothing would have happened. Nothing. As a matter of fact, *I* was the best suspect the police had. *Me!* Can you believe that? They liked me for the murders. How's that for a laugh? That's why Johnson was at my house when Joey showed up. As it turns out, you're the one responsible for your grandfather's suicide. Not me. You brought the police to his door by getting me off the hook. You showed them they'd been looking at the wrong guy. You showed them where to look. How does that make you feel?"

"Shut up!"

"Who sent Joey to New York, you or *Ralph?*"

This time she answered with a smirk. "Both of us."

I could feel the rage that had been layered over by grief rising to the surface, displacing the new fear that weakened my guts. "I know my uncle painted everything. How did it all start?"

"It was simple. May told grandpa about him once she realized he was never coming. Leland had the idea. There were ghost writers for people who couldn't write. Why wouldn't this work? He found him and made him a deal. That's all. Maxwell needed the money, like all losers."

"Was May ever a part of it?"

Amy averted her eyes for just a moment as she shook her head.

"Why did you have to murder him? He'd kept the secret for most of his life, didn't he? Why'd you have to kill him?"

"He was weak. He was always weak. From the minute he broke my grandmother's heart to the day the break-in brought the police to his wretched little apartment. He'd always been on the verge of cracking. That put him over the edge. You should have heard him on the phone. It was pathetic. It's a fucking miracle he'd held it together as long as he did."

I remembered the badgering in the station house about his missing cell phone. "How did you talk? The cops couldn't get anywhere with his phone records, and they couldn't find his cell."

She grunted with conceit. "We supplied the untraceable throwaway phone, just like we thought of everything else, including getting it back."

"What about Dana? Why did you kill my wife?"

"Joey had no choice. But what was all that *pretend* bullshit between you and her? What the fuck was that all about? Did she have to fake all her orgasms for you, or what? You even tried that crap on me, but your timing was bad, Lover Boy. You were a little early, don't you think?"

"How do you know about that?"

"Joey offered me the pendant as a souvenir, but I told him I didn't have to pretend anything—and he knew it."

I beat back the rage long enough to say, "So instead he gave it to Ralph, the greatest pretender of all time, who in turn gave it to

Mona the slut so she could pretend to love the old bastard while she fucked every serf at Glenshire. Does that sound about right?"

"Back up."

"Fuck you, Bitch. Fuck you for the things you said about my wife while your murdering scumbag pimp was waiting outside to follow me."

"You're going to back up and jump off this mountain or I'll shoot you right where you stand."

"It's got to look like an accident, doesn't it? How will it look like an accident if you shoot me? Don't you think Mike will figure it out?"

"I'll handle Mike. He'll believe anything I say."

"You're a little too full of yourself. You think you can get men to do whatever you want, is that it?"

"I know I can. I got you up here, didn't I?"

"That's as far as it'll go." I slipped off my pack and tossed it to the side. "If you want me to go off this mountain you'll have to push me off. Can you do it, Outdoor Mountain Bitch? Being a tease won't cut it anymore. Let's see what else you've got. Come on. Try to push me off. If you're such hot shit with all that athletic climbing crap in the trunk of your car, you should be able to shove a pencil-pushing architect off a cliff. Come on. I'm right here. You tried to have your pimp kill me, but instead he got what was coming to him. Besides being a low-life drug dealing ex-con, he must have been one of the dumbest motherfuckers in the history of homicide. Didn't anyone ever tell him not to take souvenirs from a crime scene? Now it's your turn to see if you can do better. Come on. What are you waiting for? If you can't rush me and drive me over the edge right here you'll spend the rest of your life in a penitentiary. You'd better remember this view because you'll never see anything like it again. Think about it. You won't be able to wear those cute little designer outfits anymore. And the wind in your hair behind the wheel of your sporty convertible will be just a memory. The only thing you'll be driving is a stinking laundry cart in the prison basement. Come on, Bitch. That's what you've got to look forward to if you can't push me off this rock. Come on! Let's go! What are you waiting for?"

She raised the gun to eye level and aimed it at my face. "Do yourself a favor and shut up. Just shut the fuck up and step off. Don't you think that'll be easier than a bullet in the head?"

"If you shoot me, there's no chance of you getting away with anything. Zero! You know that as well as I do. If your shirt hadn't pulled out of your pants you might have done it. Your plan to get me up here wasn't that bad, but unless you can push me off now, you'll be the one in the lock-up. Can you do it? Come on, Bitch. Make your scumbag con-artist prison punk grandfather finally proud. You at least need to try, don't you? After all, you're the one that brought the whole thing down on his head and put the bedsheet in his hands. I explained it to you already. Are you fucking stupid, or what? You tried to have me killed, but you killed him instead."

I hoped she would simply rush me out of anger, compelled to shut me up with her own hands, but in an instant she shifted the gun to her left hand and picked up a thick two-foot long weathered branch.

"No one will know that your skull was smashed before you went over." Then with deliberate strides she came at me, the automatic in one hand and the bough in the other, wielding it in some sort of practiced martial arts motion.

I couldn't back up, nor could I escape to either side. With no place to go, I had to stand my ground.

It felt like the first blow cracked my ribs. I tried to block the second with my left arm and the pain drove me to my knees. A third might have brought the end I'd called upon myself, but instead she tried to kick me in the head. I grabbed her boot and pulled her toward me with all the strength I had, instead of trying to push her back. She toppled over with more force than I expected, her gloved hands suddenly empty and searching for something to slow her momentum. But there was nothing. I saw her clawing at the smooth granite as she went over.

I suppose I should have scrambled to grab her, but I doubt I would have been able to save the woman. It all happened so fast. But I did have enough time to say something before she slipped from view, although it wasn't what I would have expected of myself, something like: Hold on, I'll help you. Nor was it something I would tell the police. It just came out in the moment before she disappeared. "It's your time to pretend, Amy. Pretend you can fly."

I crawled to the edge and looked over, but she was gone. I scanned the rocks beside the falls for her body, or red smears. I studied the water, white with froth far below until it swirled from view. Then I backed away from the cliff and collapsed in the sun.

I knew I had to call for help. I had to report Amy's death. My chest hurt like hell and I needed a helicopter to lift me off the mountain. I pulled out my cell and checked the signal strength. I then dialed 911, but stopped myself from touching the call button, realizing that everything entering the system is recorded. What were the right words? Which phrases would be the least incriminating? I was the one reporting the accident now, not Amy. I had nothing that could prove the things she'd said. There were no witnesses, nor any evidence. The gun had been the first to go over the edge, skidding across the level granite in the direction of the falls after it left her hand. Even the branch she'd wielded like a baton had gone over.

Considering everything that had happened, starting with the murders of my wife and uncle in New York more than a year ago, what chance did I have of convincing the police that my date had lured me to the top of Horsetail Falls to kill me, that she'd been the one guilty of orchestrating the crimes that had confounded them at both ends of the country? They would see it the way she had; that *I'd* been the one pursuing *her*—that I'd lured her to the top of the falls to commit murder instead of the other way around, that I'd been obsessed with vengeance and had planned a way to exact it on a beautiful Saturday morning in the Sierra Nevada by staging the perfect accident.

I decided to take my chances with Mike Johnson, even though he had questioned my intentions. I scrolled for his cell number and hit call, knowing that the only evidence I had was being swept away somewhere below by the spring runoff. Amy's once glorious body had to be found before whatever was left of the little orange and red flame tattoo that corroborated my story was stripped from her bones and eaten by the many delightful creatures of nature.

27

I gazed at the Maxwell Bennett paintings I'd hung around the great room, which really wasn't that great except for the artwork. I considered the display as a whole, then each one individually, working my way from one painting to the next. To be truthful, I liked some more than others, but that was only natural, wasn't it? Just because my uncle painted them didn't mean I had to rave about them all equally, did it?

Personally, I preferred the untitled street scenes that prompted the imagination to say, Paris or Nice; Bucharest or Prague. But I also liked the whitewashed unadorned houses beside the blue Aegean, as well as the colorful attached dwellings that clung to steep hills above the Italian Mediterranean. Some portrayed pleasant courtyards bathed in bright sunlight—rich with crisp detail. Others were night scenes—somber and subdued. Some depicted boulevards shrouded in rain and mist. Then I realized that *none* could be labeled American Impressionism. Not one.

While they were beautiful and equally captivating, they were all in sharper focus than any style employing the impressionism suffix. These were Mack's works; the one's he'd hung in his own apartment, the one's bearing his signature. Nothing resembled a Drake. Not even a little bit. I'd realized before that he'd created a style thoroughly recognizable as a Drake, in fact unmistakable to the keen eye, but now it was clear to me that he never mixed those elements of style with his own—neither subject nor technique.

I ambled around the apartment reviewing paintings the living room could not accommodate and realized, again, that the media varied from oil to acrylic to watercolor. I paused before a matched set of small still lifes that had been painted with a knife, the pastel flowers depicted in raised relief. Riding an ongoing tide of pride, I even considered the frames he'd chosen—the design, finish, and mass of each perfectly complementing the painting within.

The only room in the condo without a Bennett original was the bath, where I soon stared at myself in the mirror above the sink. I could have been happier. I should have been happier. I'd cheated death at least twice and was still alive. I was a free man, standing in my own place where the locks opened from the inside as well as the outside.

Mike Johnson had been in the helicopter that lifted the horse's ass from the top of Horsetail Falls. Shouting to be heard above the engine noise, I'd explained it all to him on the short ride to the ambulance that was waiting in the parking lot below, along with a variety of county and state vehicles. By the time the emergency room staff at the hospital in Tahoe had x-rayed my fractured ribs, the search and rescue team, with the help of the chopper, had found Amy wedged under a log a couple of miles downriver. Her gorgeous face had been smashed on the rocks, the pulp washed clean of blood, but the telltale little tattoo she was having professionally faded from her back was still recognizable, orange and red inks being the most difficult to erase.

Johnson reopened the investigation, finding a few women at Night Fire who, when shown photos, confirmed that Amy had worked there while she was in college, although an audit of the books and personnel records failed to document her employment. It isn't nice to speak ill of the dead, but, if I had to guess, knowing what I know now, I'd say that her income hadn't been the only thing going on under the table.

As I evaluated the jerk in the mirror, I couldn't help but feel disappointed, mostly with myself. Apparently, I'll never win any awards for being a good judge of character. And given my communication skills, it's certainly a good thing I hadn't chosen a career as a diplomat. Saying one thing and having the other party to a conversation hear something completely different could have inadvertently triggered World War III. But the most potent case for justified self-recrimination was pointed out to me by Mike Johnson, who will never be known as Mr. Subtle. "You fucked up," he'd said while we sat in his cruiser after he'd documented the truth about Amy. "You had the chance to ask, 'What happened to the painting that Joey took,' the one we couldn't find even with a stack of warrants, including the one issued subsequently for her place? You had the chance, Architect, but you blew it."

That was an argument I couldn't win. I'd suspected Mack had painted everything that made Drake rich and famous and Amy had confirmed it, but I still had no proof. The painting taken from the crime scene could have been the missing link, like the one-of-a-kind pendant that facilitated Drake's demise, but unlike the little gold filigree heart I'd had custom made for Dana, it was nowhere to be found.

One of Joey's cell phones did, however, connect the dots. And quite frankly, Johnson's police work continued to impress me. Apparently, Joey used his iPhone on a daily basis like the rest of us. On the other hand, the pre-paid bottom of the line phone, what Amy would have described as a throwaway, not unlike the one they'd given to Mack, must have been the one used exclusively for nefarious purposes. The call history on that phone contained only three phone numbers, all of which had been assigned to three other pre-paid phones, all four phones, including Joey's, bought by someone using an assumed identity. The serial numbers associated with those phone numbers revealed that all of the instruments had been purchased at the same time in the same store. Johnson found the store in San Francisco, reviewed the security camera system's digital footage shot at the time of purchase, and positively identified Joseph Fabiano at the register with the items in question.

Further scrutiny of the call history showed that Joey's phone had received an incoming call from one of the other numbers two minutes after that number had called Luigi's *Ristorante Italiano* in North Beach at 5:12 p.m. on the Friday I'd had dinner with Amy. Apparently, Amy Drake had been in such a frenzy to have me killed that she inadvertently used the wrong phone to make the reservation, the same phone she used to call Joey, so he could be waiting outside the restaurant to follow me back to Tahoe. We can only speculate that both Amy and her grandfather tossed their throwaway phones after Amy learned from May, thanks to our Saturday visit to the house by the river, that Joey had been shot at my front door, as those phones were never found.

Amy's everyday smartphone, secured in her fanny pack's second zippered compartment, had been recovered with her body. When dried out and dumped, a photo of my Porsche and its new license plate was revealed. With it, DMV records would have yielded my address for Joey. The shot was snapped when I was dropped at my car after our Bavarian lunch near the river. May's house was in the background.

I finally sat with aching ribs on the edge of the bed in the master suite having considered all of the paintings I'd inherited from my uncle except two; the strange little copy that was in an NYPD evidence locker, and the one I'd hidden away in a closet behind a stack of boxes. I'd stashed it there to be out of sight and out of mind because I couldn't bear to look at it. Not since the happiness I'd known had been ripped away. Not since Dana's murder. There was certainly no need to see it morning and night, to struggle against a tether to the past when I'd gone to such extremes to start a new life.

But now that the shit storm I'd plunged into quite by chance, the very same one I'd tried to leave behind in New York, was finally over, I thought it was time to say goodbye to Dana and Mack and to thank them for the unconditional and irreplaceable love and kindness they'd shown me. What better way, I thought, to pay homage to them both than to admire the wedding gift he'd painted for us?

I pulled the large watercolor still life from the shadows and stood it on the oak highboy, leaning it against the bedroom wall. I dusted the glass and the understated modern metallic gold frame with a T-shirt from one of the drawers below, stood back, and gazed at the muted flowers. Then I considered the message that I knew was hidden amongst the petals and stamens. Unless you knew it was there, unless you knew where to look and what to look for, it would never be noticed. *Robert & Dana, always!* I tried to control myself, but failed miserably. I should have known better.

I stepped closer again after drying the blur from my eyes, wanting to see the words skillfully camouflaged in the smallest details. If Mack hadn't proudly pointed them out, neither of us would have been aware of the message. It wasn't particularly profound or poetic, but given the backdrop, the simple sentiment was as romantic as it was to the point.

I was intrigued by the curiously misshapen characters, neatly fitting against one another like the pieces of a jigsaw puzzle. They were tiny and intricate, yet clearly identifiable if you were close enough. In fact, once you knew the phrase was there, it was hard *not* to see it.

I know it sounds like the letters and words would have spoiled the picture for the casual observer, but the funny thing about a painting is that it is meant to be viewed at a certain distance. I considered the phenomenon. Up close it may look like a mess: An assemblage of haphazard blobs, smears, and crooked lines, but as one backs away things come into focus and the painting not only gains meaning and perspective, it magically becomes beautiful. Once at the proper viewing range to appreciate this work in its entirety, the words, as if hiding in plain sight, are too small to see.

Then, oddly enough, something occurred to me for the first time. If Mack had painted a present for us, surely he must have done so for my aunt, the one person in the world to whom he was most devoted. If he had, what was the occasion and which painting was it? I'd just scrutinized each and every one. But I'd viewed them the way paintings were meant to be viewed; at the proper distance.

I made my way to the kitchen, rummaged through a drawer filled with junk until I found the magnifying glass I knew was there, and then returned to the main theater of my own Bennett gallery. I stood in the center of the room and tried to guess which painting might have been a gift Mack lovingly created for his sister. I was drawn to two French street scenes; a matched set we knew she loved. Bright and cheerful, they emphasized formal structure and color. Each sixteen by twenty inches, my uncle had formatted them vertically, ultimately setting the pair in modestly gilded identical wooden frames. Without further speculation, I approached the one on the left and began examining the areas of the scene most likely to conceal a message. I studied the shrubs and flowers through the magnifying glass, then the leaves of trees that cast lacey shadows on the street below. And then, there they were: Four words arranged in an arc, each tiny letter within oddly shaped, but recognizable with careful scrutiny. I repeated the message aloud, the way Mack might have. *"For Sid, my sister."* Then I found the same message in the other half of the set.

Dumbfounded, I started talking to myself. "I don't believe it! I've looked at those pictures for most of my life and had no idea."

Then something else struck me. With thirty-nine to choose from, what were the odds that I'd go directly to the right paintings? Things didn't work that way, especially for me. If not for bad luck, I would have no luck at all.

I stopped asking myself questions I couldn't answer and examined every Bennett in the collection the same way, which took the rest of the afternoon. I found the very same message in all but two of my uncle's paintings. One was our wedding present, which had a message all its own. The other was of the white house by the river. I found an entirely different message skillfully hidden in the tall grass along the bank, across from the mysterious blue tree. Again, I read it aloud the way Mack would have, if he'd had the chance. *"For May, the love of my life."*

28

I stood on the porch, resting the painting that had started it all on the top of my boating shoe. I had the shoes even if I didn't have the boat. I'm not sure why exactly, but that statement sounds somehow like the story of my life.

I'd driven my silver Porsche past the paparazzi camped along the river near the entrance to the pedestrian bridge and found a secluded parking space across the road. Some, microphones in hand, had rushed over and tried to stop me as I headed on foot for the crossing, while others snapped away relentlessly as if I were a celebrity instead of a mere architect. Fortunately, Mike Johnson had miraculously managed to keep my name out of it so nothing like that had happened to me outside my condo.

Johnson had broken the news to May personally. All of it; not only that Amy had perished during a struggle she'd initiated, but that she'd been involved in orchestrating a dastardly series of events culminating in murder. Apparently, he was one tough lawman who believed in the truth no matter how unkind it was or who it hurt.

He'd attended the funeral of the girl he would have probably married if he'd had the opportunity, unless his police instincts were set to kick in and warn him off. He'd mentioned in passing that the nature of her injuries necessitated a closed casket. He'd said so without batting an eye. Perhaps scraping people off the highway every other day had hardened him sufficiently, or maybe it meant he was finally over her.

I felt it was time for me to offer my condolences to May Drake, even if her granddaughter had deserved to die. I might have called it an accident and left it at that, had I been the one breaking the news. It was almost easy to imagine her saying, "At least she died in her favorite place, doing what she loved." What was to be gained by ruining the old woman's memory of a grandchild?

It was hard for me to imagine May's reaction to the truth; not only that the granddaughter she adored was just as much a murderer as Fabiano, but that the girl had conspired to murder her grandmother's one true love. I knew this wasn't going to be easy. Despite the fact that everything went to hell when I showed up in California, at least I wasn't the bad guy after all. I was the victim. That had to count for something in the old lady's eyes, didn't it?

She opened the door and said, "Please come in."

Not only had her granddaughter been alive the last time I was in her house, the fact that she'd married a swindler had not yet surfaced. How did it feel to learn that the person you married was a complete fraud, a con man, an ex-con, and ultimately a murderer? Come to think of it, probably not much different than finding out that the girl with whom you were falling in love had conspired to murder you and your family. In a crazy sort of way, that meant I had something in common with May Drake—that and the fact that Maxwell Bennett had been uniquely special to us both.

"I'm sorry about your granddaughter." I said the words, but I didn't mean them any more than when I'd told Amy I was sorry about her grandfather. "I won't stay long, but there are some things I'd like to share with you—things I think you should know."

"Sit down, won't you? It's all right, really. I'll make some tea," she said, always the gracious hostess. "I'll be back in a minute." But before she moved, she looked down at the brown paper-wrapped eighteen by twenty-four inch painting in my hands and asked, "What do you have there?"

"This is what made me stop and knock on your door in the first place."

She suddenly looked confused, so I continued. "I've got to be honest with you. I didn't set out to find the woman my uncle thought about every day of his life. I didn't come here to give you the bad news about his murder. I've looked at and loved this painting for years." I tore the paper from the framed oil, turned it around, and held it up in front of her. I studied her expression as I went on. "Something made me stop when I passed this house on the way home from my new job. It took me a week to muster the courage to step onto the porch. Believe it or not, this all started with a bizarre coincidence—nothing more." I considered explaining how her granddaughter and ex-husband thought, because they were both as guilty as sin, that I'd sought them out while conducting my own investigation, which couldn't have been further from the truth, but stopped short since there was nothing to be gained.

Her expression warmed a little as she gazed at the painting for the first time. Her smile was weak, but I believe it originated in a place reserved for things that meant something special. "Oh dear," she murmured as her eyes filled. I saw her shudder and cover her mouth. She wore black slacks and a pale yellow silk blouse buttoned to the neck. "I like your earrings," I said to lighten the moment, noticing the pearl studs.

She acknowledged the compliment with a long blink that forced out a couple of tears. She blotted them away with a hankie that had already been in her hand when she'd opened the door. "Thank you for showing it to me. Why don't you set it on the hearth? I'll be right back." She turned and headed for the kitchen without further delay, a departure that would also allow her the time to compose herself in private.

"Do you wear readers?" I asked before she was gone, knowing that she did.

She turned. "Doesn't everyone my age?"

"Bring them with you when you come back. There's something I want to show you."

"All right."

I placed the painting on the stone hearth, leaning it against the fireplace screen, and glanced up at the Bennett above the mantel, certain that it needed closer scrutiny. I saw no grasses, trees, or flowers to examine in search of tiny English characters, but the majestic square-rigger itself, richly adorned with fine wood grain, nets, and ornate period scrollwork, to say nothing of the restless sea upon which it sailed, provided a boatload of possibilities.

Then I looked at Amy's photograph just below it and wondered with guarded enmity how a face so beautiful could have been the face of such malevolence? Her death didn't bring Dana or Mack back to life, but I was glad she was dead nonetheless. Truth be told, I wanted to pull the photo out of its frame and stomp on it a few times with my heel, grinding it into the burgundy Persian rug before tearing it into a million tiny pieces. But I had work to do. I was in May Drake's home for a reason and getting thrown out would have been counterproductive.

I turned away and took a deep breath. The room was exactly

as I remembered, warmly lit by a variety of shaded lamps, but the windows facing the river, as well as the French patio doors leading to the pines behind the house, were now occluded by drapes that had previously been tied back. I knew this was because of the pitiless prying eyes with zoom lenses that were parked outside yearning for a potentially profitable photo of a fallen celebrity's ex-wife. Other than that, I saw no evidence that tragedy had reached in and upended the peace that resided here.

I focused on the knickknacks. They brought me back to the apartment in Queens, and I contemplated for a moment what my uncle would be thinking if he knew where I was and what I had in mind. Confident that he'd be pleased, I walked toward the rear of the room to examine the Drake hanging beside the French doors.

It was then that I realized what was wrong with the ground-level floor plan. It had bothered me the other times I'd been there, but I couldn't put my finger on it. I suppose I'd had more important things on my mind. But now the question seemed obvious. Where was the dining room? If there was one, it had to be on the other side of the floor-to-ceiling bookshelves running the length of the load-bearing wall that, along with the stairs and tiny water closet beneath them, separated the living room from the kitchen. I continued to the rear of the room thinking the entrance should have been immediately to my left, but it wasn't, just as there wasn't one through the kitchen. When I stopped in front of the painting on the back wall, I heard May's voice.

"That's the first painting Leland ever gave me. He learned and practiced in secret. It took him a year to get to that level. It's been sold as prints, and on calendars and greeting cards. It's been quite successful, you know."

"I remember you saying that the last time I was here." She must be in a state of denial, I thought. Johnson had told her everything. She knew Drake was dead—that he'd committed suicide in his jail cell after being indicted for double murder, his true identity revealed to the world. He'd been responsible for Mack's homicide and so had Amy. Together they'd conspired to kill the man May had presumably loved like no other. And still, with a touch of pride, she called him Leland. Clinging to the pieces of her world must be her way of coping with it all, I thought. It's a miracle she's not in a rubber room, for Christ's sake.

But if she is blocking out reality, how would she react to what I was about to tell her? On the way to her house I thought I'd be doing her a favor. Now I wasn't so sure. I turned to face her and said, "There's something I think you should know."

She looked at me and began to speak, but stopped, her thin lips quivering slightly. Hesitant, she stood there in silence, a pair of reading glasses now hanging around her neck on a gold herringbone chain.

I knew what she was thinking. As of late, every time someone came to her home with important news, it must have felt as if she'd been dragged another few inches closer to the end of her rope. I said, "Let's sit down. I'm not sure, but I think you may be happy about what I have to say." I walked to one of the floral armchairs grouped near the fireplace without waiting for a reply and seated myself. Then I waited for May to do the same.

She sat on the edge of the opposite loveseat, her hands on her lap toying with the wrinkled white linen hankie. The hearth, and the painting I'd brought, was to her left. She looked at it for a minute before turning toward me.

I was tempted to ask her opinion of the work. She was, after all, an art expert. But her opinion didn't matter, not anymore. My uncle didn't have to prove anything. I was the only one left with something to prove, and it was on his posthumous behalf.

"That painting behind you, Drake's first one," I began. "It's not what you think. I'm afraid you've been misled."

"What do you mean *misled*?"

"Leland Drake didn't paint that painting. In fact, he didn't paint any of the paintings he signed. Maxwell Bennett painted them all."

I didn't know how she'd react to the news and frankly, I didn't care, unless she'd known all along and was now willing to corroborate what Amy had said. It was no longer a matter of conjecture, but it still had to be proven.

She didn't argue, nor was she incredulous. She sat expressionless for some time before simply saying, "After hearing the truth about Leland, I suppose anything is possible."

"It's not just possible, May. It's true."

"How do you know? How can you be so certain?"

"Because Amy told me."

I could see the thin, wrinkled age-spotted skin around May's knuckles turn white as she clenched her fists around the tear-dampened hankie on her lap. Her lower lip quivered again before she forced the question, "When? When did she tell you?"

"A couple of minutes before she died."

There was no stopping the outpouring of tears now.

"I'm sorry, May. And I'm not sure how to say this, but I thought somehow you'd be pleased to know that the man who truly loved you was the one who, in a roundabout way, made your financial security possible. As it turned out, by painting everything behind the Drake fortune, he provided for you *and* his sister."

For several minutes I had no idea what she was thinking. I suspected a tumultuous continuum from gratitude to resentment and everything in between, but simply waited in silence for her to utter the next word. Then she asked something I didn't expect.

"You keep saying he loved me. You keep saying that. How do you know?"

"Because he put it in writing."

She looked pensive for a moment, peering back in time. Then she smiled a little more deeply, despite the tears. "Yes. His letters were wonderful."

"I'm not talking about the letters, May. Put on your glasses."

I stood, picked up the painting I'd brought, and held it near the shaded lamp on the end table to her right, resting it on the polished wood just behind a small leaf-shaped red glass dish trimmed with gold. I maneuvered it until the light illuminated the lower half of the canvas, which included the house's reflection on the river, the trunk of the infamous blue tree, and the grasses along both banks. "Look closely at this portion of the painting and tell me what you see," I said, pointing to the area that contained Maxwell Bennett's message.

Puzzled, she looked up at me.

"Go ahead. Study the grass right there."

She shifted closer to the end of the loveseat, set the glasses on her nose, and stared at the lower left-hand quadrant of the scene. A minute or two passed before she said, "What am I looking for?"

I reached into my pocket, pulled out the magnifying glass I'd brought, and offered it to her. "Use this. Perhaps it will help you."

She took hold of it with a trace of skepticism and held it between her face and the canvas, adjusting the focal distance. Another couple of minutes came and went before she looked up at me, a tangle of wonder, sadness, and disbelief on her seasoned face, every nuance illuminated by the lamp beside her. I could see the twinkle in her eyes—a light indubitably rekindled within.

"I've enjoyed this painting for the better part of my years," I said, "but it wasn't until yesterday that I discovered those words. I brought it for you. I'd like you to have it. If anything, it's long overdue."

"How did you find it?"

"He painted a watercolor still life of flowers as a wedding

present for Dana and me. He inscribed a similar sentiment in that one. We never would have noticed it had he not pointed it out. After everything that's happened, I took it out of the closet yesterday in a moment of tribute."

May carefully set the magnifying glass on the table next to a miniature two-handled Grecian urn. "Why was it in a closet and not on the wall?" she asked.

"I didn't think looking at it day after day would help me move on."

She considered my explanation a few seconds longer than I expected, her eyes averted in thought. Then she finally nodded. "I'm sorry. I didn't mean to interrupt you."

"Anyway, it occurred to me to examine the other paintings in the collection. This was the last one I checked."

"How many are there?"

"Thirty-nine."

"Are there words in any of the others?"

I nodded.

"How many?"

"All of them."

"Oh, my God, what do they say?" Rather than simply being inquisitive, I knew she was hopeful that her name was in those as well.

I could think of no way to spare her feelings. "It doesn't matter now."

She turned away and said, "It's really not that unusual for artists to do that sort of thing."

I picked up the magnifying glass, leaned the painting against the fireplace screen again, stood on the river rock hearth, and began examining the Bennett above the mantel. May Drake watched me in silence.

It took almost ten minutes to find the message skillfully hidden in the ship's rigging. "Would you like to read it for yourself, or shall I read it to you?"

"I... I don't... What does it say?"

"For May, I'll always love you."

I heard a gasp and turned. I thought she was going to collapse. I sat beside her and put my arm around her shoulders. I felt her shudder again and again as I considered the thoughts she'd penned in letters written more than fifty years ago, letters deemed by my uncle so precious he'd locked them away in a bank vault. Only after they'd been released to me and I'd read them all, could I appreciate the depth of the once-in-a-lifetime love that went unsatisfied. If I'd had them when Maxwell Bennett was laid to rest more than a year ago, I would have buried them with him. I think he would have wanted me to.

When the case was officially closed, the New York authorities relinquished to me the entire contents of the safe-deposit box that had raised more questions than answers until, ultimately, the cash led us to Drake's bank in San Francisco, which, you may recall, was my idea—even before I'd learned to think like a cop.

I hadn't had the presence of mind, however, to ask what else was in the box when the detectives at the One-Seventeen told me about the money and letters. I'd beaten myself up about that on the flight back to California. And if that self-recrimination wasn't potent enough, Deputy Johnson asked me if I had set forth that very question in the precinct. Now I knew the answer. In fact, I had the only other item contained therein with me now. I brought it to give to May.

But as I reached into my pocket and my free hand closed around it I began to have second thoughts. Maybe it wasn't a good idea. Maybe this wasn't the time. Maybe I shouldn't even be here. After all, how much could this woman endure? If she was near the breaking point, could this cause the snap? The last thing

I wanted was to push her so far she'd have a nervous breakdown, or something even worse—a stroke or a heart attack. I certainly didn't want to be responsible for that. And if it happened, what would the police think about me this time, especially if the woman was incapacitated or dead on the floor? I left it in my pocket and said, "It's all right, May. At least you know the truth. He told you he loved you every time you looked at that painting—in fact every time you walked into the room. You just didn't know it."

"He gave me that painting a very long time ago. I hid it when he didn't come to me and I married Leland, the same way you hid the flowers he painted for you and your wife. When Leland left me, I put it back above the mantel. I've looked at it for years and had no idea his words were there. Why, Robert? Why didn't he come to me? I couldn't wait any longer. If he loved me so much, why didn't he come to me? Our lives would have been so different."

"He couldn't abandon his sister. He tried. He made it halfway across the country on his way to you, but he couldn't do it. She was sick. She had cancer. She battled it her whole life and time after time she beat it—operation after operation, treatment after treatment. Maybe it was her brother's devotion that kept her alive, in more ways than one. If it wasn't for the bills, he never would have agreed to do anything unethical. Never! That's why he made a deal with the devil—your husband. I know it. There's only one way to look at it now. Sid needed him even more than you did."

I uncoiled my arm and pivoted to face her on the settee. "I need your help, May. I need to prove that Maxwell painted everything Leland signed."

She looked at me like a deer in the headlights before starting to shake her head slowly from side to side. "Leave it alone. I've lost too much already. I can't lose any more."

"I'm not asking you to lose anything. If you're worried about the value of Leland's estate, don't be. It can only go up. Nothing sells like controversy."

"I'm not talking about money," she protested. "I've lost everyone in my life, everyone who's been important to me, everyone I've ever loved. How much can I stand? Look outside, will you? Now I've lost my dignity and my privacy. Don't ask me to lose any more. I just can't. It'll kill me."

"My uncle painted a collection that made your husband famous for something he didn't do. And whether you knew it or not, you helped make it happen. Now it's time for you to set things right and see that credit is given where credit is due."

"Please. Leave it alone."

"The man who loved you deserves better than that. You owe him that much."

"What do you mean?"

"You forced him to make an impossible decision. You could have gone to New York. The roads go both ways, don't they? You could have gone to him if he couldn't come to you."

"I had a successful business to run. I had a life here in California."

"And his life was there. I know the struggle you put him through. I watched it on film; home movies shot on my father's camera by a neighbor the very moment he came roaring back. He almost crashed through the garage doors, for Christ's sake. He'd gotten as far as Indiana. I'll never forget the anguish on his face. I could see it, even in those crappy washed-out flickering frames. If I knew what happened to the film, I'd show it to you. I wish you could see it for yourself. If you ask me, I don't think you loved him as much as he loved you. I don't think you loved him as much as you claim. If you did, you'd want the world to know who he was. You'd shout it from the rooftops. If you did, you'd help me."

We both heard the tea kettle whistling in the kitchen and she used the diversion to excuse herself.

I grabbed the magnifier, moved to the Drake on the back wall, and began to examine it closely, but it felt like doing so without permission after she'd left the room was somehow rude. I stepped a few feet to the left and peeked out between the drawn drapes at the grounds behind the house.

"It's peaceful here, isn't it?" she said, when she saw me gazing through the glass. "Or at least it used to be." She was carrying a serving tray with a porcelain tea service for two, which included a creamer and sugar bowl set. A plate of cookies with imbedded walnuts was also aboard. She placed it on the coffee table at a knickknack clearing. "Those people outside are awful. They have no shame."

"They won't be there forever."

"No, I suppose not." She sat on the chair closest to the fireplace, which also placed her beside the painting I'd brought. Then she reached over and gently touched the blue tree, her fingertips feeling the texture of the canvas and oil paint that had been dry for decades. "What can I do to help you?"

"Knowing who really painted this," I said, pointing to Drake's first painting, "I'd like to examine it, if you don't mind. I think Maxwell may have written something in it."

"All right."

I turned on the brass lamp at the top of the gilded frame that illuminated only the upper-half of the seashore landscape and searched the picture for words that would have come from Maxwell Bennett's heart. I scrutinized the lower-half using the small tactical LED flashlight I'd bought for my hike to the falls. It took a while for them to show themselves, but they were there, silently hiding in one spot for a lifetime. They weren't what I'd hoped for; the words that would make this easier on May, but they were what I expected.

When I lowered the magnifying glass and turned off the flashlight she asked, "Did you find anything?"

I sat on the loveseat opposite May and said, "He made a deal with your ex so he would have the money to pay for my aunt's medical care. That means he painted for her."

May looked at me and understood. She began to nod slowly, apparently knowing where I was going. "What does it say?"

"For Sid, my sister."

May Drake looked away, staring off into her own fragile fine china world. A bull had run through her life now and then and she'd done a good job of picking up the pieces and making the best of things. Today was undoubtedly one of those days, and I was the one with the horns. "I like you May. I really do. If the cards had been dealt differently, you would have been my aunt. I would have liked that. I'm sorry things turned out the way they did. Truly, I am. If ever I can help you with anything, I want you to call me. I'd like to think of you as family, and I wish you would do the same." Having thrown her granddaughter off a mountain, even if it was in self-defense, I couldn't imagine her taking me up on the offer, but I meant what I said.

She turned to me and said, "I'm sorry for what they did to you, Robert."

I understood the who and what, and the totality of the statement. Stein and DiCarlo had said, "We're sorry for your loss," but that didn't count. They're detectives. They say that to grieving people daily. In the course of the year, others had offered their hollow condolences, but coming from May, this was different. "I know you are. I'm not sure how I'm going to go about it yet, but I'll figure out a way to bring the truth to light."

"Is there something I can do?"

"I'd like to examine other Drake paintings. One is good, especially the first, but more would be better. Camouflaged words will probably be easiest to decipher in the full-size originals. Because the letters are so fine, I imagine giclees could be a problem. Do you have any others, or do you know where they are?"

"Many have been sold, but some have been kept by the company."

"Do you have access?"

She shook her head.

I imagined this bogging down in a legal quagmire requiring a slew of attorneys and court orders. I filled my tea cup, sipped, and said, "I'll figure it out."

Suddenly she stood, headed for the kitchen, and returned immediately with her purse. "I'll show you something if you promise never to tell anyone."

I must have looked confused.

"Promise me and I'll trust you."

"You hardly know me." *And I tossed your granddaughter off a cliff!*

"Promise me and I'll trust you," she repeated.

"I promise."

She withdrew her keys, dropped the handbag on the loveseat, and approached the wall of bookshelves near the back of the living room where the entrance to the missing dining room should have been. She gripped two shelves and leaned back, swinging a floor-to-ceiling section of hardcover editions out of the way, the entire unit mounted cleverly on concealed hinges. This revealed a smooth stainless steel door with a keyway dead-center visible through an access hole in a hardened protective plate. She inserted a unique key and twisted it a quarter of a counterclockwise turn.

I could hear heavy bolts retracting from both jambs, as well as from the floor and ceiling.

Then she pushed the door open, turned on the overhead fluorescent lights, and we stepped in. "I live in a forest so there is always the threat of wildfire," she said. "And I live alone across a footbridge. I hated the thought of being trapped and not able to get out in time, or being victimized in my own home. Someone suggested that I have a safe room, so I had one built a long time ago, even before Amy came to live with me."

Enthralled, I started studying the construction around us. "How did they build this house in the first place? How'd they get the construction materials and equipment to this side of the river?"

"There are unpaved fire access roads through the woods behind us."

"We didn't need those in Brooklyn." I knocked on the foot-thick wall and hurt my knuckles but heard nothing.

"Reinforced concrete," she said, watching me.

Interested professionally, I noted that the panic room's door fit into an airtight seal, which explained the musty odor, as well as the cooler inside temperature. I noticed sprinkler heads in the ceiling and an air conditioning system with scrubbers on the vents. I looked down and saw a drain in the center of the concrete floor. A stainless steel sink and toilet, that made the room feel like a prison cell, hung on the unpainted cement wall that butted up against the country kitchen at the front of the house. I scanned the communications station, which was comprised of a landline telephone, a satellite phone resting in a charger, and a laptop computer. Then I was taken aback by the pump shotgun tucked in the corner created by the desk and the wall. I took a moment to look at May Drake, an elegant and refined elderly woman standing in the middle of a survivalist's dream. *Wow! You never know whom you're dealing with, do you?* Indeed, I should have learned that lesson after nearly being murdered by one of the most beautiful women I'd ever seen!

I continued the sweep, noticing a three-thousand watt generator poised to power everything, its exhaust routed up through the ceiling. I saw the gasoline can to fuel it, and a large petroleum-rated fire extinguisher. I also noticed long-term foodstuffs on pantry shelves, two five gallon jugs of spring water, one already inverted on a cooler, and a folding cot waiting to be unfolded. I considered the whole setup and felt a little unnerved.

"What's in there?" I asked, pointing to a large gray metal storage locker with bi-parting swing-out doors.

"I was to receive half of the unsold paintings as part of the divorce settlement. They're in there. Open it. It's all right."

I grasped the L-shaped chrome handles, turned them ninety degrees simultaneously, and pulled the doors toward me. The harsh light spilled inside and there it was—the first of about twenty paintings leaning against the back of the cabinet. It was the only one framed. I'd never seen it before, but I knew instantly what I was looking at. Officer Gwen Millhouse's observant and vivid description made it unmistakable. What couldn't be found, even with a stack of search warrants, was now right in front of me.

Although Deputy Mike Johnson hadn't thought May to be complicit, in an attempt to leave no stone unturned, thorough cop that he was, he'd tried to obtain a search warrant for this property as well, but couldn't. Now I wondered, for more than a moment, whether or not he would have discovered the cleverly-concealed, impregnable room in which I was standing. And if he had, what would he say and do?

My mind started running a hundred miles an hour. We'd wanted this painting to tie Leland Drake to the murders and now it was here, hidden in May Drake's home. What the hell did that mean? How did she get it? When did she get it? Why did she have it? And didn't it tie *her* inextricably to the crime scene?

I remembered Amy's silent declaration; that May had not been involved in the conspiracy. And in May's defense, she'd just taken me directly to it, voluntarily divulging her secret hiding place. I asked, "What do you know about this painting, May?"

"It was to be Leland's last work before retiring. He was going to release it with the announcement."

What choice did he have? The talent behind the empire was dead. They'd killed the goose that laid the golden egg. How could there be any more Drake originals? He had to retire. I used my little flashlight to read the signature in the lower right corner: Leland Drake. He couldn't paint, but at least the son of a bitch could sign his name.

I looked at May and said, "This was going to be Leland's last painting because it was Maxwell Bennett's last painting."

It took only three seconds for her to understand. Her face began the subtle contortions that endeavored to hold back yet another wave of tears.

"This painting was taken from an easel in Maxwell's apartment by the killer to keep the police from linking your ex-husband to my uncle. It was described to me in great detail by a police officer who had seen it there after a burglary that occurred two days before the murders. It's been a crucial piece of evidence sought by the police at both ends of the country."

Speechless, she sat down on the small office chair beside the communications desk.

"How did you get it?" I asked.

"Amy gave it to me to store. She knew about this room. She knew it would be safe here."

"Why did she give it to you?"

"She said they were having trouble with the security system at the company."

"When did she give it to you?"

"A day or two after you were here the first time."

I thought about Drake's improvised plan. Murdering the artist who actually created the paintings Drake signed clearly forced his retirement. But that wouldn't necessarily be a bad thing. Why wait to be dead, like the other famous artists in history? Promising a finite number of works would only cause the value of the existing paintings to skyrocket, particularly the last one. That's why they hadn't destroyed it. Greed wouldn't let them. After all, as far as they knew, they'd gotten it out of there in time and were in the clear. That's what they must have thought for a year… until I came along. Then an even more disturbing revelation clobbered me. Had the burglary that brought the police to Mack's door only hastened the plan? Was killing Maxwell Bennett, to eternally bury the secret, their intention all along?

I lifted the New England scene mounted in a simple resin frame out of the cabinet and set it on the communications desk, leaning it against the concrete wall. I stood back and considered the painting the way viewing was intended. It didn't appeal to me, but I understood why the franchise had been so successful. I moved in with my magnifying glass and flashlight for a closer look in search of a message, confident there'd be one. But after twenty minutes of scrutiny I found nothing.

"Well?" May asked when I gave up.

"If words are there, I don't see them."

I glanced at May Drake and thought I saw a tinge of disappointment on her face.

"Don't we need something to be in every painting to prove the allegation?" she asked.

"I don't know. But I was hoping there'd be proof in this one in particular because we do know, for a fact, that it was on an easel in the middle of my uncle's living room. He was killed in that room—right there, right where he'd painted this."

I stepped back again and studied, in its entirety, the impressionist interpretation of coastal New England. Then something about the painting began to bother me. "What's wrong with this picture?" I asked.

"What do you mean?"

"Doesn't it look a little crowded?"

"Are you talking about the subject matter?"

"No, not really. Doesn't it look like it's been crammed into this frame, like a photograph that's been cropped a little too small?"

"Now that you mention it, I think it does."

I stared at it for another minute or two before it hit me. *Son of a bitch!* Fabiano had cut it out of the stretcher and rolled it up so he wouldn't draw attention to himself carrying a full-size oil painting out of the apartment, through the building, and out to the street. He must have then broken up the stretcher and carried out the pieces because I never found them in the apartment, and the police never mentioned it.

I turned the painting around to examine the back and saw that it had been professionally sealed right to the edge with smooth black paper. I pulled out the Swiss Army knife I'd started carrying after the horse had gotten out of the barn at the top of Horsetail Falls and used one of the blades to cut the paper so I could expose the back of the stretcher. Then, utilizing the screwdriver tool, I carefully pried it from the frame.

One thing was instantly obvious to me. The canvas had been stapled to the front of the stretcher beneath the frame to minimize the loss of content, instead of being wrapped around it for strength. Even so, much of the painting's periphery had been lost.

"I'm afraid any message may have been inadvertently cut away when your ex-husband's henchman took it from the apartment, especially because many of the messages have been near the borders. Based on the way this has been jury-rigged before it was framed, it looks like it was cut from its original stretcher, doesn't it?"

May Drake examined the method used to affix the canvas to the wooden framework that normally pulls a piece of fabric into a taut paint-worthy flat surface. "It's never done this way. You must be right."

I resumed the search for a few of my uncle's last words, but it was futile.

"Do you want to give it to the police?" May asked.

"There's no point. The case is closed."

"Then I'd like you to have it. I had the joy of knowing Maxwell in the first half of his life, at least for a little while. You enjoyed the pleasure of his company in the latter half. You should keep it."

I turned and looked at the elderly woman beside me. In a legal sense, she had no right to it at all. It had been unlawfully taken from my uncle's residence. Technically, she was in possession of stolen property, a crime in itself. But I thought it was a gracious offer, nonetheless.

Then, cynical bastard that I am, my mind worked up a foreseeable scenario: I take the painting, she dies and isn't around to explain how Amy had given it to her for safekeeping, and I have to convince Mike "The Sense of Humor" Johnson that I, none other than the next of kin original suspect, didn't have it all along. "I appreciate the offer," I said, keeping my thoughts to myself. "I'll let you know."

I spent the next two hours examining the other paintings in the cabinet and found short, nearly invisible messages to my aunt in the periphery of each.

May Drake was kind and cordial with every discovery, apparently accepting of her place in the scheme of things. If she was disappointed, she was learning how to cope with it.

I said, "Speaking as someone who's been married, there's

something I don't understand. How could it be possible that the two of you were married for twenty-two years and you never actually saw him paint a painting? How can that be? You never saw a painting in progress?"

Her eyes looked away, apparently in search of moments in time when they were together. "Leland loved to surprise me, especially with a completed painting. He never let me see what he was working on until it was finished. He always made the reveal a momentous occasion. Although not for me per se, each one was like an incredible gift. As I look back on our marriage, I suppose you could say he was a little too secretive. I knew it at the time, but it was just something I was willing to accept. No one is perfect. There are things all women must deal with in a relationship. That's what I told myself while it lasted. Now that I finally know the truth, I don't know what to think about anything."

A little too secretive? Really? Considering his true identity and what he did, was that the biggest understatement to ever pass someone's lips, or what?

She walked me to the front door, and I understood her pale, hopeless hollow smile as I turned to say goodbye.

"Can I count on you when I go public with this?" I asked.

It took a moment for her to nod. "I think you're right, Robert. I owe your uncle that much."

I took her hand in mine and said, "There's another fact I think you should know."

She seemed to brace herself for the next bombshell. "Oh, God. What is it *now?*"

I paused briefly for added drama and said, "I've never liked cookies with nuts, Aunt May. The next time I come over, maybe you could serve a batch with chocolate chips instead."

"And I've never tolerated a brat, nephew or otherwise."

I kissed her on the cheek and said, "I'll bear that in mind. I'll be in touch."

I turned away and took one step, but stopped short. "There is one other thing I've wondered about for a long time," I said before she closed the door.

"What's that?"

"There's a blue tree in the painting I brought you. The whole damned thing is blue—the leaves, the branches, the trunk, everything. Do you have any idea why he did that? Does it have any significance?"

She nodded. "That was one of the first things I noticed." She stepped out of the shadows, either forgetting about the paparazzi across the river or not caring, and walked to the porch railing. "There used to be a beautiful California alder right there, near the bank." She pointed to a level open area covered with gravel between the house and the river, a few yards west of the bridge. "We would sit in the shade beneath it and talk for hours. We learned a lot about each other under that tree, its leaves rustling above. It was wonderful." She paused, gazing back in time. "Maxwell carved a heart containing our initials into the smooth pale gray bark. We'd met in San Francisco, but this is where we knew what we had was real. This is where we thought we'd ultimately live out our lives."

She fell silent for a minute or two before turning to face me. Then she looked into my eyes and said, "Finding this house was no coincidence, Robert."

"It was. That's the truth. Please believe me."

She closed her eyes momentarily and slowly swiveled her head ever so slightly. "I do believe you, but you're wrong. Moving to California wasn't by chance. None of this was by chance. Passing here wasn't an accident. Noticing this house wasn't just luck, good or bad, especially because the house in the painting only vaguely resembles this one, for whatever reason your uncle had, God rest his soul. And doing something about it certainly wasn't based on a coincidence. You may think it was, but I don't. I know better."

I felt like a student having absolutely no idea what point the professor was trying to make. "What are you saying?"

"Don't you see? You were led here."

"By whom?"

Then her expression made me feel stupid. "Who do you think?"

As confused as I was, enlightenment slowly descended upon me. I'm not particularly spiritual now, nor have I ever been, but I suppose she could have been right. All things considered, that was as good an explanation as any—perhaps better than most. Not knowing how to respond, I humbly said, "You may be right." What else could I have contributed before changing the subject? "What happened to the tree? Did it fall in a storm?"

"Leland cut it down. Then he hired someone with a backhoe to dig out the roots and remove all traces of it. Still not satisfied, he filled the hole with concrete and covered that with gravel so nothing could ever grow there—not even grass. That's the way he was."

"You mean jealous."

She moved her head again in the negative way. "Vindictive is a better word."

I shook my head slightly, too. "Asshole is even better."

She chuckled a little before noticing the cameras across the river pointed in our direction. Then she stepped back into her home.

"Wait, May. There's something else." I reached into my pocket and withdrew the small black velvet-clad box that held a diamond engagement ring. I handed it to her and said, "What you had with my uncle *was* real, and so is this. It was in his safe-deposit box, bound with a yellow ribbon to the letters you wrote. I can only imagine that he had it with him when he headed this way. I'm sure he'd want you to have it."

I'd secured the cooperation I sought, and I'd said everything there was to say, so I simply turned and walked back to my car, leaving May with the ring that was meant for her a lifetime ago.

29

They say getting there is half the fun. I don't know who *they* are, but I know they're right, especially if you like to drive as much as I do and you have a car like mine. The shorter way to get where I was going, where I'd been invited, would have been to take Interstate 5 South out of Sacramento. Or perhaps 680 toward San Jose, but I chose California 1, better known as the Pacific Coast Highway. It's a celebrated two lane blacktop that nearly runs the entire length of the state, passing places like Mendocino, Monterey, Carmel by the Sea, and perhaps most notably Big Sur. I'd even heard of it in Brooklyn, and now I know why. It's spectacular! I picked it up at Half Moon Bay and headed south along the ocean.

I was feeling all right, except for the persistent dull ache in my ribs. I lowered the windows and inhaled the fresh salt wind coming off the breaking waves. I noticed the surf crashing against huge rock outcroppings in some places and tumbling onto lonely stretches of beach in others. There was no fog, as there is so often in the summer where the water meets the shore on the Northern California coast, or so I'd been told. The sun had passed the midday mark on its arc across a crystal blue sky that was clear to the horizon. I ran the Porsche up and down through the gears a few times, watching the tachometer and listening to the growl, almost sure the engineers in Stuttgart had figured out a way to make it run on adrenaline and testosterone—both renewable resources.

I'd learned a few things of interest since my visit to May's house. I'd conferred with several art experts at the world's most reputable auction houses and learned that the value of the remaining Drake originals had hit the stratosphere since his demise, simply because a finite number of works had been established. I'd expected that. What I didn't expect was the confident and unanimous speculation by those in-the-know that the thirty-nine Bennett originals in my Tahoe Keys condo would likely go from being worthless to being virtually priceless when the truth was made public, especially because of the scandalous events surrounding the life and death of Leland Drake, his involvement in the murder of Maxwell Bennett, now a ghost artist in more ways than one, and the nature of the irrefutable proof I'd discovered within each painting.

I'd retained a high-powered law firm, which charged as much per hour as the world's finest call girls, to make it all happen. It's interesting to note that in one case you pay through the nose to get fucked, and in the other you pay *not* to. They were looking into the assets of the Drake Corporation, a family company with interests in art publishing, collectibles, greeting cards, and calendars, to name a few. Drake had left the lion's share of his estate to Amy, his granddaughter and partner in crime, and not to his slut wife, with whom he'd had a prenuptial agreement. But Amy was dead. That meant, in all likelihood, that the slut would go after everything, pre-nup or not, especially because this was California, the poster child for community property.

On the other hand, Maxwell Bennett had bequeathed all of his worldly possessions to me, his only living blood relative. If he hadn't created everything upon which the Drake Empire was based, there would be no Drake anything. Didn't that mean that I had claim to all things named Drake? It was an interesting legal question—one certain to be in the courts for years, break new ground in the ridiculous realm of jurisprudence, and likely set several legal precedents as, to my knowledge, nothing like this had ever happened before.

As I motored south beside the sea I wondered why my uncle had never stepped forward. I can only speculate, since it is impossible for me, or anyone else for that matter, to ask him. Like my father, he was a worrier. Perhaps he was afraid of being named in a conspiracy. Or more likely, he'd been frightened by Fabiano, probably the bagman sent to pick up each completed but unsigned painting. The more I thought about it the easier it was to envision Joey threatening him time after time in his own apartment. After all, I'd seen up close what the convict was capable of. Then, thinking like a cop, something Johnson had taught me, an even more infuriating possibility crossed my mind. Maybe *our* lives had been threatened too, mine and Dana's, if Mack stopped cooperating. Could my uncle have been trapped in the bad deal he'd made because he was afraid for us?

It took more than a few miles on one of America's most scenic highways for my newfound belief in karma to settle my thoughts and lower my blood pressure, thankful that, as May had pointed out, the angels had led me to her door. And that, in the end, the trash had ultimately been taken out.

In the here and now, the authorities in New York had released to me the recovered possessions heretofore held in evidence that

I'd identified in the station house in Queens, as well as the contents of the vault box. How far the sixty thousand dollars would go for legal fees toward bringing credit where credit was due was questionable, but it was a reasonable down payment, even after setting aside a third in anticipation of the likely IRS investigation. Bill Sherman was kind enough to remind me that Uncle Sam was my other uncle.

I pulled off the highway and into a parking area where the road was particularly close to the beach, pointing the car toward the Pacific and nosing it as close to the sand as the pavement would allow. I sat there for a while, staring at the restless ocean and thinking about all that had happened to me, to the people I loved, and to those who'd caused so much carnage. I'd discovered things I'd never known about my uncle and his art, which led me to the irony-laced and inescapable conclusion that, after a life of struggle, he should have still been alive to finally enjoy the full fruits of his talent. But as is the way most often in the art world, he was now worth more dead than alive.

I pulled the envelope I'd taken with me out of my pocket, extricated the letter within, unfolded it, and read it for the second time. It was from May. It was not one of the old ones from the bank vault in New York. This one was addressed to me. I'd received it only the day before, but the stationery and handwriting was eerily similar to the love letters Mack had received and saved so many years ago. Apparently she'd taken to me as the aunt I'd suggested, perhaps because she trusted me, perhaps because Mack would have wanted her to. And to my surprise, she harbored no ill will toward me for Amy's death. She thanked me for the painting I'd brought, and for uncovering the truth. Then she reiterated that I could count on her as an ally instead of an adversary in my quest to control the future of Maxwell Bennett's legacy. It was, however, the postscript that was most shocking. In it she mentioned that she had revised her last will and testament, bequeathing all the art she possessed to me. She also apparently felt the need to mention that the rest of her will would remain unchanged, the remainder of her estate to be divided amongst several art related charities, endowments, and institutions. As I held the letter in my hands, contemplating how different our lives would have been if my uncle had kept his Thunderbird pointed west instead of turning around in Indianapolis, I realized that the decisions we make extend far beyond ourselves.

I looked up, above the steering wheel, and noticed two lovers walking across the beach from left to right. They were pretty far away, near the waterline where the sand was smooth and wet, but I could see that they were holding hands. They strolled to the center of the stage, stopped, and faced each other. I saw the man touch the woman's hair as it blew in the wind. Then he cleared it from her face and kissed her. I couldn't tell how old they were, but I soon realized it didn't matter. The hormone levels may change, but the emotions are the same, aren't they? Through the windshield, I envied the embrace that made them one, holding each other beside the dangling gold filigree heart that I'd hung from the rearview mirror. Johnson had returned it to me when the criminal investigation was officially closed. My eyes shifted to the word *Pretend* artfully cut in script across the width of the pendant. I didn't have to pretend that I was going to be fabulously wealthy, the unexpected end result of recognizing the white house by the river. That was going to happen. But the empty seat to my right reminded me that happiness was still elusive.

I arrived at my destination in the evening after making a few stops along the way, including one at Laguna Seca Raceway near

Monterey to register for another three-day high performance track-school driving course, not only because it's the most fun a guy can have with his pants on, but because you simply never know when you'll have to outrun someone. I had dinner alone on a patio beneath strands of tiny white lights strung between two old red brick walls at the rear of a charming little Italian restaurant in San Luis Obispo. Then I found the motel in which I'd made a reservation. I registered at the front desk and went to bed.

The commencement ceremonies the next morning at California's Polytechnic University took place in splendid sunshine on the grass of Mustang Memorial Field, so named in honor of sixteen football players killed in a tragic plane crash in 1960, which reminded me that no one has a monopoly on heartache. I was seated between William Sherman, his wife, and youngest daughter to my left, and Heinrich Essen and his wife, the lovely *Frau* Essen, to my right, who, much to their credit, were as enthralled with the proceedings as they might have been if we were all watching the launch of the Bismarck.

"Thanks for inviting me," I said into Bill's ear while the single file procession of jubilant young graduates made their way onto the temporary stage to accept a symbolic diploma, a blank piece of rolled parchment tied with a ribbon. Some things never change.

"You're welcome," he said, without taking his eyes off the ritual. "I'm glad you could make it. Jenny would have been disappointed if you weren't here."

Really? I considered the fact that I was more than a decade her senior, but quickly dismissed the thought. After all, it wasn't like I was twenty and she was six. "Your daughter is beautiful. And she'll be a brilliant architect. You must be very proud."

"I am."

The adage, the apple doesn't fall far from the tree, came to mind one more time as I compared Leland and Amy with William and Jenny, not exactly the same family relation, but close enough. The conclusion I drew may not be particularly profound, but it was inescapable. Quality is quality and scum is scum. And you can quote me, if you like.

I soon saw hundreds of people hugging and shaking hands. If ever a throng of optimists had been assembled in one place, this was it. Still unable to leave the past behind where it belonged, I wondered briefly if anyone there, besides me, had ever heard that a pessimist is simply an optimist with experience.

The Shermans had planned to celebrate their daughter's college graduation with a grand luncheon at the town's finest restaurant, where a reservation had long ago been made and a shiny new Volkswagen was waiting for her. When Bill let me in on the surprise, I couldn't help but suspect that Heinrich had put his two Deutschemarks into the selection process. I was invited and we all made our way across the sprawling campus to the parking lot near the Performing Arts Center, where Jenny announced that she would ride with me.

As we approached the Porsche, I realized I should have pocketed the necklace still dangling behind the windshield.

She peeled off her cap and gown to reveal a vividly colored little sundress as I opened the passenger door. She tossed the ceremonial garb in the back and gracefully seated herself in the front, pivoting her slender legs and bright red pumps over the sill and into the footwell.

I started the car and opened the windows to let in the fresh air blowing inland from the nearby Pacific. As we began to roll and I upshifted through the gears, she tied her long, silky blonde hair into a ponytail and reveled in the feel of the wind. We got to know each other a little better along the way as I followed her family to the celebration. But before we got out of the car, I said, "I've got a question for you."

"What's that?"

"If graduation marks the end of your education, why do they call it commencement?"

She chuckled. "That's an easy one, Silly. It's called commencement because it's the beginning of the rest of your life."

Our eyes connected and all I could manage in reply were the words, "How about that."

She didn't turn away. Instead she said, "You knew that, didn't you? You were just being facetious."

I nodded, still looking into her enchanting blue eyes. "I just wanted to hear you say it."

Instead of getting out, she turned toward the pendant hanging from the rearview mirror, reached for it with her right hand, and stopped it from swinging by cradling it in an open palm. "This is beautiful," she said.

I expected her to ask about its origin, which I really didn't want to repeat, so I didn't reply.

But she didn't. She simply murmured the word *Pretend* slowly a couple of times before saying, "It sounds like a game."

"I never thought of it that way, but I guess you could say that."

"What are the rules?" she asked. "All games have rules."

I briefly considered what I'd learned from life's last lesson and concluded that there were none. "There are no rules."

"Really?"

I nodded.

"None at all?"

"Nope. None that I can think of. Anything goes."

"Sounds like fun," she said. Then she turned toward me again before reaching for the door and asked, "Can I play?"

A Personal Note...

   Robert Bennett and I thank you for selecting, purchasing, and reading NO FORCED ENTRY. We look forward to bringing you his ongoing story.

   Your readership and continued interest are truly appreciated. Until next time, be careful who you let in!

                    Sincerely,

                    Robert Max

ACKNOWLEDGMENTS

First and foremost, I'd like to thank my beautiful wife, Lynn, always knowing the things that are most important. My life has been enhanced immeasurably by her extraordinary sense of style, keen intuition, generosity, and selfless nature. I know this to also be true for many others fortunate enough to know her. In this respect in particular, I am a very lucky man.

A multitude of thanks must also be expressed to Lee, my brother. His police procedural know-how, the product of a multifaceted law enforcement background, combined with his talented and tireless editorial skills have made him the perfect technical advisor in this genre. The lion's share of thanks here must, however, be tied to his relentless enthusiasm, never waning through countless conversations taking place almost daily over what can only be described as a very, very long time.

I'd like to say thank you to my friend Derek for his willingness to help overcome several technical challenges in the electronic world. And if I may, I'll take this opportunity to publicly wish him the best of luck in his new career.

Robust and heartfelt thanks must also go to Jim and Patti, Louise Ann, Terry and Marion, and Joe Z. for their feedback and encouragement. My appreciation can never be adequately expressed, especially to Carol P., editor extraordinaire.

For a preview, turn the page.

Coming Next from Station House Publishing Trust

WHEN IT'S PERSONAL

Vengeance Knows No Boundary

By

ROBERT MAX

Surviving a distinguished career in the NYPD, Detective First Grade Dan Crane, sick and tired of life in the clutter and chaos, has been looking forward to just one thing: Reuniting with his only brother and spending his upcoming retirement in the wide-open spaces of Nevada beneath an unobstructed western sky. That dream is shattered when Jay, a radar development scientist employed by a major defense contractor, is brutally attacked in his Special Access Programs secure laboratory compound.

Plunged into an unthinkable nightmare with one hysterical phone call, Dan, suddenly in the same unwavering crosshairs, has yet another case to solve—this time on his own, with no jurisdiction, no backup, and the black-ops perpetrators coming for *him*.

Convinced he has nothing left to lose, he will soon shred the department policy that stops a cop from working a case **WHEN IT'S PERSONAL.**

Please visit www.robertmaxnovels.com

Made in the USA
Las Vegas, NV
05 January 2023

65054241R00217